Low, Slow, Delicious

LOW, SLOW, DELICIOUS

Recipes for Casseroles and
Electric Slow-Cooking Pots

Martha
Lomask

Faber and Faber LONDON AND BOSTON

First published in 1980
by Faber and Faber Limited
3 Queen Square, London WC1N 3AU
Printed and bound in Great Britain by
Fakenham Press Limited, Fakenham, Norfolk

British Library Cataloguing in Publication Data

Lomask, Martha
  Low, slow, delicious.
  1. Cookery
  I. Title
  641.5'88   TX717

ISBN 0–571–11384–2

Contents

List of Illustrations

Acknowledgements

Many of the recipes in this book are from my own collection of much-handled, floury, sauce-stained 3 by 5 inch index cards, typed from heaven knows how many sources and over more years than I care to think about. In some cases I have made notes on these cards of the name and the writer and the book or magazine in which the recipe appeared, but in shamefully many there's no possible clue to the origin. I can only say to James Beard, Patricia Brooks, Craig Claiborne, Elizabeth David, Theodora Fitzgibbon, Marika Hanbury Tenison, Georgina Horley, Jocasta Innes, Elizabeth Ray, Delia Smith, Katie Stewart, Mapie de Toulouse Lautrec, Harold Wilshaw – and the shades of Clementine Paddleford and Countess Morphy – thank you, again and again, for the hours of good reading and happy cooking.

More specifically, I would like to acknowledge the primary sources of the following recipes, with the *caveat* that I have necessarily changed the method and in some cases the ingredients, to fit the Pot. The inspirations are theirs, the method and any mistakes are mine.

Pot au Feu: James Beard, *The James Beard Cookbook*, Dell Publishing, New York, 1959.

Beef Rib Barolo: Ada Boni, *The Talisman Italian Cookbook*, Crown Publishers, New York, 1950.

Stracotto: Patricia Brooks, *Meals That Can Wait*, Gramercy Publishing Co., a division of Crown Publishers Inc., New York, 1970.

Brazilian Pudding, Loubia, Indian Pudding and Red Cabbage: Craig Claiborne, *The New York Times Menu Cookbook*, New York Times Publishing Co., 1966.

Haricots à la Bretonne, Poule au Pot Béarnaise and Estouffat: Elizabeth David, *French Provincial Cooking*, Michael Joseph, 1960, Penguin Books, 1964 (Revised edition, 1970).

Fricandeau of Veal and Whisky Cake: Theodora Fitzgibbon, *Theodora Fitzgibbon's Cookery Book*, Gill and Macmillan, Dublin, 1972.

Rabbit and Bacon Casserole: Georgina Horley, *Good Food on a Budget*, Penguin Books, 1969 (Revised edition, 1978).

Dry Beef Curry, Kidneys with Sherry and Rillettes: *Good Housekeeping Cookery Book*, The Hearst Corporation, 1944 (Revised editions 1966, 1972).

Pease Pudding: Jocasta Innes, *The Pauper's Cookbook*, Penguin Books, 1971.

Roast Chicken with Lemon: Mary Karay and Fannie Nome, *Hellenic Cuisine*, St Helen's Society, Detroit, 1957.

Boiled Silverside: Robin McDouall, *Cookery Book*, Michael Joseph, 1963.

Stuffed Vine Leaves: Claudia Roden, *Middle Eastern Food*, Thomas Nelson, 1968, Penguin Books, 1969.

Vegetable Curry: Delia Smith, *The Evening Standard Cookbook*, Beaverbrook Newspapers, 1974.

Tomato Casserole and Chocolate Custard: Anna Thomas, *The Vegetarian Epicure*, Vintage Books, New York, 1972, Penguin Books, 1974.

Potato Soufflé and Salmon Mould: Marian Tracy, *Casserole Cookery Complete*, Viking Press Inc., New York, 1956.

Miriam's Terrine: Miriam Ungerer, *Good Cheap Food*, Viking Press Inc., New York, 1973, Signet Books, New York, 1976.

My special thanks are due to Sue Cutts, The Prestige Group; Dianne Page, Tower Housewares Ltd; Sylvia Brunyee and Marjorie Waugh, Pifco; Mrs J. Smith, Kenwood, all of whom lent me slow-cookers of every size and type. More than that, they gave me endless advice and comfort and dealt patiently with my questions, shrieks, complaints and requests over a period of two years.

My especial gratitude goes to Helen Dore, who suggested this book; Rosemary Goad and Eileen Brooksbank, my editors, who taught me how to write a cookery book; and to my husband who ate casseroles for every meal, sometimes with silent stoicism and, more often, with enthusiasm. He bore with me while I lost sleep, lost my figure, my temper and (once) the manuscript. This book is for him, with my love.

The publishers are grateful to the following for supplying or sponsoring photographs:

British Meat (Plate 1)
Pifco Ltd (Plate 2b)
Carmel Produce (Plate 3)
Tower Housewares Ltd (Plate 4a)
Lea & Perrins Ltd (Plate 4b)
New Zealand Lamb Information Bureau (Plate 5)
James Robertson & Sons Ltd (Plate 6)
Colman's Mustard (Plate 6)
Cadbury Typhoo Ltd (Plate 8a)

also to The Prestige Group Ltd and Thorn Domestic Appliances Ltd (Kenwood) for providing electric slow cookers for photography. The casseroles in Plates 1 and 7 are from Pearsons of Chesterfield.

The line drawings on the title pages are by Nadia Roden.

Introduction

'Do you know that you have twenty-two casseroles in this kitchen?' This question came, in an unbelieving tone, from a new acquaintance. Anyone who knew me well wouldn't have bothered. Little did she know that while there were twenty-two on view, nine more were in a cupboard. Fat glossy brown earthenware ones. Neat square space-age glass/ceramic ones fitted close together. Heavy round flame-orange enamel-on-cast-iron French ones. Many hanging from butchers' hooks on a rack, some in their own wooden stand and (naturally) about four simmering in the oven. Newest, waiting to be proven: a most elegant, rather lightweight enamel-on-steel set, with non-stick interior and very ingenious detachable handles.

Finally, my trusty and well-beloved friend, the electric slow cooker, the slowest 'casserole' of them all. I had done battle with it over a period of months. Once, it had nearly gone to Oxfam. For some time, I was half-convinced of its virtues, half-sceptical. At last I was able to bend it to my will, so that now it turns out, day after day, utterly delicious slow-simmered meals. And very satisfying they are, from the more obvious pâtés and soups, to unexpected soufflé-like puddings. As you will see, I have devoted more space to it in these introductory pages than I have to the conventional casserole cookery. I hope that those who are already experienced devotees of the Pot (for the sake of clarity, I have used the single word 'Pot' to describe all the electric slow cookers: more specific words about them later) will bear with me.

In the last few years, as cooks and kitchen helpers disappeared, costs of steaks and chops leapt upward like sparks to the sky, and more and more women became more and more busy and harried, casserole cooking has become a sort of way of life. The first casseroles, I suppose, were nothing more than a bundle of wet clay slapped around fresh-killed meat and buried in the heart of a primitive fire. Modern ones can be as simple and basic as the brown glazed beanpot, or as fashionable as the flowered and gleaming Royal Worcesterware; shallow and wide for a dish of poached pears, or deep as a drum for a big pot au feu. Always they are the truest of kitchen helpers for the busy, the preoccupied; the loving cook, the careless cook; those who adore food and its preparing, even those to whom cooking is something to be fitted into scraps of spare time.

Casseroles are so blessedly undemanding. They give you the priceless gift of time to distribute as you will. Time to ferry children to a swimming lesson, time for limbering up body and mind with yoga. Secret, selfish time to finish a detective story, or generous time to give to someone who needs it. And lovely unstressed kitchen time, to put your whole mind on a new kind of sauce for a new kind of pudding, while a comforting big pot of oxtail stew sings quietly to itself.

What with all the endless magazine and newspaper pieces about the virtues of low, slow cooking, there's probably little need now to labour the point. My own little list: inexpensive cuts of meat made tender and succulent with the heel of a bottle of very ordinary wine; the earthy, elemental taste of pulses, glorified by slow cooking into something as ancient and vital as fire itself; the surprise of a cake baked moist and delicious for two hours or more; bread baked peasant-fashion in a heavy iron casserole—modern version of the Irish 'bastable' oven.

Casserole cooking, whether it's in the oven or in an electric slow cooker, can range from incredibly cheap and quick-to-do dishes (lentils and sausages, prepared in five minutes to simmer for hours) to the superb extravagance of partridge on a bed of cabbage, or duckling with green peppercorns. Many casseroles—Pyrosil, Le Creuset, some of the heavier enamel-on-steel ones—give you the luxury option of oven cooking or cooker-top simmering.

Oven cooking time can be quite flexible.

Experiment. If the recipe times and temperatures don't suit *your* schedule, try lowering heat from, say, Gas 3 (325°F, 170°C), to Gas 1 (250°F, 130°C), and doubling cooking time. Then at the end, turn oven high to brown or crisp or whatever. Exception: a whole chicken or small turkey must cook to an internal temperature of 190°F, 85°C, to be absolutely safe from the risk of salmonella poisoning. So you won't want to set your oven lower than about Gas 2 (300°F, 150°C); then cook your bird until the juices run completely clear.

In this book, almost all the ingredients and quantities are the same for oven-cooked casseroles and for electric slow cookers. However, experience has taught me to use less liquid in the electrics: because food cooks under a vapour-seal, there's almost no evaporation; the natural juices of meat, vegetables and fruits cook *into* the food instead of away in steam. (More about that in No. 3 of the Four Cardinal Points of Pot Cooking, p. 16.) In some ingredient lists, you will find in brackets larger quantities of liquid indicated; that's for oven-cooking where some evaporation is to be expected.

Flavouring and seasoning, like falling in love, is one of those intensely personal and rather emotive subjects. How *can* she use so much tarragon? What on earth does she see in that man who never sees a joke? My own feeling is that all slow cooking needs rather heightened seasoning. This is especially true of electric slow cookers, perhaps because the moisture re-condenses and slightly dilutes flavour? In the lists of ingredients in the recipes, I've based my seasoning recommendations on the needs of the electric slow cooker, because once you've started it on its way, you really shouldn't keep opening it to check the taste. For oven-cooked casseroles, use your own judgement. You may want to decrease the amount of black pepper (or nutmeg, soy sauce, mushroom sauce) at the beginning, then taste for seasoning at the end of cooking and pay heed to the dictates of your own palate.

THE ELECTRIC SLOW COOKER

'My life with the Electric Casserole' is a continuing story of transition from hate to love. Variously called a CrockPot, a CookPot, a Slo-Cooker, this new slow-simmering low-wattage casserole first appeared in England in 1976, on a wave of advertising and publicity. 'Busy Day Bonus.' 'Slow Cooking, the secret of good cooking all over the world.' 'Set it—and forget it.' Go to work in the morning, the ads suggested, come home to a gourmet meal that has cooked itself. What a wonderful idea . . . *if it were only foolproof.*

My husband gave me one; he knows how wedded I am to the 'cook it low, cook it slow' principle. I am spoiled by the luxury of an Aga cooker which in winter warms my kitchen, gently cooks endless casserole meals, and never tricks me with underdone joints or scorched pans. Each May, however, the Aga is turned off for the summer, and each year I must come to terms with my summer cooker. So—The Pot, and the beginning of the long love-hate relationship.

The Pot, supposedly, was designed to make wonderful somethings out of little nothings. Put in some stewing steak, a few carrots, minced onion, some herbs, a slosh of red wine. Go away for the day, come home to Boeuf à la Française or some such. I tried it. What came out was a wonder to behold. Grey, stringy, overcooked meat. Vegetables which I would have expected to be deliciously tender were horridly crisp. Instead of a sauce, a sort of reddish sludge.

My next attempt was an ox-tongue, cooked 10 hours as directed, in rather a lot of water. Result: a large wodge of cotton wool, all its flavour cooked away into an incredible quantity of tongue stock. (And how much tongue stock can you use up in the course of a week or a year?) The meat I salvaged with rather a lot of brandy, butter, garlic, herbs and every *terrine* in the house, turning it into much more tongue pâté than we ever expected to eat.

The Pot began to be called, in my kitchen, the Crook Pot.

But—the more I worried away at it, the more I began to believe that there must be wonderful hidden possibilities. After all, what about all those wonderful *marmites*, tightly sealed, simmering away forever in those legendary French country kitchens? For that matter, the big Dutch oven my grandmother used so much was a slow cooker. Experimenting cautiously, I came to think that these ancient well-proven methods must have some things in common. Food was never merely piled in, without some initial browning and searing. Each dish was well-seasoned at its outset.

Richness and flavour came not from indiscriminate washes of water or wine, but often from the fragrant juices of vegetables that had been turned over in butter, or from the life-enhancing touch of good oil, the deepening and darkening quality of black treacle, Worcestershire sauce, even soy sauce.

I found answers in some early American cookery books, in wine-stained French and Italian books, in my own boxes full of casserole recipes, in fraying cuttings from long-discarded newspapers and magazines. Slowly this elegant, infuriating twentieth-century 'marmite', became a standby and a joy (yes, even when my Aga is going).

The Pot can be your most useful casserole if you approach it with a mix of common sense and some very old cooking principles. It's a lifesaver in time of trouble: when dry rot ate up my kitchen floor, I cooked for a month in my dining-room with one frying-pan, a Camping Gaz cylinder, one Le Creuset casserole and my precious Pot. The electric casserole is a dream for feeding a family with no sense of time, or for those cooks who have half a dozen schedules to deal with: a Pot meal stays hot, without overcooking, stays savoury and welcoming without scorching or drying up, even when the 6.27 train is cancelled, fogbound or merely normally late.

What's in the Pot for you?
The Pot is incredibly economical. It cooks for hours for just pennies. Instead of heating up an oven to cook one dish, it will use about the same amount of electricity as a 75-watt bulb on the LOW setting, and on the HIGH only about as much as 150 watts, depending on the make. At the time of writing, a rise in gas prices of 37 per cent over the next twelvemonth has just been announced; electricity looks like going up more than 80 per cent in the next three years. We must learn to pack every corner of an oven with casseroles, or for a one-dish meal exploit the Pot. It will let you make something extraordinarily good out of cheapish cuts of meat (shin of beef, pie veal, boiling fowl). Used with intelligence and discernment, it really *will* allow you to start a meal at 8.30 in the morning, eat it with pleasure 9, 10, even 12 hours later. Your kitchen will be degrees cooler in hot weather, without an oven going. And you will find that less and less must you turn to expensive grilled and fried food (a costly way to cook,

anyway, even in an ideal world without energy problems).

The Pot is wonderfully portable: use it in a dining-room, in a bed-sitter, in a mobile home, wherever there is a power point. Think of it for student digs, for the elderly living in little space on less money.

What will it do?
It will make supremely good soups.
It will make Christmas pudding.
It will make pâté for twenty—or chicken for two.
It will make Potted Beef, Osso Bucco, Braised Oxtail, Rabbit and Bacon, Apple Crumble, Poached Salmon Trout, Greek Vine Leaves, Marrow Chutney, Marmalade, Meat Loaf, Almond Fruitcake, Indian Pudding. It will even bake bread!

But don't expect it to—
Make a true soufflé.
Roast pork with crisp crackling.
Cook peas or broccoli or spinach.
Make sauces.
But, when the main dish of a meal has been quietly simmering away, minding its own business for the whole length of a busy day, you can with an easy conscience put your whole mind on lovely rewarding things: making the perfect hollandaise sauce, cooking tiny new peas in butter for 3 or 4 minutes, even experimenting with a Soufflé Grand Marnier.

The Pot isn't a miracle-worker. I've found that it does some things infinitely better than any other cooking method. Others it does just as well, with much less cost and trouble. I hope that this book will save you some of the frustrations I felt, early on, and help you to the true pleasures of the Pot.

General Instructions on the Pot
On p. 156 you will find detailed descriptions of all electric slow cookers on the UK market at the time of writing.

If you are about to buy a Pot—or if you have one and want to explore possibilities beyond those suggested in the brochure that came with it—or if, like me, you have one and after tearing out a certain amount of hair, are about to turn it and its problems over to your favourite charity: read on.

Be Patient. For the first week or so, you will probably find that every dish is either cooked and ready somewhat earlier than you expected, or, conversely, needs an hour or more cooking time. But press on. Don't invite anyone to dinner until you have learned the ways of your own Pot. At one stage of this book, I was turning around like a waltzing mouse in a maze of Pots—six of them all cooking away. I found that every Pot on the market has its own characteristics. There are even small variations in the performance of two Pots of the same make.

Cooking times can vary for many reasons: a very warm kitchen or a draught from a window can make a difference. Electrical current and its variations can affect the behaviour of your Pot. If everyone near you suddenly switches on electric cookers at 6 p.m., the intense surge can drain the grid and cause a significant drop in current supply. All Pots on the English market are engineered for 240-volt supply; *if you happen to live in a 220-volt area, you may have to allow 10 minutes more pre-heating time*, and up to an hour longer cooking on LOW, half an hour longer on HIGH. All these things will fall into a pattern for you once you have grown familiar with your own Pot.

I have found that I have had greatest success with almost every recipe by preheating the Pot for 15 to 20 minutes on HIGH. As I am a firm advocate of preliminary browning (for meats, poultry, game, vegetables), almost all food that goes into *my* Pot is hot. It would quickly lose this essential initial heat if it went into a cold Pot. I have, therefore, prefaced nearly every recipe with a preheating instruction.

In general, it's wise to follow the makers' instructions about initial cooking on HIGH before switching to LOW. But as you grow in confidence and experience, you can work out your own best methods. Kenwood, for example, advise 2 hours' cooking on HIGH for many of their recipes, and they specify here food cold from the fridge, the Pot not preheated, but at room temperature. Alternatively, they suggest 1 hour on HIGH and the rest on LOW, with food pre-browned and liquids at boiling point.

Tower and Kenwood, at this moment, are the only manufacturers offering Automatic Pots which cook for a predetermined time on HIGH then switch themselves to LOW, but there well may be more by the time you read this. These Auto cookers do not need preheating, as the initial HIGH period comprises preheating and a certain amount of cooking at the higher temperatures. *Read the manufacturers' brochures carefully* for timings for these special Pots, and adapt recipes from this book to similar ones for the Automatic method.

With standard Pots, in most cases recipes designed to cook for very long periods (8, 10, 12 hours) on LOW, can be cooked in just under half that time on HIGH. But the converse is not true. You can make a very good fruitcake in about $3\frac{1}{2}$ hours on HIGH, whereas 7 hours' cooking on LOW leaves you with nothing but sweet spongy batter. (I speak as perhaps the only person in the world who has ever tried to cook a Marmalade Fruitcake on LOW, overnight.)

The Pot is designed for moist, low-temperature cooking, so nothing will burn, no liquid will boil away on the LOW setting. You can leave your kitchen, or indeed your house, for 8 or 10 hours with safety and an easy mind. Cooking on HIGH, however, is most emphatically not 'set it and forget it'. Treat the HIGH setting exactly as you would a slow-to-medium simmer on your cooker top. An occasional swift check into what's going on here is quite a good idea. On HIGH, food can lightly scorch to the casserole, and sauces and gravies will simmer down a good deal.

Before you use your Pot, take 10 minutes to read the instructions. Then read them again, and do exactly what they tell you about use, care, cleaning. It's the safe and sensible way.

Use Your Pot on a Level, Stable Surface. I learned this the hard way, with a Pot cooking away on a table-height deep freeze. The vibration, hardly more than a deep purr to the ear, was actually enough to shift the movable dial from LOW to HIGH over a period of 6 hours. The results, fortunately, were not disastrous, merely surprising.

Use Your Pot Safely. Make sure that it is well away from children and animals while it is cooking and, if possible, not too close to your main centre of food preparation. Don't let the flex dangle over a table edge or stretch across a space where it might be caught by somebody's unwary movement.

The Pot is Hot. The outside surface can get hot enough, even on LOW, to burn fingers. And the inner casserole is to be handled with care. Have a pair of sturdy, padded oven gloves always at hand, either to take out an inner removable casserole, or to carry the whole Pot to the table. When preheating, check the inner temperature with a cautious finger, not with the flat of your hand. Protect your hands from steam and hot water with oven gloves or a heavy towel, when you take out a steamed pudding or cake. Don't absent-mindedly hug the Pot to your bosom when you lift it. Always butter or oil the inside of the casserole *before* preheating when a recipe specifies this procedure.

Is slow cooking safe?
The answer is an unequivocal Yes. The minimum safe cooking temperature for meat, poultry and game is 190°F, 85°C. At this temperature, all bacteria are killed. The LOW setting on Pots is approximately 200°F, 100°C. If you brown your meat, etc. first, this intense initial heat will give you a considerable boost in temperature. The preheated Pot carries on from there. Even without pre-browning, however, the continuous cooking heat of the Pot is enough to ensure safety.

Always thaw frozen meat, poultry and game thoroughly before you cook it in any casserole, electric or otherwise. Let it thaw at room temperature, or overnight in the fridge. Never on the top of a heated cooker or on a radiator, as that may give you a warm, soft surface deceptively masking a dangerously frozen interior.

What about vitamins and minerals?
Slow cooking actually conserves many of the good things in food which can be driven off by high-temperature grilling, frying, boiling. There is some evidence that the slow-cooking method keeps essential amino-acids stable in the protein of meat, while high-temperature quick cooking can be destructive.

Can I reheat food in the Pot?
Not recommended. Even on the HIGH setting, reheating of chilled leftovers can only be gradual, and it isn't worth the risk. Reheat in a saucepan on top of your cooker, or in a hot oven.

May I store food in the casserole?
No—remove food from the Pot (or indeed from *any* casserole) as soon as a meal is finished; don't let it stand around, cooling at room temperature. Decant the remaining contents into a heatproof plastic or enamel basin, cool quickly—perhaps by plunging it into a sinkful of cold water—then refrigerate or freeze.

Care and Cleaning
Each manufacturer has carefully worked out the best methods for using and cleaning his particular Pot. Again, read the instructions and use them sensibly. I have found, over a longish period of use, that all Pots must be treated as you would any fine earthenware: don't put a hot casserole down on a cold surface or into cold water. Never pour icy liquid or frozen food into a preheated Pot. You can safely put pre-browned food and boiling liquids into Pot *at room temperature* or into a *preheated* Pot. Never knock a casserole against the lip of a sink or on metal taps.

Removable casseroles may be washed by hand or in a dishwasher. Pots with non-removable casseroles must never be immersed in water. Remove the flex, hold your Pot carefully under the tap, fill it with water of the correct temperature, add some mild detergent, take it away from the sink and wash it out. Be very careful not to let water get into the socket at the base.

If food has adhered to the inner surface during cooking, fill the Pot with hot water and detergent, let it stand until the food loosens, then proceed as above. For *really* hard-stuck food (yes, it can happen, with some sweet or starchy dishes cooked on HIGH), I have found that a tablespoon of household bleach in a Pot of fairly hot water works wonders. But finish it off by washing out well with detergent and lots of fresh hot water, to do away with the chemical smell.

Never use wire wool or soap-filled wire wool pads on Pot casseroles; they will make micro-fine scratches that permanently dull the pretty gloss. If you find a smudged ring around the inside (after steaming a pudding, for example), wash as usual, fill the casserole with hottish water and a tablespoon of bicarbonate of soda; let it stand for a few minutes, then very gently rub with a nylon brush or plastic (not metal) scouring pad. When dry, wipe over with kitchen paper and a very small amount of cooking oil, to bring back the gleam.

After you've cooked strong-flavoured foods (curry, sauerkraut, dishes rich in onions and garlic) you may find that the inside of the casserole retains the memory a little too long! Dissolve 2 tablespoons of bicarbonate of soda in a pint of hot water, pour into the Pot, let it stand for half an hour, then rinse out well.

THE FOUR CARDINAL POINTS OF POT AND CASEROLE COOKING

1. Browning

Do, please, forget that business about putting things bare as they were born into either Pot or casserole. What goes in, comes out. I have found that for almost all meat, chicken and game dishes, it is absolutely vital to brown the main ingredients. Sear them quickly in spitting hot fat. Then all the flavour is sealed in, instead of leaching away into the liquid in the long slow hours of cooking. This quick, hot, initial browning adds immeasurably to the rich succulence of slow-cooked foods—hot-pots, ragoûts, stews, braises. Vegetables, too, benefit from a quick turning over in hot butter or oil.

Yes, it does make one extra step. But this takes only a very few extra minutes of cooking, with another minute or two to wash out a frying pan. And in all casseroles, not just the Pot, it's often what makes the difference between rather characterless food and a richly fragrant dish.

There are, of course, a number of main-course and vegetable recipes which don't need browning first (the lovely Greek chicken, for one, or Tongue in Madeira, or Smothered Chump Chops). If you really can't face the scent of lamb sizzling in oil and garlic at breakfast time, when half your mind is on getting the children to school, or yourself to an office at 9.30, all right: just look for the recipe with a star beside the title. They don't need browning or pre-cooking.

2. Seasoning—especially for the Pot

Because food cooks so slowly in the Pot, with all the moisture kept in by the vapour seal of the lid, I've learned that you need much more flavouring than you would think. And because you shouldn't fiddle around opening and closing it during cooking, it's best to season well at the beginning. Try some unlikely agents: a teaspoon of mushroom ketchup, some black treacle, wine vinegar, a little anchovy essence in meat dishes. All have the golden virtue of enhancing flavour and colour. Swill out the frying-pan in which you seared your pigeon, or shin of beef, with a little cider, wine or stock, scrape round to get out the brown bits, and let this all make part of your cooking liquid. Which brings me to:

3. A light hand with liquid

In reading the ingredient lists, you'll find in many places two quantities of liquid specified. The smaller is for the electric slow cooker, the larger (bracketed) for casserole cooking by the oven method. For the electric Pot, use only enough to cover the food decently without drowning it. And when you adapt your own casserole recipes for the Pot, use less—perhaps even only half as much as you normally would.

I must reiterate that there is little or no evaporation from the Pot. Vegetables and meats exude a surprising amount of juice in slow cooking. On the LOW setting, you needn't worry about food cooking dry or scorching.

If, when you open the Pot at the end of cooking time you find there is still more liquid than you want—turn control to HIGH, cover the Pot, let the sauce reduce for half an hour or so. Or tip it out into a saucepan and cook down swiftly on a high flame. Thicken, if need be, at the end with *beurre manié* or a good roux (pp. 153 and 154).

4. Don't keep peering into the Pot

Wait until you think the cooking time is nearly done. Resist the natural urge to poke and prod. Each time you open the lid, the heat shoots off into the air, and it can take from 20 minutes to an hour to get the Pot back to its proper cooking temperature. The moisture inside forms a vapour seal which helps keep it at an even heat. This of course is broken each time you open the lid. Some Pots have transparent glass or plastic lids, so you can see about how much liquid is left—and I promise you, it's more than you'd think, especially on the LOW setting.

INGREDIENTS: SOME PERSONAL DECLARATIONS

Prejudices, principles, suggestions only: use them how you will for oven casseroles or electric Pots.

Pepper. Whenever it's listed, it will always mean black, always freshly milled, as to my mind the flavour is infinitely racier than the pre-ground kind. Freshly-milled *white* pepper is even sparkier in many dishes, and in some recipes it is certainly preferable for reasons of colour. Likewise, I have in certain places suggested coarsely cracked black pepper which you can buy in glass jars or make yourself by bashing captive peppercorns in a plastic bag with a meat hammer or a rolling-pin.

Salt. I like sea salt in cooking and on the table, for what seems to me its more vigorous flavour. But if free-running table salt is more convenient for you, by all means use it.

Herbs. Dried herbs are meant in all cases, with the exception of parsley, and quantities specified are on that basis. If you are lucky enough to grow fresh basil or tarragon or summer savory, by all means use them, but double the given quantities. If you use dried parsley, read the directions on the packet, as in some cases it's advisable to soak the dry flakes in water before adding.

Spices. Far better to buy them in small quantities and use them up rapidly; the little you save in buying in larger batches is lost as their flavour dies away. Put them in tight-stoppered glass jars if you can, keep them away from light and heat. Even curry powder, coriander and cumin—surprisingly—can go flat if stored too long.

Oils. I must confess to a preference for groundnut, soya and sunflower oils, rather than corn oil which always seems to me to have a slightly greasy feel and taste. In some cases, I do think that olive oil is important to the final flavour of a dish, and have so specified it. But naturally you must use your own judgement in terms of flavour, cost and family taste. For sautéing and frying, consider groundnut or soya oil; for dishes with aubergines, courgettes, green peppers, perhaps a mixture of equal quantities of soya oil and olive oil.

Butter and Margarine. I have not spelt out 'butter *or* margarine' in each list of ingredients, but have merely said 'butter'. You can of course use either as I do, except in those cases—very rare in slow cooking—where the flavour of butter is what makes the dish—and there I've said so firmly.

Tomatoes. In recipe after recipe, I have suggested as alternatives fresh ripe tomatoes or the best tinned peeled tomatoes you can find. In fact, except in high summer, I think that the latter are much richer, sweeter and more flavourful. That's because they are prepared from the lumpy, misshapen, beautifully tasty Mediterranean tomatoes, so ugly beside our pretty little picture-book fruits, so heavenly to eat. If, however, you can get (or grow) Maroc or Marmande tomatoes fresh and dripping ripe—by all means use them.

Nutmeg, Soy Sauce, Mushroom Sauce. In re-reading my own words set down in cold type, I am perhaps unjustifiably surprised to see how often the words 'freshly grated nutmeg', 'soy sauce' and 'Chinese mushroom sauce'—along with those ubiquitous Italian tomatoes—seem to recur. Let me say here that I am not, alas, in the pay of any of these flavoursome industries. Is there a Nutmeg Board? A Soy Sauce Society? Not so much as a peeled tomato or a Chinese mushroom have I ever had as a gift. But these—and all the other rich-flavoured, sweet and savoury fruits, vegetables and condiments—are what to me raise casserole cooking from mere 'convenience cooking' to something uniquely worthwhile.

Beurre Manié. Far and away the best method of thickening sauces and gravies, but a bit tricky to use. Just equal quantities of butter and flour, worked together on a saucer into a paste and stirred in lumps the size of an olive into the simmering Pot set on HIGH, or a simmering casserole. If you find it easier, tip the liquid from the Pot into a saucepan set on a medium flame and stir in the bits of *beurre manié* little by little until the sauce thickens smoothly (see p. 153).

Roux. Another good way to thicken. See p. 154 for recipe and method of making in quantity, refrigerating or freezing.

Instant Potato. Excellent as a thickener, but the liquid must be boiling wildly or you'll have ineradicable lumps. Pour the liquid into a saucepan on highish heat, stir in the potato powder cautiously and beat well.

WEIGHTS AND MEASURES

Cooking, thank goodness, is a gloriously inexact science, and nothing better demonstrates this than the current kerfuffle about changing imperial measurements into metric. Every magazine, every cookery writer, seems to have a different system. In this book I have rounded off metric quantities to the nearest 25 gram equivalent of the imperial weights and measures of the original recipes. However, they can only be taken as approximate.

Most scales now available with dual-system markings are calibrated only in 25 gram steps. An ounce is really 28 grams-plus, therefore nearer to 30 grams than to 25, but unless you are prepared to invest in a postal scale to weigh in steps of 5 and 10 grams, you'll go quietly mad trying to work out exact equivalents from imperial to metric.

The one principle which must be adhered to, firmly and without fail, is to use *either* imperial *or* metric measures in each recipe, and stay with it. *Using metric measurements, expect a result that is about 10 per cent smaller than if you had used imperial measurements.*

I have tried to train myself to go completely metric by putting a thin strip of sticky tape over all imperial measures, but it all becomes a nonsense anyway when most small measurements are naturally in teaspoons, tablespoons, saltspoons and pinches. As long as leeks persist in growing to their own perfect size instead of forcing themselves to stop at a weight of 100 grams, and a medium onion can weigh anything from 100 to 200 grams, depending on season, rainfall and soil, we must all just do the best we can.

Only in recipes where proportions of fat to flour, say, or liquid to fat, may be crucial to tenderness, crustiness or flakiness, is it important to follow directions as closely as possible.

I do advise you to invest in an inexpensive set of the new metric spoons, which come in a set of four graded from 2·5 ml to 15 ml. In imperial terms, they roughly correspond to existing imperial *measuring* spoons (not the bent and scratched old household spoons rattling around most kitchen drawers), as follows:

2·5 ml spoon more or less equals	½ teaspoon (tsp)
5 ml spoon (medicine spoon)	1 teaspoon (tsp)
10 ml spoon	1 dessertspoon (dsp)
15 ml spoon	1 tablespoon (tbs)

In measuring liquids, I have found that five 15 ml spoonfuls of water, wine or stock equal about ½ an imperial gill (2½ fl oz). Any quantity larger than that is really easier to measure out in a marked measuring jug.

All spoon measurements for solids (flour, butter, spices and herbs) in the recipes are *rounded*, unless there is a good reason to be specific about a *level* spoonful.

All recipes are to serve 4 people, unless otherwise stated; but of course everything depends on appetite, greed and whether you're thinking about a meal with 4 or 5 courses, or one main dish plus a salad and a sweet.

The following table is a reasonably close approximation to actual gram-kilo-litre measurements. Don't be disturbed by the apparently slightly illogical jump from 100 g (4 oz) to 150 g (5 oz), as both are merely attempts to come close to the true metric weight.

Dry Weights

Imperial ounces (oz)	Metric (approximate gram conversion to nearest 25 g)
1	25
2	50
3	75
4 (¼ lb)	100
5	150
6	175
7	200
8 (½ lb)	225
9	250
10	300
11	325
12 (¾ lb)	350
13	375
14	400
15	425
16 (1 lb)	450
20 (1¼ lb)	575
24 (1½ lb)	700
28 (1¾ lb)	800
32 (2 lb)	900
35	1000 (1 kg)
3 lb	1·5 kg
4 lb	1·8 kg
5 lb	2·3 kg

Liquid Measures

Imperial	Metric (approximate)
$\frac{1}{4}$ pt (5 fl. oz)	150 ml
$\frac{1}{2}$ pt (10 fl. oz)	300 ml
$\frac{3}{4}$ pt (15 fl. oz)	400 ml
1 pt (20 fl. oz)	600 ml ($\frac{1}{2}$ litre)
1$\frac{1}{2}$ pt (30 fl. oz)	800 ml
2 pts (40 fl. oz)	1000 ml (1 litre)
3 pts (60 fl. oz)	1800 ml

Other Measurements

Pudding basins, loaf tins, soufflé dishes:

Imperial (by volume)	Metric
$\frac{1}{2}$ pt	250–300 ml
1 pt	500–550 ml
2 pt	1 litre or 1$\frac{1}{4}$ litre
6 pt	3 litre or 3$\frac{1}{2}$ litre

Imperial	Metric
6 in	15 cm
7 in	18 cm
8 in	20 cm
10 in	25 cm

If you prefer to ignore the whole horrid subject of weights imperial and weights metric, you can do a sort of rough and ready calculation using household measures which you probably have in the kitchen. Even a couple of washed-clean yoghurt or cream containers can be used! And they have the virtue of having their liquid contents marked clearly and indelibly on the outside where it can be read.

A 10 fl. oz measure ($\frac{1}{2}$ an imperial pint, 300 ml) will give you:

flour:	5$\frac{1}{2}$ oz (160 g)
caster sugar:	8 oz (225 g)
rice:	8 oz (225 g)
sultanas or mixed fruit:	4 oz (100 g)
butter:	8 oz (225 g)
dry breadcrumbs:	4 oz (100 g)
grated cheddar cheese:	4 oz (100 g)
fresh breadcrumbs:	2 oz (50 g)

Tablespoons (the 15 ml metric measuring spoon is about 1 standard measuring tablespoon):

butter:	1 rounded tablespoon is 1 oz (25 g)
	1 level tablespoon is $\frac{1}{2}$ oz (12 g)
sugar:	1 rounded tablespoon is 1 oz (25 g)
flour:	2 level tablespoons is 1 oz (25 g)
	1 level tablespoon is $\frac{1}{2}$ oz (12 g)
golden syrup or treacle:	1 level tablespoon is 1 oz (25 g)

Soups and Starters

It may seem slightly eccentric to suggest making all your soups in casseroles, but once over the initial surprise, consider what good sense it is. A casserole will cook slowly, thoroughly, and on low heat at considerable saving in energy. It's a good move to pack your oven with whatever casseroles will cook happily and compatibly at the same low temperature: a major soup, a small pâté, a casserole of pork and apples, a slow-cooking fruit cake are all natural 'go-togethers'.

And if the electric Pot had been invented solely for soups, it would more than pay its way. I feel almost intolerably smug, virtuous and wise when I have made a soup from leftovers (those maddening bits which are just too small to make part of an antipasto, just too large to scrape lightheartedly into the rubbish) and the surprisingly large amount of aromatic broth left from boiling bacon; or from such unconsidered trifles as the outside leaves of cabbage, odds and ends of onion, carrot scrapings and all that liquid I'm always draining out of tins of Italian tomatoes. Soup in the Pot simmers on LOW overnight, to be cooled and reheated for an evening meal; or from just after breakfast until just before dinner; or in the space of an afternoon, if that suits the pace of your life better.

In the Pot, make a mighty beef broth that simmers for 24 hours without being watched or stirred. Learn the art of constructive hoarding: save beef-bones, both raw and cooked, and chicken carcasses; file them in the freezer for future soups. Fill yoghurt containers with the rich brown meat jelly that collects under a joint, freeze and pull out at need.

Strongly resist one temptation, however, when you become a thrifty, beady-eyed peasant soup cook: forget everything you have heard about that ever-simmering pot of soup on the back of the stove. People died young, those days, and perhaps now we know why. Don't cook and store and bring out and toss in odd bits, and cook again. By all means put in scraps, and simmer broth to a rich strength. But cool it quickly, refrigerate as soon as possible and use it all up pretty smartly. Never use your Pot as a storage container and don't let soup (or, for that matter, any other food) sit about attracting invisible hosts from the air.

You can make very, very good soups by simply combining all your ingredients in the Pot and letting them simmer on undisturbed. I have found, though, that turning cut-up vegetables in butter (or margarine or oil) until just lightly browned, gives an infinitely richer flavour. It's worth the extra 5 minutes. Do all this in your heavy-based frying-pan and swill it out with your chosen liquid (water, stock, broth left over from steaming vegetables), then transfer quickly to the Pot.

Root vegetables for soup must be cut finer than usual, in thin slices or smallish dice, so that they cook at an even pace with the other ingredients. Both flavour and cooking performance benefit, in fact, if potatoes, onions, leeks, swedes and so forth are quickly pre-cooked in the boiling soup liquid before it goes into your Pot. With this new way of cooking, soup stock doesn't simmer away in steam as it does with conventional methods, so you may want to experiment with smaller quantities than usual. Add milk, soured cream or yoghurt almost at the last, and reheat cautiously; *don't let it come to the boil*—milk products will curdle in long slow cooking: see 'To Stabilize Yoghurt', p. 155.

I have tried making dumplings in the Pot, dropping them in half an hour before serving and cooking on HIGH. But to my mind this produces a somewhat cloudy, murky soup. The highest heat capability of the Pot is not great enough for an instant sealing of the flour mixture. Far better, if a bit fiddly, is to drop the dumplings into a saucepan of boiling water, pop on a tight lid and let them cook high, light and billowy before you add them to the soup.

Rice, barley and the firmer pasta shapes such as shells and spirals cook well in the Pot, but in my experience thin noodles and very small pieces of pasta may disintegrate. Give them 5 minutes in simmering water, then add them to the Pot about a quarter of an hour before serving, so that they gently absorb a measure of flavour and contribute a bit of thickening.

In addition to the recipes in this section, there are several in the Vegetables and Pulses section (for example, Ratatouille, Loubia) which make excellent starters. For additional soup suggestions, see under 'Soups' in the Index.

Autumn Soup

serves 4

1	small (about 1 lb (450 g)) tight-leaved white cabbage, cored and shredded	1
3	large cooking apples, peeled, cored and chopped	3
3	medium onions, finely minced	3
2 tbs	butter or bacon dripping	2 tbs
2 pts	chicken stock	1 gen l
1 tsp	brown sugar	1 tsp
	salt and pepper	
	To garnish:	
4	streaky bacon rashers	4
4 tbs	double cream	4 tbs

Electric slow cooker: preheat Pot on HIGH for 20 minutes

1. In a heavy pan, sauté the onions in the melted butter or dripping for about 5 minutes until pale gold. Add the cabbage and apples, raise heat, cover and sweat for another 5 minutes. Pour on the stock, add the sugar, bring to the boil, season well and put into the Pot. Cook on LOW for 5 hours until the cabbage is very soft.
2. Turn the Pot to HIGH. Purée half the soup in a blender, then stir back into the Pot. Let it heat through. Meanwhile, fry the bacon rashers crisp and crumble into each bowl of soup.

At the table, stir in the cream: you can use single cream, of course, if you prefer.

Casserole cooking: preheat oven to Gas 3, 325°F, 170°C

As in Steps 1 and 2 above, simmering in oven in a casserole with a well-fitting lid for 3 hours. Add a little more boiling stock, or boiling water, halfway through if it looks like cooking down more than you like. When you've done the puréeing part, put the casserole back in the oven for another half an hour, then fry bacon and add to each bowl of soup.

Cassoulet Soup

serves 4 to 6

4 oz	dried haricot beans, or 13 oz (365 g) tin haricot or cannelini beans	100 g
14 oz	tin Italian peeled tomatoes	400 g
6 oz	smoked German sausage, sliced	175 g
2 tbs	oil	2 tbs
1	medium onion, minced	1
2 lev tbs	brown flour	2 lev tbs
1 pt (1¼ pt approx)	chicken stock	600 ml (750 ml approx)
	salt and pepper	

Electric slow cooker: preheat Pot on HIGH for 15 minutes

1. If using dried beans, bring to the boil in cold water in a saucepan and boil for 2 minutes. Remove from heat and leave to stand, covered, for 2 hours.
2. Heat the oil in a heavy frying-pan and sauté the onion until limp and pale gold, not brown. Stir in the flour and cook until the mixture honeycombs. Add the stock and tomatoes and bring quickly to the boil. Add the beans and sausage, put into the Pot and cook on HIGH for 30 minutes, then on LOW for 6 to 8 hours. Taste for seasoning.

Serve with great quantities of French or Italian bread, and followed by a collection of hearty cheeses and fruit. Apologies for the cliché, but this really *does* make a meal.

Casserole cooking: preheat oven to Gas 3, 325°F, 170°C

As in Steps 1 and 2, putting everything but sausages and tomatoes in a casserole (mixing the flour with a little liquid first), lidding it tightly, and cooking for about 2½ hours until beans are quite tender. After an hour, add more stock—about ¼ pt—to cover beans. After putting in sausages and tomatoes, cook another 2 hours. This is a hearty, solid soup, a December dish to cherish.

Badaczony Goulash Soup

serves 8 to 10

A recipe for a big Pot or casserole; quantities may be halved.

2 lb	shin of beef, trimmed and cut into 1 in (2½ cm) cubes	900 g
2 tbs	lard	2 tbs
1	large garlic clove, crushed	1
1	large onion, finely minced	1
1 tsp	each sweet Hungarian paprika and hot paprika	1 tsp
1 tsp	caraway seeds	1 tsp
3 pts (4½ pts)	boiling water	1·5 l (2·5 l)
3	medium potatoes, diced	3
1	large carrot, diced	1
1	large tomato, peeled, and chopped	1
½	large green pepper, de-seeded and coarsely chopped	½
	For dumplings:	
2 oz	flour	50 g
1	egg	1
2 tbs	water	2 tbs
	pinch of salt	

Electric slow cooker: preheat Pot on HIGH for 20 minutes

1. Heat the lard in a heavy frying-pan, and soften but do not brown the garlic and onion. Stir in the sweet and hot paprika. Add the meat to the onions with about ¼ pt (150 ml) boiling water. Bring to the boil and cook for about 5 minutes, until the liquid is reduced by about half. Stir in the caraway seeds and cook on moderate heat until liquid has evaporated, stirring often. Put into the Pot and add the rest of the boiling water. Cook on LOW for 8 to 10 hours or overnight.
2. Blanch the vegetables in boiling water for 2 minutes, add to the Pot and cook on HIGH for 30 minutes or until the vegetables are tender.
3. Mix the dumpling ingredients and beat to a smooth dough. Leave to stand for 30 minutes.

Have ready a large saucepan with a tight-fitting lid, and about 2 pts (1 generous litre) boiling water. Pinch the dough into pieces about the size of a pea and drop into the water. With a slotted spoon, lift them gently from the bottom of the saucepan. Cover and cook for 5 minutes, add to the Pot just before serving.

Casserole cooking: preheat oven to Gas 3, 325°F, 170°C

As in Step 1, increasing boiling water to about 4½ pts (about 2½ l), and simmering in oven about 4 hours. Then add vegetables as in Step 2, turn oven heat to Gas 6, 400°F, 200°C, and cook another 30 minutes. Finish with dumplings as in Step 3, putting them into casserole just after it's taken from oven.

Chinese Chicken Consommé

serves 6

1	chicken carcass, with some shreds of chicken clinging to it	1
2	carrots, diced	2
1	stalk celery, diced	1
2 tsp	salt	2 tsp
1 tbs	soy sauce	1 tbs
1	bayleaf	1
6	black peppercorns	6
2	eggs (size 3)	2
3 pts	water	1·8 l
2 tbs	dry sherry	2 tbs

Electric slow cooker: preheat on HIGH for 20 minutes

1. Combine all ingredients except eggs and sherry in large saucepan, bring to boil. Skim, put in Pot. Cook on LOW 8 hours.
2. Strain stock into basin, wash out Pot, turn to HIGH. Put stock back in Pot. Separate eggs, whisk in whites. Lightly whisk soup a bit, cover, cook on HIGH about 15 minutes.

3. Strain soup again, into a large saucepan, add sherry, bring to boil. Mix egg yolks with fork. Pour soup into warmed bowls, and trail strands of yolk with fork over the hot soup, just before serving. Put a small jug of soy sauce on the table, let each person add as much or as little as liked.

Casserole cooking: preheat oven to Gas 3, 325°F, 170°C

As in Steps 1 and 2 above, but use a large casserole, set the lid slightly askew, and cook in oven about 3 hours. Strain soup into basin, rinse out casserole, add egg whites, whisk gently, return to oven and cook another 15 minutes.
3. Finish as in Step 3 above.

Carrot Soup serves 4

1 lb	carrots, coarsely grated	450 g
2	large onions, coarsely grated or minced	2
2 tbs	butter	2 tbs
1½ pts (1¾ pts)	chicken stock	750 ml (1 l)
½ pt	single cream	300 ml
1	garlic clove, crushed	1
½ tsp	salt	½ tsp
	white pepper	
1 oz	*beurre manié* (see p. 153)	25 g

Electric slow cooker: preheat Pot on HIGH for 20 minutes

1. Melt the butter in a heavy frying-pan and sweat the onion and carrot for about 10 minutes. Put into the Pot. Bring the stock to the boil and add, with the crushed garlic, salt and pepper. Cook on HIGH for 30 minutes, then on Low for 3 to 4 hours.
2. Turn the Pot to HIGH until the liquid is bubbling, then whisk the *beurre manié* a little at a time into the soup.

Do not sieve this soup, as its slightly grainy texture is one of its charms. Stir in the cream about 15 minutes before serving; do not let it curdle.

Casserole cooking: preheat oven to Gas 2, 300°F, 150°C

As in Steps 1 and 2, increasing liquid to about 1¾ pts (1 l), and simmering in casserole in oven 3 hours. To finish, put casserole on metal mesh mat on cooker top, and on medium heat add *beurre manié*, stir until thickened and smooth. Finish with cream, off the heat.

Beef Tea serves 4 to 8

This is a wonderful soup for slimmers, or for anyone recovering from an illness.

2 lb	shin of beef, trimmed and cut into ½ in (1 cm) cubes	900 g
1	small onion, minced	1
1	carrot, minced	1
2 pts	boiling water	1 gen l
1	bay leaf	1
	dash of soy sauce	
	salt and pepper	
	Optional: brown bread	
	Cheddar cheese, grated	

Electric slow cooker: preheat Pot on HIGH for 20 minutes

1. Bring all the ingredients to the boil in a saucepan and put into the Pot. Cook on LOW for 10 to 12 hours or overnight. Strain and allow to cool.
2. Skim off the fat and reheat in a saucepan.

You can float pieces of well dried brown bread or toast on top of the hot soup, and sprinkle in grated cheese. If the broth seems a little colourless, stir in a teaspoon of home-made browning (p. 153).

Casserole cooking: preheat oven to Gas 2, 300°F, 150°C

As Steps 1 and 2, simmering in a casserole with a very well-fitting lid (put a piece of foil under lid, if it's not really tight), for 3–4 hours until meat is falling to bits. At Gas 1, 250°F, 130°C, it can be cooked 6–8 hours if you are doing an ovenful of casseroled, very slow-cooking dishes.

Cold Curry Soup serves 6 to 8

This soup can be cooked overnight in the Pot on LOW, or beforehand in the casserole, then cooled in the morning and chilled all day in the fridge or larder. It has a mysterious flavour and very few people—unless they are devoted readers of Delia Smith in the Evening Standard, *from whom the original recipe came—ever guess the secret.*

1	medium onion, finely minced	1
1	medium carrot, diced small	1
3 oz	butter	75 g
3 tbs	flour	3 tbs
2 pts	chicken stock	1 gen l
1 tbs	+ 1 extra tsp mild curry powder	1 tbs
1 dsp	apricot jam	1 dsp
$\frac{1}{4}$ pt	double cream	150 ml
	salt and pepper	
	a few very small raw cauliflower florets, or 2 thin celery stalks, diced	

Electric slow cooker: preheat Pot on HIGH for 20 minutes

1. Heat the butter to foaming in a heavy pan, sauté the onion and carrot, but do not let them brown. Stir in the flour and 1 tablespoon curry powder, and add the stock slowly, stirring with a wooden spoon. Season. Put into the Pot and cook on LOW for 6 hours.
2. Remove and sieve or liquidize. Cool quickly, then chill thoroughly for 4 hours. Mix the extra teaspoon of curry powder with the apricot jam, whisk the cream lightly and blend with the curry powder and jam. Put a few sprigs of cauliflower or cubes of celery into each bowl, ladle in the soup, and top with a float of the cream mixture.

Casserole cooking: preheat oven to Gas 3, 325°F, 170°C

As in Step 1, but simmer gently in covered casserole in oven for about 2 hours, then cool and chill and finish as in Step 2. In a flameproof casserole, and if you can trust your cooker rings to simmer low and slow, cook for about 45 minutes, stirring once in a while, then finish as above.

Soupe au Pistou serves 4

This is like a very simple version of the most primitive minestrone, found all along the Ligurian coast of Italy, and sometimes in the South of France.

1 lb	French beans, cut into 1 in (2·5 cm) pieces	450 g
4	medium potatoes, peeled and diced	4
4	tomatoes, peeled and chopped, or their equivalent in tinned Italian peeled tomatoes	4
1	medium onion, finely minced	1
1$\frac{1}{2}$ pts (1$\frac{3}{4}$ pts)	boiling water	900 ml (1 l)
	salt and pepper	
4 oz	small pasta shells or stars	100 g
3	garlic cloves	3
2 tbs	basil	2 tbs
1 tbs	tomato paste	1 tbs
	dash of hot pepper sauce	

Electric slow cooker: preheat Pot on HIGH for 20 minutes

1. Put the prepared vegetables and boiling water into the Pot with salt and pepper, cook on HIGH for 30 minutes, then on LOW for 6 to 8 hours. One hour before serving, add the pasta, turn the Pot to HIGH and cook until soft.
2. Crush the garlic with the basil, add to the tomato paste and hot pepper sauce, stir well, then mix in 4 tablespoons of the hot soup. Stir back into the soup, or pass the garlic mixture at the table if preferred.

Casserole cooking: preheat oven to Gas 3, 325°F, 170°C

Bring vegetables, seasoning and water to boil in saucepan, tip into a large casserole, and cook, covered, in oven about 2$\frac{1}{2}$ hours. Add another $\frac{1}{4}$ pt (150 ml) boiling water halfway through cooking time. Half an hour before serving time add pasta and increase oven heat to Gas 6, 400°F, 200°C. Make the 'pistou sauce' as in Step 2, and put it into the soup at the last moment just before serving.

Toupin

serves 4

This is an immensely comforting soup, whether it is life or a cold climate that has chilled your blood. I make it in largish quantities up to the point of adding the egg yolks, and freeze it. You can then finish it off on top of your cooker while the French bread is crisping.

3	large sweet Spanish onions, sliced very thin	3
1	garlic clove, crushed with ½ tsp salt	1
4 tbs	melted pork fat	4 tbs
2 pts (2½ pts)	chicken stock	1 gen l (1·5 l)
4	egg yolks	4
	salt and black pepper	
	nutmeg, freshly grated	
	French bread	

Electric slow cooker: preheat Pot on HIGH for 15 minutes

1. Heat the fat in a heavy pan. Cook the onions and garlic, covered, very slowly, to a soft purée, stirring from time to time. Add the stock and bring to the boil. Cook on LOW for 4 to 6 hours. Season.
2. Beat the egg yolks, blend a little of the hot soup into them and whisk this back into the Pot. Cook on HIGH for another 15 minutes.
3. In the meantime, slice a loaf of French bread, and crisp slices in a medium oven (watch them, they burn easily). Put a slice in each bowl, pour soup over and serve very hot.

Casserole cooking: preheat oven to Gas 3, 325°F, 170°C

As in Steps 1 and 2, using a large—preferably French glazed inside, rough beige outside—casserole, and cooking in oven about 2 hours. Then add egg yolks and return to oven, uncovered, for another 10–15 minutes. You may want to increase stock to 2½ pts (1·5 l), which makes a most generous soup. I seem to have eight recipes for what I was taught to call 'Toupin', in my files—and have now acquired two more very similar ones called 'Tourin', one of which apparently can be made in less than half an hour! As you can see, an extraordinarily flexible soup.

Cotriade

serves 4 to 6

2 lb	any firm fish, such as bream	1 kg
1 lb	fish trimmings (sole, plaice or any other white, non-oily fish)	450 g
3 oz	unsalted pork fat	75 g
1	large onion, thinly sliced	1
6	fennel seeds	6
4	black peppercorns	4
3 pts	water	1·5 l
	salt and pepper	
1	bay leaf	1
	peel of a small lemon	
1 lb	potatoes, peeled and sliced	450 g
1	small garlic clove, crushed	1

To garnish:
parsley and/or chives, finely chopped

Electric slow cooker: preheat Pot on HIGH for 20 minutes

1. Melt the fat in a frying-pan and sauté the onion until limp but not coloured. Bring the water to the boil in a saucepan, add the fish trimmings, peppercorns, fennel, salt, pepper, bay leaf and lemon peel. Put into the Pot, add the onions and melted fat and cook on LOW for 6 hours. Strain. (This can be done well in advance, cooled and refrigerated or frozen.)
2. Blanch the potato slices in boiling water for 1 minute and drain. Bring the fish stock to the boil in a large saucepan. Turn the Pot to HIGH. Put the stock, potatoes and cleaned fish, cut into 2 inch (5 cm) pieces, into the Pot and cook on HIGH for 1 hour. Add the crushed garlic. Taste for seasoning.
3. To serve, remove the fish and potato pieces with a slotted spoon, put some into each soup plate and pour on the fish soup.
   Garnish with parsley and chives if liked.

Casserole cooking: preheat oven to Gas 5, 375°F, 190°C

As in Step 1, using a heavy ovenproof casserole, cook in oven 1½ hours. Then strain, add thinly sliced potatoes, fish, and boiling stock, and cook on another 45 minutes. Finish as in Step 3.

Cucumber Vichyssoise

serves 4

This recipe is for 4. But once, having 7 to feed, only one cucumber, no spring onions, and just the long green top shoots of garden onions, I made a rather odd but good version of this soup by increasing the potatoes to 1½ lb (675 g) and mincing the onion tops very fine. It was an extraordinary colour, like a thunderous sky, but had a lovely fresh taste—much nicer than conventional vichyssoise. All this preamble is to assure you that you can go your own way with quantities. But do use plenty of butter. You cannot substitute margarine in this recipe.

1	large cucumber, peeled and diced	1
2 tbs	butter	2 tbs
8 oz	potatoes, peeled and diced	225 g
6	spring onions, chopped	6
1½ pts (2 pts)	chicken stock	750 ml (1·2 l)
	salt and pepper	
4 tbs	single cream	4 tbs
	chives, minced (*optional*)	

Electric slow cooker: preheat Pot on HIGH for 20 minutes

1. Heat the butter to foaming in a heavy pan, but do not let it brown, and turn all the vegetable pieces over in it until hot and well coated. Lower the heat, cover and simmer for about 10 minutes. Bring the stock to the boil in a saucepan. Put the stock and vegetables into the Pot and cook on LOW for 4 hours, until the vegetables are tender. Taste for seasoning.
2. Liquidize or press through sieve, cool in basin in a sinkful of cold water. Chill for 3 hours or more.

  Serve with a tablespoon of cream in each soup bowl and, if possible, freshly minced chives.

Casserole cooking: preheat oven to Gas 3, 325°F, 170°C.

As in Steps 1 and 2 above, using a heavy casserole, increasing chicken stock to about 2 pts (1·2 l), and cooking about 1½ hours until vegetables are very soft. In a flameproof casserole, you may simmer it on your cooktop for 50–60 minutes.

Lentil Soup with Pasta

serves 4

If you can, give everything an occasional quick stir, during the LOW cooking period if using the electric slow cooker, and clap the lid back on instantly.

6 oz	brown lentils	175 g
1 tbs	oil	1 tbs
1	large onion, finely minced	1
2	garlic cloves, crushed	2
2 oz	diced bacon, or a ham bone	50 g
2	celery stalks, diced	2
3	large tomatoes, peeled and chopped, or their equivalent in tinned Italian peeled tomatoes	3
1 tsp	basil	1 tsp
	salt and pepper	
2 pts (2½ pts)	boiling water	1 gen l (1·2 l)
2 oz	pastina, or fine spaghetti, broken up	50 g
	fresh parsley, chopped (*optional*)	

Electric slow cooker

1. Wash and pick over the lentils. Cover with cold water in a saucepan, bring to the boil, remove from heat and leave to stand for 2 hours. Strain and throw away the water.
2. Preheat Pot on HIGH for 20 minutes.
3. Heat the oil in a frying-pan and gently sauté the onion, garlic and chopped bacon, or ham bone. Add the celery, tomatoes, herb and seasonings, bring to the boil and put into the Pot. Stir in the lentils and pour on the boiling water. Cook on HIGH for 30 minutes, then on LOW for 8 to 10 hours.
4. Half an hour before serving, add pastina or fine spaghetti broken into little bits. Turn the Pot to HIGH and cook until pasta is tender. Remove the ham bone, if used.

  Serve with quite a lot of fresh parsley if you like.

Casserole cooking: preheat oven to Gas 3, 325°F, 170°C

As in Steps 1 and 3 above. Put everything but the

pasta in a large casserole, add about 2½ pts (1·2 l) boiling water, stir it all up, set on casserole lid slightly askew so that lentils won't boil over, and cook 3 hours. Finish as in Step 4.

Creamy Fish Soup (Cold)

serves 4

6 oz	frozen cooked prawns	175 g
6 oz	white fish, cut into pieces	175 g
1 tbs	butter	1 tbs
1	small onion, finely minced	1
1	garlic clove, crushed	1
½ pt	light stock	300 ml
	salt and pepper	
1 pt	milk	600 ml
¼ pt	single cream	150 ml
2 oz	*To garnish:* peeled prawns	50 g
1 tsp	dillweed	1 tsp

Electric slow cooker: preheat Pot on High for 20 minutes

1. Melt the butter in a heavy pan and gently cook the onion and garlic until just translucent but not brown. Add the prawns, fish, stock, salt and pepper. Bring to the boil and put into the Pot. Cook on LOW for 4 hours.
2. Add the milk and liquidize for a few seconds only, so that the soup isn't completely puréed. Chill.

Just before serving, stir in the cream and garnish each soup bowl with some extra prawns and dillweed to your taste.

Casserole cooking: preheat oven to Gas 3, 325°F, 170°C

As in recipe above, simmering in oven about 2 hours. Finish with milk and cream; prawns and dillweed. In a flameproof casserole on your cooker top, it should simmer for about 1¼ to 1½ hours, before stirring in milk.

Garbanzo Soup

serves 6

8 oz	dried chick peas, or 2 tins	225 g
1	ham bone with a little ham clinging to it	1
4 oz	salt pork, cut into 2 in (5 cm) cubes, or a piece of unsliced streaky bacon	100 g
8 oz	Spanish chorizo sausages, Kabanos or pepperoni	225 g
2	medium onions, minced	2
1 tsp	paprika	1 tsp
1 lb	potatoes, peeled and diced	450 g
4 tbs	olive oil	4 tbs
1¾ pts (3½ pts)	cold water	1 l (2 l)
	salt and pepper	

Electric slow cooker

1. Wash the dried chick peas thoroughly and soak overnight in salted water. In the morning drain well, cover with fresh cold water in a saucepan, bring to the boil, boil for 2 minutes and leave to stand for 2 hours.
2. Preheat Pot on HIGH for 20 minutes.
3. Add the ham bone, salt pork cubes, sausages, onions, potatoes, paprika and oil to the saucepan, cover with the water, bring to the boil and put into the Pot. Cook on HIGH for 30 minutes, then on LOW for 8 to 10 hours, until the chick peas are tender.
3. Discard the bone, remove the salt pork and sausages and cut into small pieces. Turn the Pot to HIGH. Purée half the soup in a food mill or blender, return it to the Pot, put in the pork and sausages and reheat. Taste for seasoning; it may need a little or a lot of salt. When cooking chick peas, always add salt at the end of cooking, otherwise they may be tough.

Casserole cooking: preheat oven to Gas 3, 325°F, 170°C

As in Steps 1 and 3, simmering in a covered casserole about 3 hours until chick peas are soft. Finish as in Step 3.

Minestrone

serves 4

This is the simplest, basic minestrone from Genoa. There are about 80 versions, which can include celery, peas, rice, even marrow and French beans.

3 tbs	oil	3 tbs
2	large onions, coarsely chopped with 1 garlic clove, crushed with 1 tsp salt	2
2	medium carrots, diced	2
2	streaky bacon rashers, or about 3 oz (75 g) bacon ends, chopped	2
3 pts (4 pts)	stock or water	1·5 l (2 l)
8 oz	peeled tomatoes, chopped, or their equivalent in tinned Italian peeled tomatoes	225 g
4 oz	dried haricot beans, pre-cooked, or a tin of Italian cannelini beans	100 g
1 tsp	*each* of basil and oregano	1 tsp
½	small cabbage	½
2 oz	pasta shells or stars, or short-cut macaroni	50 g
	salt and black pepper	
	To garnish:	
1	garlic clove	1
1 tsp	basil	1 tsp
1 tbs	olive oil	1 tbs
1 tbs	Parmesan cheese, grated	1 tbs

Electric slow cooker: preheat Pot on HIGH for 20 minutes

1. Heat the oil in a frying-pan and lightly brown the onion, garlic and carrots. Sauté the bacon in the same oil. Put into the Pot. Bring the stock and tomatoes to the boil in a saucepan and add to the Pot. Put in the haricots, basil and oregano. Cook on LOW for 8 hours. All this can be done overnight, or the day before you want to serve the minestrone.
2. Two hours before you are ready to serve, shred and wash the cabbage and add to the Pot. Turn the Pot to HIGH. One hour before serving, stir in the pasta. Cook until the pasta and cabbage are tender. Season.

3. Garnish, if you like, with Pesto. To make this, crush the garlic clove and mix with the basil, olive oil and grated Parmesan to a thick, grainy sauce. Put a blob in each soup plate, and pass a bowl of grated cheese.

Casserole cooking: preheat oven to Gas 4, 350°F, 180°C

As in Step 1, but increase stock or water to about 4 pts (2 l) and cook about an hour. Then add shredded, washed cabbage, cook another half hour and stir in pasta. Cook another 30 minutes until pasta is tender but not mushy. If you opt for cooking on a boiling ring, the basic timing is about the same, but the final simmering after putting in the pasta will be only about 15–20 minutes.

Luxurious Chicken Soup

serves 4

This is still a good soup without the crabmeat and cream but, of course, not so luxurious.

3	chicken pieces (total weight 10 oz (300 g)): thighs or legs are best, not the bonier bits	3
4 oz	cooked crabmeat	100 g
2 pts	chicken stock	1 gen l
1	small onion, finely minced	1
2	celery stalks, diced	2
1	small garlic clove, crushed	1
½ tsp	tarragon	½ tsp
	salt and pepper	
	For the roux:	
2 tbs	butter	2 tbs
2 tbs	flour	2 tbs
	To garnish:	
2 tbs	cream	2 tbs

Electric slow cooker: preheat Pot on HIGH for 20 minutes

1. Bring the stock to the boil in a saucepan, add the chicken pieces, minced onion, garlic, celery, tarragon, salt and pepper. Put into the Pot and cook on LOW for 6 hours or overnight.
2. Remove the chicken and dice the flesh finely.

Turn the Pot to HIGH. Strain and skim the fat from the stock.

3. Melt the butter in a small frying-pan and stir in the flour gradually. Cook until it honeycombs, do not let it brown. Stir in the hot stock, return to the Pot and cook on HIGH until thickened and smooth. Stir in the chicken flesh, add the cream and crabmeat and taste for seasoning.

Casserole cooking: preheat oven to Gas 3, 325°F, 170°C

As in Steps 1 and 2 above, simmering in casserole with lid slightly tilted in oven for about 3½ hours. Skim surface once in a while. When you've made the roux as in Step 3, pour it back into casserole and cook on in oven another 15 minutes, or—using a metal mesh or asbestos mat—simmer on the top of your cooker just until thickened.

Ciorba
serves 4 to 6

This is a recipe to make when you have had a great rush of tomatoes which have been made into tomato juice (see p. 148), or you can use the excellent tinned Israeli juice.

1 lb	onions, finely minced	400 g
2 tbs	butter	2 tbs
2	garlic cloves, crushed	2
2 pts	tomato juice	1 gen l
½ tsp	celery seed	½ tsp
	salt and pepper	
	To garnish:	
2 tbs	dillweed	2 tbs
8 fl oz	plain yoghurt, stabilized if possible (see p. 155)	225 ml

Electric slow cooker: preheat Pot on HIGH for 20 minutes

1. Heat the butter in a heavy saucepan and gently sauté the onion and garlic until just soft. Add the tomato juice, celery seed, salt and pepper, and bring to the boil. Put into the Pot and cook on LOW for 4 to 6 hours.
2. Taste for seasoning and stir in the dillweed and yoghurt. Turn the Pot to HIGH and cook for no longer than 10 minutes if using unstabilized yoghurt, or it may curdle.

Casserole cooking: preheat oven to Gas 3, 325°F, 180°C

As in Steps 1 and 2, putting all ingredients except yoghurt into a large casserole, cover tightly, simmer 3 hours, then finish as in Step 2.

Lentil Cream Soup
serves 4

8 oz	red lentils	225 g
2 tbs	butter	2 tbs
1	bacon rasher, or some bits of cooked ham	1
1	medium onion, diced	1
1	bay leaf	1
	salt and pepper	
¾ pt	water	400 ml
½ pt	milk	300 ml
1 tsp	curry paste (*optional*)	1 tsp

Electric slow cooker: preheat Pot on HIGH for 20 minutes

1. Pick over the lentils and wash them well. Heat the butter in a heavy frying-pan and sauté the cut-up bacon for about 2 minutes, then add the diced onions and turn them over and over in the same pan until well coated. Add the water and bring to the boil. Season, put all the ingredients (except milk and curry paste), including the water in which the bacon has been boiled, into the Pot and cook on LOW for 6 to 10 hours according to your convenience.
2. Taste for seasoning. Remove the bay leaf, liquidize or sieve. Put into a saucepan, add enough milk to bring the soup to the consistency you like best and reheat gently.

If you have some curry paste at hand, a teaspoon stirred in before you add the milk makes an interesting variation.

Casserole cooking: preheat oven to Gas 3, 325°F, 170°C

As in Steps 1 and 2 above, but use a casserole with a lid that can be tilted slightly while the soup cooks in the oven, as lentils tend to boil over all too quickly if tightly covered. Cook about 2 hours, adding a little boiling water at half time if soup seems to be too thick.

Pot au Feu I

serves 8

This is not the absolutely classic French recipe, which includes a boiling fowl as well as beef. But it does yield a delicious boiled dinner (see also Pot au Feu II, p. 74) and a large quantity of superb broth for future soups, such as an old-fashioned vegetable soup or a French onion soup; or the broth can be boiled down to half its quantity for a rich consommé.

4 lb	shin of beef cut off the bone, and the beef shin bone	1·8 kg
8 oz	salt pork	225 g
1	garlic clove, crushed	1
1	onion, stuck with 2 cloves	1
4	leeks, well washed and sliced	4
4	carrots, scraped	4
2	small white turnips, peeled and cut up	2
1 tbs	salt	1 tbs
4 pts (6 pts)	water	2 l (3 l)
	bouquet garni	
	pepper	

Electric slow cooker: preheat Pot on HIGH for 20 minutes

1. Put everything into a very large saucepan, bring to the boil and skim off the scum that rises to the surface. Put into the Pot and cook on LOW for 12 hours or overnight.
2. Cool quickly (pour into a large saucepan and plunge into a sinkful of cold water), strain and skim the fat from the surface. Reheat in the saucepan and serve; a bowl of the broth first, then slices of meat, vegetables, with coarse sea salt, horseradish sauce, gherkins, several kinds of mustard. Any cold meat left over makes a memorable salad, with a highly seasoned potato salad, paper-thin onion rings, capers and suchlike.

Casserole cooking: preheat oven to Gas 2, 300°F, 150°C

As in Step 1, bring all ingredients, plus 2 additional pints of water (about 1 generous litre) to boil in big saucepan, skim the thick brownish scum that rises to the top, and transfer to a very large casserole. Put lid on, slightly tilted so steam can escape, and simmer in the oven a good 4–5 hours. Strain, and keep meat warm while you skim fat from the surface of the broth. Reheat, and serve as above.

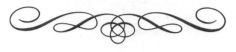

Mushroom and Barley Soup

serves 4

6 oz	mushrooms (preferably dark, open 'field' mushrooms) washed and chopped	175 g
3 oz	butter	75 g
1	medium onion, finely minced	1
1	medium carrot, coarsely diced	1
3 pts	chicken stock	1·8 l
2 oz	pearl barley, rinsed	50 g
1 tsp	Chinese mushroom sauce (*optional*)	1 tsp
	salt, pepper	
	To finish:	
1 tbs	flour	1 tbs
	dillweed (fresh or dried)	
4 tbs	sour cream	4 tbs

Electric slow cooker: preheat Pot on HIGH 20 minutes

1. Heat half the butter to foaming in a heavy frying-pan. Gently cook mushrooms, onion and carrot, about 10 minutes. Rinse barley, add to frying pan. Bring stock to boil and put in Pot with vegetables and barley. Season and cook on HIGH 30 minutes, then on LOW 6 hours.
2. Melt remaining butter in small saucepan, stir in flour to make a blond *roux*. When the mixture honeycombs, gradually add about $\frac{1}{4}$ pt (150 ml) of the hot soup, and stir until well-blended. Stir back into Pot. Turn to HIGH and cook until lightly thickened. Add dillweed just before serving, and swirl a tablespoonful of soured cream into each soup bowl. (Or pass a little bowl of it, for individual choice.)

Casserole cooking: preheat oven to Gas 2, 300°F, 150°C

As in Step 1, putting all the ingredients after their preparation into a large casserole. Simmer, covered, in oven 3 hours. About halfway through, add a little more stock or water (barley swells alarmingly). Finish as in Step 2.

Irish Oatmeal Soup   serves 4

2 tbs	oatmeal, heaped (pinhead is best)	2 tbs
2 tbs	butter	2 tbs
2	medium onions, finely minced	2
	salt and pepper	
1 pt (1¼ pts)	good chicken stock	500 ml (650 ml)
¼ pt	rich milk or single cream	150 ml
	To garnish: chives or spring onion tops	

Electric slow cooker: preheat Pot on HIGH for 20 minutes

1. Heat the butter to foaming in a heavy frying-pan and gently sauté the onion. Stir in the oatmeal, salt and pepper. Add the stock, bring to the boil and put everything into the Pot. Cook on LOW for 6 hours.
2. Press through a food mill or whirl briefly in a liquidizer. Turn the Pot to HIGH and cook for another 15 minutes, stir in milk or cream and heat, but do not allow to curdle.

Garnish with chopped chives or snipped spring onion tops.

Casserole cooking: preheat oven to Gas 3, 325°F, 170°C

As in Step 1, but put the ingredients in a large casserole, increase the liquid by about another ¼ pt (150 ml), and simmer in oven 1½–2 hours. Finish as in Step 2. This soup can be made in a flameproof casserole, on a steady slow simmer on top of your cooker, for about 45 minutes, but the oven method is easy and foolproof.

Pasta Fagiole   serves 4

8 oz	dried haricot beans	225 g
1	large onion, minced	1
2	garlic cloves, crushed with 1 tsp *each* salt and basil	2
2 tbs	oil	2 tbs
1	ham bone with some ham still clinging to it	1
3 tbs	tomato purée	3 tbs
4 oz	short-cut macaroni	100 g
	To garnish: parsley, chopped	
	cheese, grated	

Electric slow cooker

1. Cover the beans with cold water in a saucepan and bring to the boil for 2 minutes, remove from heat, leave to stand, covered, for 2 hours.
2. Preheat Pot on HIGH for 20 minutes.
3. Heat the oil in a frying-pan, soften the onions and garlic and add to the well drained beans. Put into the Pot, add the ham bone and boiling water to cover, then stir in the tomato purée. Cook on HIGH for 30 minutes, then on LOW for 8 to 10 hours.
4. An hour before serving, purée half the soup, turn the Pot to HIGH, return the soup to the Pot, add the pasta and cook until it is soft. If stages 1–3 have been done in advance, stage 4 should be done in a saucepan, not the Pot.

If you like, sprinkle some chopped parsley into each soup bowl, and pass a dish of grated cheese (Parmesan for choice, but a dry Cheddar does nicely).

Casserole cooking: preheat oven to Gas 4, 350°F, 180°C

As in Steps 1 and 3 above, bringing to boil on top of cooker, then putting into a large casserole. Add about another ½ pt (300 ml) boiling water so that vegetables are well-covered with liquid. Cook 3 hours, then purée half the soup, stir it back into casserole, add macaroni and cook on until it is soft, about another 45 minutes. Serve with grated cheese and minced parsley in each bowl.

Petite Marmite

serves 4

A recipe to begin the day before it is wanted; or, if using the electric slow cooker, to cook overnight, chill during the day, and finish just before dinner.

¾pt (2 pts)	rich beef stock	450 ml (1·2 l)
¾pt	boiling water	450 ml
1 lb	lean, unsalted brisket of beef	450 g
1 tsp	salt	1 tsp
2	chicken wings	2
2	carrots, sliced	2
1	small turnip, sliced	1
	Parmesan cheese, grated	

Electric slow cooker: preheat Pot on HIGH for 20 minutes

1. In a large saucepan, combine the stock, water, salt, chicken and beef. Bring to the boil, skim, and put into the Pot. Cook on LOW for 8 hours or overnight. Remove the meat and refrigerate.
2. Chill the broth and, when cold, lift the fat from the surface. Put into a saucepan, bring to the boil, add the carrots and turnips, cover and simmer for 15 minutes. Cut the meat into small pieces (discarding the skin and bone from the chicken wings) and put into the soup to heat through. Taste for seasoning.

Pass coarsely grated Parmesan cheese with the soup; it should melt into a sort of delicious thatched covering.

Casserole cooking: preheat oven to Gas 3, 325°F, 170°C

As in Step 1, but increase liquid to about 2 pts (1·2 l), and don't put the chicken wings in at the beginning. Simmer in a casserole in the oven, tightly lidded, about 2½–3 hours, until beef is tender, then add chicken and cook another 45 minutes. Finish as in Steps 1 and 2. Of course, a flameproof casserole simmering on top of your cooker will make your Petite Marmite, but you must have a steady, unaltering heat and keep the liquid just moving, not boiling.

Potato Soup with Bacon

serves 4 to 6

This can all be made the night before (up to the bacon-frying stage), chilled and refrigerated, then reheated in a saucepan.

2 oz	butter	50 g
1 lb	potatoes, peeled and diced	450 g
3	celery stalks, diced	3
1	small parsnip, scraped and diced	1
1	large onion, finely minced	1
1½ pts (gen 2 pts)	beef stock	900 ml (1·2 l)
½ tsp	marjoram	½ tsp
	salt and pepper	
2	streaky bacon rashers	2

Electric slow cooker: preheat Pot on HIGH for 20 minutes

1. Melt the butter in a heavy pan, add the prepared vegetables, stir well and cook for about 5 minutes on medium heat. Add the stock, marjoram, salt and pepper, bring to the boil and put into the Pot. Cook on LOW for 8 hours.
2. Purée half the vegetables in a blender, or force through a food mill. Turn the Pot to HIGH. Return the purée to the Pot to reheat.
3. Fry the de-rinded bacon rashers crisp at the last minute and crumble into the soup at the table.

A scattering of paprika looks pretty on the pale surface of the soup.

Casserole cooking: preheat oven to Gas 4, 350°F, 180°C

As in Steps 1, 2 and 3 above, but increase stock to a generous 2 pts (1·2 l), and simmer in casserole, uncovered, in oven about 2½ hours until vegetables are meltingly tender. After puréeing half the soup, turn oven heat to Gas 6, 400°F, 200°C, to reheat while you fry the bacon.

Real Chicken Soup

serves 4

2 lb	boiling chicken, jointed (freeze the rest of a large boiling fowl, or use for Chicken Fricassee, p. 55)	900 g
1	small onion or 3 spring onions, finely minced	1
1	celery stalk with leaves, chopped	1
1 tbs	salt	1 tbs
6	parsley sprigs	6
2 pts	boiling water	1 gen l
2 oz	mushrooms	50 g
	white pepper	
	dash of soy sauce	

Electric slow cooker: preheat Pot on HIGH for 20 minutes

1. Put the chicken, onion, celery, salt and parsley into a large saucepan, add the boiling water, bring it all to the boil and put into the Pot. Cook on LOW for 6 to 7 hours or on HIGH for 3½ to 4 hours.
2. Strain and set the broth aside. Skim off the fat. Skin and bone the chicken, cut the flesh into small pieces, return to the broth and reheat in a saucepan. Taste for seasoning, add white pepper to taste.
3. Slice the washed mushrooms downwards from top to bottom and put some into each soup plate. Add a dash of soy sauce—2 or 3 drops—to each dish; it does something very good for this soup.

Casserole cooking: preheat oven to Gas 3, 325°F, 170°C

As in Steps 1, 2 and 3 above, using a large casserole in oven and cooking for 4 hours; you may want to add more boiling water halfway through the time. With a flameproof casserole, and reliable boiling rings on top of your cooker, you can simmer this soup for about 3 hours, skimming occasionally and making sure liquid is not reducing too rapidly.

Sauerkraut Soup

serves 4

This is, I think, best made the day before you want it (the extra time will not spoil it), cooled, then refrigerated. Reheat in a saucepan, not in the Pot, or use a casserole in the oven.

12 oz	sauerkraut left over from Choucroute Garni (see p. 97) or a small tin of good Polish sauerkraut	350 g
1 tbs	bacon dripping	1 tbs
½	medium onion, finely minced	½
1	celery stalk, diced	1
1	large carrot, thinly sliced	1
1	potato, peeled and diced	1
¼ pt	beer	150 ml
¼ pt	*tomato juice	150 ml
¾ pt (1¼ pt)	boiling water	400 ml (650 ml)
	salt and pepper	
¼ pt	soured cream *(optional)*	150 ml

Electric slow cooker: preheat Pot on HIGH for 20 minutes

1. Heat the bacon dripping in a heavy pan until very hot, sauté the onion, celery and carrots for 5 minutes, but do not let them brown. Add all the other ingredients except sour cream, bring to the boil and put into the Pot. Cook on LOW for 5 hours.

If you like, stir in some soured cream just before serving.

* The juice strained from tinned Italian peeled tomatoes used in another dish is excellent.

Casserole cooking: preheat oven to Gas 2, 300°F, 150°C

As in method above, putting in heavy, tight-lidded casserole, and simmering in oven about 2–2½ hours. Look at it after an hour, and add another ½ pt boiling water if soup is getting too thick. This can be simmered for an hour in a flameproof casserole on your cooker top, but make sure the heat is very low, very steady, and stir from time to time.

Simple Lentil and Bacon Soup

serves 4

This is the easiest lentil soup I know. It is made with the readily available red lentils, but is equally good with brown lentils—these, however, must be well picked over and soaked overnight, or boiled for 2 minutes, then left to stand for 2 hours.

1 lb	bacon knuckle, soaked overnight	450 g
6 oz	red lentils	175 g
4	onions, peeled and thinly sliced	4
4	medium carrots, thinly sliced	4
2	celery stalks, diced	2
	salt and pepper	

Electric slow cooker: preheat Pot on HIGH for 20 minutes

1. Drain the bacon well, put into a saucepan, cover with fresh cold water and bring slowly to the boil. Wash the lentils and check them for grit.
2. Put all the ingredients, including the bacon liquor, into the Pot. Cook on LOW for anything from 6 hours to overnight, according to your convenience. Remove the bacon knuckle and cut the meat into small pieces, stir back into soup. Taste for seasoning.

If you like a thickish soup, purée half the lentils (after the bacon has been taken out) in a blender or food mill and heat in a saucepan for about 20 minutes.

Casserole cooking: preheat oven to Gas 2 or 3, 300–325°F, 150–170°C

If using brown lentils, wash well, bring slowly to boil in cold water to cover, then remove from cooker and let stand, covered, for 2 hours. Red lentils need no soaking but should be well washed in several changes of cold water. Proceed as in Step 1, but after bacon has been brought to boil in fresh cold water, add lentils and all other ingredients, and heat to boiling again. Then put in casserole, set lid slightly askew, and cook in oven 4 hours, until bacon is cooked and lentils are soft. Finish as above.

Potage Parmentier

serves 4

1 lb	potatoes, peeled and diced	450 g
½ lb	leeks, well washed	225 g
3 oz	butter	75 g
1¼ pts (1½ pts)	stock	650 ml (900 ml)
	salt and white pepper	
2 oz	flour	50 g
¼ pt	milk	150 ml
	Optional garnish: croutons	
	cream or yoghurt	
	chives	
1	egg yolk	1

Electric slow cooker: preheat Pot on HIGH for 20 minutes

1. Melt 1 oz (25 g) of the butter in a heavy frying-pan and soften the leeks for about 5 minutes on low heat. Bring the stock to the boil in a saucepan and add the leeks, potatoes and about half a teaspoon of salt. Put into the Pot and cook on LOW for 10 to 12 hours or overnight.
2. Half an hour before you want to serve the soup, liquidize in a blender or press through a food mill. Wash out the Pot, turn to HIGH, taste the soup for seasoning and return it to the Pot.
3. Melt the remaining butter in a small saucepan, add the flour and milk and bring to the boil, stirring continuously, until it thickens smoothly. Simmer for 2 minutes on low heat. Stir some of the soup from the Pot into the roux and, when well blended, tip it all back into the Pot.

To make a velvety, extra-rich soup, beat an egg yolk, add about a tablespoon of the hot soup liquid to it, stir smooth, then blend back into the Pot; do not let the soup boil after this addition.

A tablespoon of cream, yoghurt or chives, or some croutons of crisply fried bread in each serving plate is pleasant but not essential. Freshly milled *white* pepper is best for this soup, but black will do.

Casserole cooking: preheat oven to Gas 2, 300°F, 150°C

As in Step 1, putting the vegetables and stock in a heavy casserole, and increasing liquid to about

1½ pts (900 ml). Simmer about 3–4 hours, then finish as in Steps 2 and 3. You may want to add a little more milk. This can be made much more quickly, in a flameproof casserole on top of the cooker, if you're in a hurry—simmer about 45 minutes, then finish as in Steps 2 and 3, but the oven casserole does seem to blend and mellow the flavours.

Cock-a-Leekie   serves 8

This is a recipe for a large Pot or casserole.

1	boiling fowl, about 5 to 6 lb (2½ kg)	1
1	good beef marrow bone, cracked	1
4	lean bacon rashers	4
2 lb	leeks, well washed and cut up	1 kg
4 oz	prunes, cooked and stoned	100 g
2	bay leaves	2
	salt and pepper	
3 pts (4 pts)	boiling water, approx.	1·5 l (2 l)

Electric slow cooker: preheat Pot on HIGH for 15 minutes

1. Cut the chicken into serving-size pieces. Put everything except the prunes and 2 or 3 leeks into the Pot, and cook on LOW for 8 to 9 hours or overnight.
2. Season to taste, skin and bone the chicken pieces and strain the broth. Return the chicken and broth to the Pot, turn to HIGH, add the cooked prunes and finely chopped leeks and cook for 30 minutes longer.

Casserole cooking: preheat oven to Gas 4, 350°F, 180°C

As in Steps 1 and 2, but bring all ingredients except prunes and leeks to galloping boil in saucepan (or flameproof casserole) on top of cooker, then put casserole, tightly lidded, into oven and cook about 4 hours. Season broth, skin and bone chicken, strain broth into basin, then return chicken and broth to rinsed-out casserole, add cooked prunes and chopped leeks. Cook another 45 minutes in oven.

Red Bean Purée   serves 4

As an alternative to soup, this can be served as a puréed vegetable, with thin rings of mild onion and a dollop of sour cream on each serving.

1 lb	dried red beans	450 g
1	large onion, finely minced	1
¼ pt	olive oil	150 ml
1	garlic clove, crushed with 1 tsp salt	1
3 dsp	wine vinegar	3 dsp
1	bay leaf	1
	black pepper	
½	*To garnish:* large lemon, thinly sliced	½
	sherry	

Electric slow cooker: preheat Pot on HIGH for 15 minutes

1. Pick over the beans for bits of straw and grit, and wash them thoroughly. Cover with cold water in a saucepan, bring to the boil, remove from heat, cover and leave to stand for 2 hours.
2. Heat the oil in a frying-pan and sauté the minced onion and crushed garlic until soft. Drain the beans, cover with fresh cold water in a saucepan and bring to the boil. Remove from heat and stir the onions and garlic into the beans. Put everything but the vinegar into the Pot and cook on HIGH for 30 minutes, then on LOW overnight or for 8 to 10 hours.
3. Discard bay leaf. Purée half the mixture in a blender or food mill, return to washed-out Pot and reheat on HIGH for 30 minutes. Stir in vinegar.

Serve with the lemon and a dash of sherry in each bowl.

Casserole cooking: preheat oven to Gas 3, 325°F, 170°C

As in Steps 1 and 2, using a large heavy casserole with a good tight lid, and simmering in the oven (after preliminary boiling) for at least two hours, until beans are tender. Top up with water, if needed. Or, in a flameproof casserole on a low, steady heat, cook 2 hours on top of cooker, adding water as necessary to keep the beans from sticking to the casserole. Finish as in Step 3.

Twelve-hour Vegetable Soup

serves 4

The black treacle and soy sauce help to darken and enrich this soup, but be careful not to overdo it with them.

2 lb	shin of beef on the bone	900 g
	or	
1 lb	brisket and a marrow bone	450 g
1	large onion, sliced thin	1
3	carrots, diced	3
2	celery stalks, diced	2
$\frac{1}{2}$ tsp	black treacle	$\frac{1}{2}$ tsp
$\frac{1}{2}$	small white cabbage *(optional)*	$\frac{1}{2}$
$1\frac{3}{4}$ pts ($2\frac{1}{2}$ pts)	boiling water	1 l (1·5 l)
1	bay leaf	1
1	clove	1
1 tsp	salt	1 tsp
1 tsp	soy sauce, or Chinese mushroom sauce	1 tsp

Electric slow cooker: preheat Pot on HIGH for 20 minutes

1. Combine all the ingredients except the cabbage in a large saucepan and bring to a rolling boil. Put into the Pot and cook on HIGH for 30 minutes, then on LOW for 12 to 18 hours.
2. Remove the meat, bay leaf and clove if possible; dice the meat finely and return to the soup. Turn the Pot to HIGH to reheat. If you like cabbage in soup, shred it fine and blanch in boiling water for 2 minutes, add to the Pot and cook on HIGH for another 30 minutes.
3. You may want to chill the soup and skim off the fat, and then reheat in a saucepan on top of the cooker.

You can add diced potatoes to this basic vegetable soup halfway through the cooking time, and some good, flavourful fresh or tinned peeled tomatoes. Some people like a diced turnip but I myself think it makes for too strong a flavour.

Casserole cooking: preheat oven to Gas 3, 325°F, 170°C

As in Step 1, using a big casserole with tight lid, increasing boiling water to $2\frac{1}{2}$ pts (1·5 l), and simmering in oven about 6 hours. Finish as in Step 2, increasing oven heat to Gas 7, 400°F, 200°C, to cook the cabbage.

I think my grandmother invented oven-cooking of soup, as a way of using every corner of a wood-burning 'kitchen range' and filling every corner of a greedy family: and this was her standby soup for all seasons. I have changed it only by adding soy sauce.

Soupe aux Choux

serves 4–8

As Delia Smith of the Evening Standard, *from whom I had the original of this recipe, says: 'Cabbage Soup just doesn't sound very inviting.' It is a sort of universal, comforting soup—so call it what you will.*

$\frac{1}{2}$	firm white cabbage	$\frac{1}{2}$
2 oz	butter	50 g
8 oz	lean belly of pork, diced	225 g
1	large mild onion, finely minced	1
1	potato, peeled and diced	1
1	leek, well washed and sliced	1
1	garlic clove, crushed with 1 tsp salt	1
2 pts (3 pts)	good stock	1 gen l (1·8 l)
	salt and pepper	
	nutmeg, freshly ground	
3	thick slices of granary bread, several days old	3
1	garlic clove, cut in half	1
	cheddar cheese, grated *(optional)*	

Electric slow cooker: preheat Pot on HIGH for 20 minutes

1. Cut the cabbage into strips and blanch in boiling water for 1 minute. In a large, heavy frying-pan, heat the butter and fry the diced pork until the fat runs, then tip in all the other vegetables and cook them for about 5 minutes until they begin to soften. Put into the Pot. Bring the stock to the boil in the same frying-pan and pour into the Pot, scraping out any bits that cling to the pan. Cook on HIGH for 30 minutes, then on LOW for 6 to 8

hours. Season well with salt, pepper and a little nutmeg.

2. While the soup is cooking rub the bread with cut garlic and dry it out in the oven. Put a piece of bread in each soup bowl and pour the soup in.

You can pass some grated cheese with it, but it's not all that necessary.

Casserole cooking: preheat oven to Gas 4, 350°F, 180°C

As in Step 1, but increase the stock to 3 pts (1·8 l), and cook in oven, in a good big casserole without lid, for about 1½–1¾ hours. Test some of the vegetables and taste the broth—everything should still have some 'bite'. Cook longer if it suits you. Make the dry garlic bread as in Step 2, put a piece in each soup bowl and pour on the soup.

Viola Keats' Vegetable Broth   serves 4

A wonderful slimmer's soup.

8 oz	tomatoes, peeled or their equivalent in tinned Italian peeled tomatoes	225 g
8 oz	celery with its leaves	225 g
4 oz	onion, finely minced	100 g
1 tbs	parsley, chopped	1 tbs
2 pts (2½ pts)	cold water	1 gen l (1·5 l)
	salt and pepper	
1	bay leaf	1

Electric slow cooker: preheat Pot on HIGH for 20 minutes

1. Combine everything in a saucepan. Bring to the boil, put into the Pot and cook on LOW for 8 hours.
2. Check for seasoning, strain and serve very hot.

Casserole cooking: preheat oven to Gas 4, 350°F, 180°C

Combine everything in saucepan, increasing water to about 2½ pts (1·5 l), bring to boil and put in large casserole. Cover, cook in oven 2 hours, strain—and that's it. This lovely broth can be

made in a flameproof casserole on top of cooker, simmering about 45 minutes, but the oven method gives a richer, deeper flavour.

Tomato and Courgette Soup   serves 4

A summer soup, to be made when tomatoes are dripping ripe, cheap and flavourful, and courgettes abound. I have, however, made it with the ever-useful tinned Italian peeled tomatoes, using all their juice, and it's very good.

1½ lb	courgettes, sliced	700 g
1½ lb	tomatoes, peeled	700 g
1	large onion, finely minced	1
1 pt (1¼ pt)	chicken stock	600 ml (750 ml)
1½ tbs	olive or groundnut oil	1½ tbs
1	garlic clove, crushed	1
1 tsp	basil	1 tsp
1 tsp	whole coriander seeds, crushed	1 tsp
	salt and pepper	

Electric slow cooker: preheat Pot on HIGH for 20 minutes

1. Heat the oil in a frying-pan and sauté the onions until golden but not brown. Add the tomatoes, courgettes, garlic, basil and coriander seeds. Pour in the stock, bring to the boil, season and put into the Pot. Cook on HIGH for 2 hours or on LOW for 5 hours.
2. Sieve or liquidize almost all the soup: reserve some of the courgette slices whole to add texture to the finished soup. It will be thick; if you prefer it thinner, add more chicken stock.

Serve with sippets of bread fried crisp in olive oil.

Casserole cooking: preheat oven to Gas 4, 350°F, 180°C

As in Steps 1 and 2 above, using a casserole with a well-fitting lid, and increasing stock by about ¼ pt (150 ml), cook about 2–2½ hours. Look in at half-time, and add a little more hot stock if you like.

German Bean Soup   serves 4

8 oz	large white dried beans	225 g
8 oz	German sausage	225 g
	bouquet garni	
3	medium carrots, scraped and sliced	3
3	medium leeks, well washed, cut into 2 in (5 cm) lengths	3
1	garlic clove, crushed	1
1 tbs	oil	1 tbs
3 pts	stock	1·5 l

Electric slow cooker

1. Wash the beans, put them into a saucepan, cover with cold water and bring to the boil. Cook for 2 minutes, remove from heat and leave to stand, covered, for 2 hours. Drain well.
2. Preheat Pot on HIGH for 20 minutes.
3. Put the beans and bouquet garni into the Pot. Heat the oil in a frying-pan and sauté the carrots, leeks and garlic for about 5 minutes. Add to the Pot. Bring the stock to the boil and put into the Pot. Cook on LOW for 6 hours or overnight until the beans are tender.
4. One hour before serving, cut the sausage into 1 inch (2·5 cm) lengths and add to the Pot. Turn the Pot to HIGH and finish cooking. Don't cook too long, or the sausage slices will go into funny dished-in shapes; this doesn't affect their flavour but does mar the appearance of the finished soup.

Casserole cooking: preheat oven to Gas 2, 300°F, 150°C

As in Steps 1 to 4 above, simmering in casserole in oven for 3 hours, before adding sliced sausages. Return to oven for about half an hour. (This is a soup that can be cooked for as long as 6 hours in an oven at Gas 1, 250°F, 130°C. The casserole must have a well-fitting lid.) If you have a flameproof casserole, cook it on low heat for about 2 hours, adding a little more stock if necessary.

Chicken Liver Pâté   serves 4

8 oz	chicken livers, washed and trimmed	225 g
1 oz	butter (not margarine)	25 g
¼ pt	double cream *or*	150 ml
4 oz	cream cheese	100 g
1	garlic clove, crushed with ½ tsp salt	1
1 tbs	brandy	1 tbs
1 tbs	lemon juice	1 tbs
	pinch of mixed spice	
	Optional garnish: a little concentrated tinned consommé	
	juniper berries	
	lemon slice	

Electric slow cooker: preheat Pot on HIGH for 15 minutes

1. Heat the butter in a frying-pan and cook the well trimmed livers on a lowish heat until they are slightly pink when pierced with a sharp knife. Press through a sieve or purée in a blender, then add the cream or cream cheese, garlic, brandy, lemon juice and spice.
2. Put in a lightly oiled soufflé dish that will fit your Pot and cover with aluminium foil. Use the aluminium foil 'lifter straps' as suggested on p. 126. Set on a trivet or an inverted saucer and pour boiling water halfway up the soufflé dish. Cook on HIGH for 30 minutes, then on LOW for 3 hours. Chill well.

This pâté is prettier if you have time to run a thin layer of undiluted tinned consommé (the double-strength kind) over the top, and garnish with a few juniper berries and a very thin slice of lemon, quartered and pressed into the consommé as it sets.

Casserole cooking: preheat oven to Gas 2, 300°F, 150°C

As in Steps 1 and 2, putting pâté mixture into a soufflé dish, or loaf tin. Cover with foil. Set in a baking tin with 1 inch of boiling water and cook for 1½ hours until pâté shrinks slightly from edge of tin. Chill well.

Rabbit Pâté

serves 4

This pâté improves with keeping.

1 lb	rabbit (the frozen Chinese rabbit available in supermarkets is good)	450 g
½ glass	white wine	½ glass
2 oz	rabbit liver if available, or chicken liver	50 g
1	garlic clove, crushed	1
6 oz	streaky bacon	150 g
½	lemon peel, grated	½
	salt and pepper	
	nutmeg, freshly ground	
½ tsp	thyme	½ tsp

Electric slow cooker

1. Cut the best parts of the rabbit into neat fillets and marinate in the wine and garlic for about 3 hours. Mince the rest of the meat with the liver, quite finely. Cut the rinds from the bacon, keep three rashers aside to cover the pâté and dice the rest. Mix the bacon with the minced meat and season well with the salt, pepper, nutmeg and thyme. Mix the grated lemon peel through the minced meat.
2. Preheat Pot on HIGH for 20 minutes. Butter an oblong dish that will fit into your Pot, and put into it layers of the rabbit fillets and the minced mixture. Stretch the bacon rashers thin with the back of a knife and lay across the pâté. Pour on the wine marinade and cover with buttered aluminium foil. Use the aluminium foil 'lifter straps' as suggested on p. 126. Put on a trivet in the Pot, pour in boiling water halfway up the dish, and cook on HIGH for 4 hours or on HIGH for 30 minutes and on LOW for 6 hours.
3. The pâté is done when it shrinks from the sides of the dish. Press down with a piece of wood and a weight and allow to cool.

Casserole cooking: preheat oven to Gas 4, 350°F, 180°C

As above, butter an oblong, round or oval terrine—a casserole of about 3 pts (1·8 l) capacity—and fill it as described. Cover with foil, set in a deep oven tin with boiling water halfway up sides of casserole. Cook on a low shelf of oven about 1 hour 45 minutes (oblong terrines take less time than the others, for what reason I don't know.) Pâté will have shrunk away from casserole sides, and its juices should be clear and pale without any tinge of red. Finish as in Step 3.

Fasoulathia

serves 8

Fasoulathia will keep for a week, covered, in the fridge, therefore I have suggested making this rather large quantity, but you can, of course, make a half recipe. It is a hearty appetizer by itself, or wonderful as part of a cool summer meal with a distinct mid-Eastern flavour: sliced tomatoes, stuffed aubergines, rice salad, olives, feta cheese or white Stilton.

1 lb	dried haricot beans	450 g
4	large, very ripe tomatoes, or their equivalent in tinned Italian peeled tomatoes, well drained	4
3	carrots, finely chopped	3
¼ pt	olive oil, or a mixture of olive and sunflower oils	150 ml
½ teacup	fresh celery leaves, minced	½ teacup
2	garlic cloves, crushed with 1 tsp salt	2
	pepper	
	dash of hot pepper sauce	

Electric slow cooker

1. Cover the beans with cold water, bring to the boil, boil for 2 minutes, remove from heat and leave to stand, covered, for 2 hours. Drain well.
2. Preheat Pot on HIGH for 20 minutes.
3. Add the drained beans to all the other ingredients, bring to the boil, in a saucepan, put into the Pot and cook on HIGH for 6 hours, stirring once in a while. Put the contents of the Pot into a basin and cool quickly in a sinkful of cold water.

Casserole cooking: begin as in Step 1, then preheat oven to Gas 2, 300°F, 150°C

Continue as in Step 3, cooking in a large casserole, tightly lidded, for 3–3½ hours until beans are tender.

Chicken Liver Timbales

serves 4

This is a rich and concentrated dish. It can be served for lunch with a savoury sauce.

1½ dsp	butter	1½ dsp
2 dsp	flour	2 dsp
8 fl oz	milk	225 ml
½ tsp	salt	½ tsp
	black pepper	
6 tbs	single cream	6 tbs
8 oz	chicken livers, well trimmed	225 g
2	whole eggs and 2 egg yolks (size 3)	2
1 dsp	brandy	1 dsp

Electric slow cooker: preheat Pot on HIGH for 20 minutes

1. Melt the butter in a frying-pan, stir in the flour, add the milk slowly, season with salt and pepper, bring to the boil and boil, stirring, for 1 minute. Cool, stirring occasionally.
2. Put the cut-up chicken livers, eggs, egg yolks, and some freshly milled black pepper into a liquidizer and blend for 1 minute only. Or mix the eggs and egg yolks very well, then mince the livers very, very fine with a sharp knife, and combine. Add the cooled sauce, cream and brandy and liquidize for about 10 seconds.
3. Strain into 4 well buttered ramekins. Set on a trivet in the Pot, pour in boiling water halfway up the ramekins and cover each tightly with aluminium foil. Use the aluminium foil 'lifter straps' as suggested on p. 126. Cook on HIGH for 3 hours.

To serve, run a knife around the edge of each ramekin and turn out on to a warm plate.

Casserole cooking: preheat oven to Gas 4, 350°F, 180°C

As in Steps 1 and 2, putting the mixture into well-buttered ramekins, and setting these on a trivet in a large casserole with hot water. Bake 40 minutes, until set (a thin skewer thrust into the centre of timbale comes out clean). Then leave in turned-off oven, with door slightly ajar, for another 15–20 minutes, before turning out on warmed plate.

Miriam's Terrine

serves 4 to 8

This makes a great meat loaf if served hot.

1 lb	lean beef, minced	450 g
8 oz	pork (shoulder or leg), minced	225 g
8 oz	pie veal, trimmed and minced	225 g
2 tbs	bacon dripping	2 tbs
1	medium onion, finely minced	1
1	large garlic clove, crushed with 2 tbs salt	1
4	thin slices day-old bread, trimmed and crumbled	4
	handful of fresh parsley, minced	
3 tbs	brandy or whisky	3 tbs
1	egg	1
½ tsp	pepper	½ tsp
¼ tsp	ground allspice	¼ tsp
¼ tsp	thyme	¼ tsp
1	bay leaf	1
2	rashers streaky bacon, sliced into strips, or thin strips of ham	2

Electric slow cooker: grease and preheat Pot on HIGH for 20 minutes

1. With your hands, mix the minced meats together thoroughly. Heat the bacon dripping in a frying-pan and sauté the onions and garlic until translucent. Mix with the meat, then work in the breadcrumbs, brandy, egg, parsley, thyme and spices.

Shape into a neat loaf: it will be a soft, rather floppy assemblage, so lift it into the greased Pot with care, making sure you don't burn your fingers. Pinch and press it back into shape.
2. Break the bay leaf into quarters and lay on the meat, then cover with the strips of bacon. Cover with aluminium foil and cook on HIGH for 30

minutes, then on LOW for 6 to 7 hours. It will be well cooked but moist, not crusty.

3. Turn off the Pot, leave the terrine to stand for 1 hour before removing. Put in a small bread tin, press down foil and weigh down. Chill for about 4 hours.

Do not serve straight from the refrigerator, or it will seem too bland.

Casserole cooking: preheat oven to Gas 4, 350°F, 180°C

Mix ingredients as in Step 1, and shape into a loaf that will fit into a greased, round or oblong casserole. Break bay leaf in quarters and lay on surface of meat, then cover with bacon strips. Bake on middle shelf of oven 1½ hours. Remove, let stand in casserole in warm place for half an hour. Then weigh it down as in Step 3 above, and chill 4 hours. To serve hot: turn out of casserole after its 30-minutes rest, and slice.

Tongue Pâté

serves 4

This is not a Pot or casserole recipe, but a way of using up any tongue you may have left over (see Braised Tongue in Madeira, p. 99).

8 oz	cooked tongue	225 g
8 oz	cream or curd cheese	225 g
4 tbs	top of milk	4 tbs
1	garlic clove, minced	1
½ tsp	salt	½ tsp
½ tsp	mixed herbs	½ tsp
1 tsp	made mustard	1 tsp
1 tsp	tomato purée	1 tsp
1 tsp	Worcestershire sauce	1 tsp

Finely chop the tongue with a sharp knife. Beat together all other ingredients, then blend well with the tongue. (For a very smooth pâté, do all this in a blender.) Pack into a small terrine and chill for at least 1 hour.

The pâté may be dressed up with thin slices of lemon or strips of pickled red pimento.

Peperonata

serves 4

This will serve 8 if it forms part of an antipasto (hors d'oeuvre).

4	large green peppers, de-seeded	4
1	large onion, peeled and sliced very thin	1
4 tbs	olive oil	4 tbs
1 lb	ripe tomatoes, or their equivalent in tinned Italian peeled tomatoes, well drained	450 g
2	level tsp salt	2
	vinegar (cider or wine)	

Electric slow cooker: preheat Pot on HIGH for 20 minutes

1. Cut peppers in strips about ½ inch wide and 1 inch long, making sure that all the white pithy bits have been pared away. Heat the oil in a frying-pan and gently sauté the onions until limp and translucent but not brown. Add the pepper strips, cover and sweat for about 10 minutes on low heat. Add the tomatoes, bring to the boil and put into the Pot.

2. Cook on LOW for 4 hours. If at the end you have too liquid a result, drain off the excess and save it for soup. Taste for seasoning and very cautiously add a little vinegar—about ½ a teaspoon.

Caponatina: to turn Peperonata into even more of an Italian thing, add about 1 teaspoon capers and omit the vinegar—the capers are sharp enough in their own right. Or mix in a tablespoon of chopped anchovy bits.

Casserole cooking: preheat oven to Gas 3, 325°F, 170°C

As in Step 1 above, but put all ingredients, except vinegar, in shallow casserole and cook, uncovered, for about 2 hours. If it seems to be cooking down to a pulpy mass, stir in a little boiling water about halfway through cooking time. Taste for seasoning, add a little bit of vinegar, taste again; add capers or minced anchovy if you feel so inclined.

Terrine of Pork Liver serves 8

This tastes astonishingly like pâté de foie gras, and if made with the very good Irish pork liver to be found in supermarkets, it's very cheap to make. But you must be able to mince the pork, pork fat, liver and breadcrumbs extremely fine and smooth. Serve it in slices with baby gherkins and lemon, as a first course; as elegant picnic food with good French bread; or spread, fairly thin, on wholeweat bread for sandwiches.

4 oz	unsalted pork fat	100 g
8 oz	belly of pork, boned and rinded	225 g
6 oz	pork liver	175 g
3 oz	very fine soft breadcrumbs	75 g
1	egg, size 3	1
1 tbs	brandy	1 tbs
½ tsp	black pepper	½ tsp
	pinch of cayenne and some freshly milled nutmeg	
	some unsalted pork fat strips for lining terrine	

Electric slow cooker: preheat Pot on HIGH 20 minutes

Beat strips of pork fat as thin as you can, between sheets of greaseproof paper, and line an oblong casserole (or a round one) that will fit into your Pot. Save out one or two pieces to cover pâté. Mince pork fat, pork liver and pork belly very fine (put through blade of mincer several times), then mince again with fine breadcrumbs. Beat in the rest of the ingredients and press into the casserole. Cover with reserved pork fat strips, a sheet of foil and casserole lid. Set on a trivet in the Pot, pour in hot water to come halfway up sides of casserole, cook on HIGH 30 minutes then on LOW 6 hours. At the end of the cooking time, the juices that run when you take out and tip the casserole slightly should be clear and straw-coloured, no tinge of pink. Take off casserole lid, and weigh down pâté with plate or piece of wood that will fit in snugly, and top it with a heavy tin of food. Cool, then refrigerate (2 or 3 days in fridge greatly enhances the flavour). Remove pork strips from top and bottom before serving.

Casserole cooking: preheat oven to Gas 4, 350°F, 180°C

As above, putting the casserole in a deep oven tin with boiling water halfway up its sides. Cook in centre of oven 3 hours, until juices are pale yellow. Finish as above.

Potted Shin of Beef serves 4

A highly simplified version of Boeuf à la Mode, which goes well with a salad after a hearty soup.

1 lb	lean shin of beef	450 g
5 oz	streaky bacon	150 g
	salt and pepper	
	nutmeg	
	bouquet garni	
1	bay leaf	1
¼ pt (6 fl oz)	stock	150 ml (175 ml)
1 tsp	soy sauce	1 tsp

Electric slow cooker: preheat Pot on HIGH for 20 minutes

1. Cut the beef into very thin slices, about 2 inches (5 cm) square. Cut off the bacon rinds and set aside. Dice the bacon finely. Put a layer of beef slices in the bottom of the Pot, then a layer of bacon, with salt, pepper and nutmeg. Repeat until both beef and bacon are used up.
2. Bring the stock to the boil in a saucepan and add the soy sauce. Put the bouquet garni and bay leaf into the Pot. Strew the bacon rinds over the meat and add just enough stock to cover (this will vary with the depth of your Pot). Cover tightly with aluminium foil and cook on LOW for 8 hours, until the meat is fork-tender.
3. Take out the bacon rinds, bouquet garni and bay leaf. Tip the meat and juices into a basin and cool quickly, weigh down and refrigerate until the juices have jellied.

Casserole cooking: preheat oven to Gas 4, 350°F, 180°C

As above, putting the mixture into a heavy casserole with tight-fitting lid. Increase hot stock to 6 fl oz (175 ml). Cook in centre of oven 2½ hours, until meat is very tender. Finish as in Step 3.

Rillettes serves 12

This is very rich, and keeps well if the layer of fat on top is undisturbed. You may want to fill several small containers rather than one large one. Prepare rillettes *the day before it is to be cooked.*

2 lb	belly of pork, rinded and boned	scant 1 kg
1	large clove garlic, crushed with 1 tsp salt	1
1 lb	pork fat, unsalted	450 g
	bouquet garni	
	black pepper	

1. Rub meat well with the garlic and salt, and leave it to stand overnight in a cool place. Cut into thin, small strips, against the grain of the meat. Dice the pork fat very small.

Electric slow cooker: preheat on HIGH 20 minutes

2. Put all ingredients in Pot, add about 4–5 tbs boiling water. Cover with aluminium foil. Cook on HIGH 30 minutes, then on LOW 10 hours or overnight.
3. Discard bouquet garni. Season well with additional black pepper if necessary. Pour melted fat through sieve into a basin. Pull meat into very fine shreds with two forks. (This is fiddly, and takes time, but it can be done. Just be patient.) Lightly press meat into earthenware or glass bowl, pour on strained fat to form a complete seal. Cover with foil, refrigerate. Serve at room temperature, not cold, with good French or homemade coarse brown bread, a few little gherkins, some French mustard.

Casserole cooking: prepare meat as in Step 1

Then preheat oven to Gas 1, 250°F, 130°C. Put meat, seasonings and a scant ¼ pt (150 ml) boiling water in heavy casserole. Cover with aluminium foil, lid it tightly, cook about 5–6 hours until meat is very tender. Taste for seasoning. Finish as in Step 3.

Terrine de Chatignon serves 4

You may like to make a double recipe and freeze half of it.

8 oz	chicken livers	225 g
8 oz	pork (shoulder or leg)	225 g
4 oz	pork fat	100 g
½ tsp	salt	½ tsp
2	shallots, or half a small mild onion	2
1	garlic clove, crushed	1
1 tbs	sherry	1 tbs
½ tbs	melted pork fat	½ tbs

Electric slow cooker: preheat Pot on HIGH for 15 minutes

1. Trim the chicken livers of all yellowish bits. Mince the pork, pork fat and onion, not too finely. Then chop the chicken livers finely with a sharp knife and mix with the pork. Blend in all the other ingredients except melted fat.
2. Put a thin layer of melted pork fat on the bottom of an earthenware terrine that will fit into your Pot, and let it set in a cool place. Put in the pâté mixture and cover with the remaining melted fat. Lay a piece of aluminium foil on top. Use the aluminium foil 'lifter straps' as suggested on p. 126. Put on a trivet in the Pot and pour in boiling water halfway up the side of the terrine. Cook on HIGH for 4 hours.
3. Remove carefully from the Pot. Put a small saucer on the aluminium foil and weigh down with something heavy. Cool thoroughly and turn out.

Casserole cooking: preheat oven to Gas 4, 350°F, 180°C

As above, putting mixture into a loaf tin or earthenware casserole lined with the melted, cooled pork fat, set in baking tin and pour in hot water about two thirds of the way up. Cover, cook about 1½–2 hours—longer for a deep casserole, less time for a shallow one. Finish as in Step 3.

Fish

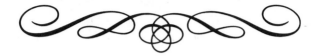

★ No initial browning needed

1. **Sarah Morphew's Brown Stew** (p. 78): brown ale, braising steak and a little brown sugar, cooked for hours to a mahogany richness

(*British Meat*)

2a. **Cod Chowder** (p. 51) and **Terrine of Pork Liver** (p. 44): a richly flavoured soup and a hearty pâté, both benefit from cooking at a controlled low temperature (*Fred Mancini*)

2b. **Chicken Korma** (p. 58): gentle cooking preserves its mild and delicate curry flavour

(*Pifco Ltd*)

Cioppino

serves 8

You can make half quantities of this recipe for a smaller Pot or casserole or for smaller appetites.

1½ lb	firm-fleshed fish (sea bass, halibut)	700 g
8 oz	peeled prawns or shrimps	225 g
12	mussels, well scrubbed	12
4 fl oz	olive oil	100 ml
2	medium onions, finely minced	2
2	large garlic cloves, crushed with 1 tsp *each* salt, oregano, basil	2
28 oz	tin Italian peeled tomatoes	780 g
12 oz	tomato purée	350 g
¾ pt	white wine	450 ml
3 oz	green pepper, de-seeded and diced	75 g
6 tbs	parsley, chopped	6 tbs

Electric slow cooker: preheat Pot on HIGH for 20 minutes

1. Heat the olive oil in a large frying-pan and sauté the onion, garlic, salt and herbs until the onion is just limp. Add the tomatoes, tomato purée, half the wine, the green pepper, half the parsley and boiling water just to cover. Arrange the shrimps or prawns and fish on the bottom of the Pot, add the boiling mixture and cook on LOW for 6 hours.
2. Half an hour before serving, turn the Pot to HIGH and add the cleaned mussels. Cover and steam until they open. Discard any that do not open. Add the remaining wine and sprinkle with chopped parsley just before serving.

Casserole cooking: preheat oven to Gas 3, 325°F, 170°C

As in Step 1, using a big casserole that can go from oven to table. Increase liquid by adding about ¾ pt (450 ml) boiling water to the fish mixture. Simmer about 2½–3 hours. Taste for seasoning. Finish as in Step 2, adding mussels and raising oven heat to Gas 6, 400°F, 200°C. Add more salt if necessary at the last minute.

Salmon Mould with Cucumber Sauce★

serves 4

7½ oz	tin salmon, flaked	210 g
2	medium onions, finely minced	2
2	large celery stalks, minced	2
4 oz	cream crackers, crushed fine	100 g
2	eggs (size 3), beaten	2
8 fl oz	milk	225 ml
	salt and pepper	
	For the cucumber sauce:	
1	medium cucumber, peeled and diced	1
3 tbs	butter	3 tbs
2 tbs	flour	2 tbs
¼ pt	boiling water	150 ml
2	egg yolks, whisked with ½ tsp salt	2
	juice and rind of half a lemon	

Electric slow cooker: preheat Pot on HIGH for 20 minutes

1. Lightly mix all the ingredients for the mould and pile into a buttered casserole, soufflé dish or tin that will fit your Pot. Cover the dish with aluminium foil, use the aluminium foil 'lifter straps' as suggested on p. 126, set on a trivet in the Pot, pour in about ¼ pt (150 ml) boiling water half-way up the dish, and cook on HIGH for 5 hours.
2. About 20 minutes before you are ready to serve, cook the diced cucumber in a small amount of boiling water until just translucent. Melt the butter in small saucepan, stir in the flour, and when it honeycombs, add the boiling water. Simmer until thick, stir in the lemon juice and rind and the drained cucumber. Remove from heat and little by little whisk in the egg yolks.
3. Remove the soufflé dish carefully from the Pot and serve the mould hot with the sauce.

Casserole cooking: preheat oven to Gas 4, 350°F, 180°C

Mix as in Step 1, pouring ingredients into well buttered casserole (or a pretty soufflé dish if you prefer). Bake on middle shelf of oven 45 minutes until it rises in a moderate sort of way, and is lightly browned. Serve with cucumber sauce.

Cod Naidu

serves 4

4	large cod (or hake) steaks, ¾ inch thick	4
4 tbs	oil	4 tbs
1	clove garlic, finely minced	1
1	large onion, finely minced	1
1 tbs	parsley, minced	1 tbs
8 fl oz	dry white wine or dry cider	225 ml
2 dsp	mild curry powder	2 dsp
1 tbs	butter	1 tbs
¼ pt	stabilized yoghurt	150 ml
	juice of 1 lemon	
	salt and black pepper	

Electric slow cooking: preheat Pot on HIGH 20 minutes

Heat oil in frying-pan, sauté onions and garlic until translucent but not brown. Spread in bottom of Pot, sprinkle on parsley and lay in the fish steaks. In frying-pan, mix wine or cider with curry powder, bring to boil, stir in yoghurt and pour over fish. Cut butter in flakes over fish. Cook on LOW 4–5 hours. Season, and just before serving pour on lemon juice.

Casserole cooking: preheat oven to Gas 2, 300°F, 150°C

As above, using a shallow fairly wide casserole, and cooking 2 hours. For a richer sauce, in this version you may use double cream instead of yoghurt.

Rossbrin Mackerel★

serves 4

4	filleted mackerel	4
3	bay leaves	3
2 dsp	mixed herbs: parsley, thyme, fennel	2 dsp
3 tsp	caster sugar	3 tsp
1	small onion, finely minced	1
¼ pt (½ pt)	cider vinegar (cider vinegar and water)	150 ml (300 ml)
	salt and pepper	

Electric slow cooker: preheat Pot on HIGH for 20 minutes

1. Be sure that all the bones are removed from the fish. Put the fillets flat on a plate and sprinkle each with salt, pepper and sugar and about one teaspoon of herbs. Roll up the fillets and put them side by side in the Pot. Scatter the rest of the herbs over, and then the minced onion. Bring the vinegar to the boil and pour into the Pot. Cover tightly with aluminium foil, tucking the foil round the fish. Cook on HIGH for 30 minutes, then on LOW for 3 hours.
2. Remove carefully; put in a flat dish with all the liquid and allow to cool. Chill.

Casserole cooking: preheat oven to Gas 4, 350°F, 180°C

As in Step 1, increasing liquid to ½ pt (300 ml), half cider vinegar and half water. Put fish fillets in ovenproof shallow casserole, cover with foil and a well-fitting lid, put in oven and at once lower heat to Gas 2, 300°F, 150°C, for about 1 hour. Take out of oven, remove foil and lid, let cool, then chill well.

Salmon Trout in Cider★

serves 4

This recipe is only suitable for a wide Pot or casserole.

1	salmon trout, about 2 lb	900 g
1 tbs	butter	1 tbs
1 dsp	mixed fresh herbs: parsley, lemon thyme, fennel, or ½ tsp dried fennel seeds	1 dsp
½	a lemon	½
	salt and pepper	
¼ pt (½ pt)	dry cider	150 ml (300 ml)

Electric slow cooker: butter Pot well and preheat on HIGH for 20 minutes

1. Clean the fish very thoroughly, removing the head, put the herbs inside and place in the Pot. Squeeze the lemon over the fish, season, and dot with the remaining butter.

2. Bring the cider to the boil and pour into the Pot. Cook on LOW for 3 hours. Halfway through cooking time, baste well with liquid.

This can be served hot, but is also most delicious cold with a lemony mayonnaise.

Casserole cooking: preheat oven to Gas 2, 300°F, 150°C

As in Steps 1 and 2, putting the salmon trout in a shallow casserole, fairly form-fitting. Increase amount of cider to ½ pt (300 ml), boil it up and add to casserole. Cover and cook in oven 1½ hours, glancing at it once during the cooking time to see that cider is at a steady, murmuring simmer and not boiling.

Cod Chowder★   serves 4

I suppose properly speaking this is a soup—but it's such a hearty dish that it can very easily be the centrepiece of a meal.

1½ lb	cod fillets	700 g
2	medium potatoes, peeled and sliced thin	2
1	medium onion, sliced thin	1
3	tomatoes, peeled and chopped, or their equivalent in Italian tinned tomatoes, well drained	3
1 tsp	tomato purée	1 tsp
1 tsp	soy sauce	1 tsp
	salt and pepper	
	juice of 1 lemon	
1 tsp	or more Worcestershire sauce	1 tsp
2 pts (3 pts)	water	1·2 l (1·5 l)

Electric slow cooker: preheat Pot on HIGH for 20 minutes

1. Bring the water to the boil in a saucepan, put in all the vegetables and put into the Pot with the salt, pepper, tomato purée and soy sauce. Cook on LOW for 6 hours.
2. Wash and skin the fish, cut into 2 inch (5 cm) cubes, add to the Pot and cook on HIGH for 2 hours. Add the lemon juice and Worcestershire sauce just before serving.

Casserole cooking: preheat oven to Gas 3, 325°F, 170°C

As in Step 1, simmering in a big casserole in oven 2 hours. Then add fish and raise oven heat to Gas 5, 375°F, 190°C, and cook another 45 minutes to 1 hour. Taste for seasoning, add lemon and Worcestershire sauce.

Stuffed Herrings or Mackerel   serves 4

4	large herrings or mackerel	4
1–2 tbs*	butter	1–2 tbs*
¼ pt	single cream	150 ml
2	*For the stuffing:* streaky bacon rashers, coarsely chopped	2
½ tsp	butter	½ tsp
2 oz	mushrooms, chopped	50 g
1	garlic clove, crushed	1
3 tbs	fresh white breadcrumbs	3 tbs
2	hardboiled eggs, chopped	2
	salt and pepper	

Electric slow cooker: butter and preheat Pot on HIGH for 20 minutes

1. Slit the fish down the centre and clean them, leaving the heads on. Press along the backbone with your thumbs and lift out the bones. In a frying-pan fry the bacon in the ½ teaspoon butter until limp. Add the mushrooms, garlic, breadcrumbs and chopped eggs, season well and bind with a little of the cream. Stuff the fish with the mixture and secure with cocktail sticks.
2. Lay the fish in the buttered Pot, pour on *2 tablespoons melted butter for herrings and 1 tablespoon for mackerel, and the rest of the single cream. Cook on HIGH for 30 minutes, then on LOW for 4 hours. The cream and butter will look slightly curdled, but this can't be avoided.

Casserole cooking: preheat oven to Gas 2, 300°F, 150°C

As in Steps 1 and 2, bake in a shallow buttered casserole with a well-fitting cover for 1¼ hours.

Terrine Dieppoise   serves 8

As a starter this will give about 8 servings.

8 oz	white fish (sole, turbot, halibut) boned	225 g
8 oz	cooked shrimp	225 g
3	eggs, size 3	3
2 oz	butter	50 g
1 oz	shallot or mild onion, finely minced	25 g
2 tbs	lemon juice	2 tbs
2 tbs	plain flour	2 tbs
½ pt	single cream	300 ml
6 oz	piece of fresh salmon, or very good tinned salmon, drained	175 g
½ tsp	tarragon	½ tsp

Electric slow cooker: preheat Pot on HIGH 20 minutes

1. Melt butter, gently sauté shallot or onion until soft. Stir in tarragon, lemon juice, and flour. On very low heat, add cream and bring slowly to boil, stirring. Remove from heat and whisk in eggs which have been lightly beaten.
2. In liquidizer, blend shrimp and white fish, adding some of the hot sauce to make it all blend smoothly. Mix fish purée with rest of sauce. Pour half this mixture into a round or oval casserole that will fit into your Pot; lay salmon pieces evenly down the middle, add the rest of the fish mixture. Cover casserole, put in Pot with boiling water halfway up sides. Cook 3 hours on HIGH. Remove, cool and chill. Cut in thick slices and serve on lettuce leaves, with a cooled hollandaise sauce or a mustardy mayonnaise.

Casserole cooking: preheat oven to Gas 3, 325°F, 170°C

As in Steps 1 and 2, setting casserole in a deep oven tin with boiling water halfway up sides. Bake in oven about 1 hour, test the centre with a skewer, the fish mixture should be firm to the touch. Cook another 15 minutes if necessary. Cool, then chill and serve as above.

Tuna Divan   serves 4

2	packages (8 oz (225 g) each) frozen broccoli, cooked for about 5 minutes	2
2	7½ oz (210 g) tins tuna, flaked	1
2 tbs	butter	2 tbs
2 tbs	flour	2 tbs
¾ pt	chicken stock	450 ml
1	egg yolk, whisked with juice of 1 lemon	1
	salt and pepper	
2 oz	buttered breadcrumbs	50 g

Electric slow cooker: preheat Pot on HIGH for 20 minutes

1. Melt the butter in a saucepan, stir in the flour and cook until it honeycombs. Add the stock gradually, stirring, until the mixture is slightly thickened. Remove from heat and stir in the egg yolk and lemon, salt and pepper.
2. Drain the partially cooked broccoli very well and mix half the sauce with it. Put into a buttered casserole, soufflé dish or baking tin that will fit your Pot. Add the flaked tuna and pour on the rest of the sauce. Cover thickly with breadcrumbs. Cover tightly with aluminium foil. Place on a trivet in the Pot and also use the foil 'lifter straps' as suggested on p. 126, and pour about ½ pt (300 ml) boiling water around the dish. Cook on HIGH for 3 to 4 hours, until firm; or on HIGH for 1 hour, then on LOW for 5 hours.

You may, if you like—and if your Pot has a removable casserole—brown the dish under a hot grill or in a hot oven before serving.

Casserole cooking: preheat oven to Gas 4, 350°F, 180°C

As in Steps 1 and 2, putting all ingredients in a round or oval casserole that is not too wide: you want a good layer of breadcrumbs on the top. Cover with foil, cook in centre of oven about 1 hour 45 minutes. Remove foil, raise oven heat to Gas 6, 400°F, 200°C, to crisp the crumbs.

Poultry and Game

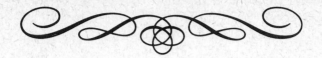

★No initial browning needed

You will see that very few chicken recipes here take more than about 2½ hours in a casserole, or 5 or 6 hours in the Pot. So think of slow-cooked chicken as promising you a free afternoon rather than a whole day. On the whole, my most successful results have been with chicken joints. But even in the very slow-cooking Pot, you can make a superbly tender whole roast chicken, once you accept its pale-gold surface rather than the crisply finished skin of an oven-roasted bird. Rather elderly boilers (always a good buy) give their all to casserole cooking. They are especially suited to the electric Pot. You have at the end of 5 or 6 hours an astonishing quantity of tender meat, for Chicken Divan, Chicken à la King, or your own favourite chicken salad. And the bliss of having a Pot full of rich, real chicken broth!

Free-range, unfrozen chicken would of course be the ideal. But facing facts, one must say that casserole cooking—oven or Pot—with the addition of such treasures as wine, oil, Italian plum tomatoes, fennel, shallots, paprika, lemon, can make the very most of plump, pale battery birds.

Pheasant, partridge, rabbit, hare and pigeon are all 'naturals' for the Pot. As venison is now being ranched like cattle, we can expect a sharp drop in the price of this most delicious and unusual meat; the Pot does well by it. Casserole birds, fortunately, always cost considerably less than the little young grilling ones. Again, brown them well, season them highly, cook very thoroughly.

Duck, surprisingly enough, is excellent cooked in this unorthodox way. But you must stab it all over, every inch, with a really sharp knife or kitchen fork, to let a lot of the fat run off; set it on a rack or trivet; and be prepared to drain off the fat from the Pot from time to time, preferably with the invaluable bulb baster gadget that looks like a giant syringe.

Chicken Fricassee★ serves 4

Split a 5–6 lb boiling fowl, use half for a Fricassee and the rest for Real Chicken Soup (p. 35), or a Chicken à la King.

2–3 lb	boiling fowl, jointed	1½ kg
2	medium onions, finely minced	2
2	carrots, finely diced	2
4 oz	mushrooms, sliced	100 g
	bouquet garni	
2 tbs	butter	2 tbs
2 tbs	flour	2 tbs
	salt and pepper	
	Optional:	
1	egg yolk	1
3 tbs	cream	3 tbs
	juice of half a lemon	

Electric slow cooker: preheat Pot on HIGH for 20 minutes

1. Put the chicken joints, vegetables and bouquet garni in a large saucepan and add just enough water to cover. Bring to the boil, put into the Pot, cook on HIGH for 30 minutes, then on LOW for 6 to 7 hours, until the chicken is tender.
2. Remove the chicken, cut the meat from the bones and strain the stock. Skim off the fat. Melt the butter in a large saucepan, stir in the flour, and when it reaches the honeycomb stage gradually stir in 1 pt (500 ml) strained stock. Bring to the boil and cook, stirring, until thick. Add the chicken and vegetables and reheat. Season.
3. For a richer sauce, whisk the egg yolk with the cream, beat in a little of the hot stock, then stir it all back into the chicken mixture and heat gently. Do not allow to boil. At the last minute add the lemon juice.

Casserole cooking: preheat oven to Gas 4, 350°F, 180°C

As in Step 1, but in a casserole with very tight fitting lid (or slip a sheet of foil under lid to seal). Cook 4 hours until meat is ready to leave bone at the touch of a fork. If you have a flameproof casserole with a well-fitting lid, simmer 3–4 hours on top of your cooker on very low heat. Finish as above.

Pennsylvania Dutch Chicken serves 4

It must be explained that, in American cookery, 'Pennsylvania Dutch' really means a recipe that is German, not Dutch, in origin, often with this sweet-sour sugar, mustard and vinegar sauce. The original recipe specifies only half as much vinegar and twice as much sugar, but I found that in Pot cooking all the sharpness had cooked away, leaving only a curious sweetened mustard sauce. So don't be tempted to reduce the amount of vinegar.

4	chicken joints (about 2½ lb, 1 gen kg)	4
1 tbs	dry mustard	1 tbs
2 tbs (2½ tbs)	caster sugar	2 tbs (2½ tbs)
1 tbs	cornflour	1 tbs
¼ pt	milk	150 ml
1	egg yolk, beaten	1
3 tbs	butter	3 tbs
4 tbs (2 tbs)	tarragon vinegar, mixed with 2 tbs water	4 tbs (2 tbs)
	salt and pepper	

Electric slow cooker: preheat Pot on HIGH for 20 minutes

1. Mix the mustard, sugar and cornflour with 2 tablespoons of the milk to a smooth paste. Bring the rest of the milk to the boil and slowly stir in the paste. Remove from heat, stirring well, stir 1 tablespoon of the hot mixture into the beaten egg yolk, then whisk this back into the saucepan. Add the vinegar and water and cook on a low heat for about 2 minutes, stirring until blended. Season.
2. Heat the butter in a heavy frying-pan and sauté the chicken joints until light brown. Put into the Pot, pour on the sauce and cover tightly with aluminium foil. Cook on HIGH for 4 hours.

Casserole cooking: preheat oven to Gas 4, 350°F, 180°C

As in Steps 1 and 2, but reduce vinegar to 2 tbs, and use about 2½ tbs sugar. Cook in covered casserole 45 minutes to an hour, until chicken joints are tender. Taste for seasoning, and if you like a sharper sauce, spoon out about half a teacup, mix in a little more vinegar, then stir it all back together and cook another 15 minutes in the oven.

Brunswick Stew★   serves 6 to 8

The original recipe from Georgia calls for 'tender little wild rabbits' and adjures the cook to 'pick out all pieces of buckshot'—chicken somehow seems tamer but safer.

This is a two-stage recipe: Part One can be done a day in advance. Only make it if you have a large Pot or casserole; it's not really worth making with a small bird.

5 lb	fat boiling chicken	2½ kg
28 oz	tin Italian peeled tomatoes, well drained	780 g
1 tbs	olive oil	1 tbs
1½ tbs	flour	1½ tbs
3 tbs	butter	3 tbs
1	large onion, diced	1
2	garlic cloves, minced	2
2	celery stalks, diced	2
6 to 8	spring onions, coarsely minced	6 to 8
	salt and pepper	
1 tbs	red pimento, minced	1 tbs
8 oz	mushrooms	225 g
4	hardboiled eggs	4

Electric slow cooker: preheat Pot on HIGH for 20 minutes

1. Thoroughly wash the chicken, inside and out. Put into the Pot with boiling water to cover and cook on HIGH for 5 hours or until completely tender. Strain the broth and measure out ¾ pt (400 ml). Remove the flesh from the bones and cut into small pieces.
2. Heat the olive oil in a pan, add the tomatoes and cook for a few minutes. Make a roux, in a small saucepan, with the flour and butter, then stir in the onions, garlic, chopped celery and chicken broth.
3. Again, pre-heat Pot on HIGH for 20 minutes. Put all the ingredients except mushrooms and hardboiled eggs into the Pot, with the chicken pieces. Cook on LOW for 3 hours. One hour before serving, stir in the whole mushrooms.

Just before serving, top with quartered hardboiled eggs.

Casserole cooking
As in Step 1 above, cooking the chicken at a gentle simmer for 2½ hours, in salted water. Strain broth, cut up chicken. Then as in Step 2, while you preheat oven to Gas 4, 350°F, 180°C.

Put all ingredients except mushrooms and eggs in large casserole, cover, and cook in oven 1½ hours. Half an hour before serving, stir in mushrooms, and at the last minute garnish with hardcooked quartered eggs.

Greek Chicken★   serves 4

This is one of the most delicate and perfect chicken dishes I know; the garlic and lemon flavours all but vanish, leaving a moist, tender flesh and a pale-gold skin. It is wonderful cold, with a mayonnaise strong in lemon.

3–3½ lb	chicken	about 1½ kg
1	lemon	1
1	large garlic clove	1
3 oz	butter	75 g
1 tbs	sea salt, coarse	1 tbs
	beurre manié (see p. 153) (*optional*)	

Electric slow cooker: preheat Pot on HIGH for 20 minutes

1. Clean the chicken very well inside. Cut the garlic into large slivers and rub the outside of chicken well, then put into the cavity. Rub the chicken inside and out with the sea salt. Cut the lemon into quarters and put half of it inside chicken, saving the rest for the sauce. Soften the butter and thickly coat the breast, thighs, and legs with it; put any remaining butter into the cavity. Cook on HIGH for 4 hours, or until the thigh joint moves easily in its socket when gently pulled, and the juices run almost clear.
2. If you want a sauce, remove the chicken gently with wooden spoons, and keep warm; pour off the juices into a saucepan, skim off most of the fat. Thicken with *beurre manié* then blend in the juice of the remaining half lemon. Or simply strain off the juices and freeze for a basis for a future sauce.

Casserole cooking: preheat oven to Gas 5, 375°F, 190°C
As in Steps 1 and 2 above, putting chicken in a lightly-buttered casserole. Baste occasionally, and cook 1½–2 hours, until thigh joint loosens.

Poule au Pot Béarnaise

serves 6

This recipe can be made equally well with a smaller roasting chicken, in which case reduce the amount of vegetables by about one-third. The meat is moist and delicious and any leftovers make excellent sandwiches.

5 lb	fat boiling chicken	2½ kg
	handful of soft breadcrumbs soaked in milk	
5 oz	sausage meat	150 g
1 tbs	oil	1 tbs
2	large carrots, finely minced	2
6	small carrots, peeled	6
1	white turnip, diced	1
1	medium onion, minced, and	1
6	small onions, peeled	6
1	leek, sliced	1
1	celery stalk, diced	1
	salt and pepper	

Electric slow cooker: preheat Pot on HIGH for 20 minutes

1. Thoroughly wash the chicken, inside and out.
2. Mince the chicken liver very finely and mix with the breadcrumbs, squeezed quite dry, and the sausage meat. Stuff the chicken with this mixture and truss it securely. Heat the oil in a large pan and brown the chicken all over. Put into the Pot. Turn the chopped vegetables only over in the remaining oil and add to the Pot. Pour in fiercely boiling water to half-cover the chicken, cover with aluminium foil and cook on HIGH for 6 to 7 hours. Turn the chicken over halfway through cooking time. Season.
3. Half an hour before serving, remove the vegetables which will have cooked to rags. Remove the chicken with two spoons, strain the broth and put both back into the Pot. Cook small carrots and onions in boiling water in a saucepan and add to Pot just before serving. Strain the broth again through a sieve, then through muslin, and skim fat. Serve as a first course, or save to make a soup.

Casserole cooking: preheat oven to Gas 3, 325°F, 170°C

As in Step 1, putting browned chicken and vegetables and boiling water in heavy *warmed* ovenproof casserole. Skim surface with kitchen paper or slotted spoon, and lid casserole tightly. Cook 3 hours. Finish as in Step 3.

Gallina de Jerez

serves 2

I have included this recipe to demonstrate that your Pot, or casserole, will cook for a small family; quantities, of course, may be doubled, depending on the shape and size of your Pot or casserole. It must be shallow enough for the chicken breasts to lie in one layer.

2	chicken breasts* (about 6 oz (170 g) each)	2
2 oz	butter, or very good margarine	50 g
1	small onion, finely sliced	1
4 oz	tin liver pâté	100 g
2 tbs	soft brown breadcrumbs	2 tbs
3 tbs	parsley, chopped	3 tbs
4 tbs	medium sherry	4 tbs
2 tbs	Parmesan cheese, grated	2 tbs
	salt and black pepper	

Electric slow cooker: preheat Pot on HIGH for 15 minutes

1. Melt half the butter in a heavy frying-pan and brown the chicken breasts on both sides. (*You can use chicken thighs with equal success.) Melt the rest of the butter and sauté the onion until limp and translucent. Mix in the pâté, breadcrumbs, parsley, salt and pepper.
2. Put the chicken breasts into the Pot, spoon the pâté mixture over them, pour on the sherry and sprinkle with the grated cheese. Cover and cook on HIGH for 30 minutes, then on LOW for 5 hours.

Casserole cooking: preheat oven to Gas 4, 350°F, 180°C

Begin as in Step 1, put chicken breasts in small close-fitting casserole with pâté mixture and sherry, slip a sheet of aluminium foil under lid, and bake about half an hour until chicken is meltingly tender.

Chicken Cacciatore serves 4

Anglicized, this means Hunter's Chicken, originally a one-dish meal of chicken and available vegetables, perhaps cooked over a camp-fire.

3 lb	chicken joints	1½ kg
3 tbs	oil (olive if possible)	3 tbs
1	large onion, thinly sliced	1
1	large garlic clove, crushed with 1 tsp salt and 1 tsp oregano	1
14 oz	tin Italian tomatoes, well drained	400 g
1 tsp	basil	1 tsp
1	bay leaf	1
¼ pt (½ pt)	rough red wine	150 ml (300 ml)
1 tbs	butter	1 tbs
4 oz	mushrooms, sliced	100 g
	Parmesan cheese, grated (*optional*)	

Electric slow cooker: preheat Pot on HIGH for 20 minutes

1. Heat the oil in a frying-pan until quite hot, and brown the chicken joints well. Put into the Pot. In the oil in the pan, lightly sauté the onion and garlic until just pale gold. Add to the Pot and stir in the basil. Heat the wine and tomatoes with the bay leaf and add to the chicken. (I have here specified Italian tomatoes for their richer, fuller flavour, which is much needed in this dish.) Cook on HIGH for 30 minutes, then on LOW for 4 to 5 hours.
2. Ten minutes before you are ready to dish up, heat the butter in a frying-pan and quickly sauté the mushrooms. Taste the chicken for seasoning and add the mushrooms to the Pot. If the sauce seems thin, remove the chicken and mushrooms and keep warm, pour the sauce into a saucepan and reduce it quickly over a high flame. The consistency of the sauce depends very much on the amount of liquid produced by the tomatoes.

   If you like, pass a dish of grated Parmesan at the table.

Casserole cooking: preheat oven to Gas 3, 325°F, 170°C

As in Steps 1 and 2 above, with chicken and vegetables in a heavy, tightly-lidded casserole. Add about ¼ pt (150 ml) rough red wine to the quantity specified. Cook in centre of oven 2 hours, then add mushrooms and finish as in Step 2.

Chicken Korma serves 4

3 lb	chicken joints	1½ kg
	seasoned flour	
1 tbs	butter	1 tbs
2 tbs	groundnut or soya oil	2 tbs
2	medium onions, finely minced	2
1	large green pepper, de-seeded and minced	1
1	large garlic clove, minced	1
1 tbs	mild curry powder	1 tbs
14 oz	tin Italian peeled tomatoes, well drained	400 g
1 tsp	salt	1 tsp
4 tbs	or more plain yoghurt	4 tbs

Electric slow cooker: preheat Pot on HIGH for 20 minutes

1. Toss the chicken joints in seasoned flour. Heat the butter and oil in a heavy frying-pan and sauté the chicken until quite brown. Put into the Pot. In the same pan, gently sauté the onions, green pepper and garlic in the remaining oil for about 5 minutes, stir in the curry powder and mix well. Add the drained tomatoes, bring to the boil and put into the Pot. Cook on HIGH for 30 minutes, then on LOW for 3 to 4 hours.
2. Just before serving, stir in the salt and yoghurt.

Casserole cooking: preheat oven to Gas 4, 350°F, 180°C

As in Step 1, but put everything in a heavy casserole, add 3 tbs hot water and cook without a lid for about an hour, until chicken is tender. The sauce should be thick but still moist. You can cook this dish, covered, for about 1½ hours if you prefer, then take off lid, raise heat to Gas 6, 400°F, 200°C, to reduce the sauce a bit. Finish as in Step 2.

Butter-Roasted Chicken★

serves 4

This is superb cold, when the buttery herb flavour has permeated all the flesh.

3¼ lb	plump roasting chicken	1½ kg
2 tbs	butter (*not* margarine)	2 tbs
1	medium onion, thinly sliced	1
2 tbs	olive or soya oil	2 tbs
2	sprigs fresh tarragon, or ½ tsp dried	2
	pinch of lemon thyme, chervil or summer savory	
1 tbs	sea salt	1 tbs
	black pepper	
5 tbs	sherry	5 tbs

Electric slow cooker: preheat Pot on HIGH for 20 minutes

1. Thoroughly wash the chicken, inside and out. Dry it well. Boil up the giblets in a saucepan with water to cover and the sliced onion and a little salt. Cook for 15 minutes and set aside. Soften the butter, mixed with the herbs, sea salt and black pepper, and put half of it inside the chicken. Mix the remaining herb butter with the oil and rub well into the chicken skin. Put into the Pot and cook on HIGH for 3 to 4 hours, until the thigh joint moves easily in its socket when gently poked.
2. Remove the chicken and keep warm. Tip the juices out into a saucepan, scraping out any brown bits from the Pot. Skim off the fat and add the sherry and giblet stock. Bring to the boil and pour over the chicken.

Casserole cooking: preheat oven to Gas 7, 425°F, 220°C

As in Step 1, but put it in an uncovered casserole and roast at the above temperature for 15 minutes, turning twice, and basting as you go. Then lower heat to Gas 3, 325°F, 170°C, and cook another hour and 20 minutes—total cooking time should be about 1 hour 35 minutes. Finish as in Step 2.

West Country Chicken

serves 4

4	plump chicken joints	4
1 tbs	seasoned flour	1 tbs
3 tbs	groundnut or soya oil	3 tbs
2	medium carrots, sliced	2
1	medium onion, thinly sliced	1
1 tbs	calvados or brandy	1 tbs
½ pt	dry cider	300 ml
3 oz	mushrooms, sliced	75 g
1 tbs	butter	1 tbs
1 tbs	lemon juice	1 tbs
	salt and pepper	

Electric slow cooker: preheat Pot on HIGH for 20 minutes

1. Toss the chicken joints in the seasoned flour. Heat the oil in a heavy frying-pan and sauté the chicken pieces until light brown. Put into the Pot. In the remaining oil, sauté the carrots until just coloured, push them to one side and gently sauté the onion. Add the calvados or brandy and set aflame. Pour in the cider, bring to the boil and scrape everything into the Pot. Cook on HIGH for 30 minutes, then on LOW for 4 to 5 hours, until the chicken is tender. Taste for seasoning: it will undoubtedly need more salt.
2. Just before serving, heat the butter in a pan and fry the sliced mushrooms. Squeeze in the lemon juice and add to the chicken in the Pot.

Casserole cooking: preheat oven to Gas 4, 350°F, 180°C

As in Steps 1 and 2, but return chicken to frying-pan after sautéing carrots and onions, flaming the calvados and boiling the cider: bring everything back to boil and put in heavy casserole. Cook in oven 1 hour. (With a flameproof casserole, the whole process can be done—gently simmering—on a low flame for 45 minutes to an hour.) Finish as in Step 2.

Poulet en Demi-Deuil★

serves 6

There should be a better name in English for this most delicious and attractive dish than the rather silly-sounding Chicken in Half-Mourning. The French recipe calls for black truffles slivered and set in a decorative lozenge pattern under the loosened skin of the chicken, but with truffles at £3.75 for a ¾oz tin at this moment, this is pure wishful thinking and mushrooms must do instead.

4–5 lb	chicken	2–2½ kg
½ lb	field mushrooms	225 g
2 tbs	butter	2 tbs
1 lb	potatoes of even size	450 g
1 lb	pickling-size onions	450 g
	bouquet garni	
	salt and pepper	
¼ pt (½ pt)	chicken stock	150 ml (300 ml)

Electric slow cooker: preheat Pot on HIGH for 20 minutes

1. Gently pinch the chicken skin around the breast and upper thighs, until you can loosen it enough to slip your fingers between flesh and skin. Wash the mushrooms and cut the tops into flat slivers about ½ inch long. Push them gently under the chicken skin, in a single layer. This is fiddly and time-consuming, but the result is very pretty. Rub the outside of the chicken with the softened butter.
2. Put a trivet in the Pot, or a round, flattish oven-glass casserole lid, to hold the chicken off the bottom, and stand the chicken on this. Cut the potatoes in half and blanch them in boiling water for 3 minutes. Put them in a ring around the chicken. Blanch the onions in boiling water for 2 minutes, drain and drop into cold water; the skins should then slip off neatly. Put them around the chicken. Add the bouquet garni, salt and pepper. Bring the stock to the boil and pour gradually into the Pot, just to the top of the trivet or casserole lid.
3. Cook on HIGH for 3 to 4 hours, until the thigh joint moves easily in its socket when gently pulled. Take out the chicken, keep warm.

4. Strain stock into a saucepan, skim off some of the fat, and reduce over high heat to half its original quantity. Put the vegetables around the chicken on a heated serving dish, pour over some of the sauce, and pass rest in a warm sauce-boat.

Casserole cooking: preheat oven to Gas 4, 350°F, 180°C

Prepare as in Steps 1 and 2, increasing hot stock to ½ pt (300 ml), and using a tightly-lidded casserole. Cook 25 minutes per pound, and test for 'doneness' about half an hour before you think cooking time should end, as much depends on the stability of your oven heat! Finish as in Step 4. (This delicate classic dish can also be done by poaching in chicken stock, on lowest possible heat on your cooker top, for about the same length of time.)

Poulet à l'Estragon

serves 4

4	chicken joints, about 1¾ lb (800 g)	4
2 tbs	butter	2 tbs
½ pt (¾ pt)	dry white wine or dry cider	300 ml (450 ml)
12 oz	small mushrooms	350 g
1 tsp	dried tarragon	1 tsp
3 fl oz	double cream	75 ml
2	egg yolks (size 3 or 4)	2
	salt and pepper	

Electric slow cooker: preheat Pot on HIGH for 20 minutes

1. Wash and dry the chicken joints and sprinkle them with salt. In a heavy frying-pan, heat the butter till foaming but not brown and sauté the chicken until quite brown all over. Put into Pot. Heat the wine in the same pan, pour into the Pot, scraping out any brown bits. Cook on HIGH for 30 minutes, then on LOW for 4 hours.
2. About 20 minutes before serving pour a little of the hot liquid from the Pot into a small, heavy frying-pan, and cook the well washed mushrooms on a rather high heat until they soften and most of the liquid has disappeared. Mix the tarragon and cream into the mushrooms, increase heat until the mixture almost boils. Take off the heat. Lightly beat the egg yolks and stir in a teaspoon of the hot mixture, then stir all this back into the mushrooms. Reduce heat to the very lowest and stir

constantly until the sauce just thickens. Don't answer the telephone, scrape carrots, or do the washing-up—*stir the sauce*. Season. Pour over the chicken, in the Pot, and serve at once.

Casserole cooking: preheat oven to Gas 3, 325°F, 170°C

As in Step 1, putting in casserole and setting lid so that it is slightly askew: cook 1½ to 1¾ hours. Liquid in casserole must stay at the gentlest simmer. You may need to add a little more wine or cider (boiling) up to about ¾ pt (350 ml) total. Then finish as in Step 2.

Chicken in Peanut Sauce

serves 4

4	chicken quarters	4
3 tbs	groundnut or soya oil	3 tbs
1 tbs	flour, mixed with ½ tsp salt and a pinch of pepper	1 tbs
1 tsp	paprika	1 tsp
2 tbs	tomato purée	2 tbs
½	bay leaf	½
¼ pt	boiling water	150 ml
5 oz	crunchy peanut butter	150 g
	salted peanuts (*optional*)	

Electric slow cooker: preheat Pot on HIGH for 20 minutes

1. Toss the well washed and dried chicken joints in seasoned flour. Heat the oil in a heavy frying-pan and brown the chicken very well. Add the paprika, tomato purée and bay leaf and stir thoroughly. Add the water and put into the Pot. Cook on HIGH for 20 minutes. Remove about half the sauce into a small bowl, mix in the peanut butter, then put back into the Pot.
2. Cook for 5 hours on LOW.

You can, if you like, scatter a tablespoon or two of slivered, salted peanuts over the finished dish just before serving, but if so, reduce the amount of salt in the seasoned flour in Step 1.

Casserole cooking: preheat oven to Gas 3, 325°F, 170°C

As in Step 1, but use a casserole with a snug-fitting

lid, and mix the peanut butter into the sauce when you are ready to put it all in the oven. Cover, cook 2 hours, having a quick look about halfway through and adding a little more boiling water, to keep the sauce smoothly liquid.

Chicken Bonne Femme

serves 4

2½ lb	chicken joints	1 gen kg
2 oz	butter (*not* margarine)	50 g
2 oz	shallots or spring onions, finely minced	50 g
1 tbs	parsley, minced	1 tbs
1 tsp	tarragon	1 tsp
1 tsp	chervil	1 tsp
¼ pt	white wine	150 ml
	salt and pepper	
	To garnish: watercress	

Electric slow cooker: preheat Pot on HIGH for 15 minutes

1. Sprinkle the chicken joints with salt and sauté in the hot butter in a large pan. Remove the chicken and put into the Pot. Gently sauté the shallots and herbs in the butter remaining in the pan, until the shallots are just translucent but not brown. Add to the Pot. Heat the wine to just below boiling-point in the same pan, and pour into the Pot. Season.
2. Cook on HIGH for 30 minutes, then on LOW for 4 hours, until the chicken is tender.

Place on a warm serving dish, skim as much fat as you can from the sauce, pour over the chicken, and garnish plentifully with well washed, very fresh watercress. Do not be tempted to add cream, lemon or more herbs to alter the flavour of this perfect and perfectly simple dish.

Casserole cooking: preheat oven to Gas 3, 325°F, 170°C

As in Step 1, using a snug-fitting ovenproof casserole. Put a layer of aluminium foil under lid, and cook about 1 hour until chicken is tender. Then finish as in Step 2.

Normandy Chicken★ serves 6

Another recipe for a large Pot or casserole, unless you choose to use a smaller roasting chicken.

5 lb	boiling fowl	2½ kg
1 lb	dessert apples, peeled and cored	450 g
	salt and pepper	
1	large onion, thinly sliced	1
½ pt	dry cider	300 ml
2	egg yolks	2
(¼ pt)	(chicken stock or boiling water)	(150 ml)

Electric slow cooker: preheat Pot on HIGH for 20 minutes

1. Cut the apples in half and stuff them into the chicken cavity. If you have some left over, put them into the Pot and around the chicken. Rub the chicken skin with salt and pepper. Put into the Pot. Blanch the onion in boiling water for 1 minute, drain and lay around the chicken. Bring the cider to the boil and pour into the Pot. Cook on HIGH for 5 hours, until the leg joint moves easily in its socket when gently pulled.
2. Remove the chicken and keep warm. Pour the liquid from the Pot into a saucepan and bring to the boil. Whisk the egg yolks, stir a tablespoon of the hot stock into them and blend well; do this two or three times until the egg yolks are heated. Remove the saucepan from heat, beat in the egg yolk mixture slowly, whisking all the time until it thickens. Cut the meat from the chicken in neat slices and pour on the sauce.

Casserole cooking: preheat oven to Gas 3, 325°F, 170°C

As in Steps 1 and 2, but increase the liquid by adding about ¼ pt (150 ml) chicken stock or boiling water. Put in casserole just big enough to hold the chicken and onion snugly. Cook 2½ to 3 hours and test for 'doneness' as above. Then finish as in Step 2.

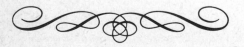

Roast Duckling with Green Peppercorns   serves 4

The interplay of the sharp 'green' taste against the richness of the duck makes this a rare and special dish. It is not for those who are out all day, nor for a small Pot or casserole.

5 lb	duckling, completely thawed, if frozen	2½ kg
1	small mild onion, finely minced	1
4 tbs	red wine vinegar	4 tbs
1 tsp	tarragon	1 tsp
½ tsp	thyme	½ tsp
4 tbs	green peppercorns	4 tbs
2 tsp	Dijon mustard	2 tsp
½ pt	beef stock	300 ml

Electric slow cooker: preheat Pot on HIGH for 15 minutes

1. Prick the duck skin all over with a very sharp fork or thin knife, at 2 inch (5 cm) intervals. Place on a trivet or wire rack in the Pot. (If your Pot is wide and shallow, you may have to cut the duck into 8 pieces for a better fit.) The duck must not rest on the base of the Pot, unless you want it to stew in its own fat.
2. Bring the vinegar, herbs and onion to the boil and cook until almost all the liquid is evaporated. Drain the peppercorns, rinse in cold water and add to the onion mixture. Add the mustard and beef stock and boil fiercely for a few minutes, to reduce slightly. Pour *half* this sauce over the duckling. Cook on LOW for 7 to 9 hours.
3. Halfway through cooking time, remove as much fat as you can with the invaluable bulb baster. (You will probably have to lift out the duck to do this.) Return the duck to the Pot, turn to HIGH for 30 minutes, then cook on LOW for the remaining time. I'm sorry, but you will probably have to repeat the fat-skimming process once more. If, at the end of the time, you seem to have too much sauce, pour it into a saucepan and boil rapidly to reduce to about ½ pint (300 ml). For a crisper finish, cut the duckling into serving pieces and put it high up in a hot oven, while you do your vegetables. Pass remaining sauce separately.

Casserole cooking: preheat oven to Gas 3, 325°F, 170°C

As in Step 1, but first you should brown duck in about 3 tbs very hot oil, in a frying-pan, then put in casserole on a rack or trivet. Proceed as above, cooking onion, vinegar and herbs in the frying-pan used for browning the duck, then add peppercorns and stock, tip it all into the casserole, cover and let braise for about 2 hours. Halfway through cooking time, skim the fat from surface. (Repeat towards end of cooking time if necessary.) Finish as above.

Belgian Pigeon
serves 4

4	large pigeons, halved	4
4 tbs	oil	4 tbs
6 oz	pickling-size onions	175 g
2 tbs	Chinese mushroom sauce	2 tbs
6 tbs	dry sherry	6 tbs
6 oz	mushrooms, washed	175 g
1 lb	frozen peas	450 g
1	round lettuce	1
	salt and pepper	
2 oz	*beurre manié* (see p. 153)	50 g
	mint *(optional)*	

Electric slow cooking: preheat Pot on HIGH for 20 minutes

1. Season the well cleaned pigeons with salt and pepper. Heat the oil in a frying-pan and fry the birds all over. Drain on kitchen paper and put into the Pot. Peel and blanch the onions in boiling water for 2 minutes. Drain and add to the Pot with the mushroom sauce, sherry and mushrooms cut into quarters if large. Cook on HIGH for 30 minutes, then on LOW for 7 hours.
2. While the pigeons are cooking, thaw the frozen peas. Half an hour before you are ready to serve, wash and shred the lettuce and put into the Pot with the peas. Turn the Pot to HIGH and cook for 30 minutes more. Thicken the sauce with *beurre*

manié and, if you like, snip in a bit of fresh mint at the last minute.

Casserole cooking: preheat oven to Gas 3, 325°F, 170°C

Cook as above, in tightly-lidded casserole for about 1½ hours. Half an hour before end of time, do the lettuce and pea business as in Step 2, return to oven until peas are tender.

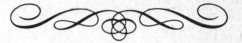

Partridge with Cabbage
serves 4

2	old partridges	2
	oil or bacon dripping	
2	small cabbages	2
8 oz	bacon rashers, trimmed	225 g
4	large carrots, sliced	4
8	small smoked sausages	8
¼ pt (8 fl oz)	stock	150 ml (225 ml)
6	juniper berries	6
2	garlic cloves, crushed	2
	peel of half a lemon	
	salt and pepper	

Electric slow cooker: preheat Pot on HIGH for 15 minutes

Brown the partridges in the oil or bacon fat in a frying-pan. Cut the cabbage into slices, blanch in boiling water for about 10 minutes and lay in the bottom of the Pot. Add the bacon. Blanch the carrots in boiling water for 3 minutes and add, then top with the sausages and the partridges. Add all the other ingredients. Cook on HIGH for 15 minutes, then on LOW for 10 hours.

Casserole cooking: preheat oven to Gas 4, 350°F, 170°C

As above, but cook about 3 hours in oven, in heavy, wide casserole, increasing stock to about 8 fl oz (225 ml). Check from time to time adding more liquid if needed.

Jugged Hare

serves 4 to 6

1	hare (or rabbit) jointed and marinated for 24 hours in half a bottle of cheap red wine	1
3 oz	butter	75 g
1	large onion, sliced	1
½ tsp	thyme	½ tsp
1 tbs	redcurrant jelly	1 tbs
6 oz	sage and onion stuffing (or a packet of sage and onion stuffing balls)	175 g
	salt and pepper	

Electric slow cooker: after marinating, preheat Pot on HIGH for 20 minutes

1. Remove the hare joints from the marinade and wipe very dry. Heat the butter in a heavy frying-pan and brown the hare. Put into the Pot. Bring the marinade to the boil in the frying-pan and pour into the Pot. Add the onion, thyme, salt, pepper and redcurrant jelly. Cook on HIGH for 30 minutes, then on LOW for 8 to 10 hours; cook for the shorter period if you have used rabbit, the longer for hare.
2. One hour before the end of cooking, make your sage and onion into small balls and add to the sauce. Just before serving, crush one or two of the stuffing balls and stir well to thicken the sauce.

Casserole cooking: preheat oven to Gas 3, 325°F, 170°C

Prepare marinated hare as in Step 1 above, and brown it. Then put hare joints, onion, thyme and seasoning in heavy casserole with tight lid. Cook 2½–3 hours in oven, until very tender. Half an hour before serving, stir in redcurrant jelly.

About 15 minutes before serving, add sage-and-onion balls, crushing two to thicken sauce.

Hasenpfeffer (Rabbit, German-style)

serves 4

1	rabbit, cut into joints	1
2 tbs	oil	2 tbs
1 tbs	flour	1 tbs
2	large onions, thinly sliced	2
½ pt	stout	300 ml
8 oz	prunes, soaked and pitted	225 g
	salt and pepper	

Electric slow cooker: preheat Pot on HIGH for 20 minutes

1. Heat the oil in a heavy frying-pan until very hot, and brown the rabbit joints well. (For a milder flavour, you may want to blanch them instead: put them into a saucepan of cold water, bring to the boil, boil for 2 minutes, drain well and dry.) Remove rabbit. Stir in the flour and cook, stirring, for 2 minutes. Blanch the onion in boiling water for 1 minute, drain and put into the bottom of the Pot. Lay in the rabbit joints.
2. Pour the stout into the frying-pan, bring to the boil and add to the Pot, scraping in the brown bits. Add the prunes, salt and pepper. Cook on HIGH for 30 minutes, then on LOW for 6 to 7 hours.

Casserole cooking: preheat oven to Gas 5, 375°F, 190°C

As in recipe above, but use a snug-fitting casserole. Cook in oven about 2 hours, tightly covered, checking occasionally to see what is going on, adding more liquid (boiling water or a little more stout if it is at hand) when needed.

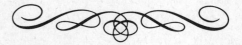

3. **Ratatouille** (p. 111): the sunny Mediterranean flavours of aubergine, green peppers, onions and tomatoes are brought out to perfection   (*Carmel Produce*)

4a. All the flavours of good ingredients are enhanced by low and gentle simmering

(Tower Housewares Ltd)

4b. **Navarin of Pork** (p. 92): an unusual blend of vegetables and pork in a lively spicy sauce

(Lea & Perrins Ltd)

Rabbit and Bacon Casserole

serves 4

2 lb	rabbit joints	900 g
1 tbs	seasoned flour	1 tbs
	salt and pepper	
1	large onion, finely minced	1
4	rashers streaky bacon, cut up	4
1 tbs	oil	1 tbs
½ pt	chicken stock	300 ml
2 tbs	parsley, chopped	2 tbs
	Optional:	
2 tbs	*beurre manié* (see p. 153)	2 tbs
	lemon juice	

Electric slow cooker: preheat Pot on HIGH for 20 minutes

1. Wash and dry the rabbit joints very thoroughly and toss in the flour. Heat the oil in a heavy frying-pan and sauté the rabbit until well browned. Put into the Pot. Fry the bacon and minced onion in the same oil for about 5 minutes. Add to the Pot. Bring the stock to the boil in the frying-pan, scrape up the good brown bits, add to the Pot with some freshly milled black pepper. Cook for 30 minutes on HIGH, then for 8 hours on LOW, until rabbit is falling off the bones. Season.
2. If you like, you may thicken the sauce with *beurre manié*. A squeeze of lemon juice at the last minute gives a pleasant little sharpness to the dish.

Sprinkle with parsley just before serving.

Casserole cooking: preheat oven to Gas 2, 300°F, 150°C

As in Step 1 above, putting everything except *beurre manié* and parsley in ovenproof casserole with a well-fitting lid. Cook 1 hour at this temperature, taste the liquid—if it's very salty, pour off half of it into a measure and replace it with an equal quantity of boiling water. Reduce heat to Gas 1, 250°F, 130°C, and cook 2 or 3 hours more until very tender indeed. Finish as in step 2 above.

Meat

★ No initial browning needed

In addition to the recipes given in this section, other recipes using small quantities of meat appear in the Vegetables and Pulses section: for example, Lentil Pot and Haricot Beans with Bacon.

Beef Rib Barolo

serves 8

This dish must be started the day before serving, and because of the high proportion of meat to bone in a rib joint, it is hardly worth making for fewer than 8 people. It can only be made in a deep, wide Pot or casserole that will accommodate this quite massive piece of beef.

4 lb	rib of beef on the bone	1·8 kg
1	bottle Barolo, or other heavy, characterful red wine	1
1	medium onion, thinly sliced	1
1	large carrot, diced	1
1	celery stalk, chopped	1
1	bay leaf	1
4	peppercorns	4
1 tbs	butter	1 tbs
2	streaky bacon rashers, chopped	2
	salt and pepper	

Electric slow cooker

1. Marinate the meat for 24 hours in the wine with the onion, carrot, celery, bay leaf and peppercorns. Turn once or twice. Remove from the marinade, wipe thoroughly dry and tie into a good shape that will fit into your Pot or casserole.
2. Preheat Pot for 20 minutes on HIGH.
3. Heat the butter and chopped bacon in a heavy frying-pan to sizzling-point, add the meat and brown well on both sides. Strain the marinade into a saucepan and boil briskly until it is reduced by half. Season the meat, put into the Pot, pour on the boiling liquid and cook on HIGH for 30 minutes, then on LOW for 7 hours. The meat should be so well cooked that it can be cut with a spoon. Pour over some of the sauce and hand the rest in a sauceboat.

To serve cold, cut the remaining meat off the bones, put into a smallish casserole or basin and pour on the sauce: the next day, it will be exceedingly odd-looking, but the scrappy bits of meat, set in wonderful jellied stock, make a most savoury spread for unbuttered, coarse brown bread.

Casserole cooking: preheat oven to Gas 3, 325°F, 180°C

As above, in casserole large enough to give house-room to the beef. Cook 3½ hours or until meat is absolutely tender when prodded with a cooking spoon.

Swiss Steak

serves 4 to 6

An American recipe despite its name; sometimes called Country Steak, or Grandmother's Steak.

2 lb	lean braising steak	900 g
3 tbs	brown flour, mixed with salt, pepper and 1 tsp paprika	3 tbs
3 tbs	oil, or good beef dripping	3 tbs
1	medium onion, thinly sliced	1
1 tsp	soy sauce, or Chinese mushroom sauce	1 tsp
½ pt	boiling water	300 ml

Electric slow cooker: preheat Pot on HIGH for 20 minutes

1. Cut the meat into pieces about 4 or 5 inches (10 or 12·5 cm) square. Roll them in the seasoned flour, then pound them unmercifully with a meat mallet until they are about double the original size. Turn them over several times as you beat them. Slash the edges of each piece two or three times. Heat the oil until very hot in a frying-pan and brown the meat well. Blanch the onions in boiling water for 1 minute and put them into the bottom of the Pot. Lay in the steak pieces and sprinkle with any remaining flour. Pour the boiling water into the frying-pan and swish out all the brown bits into the Pot. Add the soy sauce.
2. Cook on HIGH for 30 minutes, then on LOW for 5 to 6 hours. The meat should be almost falling to bits and have a rich, dark-brown flavour.

Casserole cooking: preheat oven to Gas 3, 325°F, 170°C

As in Step 1, putting everything in a casserole with a well-fitting lid. Cook 2 hours, checking from time to time and adding a little more boiling water if necessary. The sauce should be thick, dark, and savoury.

Daube à la Montigny★

serves 6 to 8 or more

This is to be started at least 36 hours before you serve it, and as it is a cold dish, rather like Boeuf à la Mode, it will feed any number from 6 to 10, depending on what else is on the table.

3 lb	lean beef (top round, rump or chuck)	1½ kg
12 oz	cooked ham, or boiled bacon or gammon, diced	350 g
1	large carrot, minced	1
1	large onion, finely minced	1
1	calf's foot *or*	1
2	pig's trotters	2
¼ pt	dry white wine or cider	150 ml
½ pt	beef stock *or*	300 ml
10½ oz	tin concentrated consommé, undiluted	290 g
1 tsp	salt	1 tsp
1 tbs	thyme	1 tbs
	black pepper	

Electric slow cooker: preheat Pot on HIGH for 20 minutes

1. Mix the diced ham, carrot and onion and put into the Pot. Add the tightly rolled and tied piece of beef and pig's trotters or calf's foot. Bring the wine and consommé or stock to the boil with the seasoning and thyme, and pour over the meat. Cook on HIGH for 30 minutes, then on LOW for 10 to 12 hours. If possible, turn the meat once halfway through cooking time.
2. When the meat is completely tender, pour everything into a large metal saucepan and plunge it into a sink of cold water. Cool it as quickly as you can, then refrigerate until you can skim off the quite large amount of fat on top. Remove the trotters or calf's foot. Put the meat and sauce into a small deep casserole or basin so that the meat is completely submerged. You can, if you like, strain the vegetables out of the sauce before this step—all their flavour has gone into the sauce.

Refrigerate for at least 12 hours, then slice and serve cold with salad.

Casserole cooking: preheat oven to Gas 2, 300°F, 150°C

As in Steps 1 and 2, cooking 6 hours in a rather close-fitting casserole so that the meat does not swim around. Turn meat halfway through cooking time, and taste seasoning at this point.

Austrian Boiled Beef★

serves 6

3–4 lb	brisket, or unsalted silverside	1½–2 kg
3 pts	beef stock	1·5 l
2	carrots, quartered	2
2	sprigs thyme *or*	2
1 tsp	dried thyme	1 tsp
2	celery stalks, chopped	2
1	leek, well washed and thinly sliced	1
1	large onion, minced	1
1 tbs	salt	1 tbs
6	peppercorns	6

Electric slow cooker: preheat Pot on HIGH for 20 minutes

1. Put everything into a big saucepan, bring to the boil and put into the Pot. Cook on LOW for 10 to 12 hours, until the meat is very tender. (I think it is wise to test the meat after about 8 hours of cooking, as some cuts—and some Pots—cook more quickly than others.)
2. Remove the meat, strain the stock and set aside for soup.

Serve with caper sauce, horseradish sauce or a warm vinaigrette sauce. With plainly boiled meat like this, always have a small dish of coarse sea salt to hand.

Casserole cooking: preheat oven to Gas 3, 325°F, 170°C

As in Steps 1 and 2, using a large ovenproof casserole and making sure everything is boiling hot when it goes into oven. Cover, cook 3–4 hours until meat is tender when stabbed with a sharp kitchen fork. Taste broth and add more salt if necessary. The strained stock, de-fatted, is perfect for making lentil soup. Serve as above.

Dry Beef Curry

serves 4

1 lb	good braising steak, trimmed and cut into 2 inch (5 cm) cubes	450 g
1 lev tbs	*each* powdered coriander and turmeric	1 lev tbs
1 tsp	curry paste, *or* mild Madras curry powder	1 tsp
½ lev tsp	*each* Indian chili and cumin	½ lev tsp
2	cloves	2
½ in	piece whole cinnamon	2·5 cm
2 tbs	cider vinegar *or* *tamarind water	2 tbs
2 tbs	butter	2 tbs
1	medium onion, finely minced	1
1	garlic clove, crushed	1
¼ pt (½ pt)	boiling water	150 ml (300 ml)

Electric slow cooker: preheat Pot on HIGH for 20 minutes

1. Mix the spices with the vinegar or tamarind water to make a thick paste. Melt the butter in a frying-pan and gently sauté the onion and garlic. Push them to one side and stir in the spice paste. Blend in the curry powder and cook for 5 minutes on a very low heat.
2. Dry the meat well and turn the cubes over and over in the frying-pan until they are well coated. Put everything into the Pot and add slightly less than the given amount of boiling water—you may want to thin the sauce later, but it is better to let the meat cook in as little liquid as possible. Cook on LOW for 6 hours or until the meat is tender.
3. If sauce seems thin at the end, tip into saucepan and reduce by boiling to desired consistency.

Serve with Dhal (p. 113), chutney, sliced bananas sprinkled with lemon juice, and a bowl of natural yoghurt with cucumber sliced paper-thin and well salted.

* Tamarind water: Indian and Pakistani shops sell dried tamarind in small packets. Soak 1 oz (25 g) in ¼ pt (150 ml) boiling water for an hour, strain off and use as liquid.

Casserole cooking: preheat oven to Gas 4, 350°, 180°C

As in Steps 1 and 2, putting ingredients in casserole without any liquid and baking for an hour. Then add ½ pt (300 ml) boiling water, and cook a further hour until liquid is absorbed, into a thick rich sauce.

Nameless Casserole

serves 4

2 lb	skirt steak, trimmed	900 g
2 tbs	seasoned flour	2 tbs
3 tbs	good beef dripping, or oil	3 tbs
1	large mild onion, minced	1
2 tbs	flour	2 tbs
¼ pt	beef stock, or undiluted tinned concentrated consommé	150 ml
¼ pt	dry cider	150 ml
1 lev tbs	dark brown sugar	1 lev tbs

Electric slow cooker: preheat Pot on HIGH for 20 minutes

1. Cut the steak into strips about 3 inches (7·5 cm) long and 1 inch (2·5 cm) wide and toss in the seasoned flour. Heat 2 tablespoons of the dripping or oil until very hot in a heavy frying-pan and brown the steak very well, in small batches. Put a layer of steak pieces in the bottom of the Pot. Sauté the onions until limp and medium brown, taking care not to let them burn. Spread half the onions on the meat, then repeat until all is used up.
2. In a small, clean frying-pan, melt the remaining tablespoon of dripping or oil and gently brown the flour, stirring all the time. (Watch it, it burns easily.) Stir in the stock and cider very gradually and cook until thickened. When completely blended, stir in the sugar and pour into the Pot. Cook on HIGH for 30 minutes, then on LOW for 6 hours. It will be dark and savoury, not sweet, excellent with plain steamed potatoes.

Casserole cooking: preheat oven to Gas 2, 300°F, 150°C

As in Steps 1 and 2, putting all ingredients in heavy casserole with a really well-fitting lid. Cook in oven 3 hours, until meat is tender and sauce is richly flavoured.

Beef Bracciole★   serves 4 to 6

Most suitable for a wide, shallow Pot or casserole.

   This is a version of a classic Italian recipe which has many variations. You can use 2 oz (50 g) cooked drained spinach instead of breadcrumbs, in which case leave out the sage and use ¼ teaspoon grated nutmeg. Or coarsely mince 2 to 4 oz (50 to 100 g) mushrooms and add to the breadcrumb mixture. Bracciole is very good served cold, with tomatoes, thinly sliced cucumbers and a good sharp mayonnaise.

1¾ lb	skirt steak, trimmed	800 g
4 oz	fresh breadcrumbs	100 g
4 oz	lean streaky bacon, chopped	100 g
	rind of half a lemon, grated	
½ tsp	basil	½ tsp
½ tsp	sage	½ tsp
2 oz	shallots, minced	50 g
1 tsp	olive oil	1 tsp
1	egg (size 4)	1
	salt and pepper	
¼ pt (6 fl oz)	white wine	150 ml (175 ml)

Electric slow cooker: butter and preheat Pot on HIGH for 20 minutes

1. Beat out the steak as thin as possible without tearing it; it is to be rolled up in one piece, like a Swiss roll. Mix together the crumbs, bacon, lemon rind, herbs, shallots and oil, then lightly beat the egg and bind the crumb mixture with it. Season. Spread on the meat, all the way to the edge, and roll up firmly. Fasten with cocktail sticks or short, thin metal skewers (longer ones will keep the roll from lying flat in the Pot). Lay the Bracciole in the Pot and pour on half the white wine. Cook on HIGH for 30 minutes, then on LOW for 4 hours, or on HIGH for 2½ hours.
2. Half an hour before serving, pour in the rest of the wine, and with a wooden spoon scrape up any brown bits from the bottom of the Pot and place on the meat. Cook for 30 minutes on HIGH.

Casserole cooking: preheat oven to Gas 4, 350°F, 180°C

As in Steps 1 and 2 above, but increase wine to a total of 6 fl oz (175 ml). Use casserole into which the rolled beef will fit rather snugly (an oval one if you have it). Cover tightly, cook 1½ hours, taste sauce for seasoning. Add remaining half measure of wine, scrape brown bits from bottom of casserole and run them over top of meat. Cook 30 minutes longer until meat is tender but not falling to bits.

Boiled Silverside★   serves 6 to 8

This also makes a sublime cold beef—rather like the best American corned beef.

3–4 lb	salted silverside	1½–2 kg
1 pt	boiling water	600 ml
4 oz	dark brown sugar	100 g
1	saltspoon ground cloves	1
2 tsp	dry mustard	2 tsp
1	medium onion, finely minced	1
2	bay leaves	2
¼ pt	cider vinegar	150 ml
1	small cabbage *(optional)*	1

Electric slow cooker: preheat Pot on HIGH for 20 minutes

1. Trim any excess fat from the meat. Put everything into a saucepan and bring to the boil, then put into the Pot and cook on LOW for 10 to 12 hours, until the meat is tender to the fork.
2. If you like, you can then turn to HIGH, remove the meat and keep it warm, and cook a small cabbage, quartered, in the broth.
   Serve with a bowl of coarse sea salt and horseradish sauce.

Casserole cooking: preheat oven to Gas 2, 300°F, 150°C

It's not usual to cook Silverside (or American Corned Beef) in the oven, but I find it works very well and is worry-free; everything as in method above, popped into a casserole that is deep rather than wide so meat is submerged. Cook about 5 hours to fork-tenderness. Twenty minutes before serving, pour liquid into saucepan, set meat to keep warm, and cook your quartered cabbage until just done but not limp and soggy.

Beef Stew with Orange

serves 4

2 lb	braising steak	900 g
2 tbs	oil	2 tbs
1	large onion, finely minced	1
	or	
10	button onions, peeled	10
1 tbs	flour	1 tbs
¼ pt	*red wine	150 ml
½ pt	beef stock	300 ml
	pinch of marjoram	
	sprig of fresh thyme, or a pinch of dried thyme	
2	bay leaves	2
2 tbs	Chinese mushroom sauce	2 tbs
3	celery stalks, cubed	3
1 tbs	orange peel, finely shredded	1 tbs

Electric slow cooker: preheat Pot on HIGH for 20 minutes

1. Heat the oil until very hot in a large frying-pan. Trim as much fat as possible from the meat and brown very well. Remove from the pan, drain on kitchen paper and put into the Pot. Sauté the minced onion (or small peeled onions) in the remaining fat until pale gold. Turn the celery cubes over in the fat. Put into the Pot.
2. Stir the flour into the fat in the pan, add the wine, stock, herbs, bay leaves and mushroom sauce, and bring to the boil. Pour into the Pot and stir in the orange peel. Cook on HIGH for 30 minutes, then on LOW for 6 to 8 hours.

   * You can use beer instead of red wine, but the flavour is not quite as good.

Casserole cooking: preheat oven to Gas 7, 425°F, 220°C

As in Steps 1 and 2, using an ovenproof casserole (heavy, please). Put it into oven at the high temperature for 10 minutes, then lower heat to Gas 3, 325°F, 170°C, and cook at a gentle simmer 3–4 hours. Peep in once in a while, and add a few tablespoons of hot stock, wine or water if sauce seems to be reducing too much for your taste. Skim or blot fat from surface. This stew reheats well, but may need salt the second time around.

Polly's Jamaica Pot Roast

serves 6

This recipe came to me from my friend Polly Rowles.

3 lb	chuck beef, in one piece, trimmed	1½ kg
	powdered ginger (see step 1)	
2 tbs	oil	2 tbs
2 tbs	soy sauce	2 tbs
¼ pt (8 fl oz)	(about) boiling water	150 ml (200 ml)
	salt and pepper	
1	medium onion, very thinly sliced	1
3	carrots, sliced	3
2	garlic cloves, slivered (optional)	2

Electric slow cooker: preheat Pot on HIGH for 20 minutes

Rub the meat with salt and pepper and quite a bit of powdered ginger (you heard me), and make a few pockets in the meat into which you insert small slivers of garlic (optional, naturally). Brown this on all sides in hot oil, put it into the Pot, place the onion on top and add the soy sauce and some boiling water. Cook gently on HIGH until the meat is done, which takes about 3 hours. (Or cook for 30 minutes on HIGH, then overnight on LOW.) Blanch some carrot slices in boiling water and add after about 2½ hours of cooking time. Test for seasoning.

The sauce is to be poured over baked, mashed or boiled potatoes. This is delicious for leftovers (if there are any). It can be refrigerated, the fat skimmed off, and the meat reheated in a saucepan.

Casserole cooking: preheat oven to Gas 2, 300°F, 150°C

As above, increasing boiling water to 8 fl oz (200 ml), and putting all ingredients into a heavy ovenproof casserole. Cook at least 3 hours, or until meat is very tender. It may with equal success be simmered, slowly, in a flameproof casserole with a tight lid on low heat on top of your cooker.

Pot au Feu II★

serves 6

This differs from the classic French recipe in omitting the usual boiling fowls; I haven't been able to cook everything together in the Pot or casserole without stewing the chicken to rags. It might be possible partially to cook a jointed fowl, and add it during the last hour or two, but this rather defeats the object of the dish.

3 lb	lean brisket	1½ kg
4 oz	piece salt pork	100 g
1	onion, stuck with 2 cloves	1
4	leeks, well washed and thinly sliced	4
2	celery stalks, sliced	2
9	carrots, peeled and sliced	9
1	turnip, peeled and sliced	1
1 tsp	thyme	1 tsp
6	potatoes, peeled and quartered	6
1	small head cabbage, cut into eighths	1
18	pickling onions	18
3 oz	butter	75 g
1 tbs	salt	1 tbs
1 tbs	sugar	1 tbs

Electric slow cooker: preheat Pot on HIGH for 20 minutes

1. Put the brisket, salt pork, onion, leeks, celery, 3 carrots, potatoes, turnip and thyme into a large saucepan. Bring to the boil with just enough water to cover and put into the Pot. Add the salt. Cook on HIGH for 30 minutes, then on LOW for 10 to 12 hours or overnight.
2. An hour before serving, blanch the remaining 6 carrots and the cabbage in boiling water for about 5 minutes, then turn the Pot to HIGH and add. While this is going on, cook the little onions in the butter in a heavy saucepan, shaking often, until they are brown and soft, then add the sugar.

To serve, remove the beef and cut into slices. Put a slice of beef, a bit of salt pork, some broth and some vegetables into large soup plates. Always have coarse salt and a variety of mustards to hand.

For cold boiled beef, take whatever beef is left from the Pot au Feu, put it into a deep dish or casserole and cover with foil and a saucer or plate that will just fit into the top of the dish. Weigh down with a tin of food or a brick, leave to cool at room temperature, then chill, still weighted down. It will set firmly into a good sliceable piece of meat.

Casserole cooking: preheat oven to Gas 2, 300°F, 150°C

As in recipe above, using a large, heavy casserole with a tight lid, and increasing water if necessary to cover ingredients when in casserole. Cook in oven 5–6 hours; or simmer in a flameproof casserole on top of cooker, on lowest possible heat, for 5 hours.

About 45 minutes before serving, blanch carrots, cabbage and potatoes in boiling water for a scant 5 minutes, and add to simmering casserole.

Blazing Hot Texas Chili

serves 8

This recipe came from a man with the entrancing name of Jake Pickle, and won a contest as 'the most authentic Texas Hot Chili'. The operative word here is hot. It will not seem a typical chili because it is made without the usual red kidney beans, but I have the (published) word of a Mexican Ambassador to the United States that chili should never have beans. Be warned: it is very, very hot, as you can see from the quantities of cayenne, tabasco and chili powder.

3 lb	beef, coarsely minced	1½ kg
3 tbs	oil	3 tbs
1	large onion	1
2	garlic cloves	2
15 oz	tomato purée	425 g
1 tsp	salt	1 tsp
1 tsp	cayenne pepper	1 tsp
1 tsp	tabasco	1 tsp
1 tbs	paprika	1 tbs
1 tbs	cumin	1 tbs
4 tbs	*American* chili powder	4 tbs
2 tbs	flour	2 tbs

Electric slow cooker: preheat Pot on HIGH for 20 minutes

1. Heat the oil until very hot in a large, heavy frying-pan. Brown the meat just until it loses its red colour, add all the other ingredients except the flour, and pour in a little boiling water—to come just below the top of the mixture. Cook on LOW for 8 to 10 hours.

2. Blot any excess fat from the top with kitchen paper towels, and taste for seasoning. Stir in the flour, turn the Pot to HIGH and cook for about another 30 minutes.

Serve with plenty of long-grain rice and gallons of cold beer.

* Do *not* use the kind of 'chili powder' you find under that name in English or Indian shops—it merely adds heat without flavour. What you want is the American kind (one brand available here is Gebhardt's), which is a special blend of dried, powdered chili peppers, cumin, garlic and salt, and is made for Chili con Carne.

Casserole cooking: preheat oven to Gas 2, 300°F, 150°C

As Steps 1 and 2, putting all the ingredients except flour in a really big heavy ovenproof casserole. Cook for 4 hours, or longer if it suits your convenience. Skim or blot fat, and thicken lightly with flour in the last half hour of cooking.

Kalahaui Beef   serves 4 to 6

This recipe came, as far as I can remember, from a Hawaiian source, which must mean that it has a vaguely Polynesian origin. It is one of the many beef stews that actually taste better served moderately, not intensely, hot for the full flavour of the spices to be appreciated. If you prefer, it may be completely cooked one day, refrigerated, and the solidified fat scraped off, then reheated gently in a saucepan half an hour before serving.

2 lb	beef, trimmed and cut into 2 inch (5 cm) cubes: good lean braising steak	900 g
1	large garlic clove	1
1 tsp	salt	1 tsp
1 tbs	lard, or groundnut oil	1 tbs
1	medium onion, minced	1
1 lev tbs	flour	1 lev tbs
1 lev tsp (½ tsp)	*each* ginger and mace	1 lev tsp (½ tsp)
¼ pt (½ pt)	cheap red wine	150 ml (300 ml)
½ tsp	mixed herbs	½ tsp
	black pepper	
3 tbs	cheap brandy	3 tbs

Electric slow cooker: preheat Pot on HIGH for 20 minutes

1. Crush the garlic with salt and mix through the meat cubes. Heat the lard in a heavy frying-pan until very hot and brown the meat—in small batches—all over. It must be thoroughly seared, so keep the heat high. Lift out with a slotted spoon and put into the Pot. Sauté the onions in the remaining fat until soft but not brown. Push the onion under the meat in the Pot.

2. Stir the flour into the frying-pan, slowly add the wine, stirring, and bring to the boil. Add the ginger, mace, herbs and pepper, and pour into the Pot. Cook on LOW for 8 hours. Blot or skim fat and taste for seasoning.

3. Heat the brandy in a small saucepan and set alight, pour over the meat and simmer for 30 minutes more.

Casserole cooking: preheat oven to Gas 3, 325°F, 170°C

As in Steps 1 and 2, but increasing wine to about ½ pt (300 ml), and decreasing ginger and mace to ½ tsp each. Put it all in a casserole with well-fitting lid, and distribute the onion slices over top of meat. Cook 3 hours, checking halfway through and adding a little boiling water if casserole seems dry. Taste for seasoning, and if you feel like adding more ginger or mace, dip out a little hot sauce and mix with spices before stirring it all together. Add brandy as above.

Chinese Fragrant Beef★

serves 6 to 8, with several other Chinese dishes

This is a lovely dish for a picnic, if you wrap the whole meat plate in clinging plastic film and take along a jar of the thin, pungent sauce.

2½–3 lb	boneless lean beef (chuck or shin)	1–1½ kg
1 pt	water	500 ml
1 tsp	star anise	1 tsp
3 tbs	dry sherry	3 tbs
3 tbs	soy sauce	3 tbs
3	slices fresh ginger, paper thin	3
3	garlic cloves, whole	3
1 tsp	salt	1 tsp
1 tsp	brown sugar	1 tsp

Electric slow cooker: preheat Pot on HIGH for 15 minutes

1. Trim any visible fat from the beef. Put all the ingredients together into a large saucepan and bring to the boil, then pour into the Pot. Cook on HIGH for 30 minutes, then on LOW for 6 to 8 hours. (Or cook overnight, on LOW for about 10 hours without the preliminary 30 minutes on HIGH. But make sure, in this case, that the ingredients are very hot, and the liquid is at a galloping boil, before you put them into the preheated Pot.) Turn the meat once during the cooking, if it is not wholly submerged: this depends on your Pot, as a wide, shallow casserole will leave part of the meat exposed.
2. Remove the meat, reserve the liquid, cool both thoroughly, wrap the meat in foil and refrigerate for at least 4 hours.
3. Thinly slice the meat, against the grain, with the sharpest possible knife. Lay the slices, over-lapping, on a large meat plate, and spoon over about 6 tablespoons of the reserved liquid.

Serve with hot pitta bread (which may be steamed in a colander for 2 minutes over boiling water, if you want to come close to the original Shanghai idea of Fragrant Beef with steamed buns).

Casserole cooking: preheat oven to Gas 2, 325°F, 170°C

As above, but cooking in oven in large casserole for 3–4 hours, turning once during the process, and checking to make sure there's enough liquid to make it all very moist.

L'Estouffat Lamande   serves 6

This may sound rather like Daube à la Montigny, but in fact the flavour—because of the brandy and red wine—is quite different. It freezes well.

4½ lb	beef (topside or top rump)	2 kg
2 tbs	good beef dripping, or lard	2 tbs
2	very large onions, thinly sliced	2
6	small carrots, cut into slivers	6
2	garlic cloves, crushed with 1 tsp salt	2
2 fl oz	brandy	50 ml
½ pt (¾ pt)	coarse red wine	300 ml (400 ml)
8 oz	salt pork, diced	225 g
2	pig's trotters	2
	bouquet garni	
	black pepper	

Electric slow cooker: preheat Pot on HIGH for 20 minutes

1. Roll and tie the beef and lightly brown in hot dripping or lard in a frying-pan. Put into the Pot. Cook the onions and carrots in the remaining fat until they begin to colour, and stir in the garlic, salt and brandy. Leave to cook for a minute or two, turn up the heat and add the wine, salt pork and pig's trotters. Bring to the boil, add the bouquet garni and pepper and put into the Pot. Cook on HIGH for 30 minutes, then on LOW for 8 to 10 hours.
2. The sauce is rich in fat and you may want to skim it with the ever-useful bulb syringe; or, when it is completely cooked, pour the contents of the Pot into a basin, submerge that in cold water and chill until the fat rises and can be skimmed off. Then reheat in a saucepan on low heat.

Serve with good, plainly boiled potatoes.

To serve cold, remove and throw away the veg-etables and pig's trotters, chill, remove fat, and leave to stand until the sauce is a deep amber jelly.

Casserole cooking: preheat oven to Gas 3, 325°F, 170°C

As in Steps 1 and 2, using a casserole of a size that will snugly fit the meat and vegetables. You may want to increase the red wine to about ¾ pt (400 ml). Cook for 5 hours, turning meat over once during that time.

Carbonnade of Beef Flamande

serves 4

1 lb	chuck steak, well trimmed and cut into 2 inch (5 cm) cubes	450 g
2	streaky bacon rashers	2
3	large onions, finely diced	3
1 tbs	black treacle	1 tbs
2	cloves	2
2	bay leaves	2
½ pt	brown ale	300 ml
	boiling water	
	seasoned flour	

Electric slow cooker: preheat Pot on HIGH for 20 minutes

1. Toss the meat in the seasoned flour. Fry the bacon in a frying-pan until the fat runs, remove and dice. Fry the meat in the bacon fat until well browned. Put into the Pot. Soften the onions in the fat in the pan, but do not brown. Add to the Pot with the treacle. Bring the ale to the boil and put into the Pot. Cautiously add some boiling water to the Pot—you need barely enough liquid in all to cover the meat but not drown it. Add cloves and bay leaves. The total quantity of water depends greatly on the size and shape of your Pot.
2. Cook on HIGH for 3 hours, then on LOW for 4 to 6 hours until the meat is completely tender.

Casserole cooking: preheat oven to Gas 3, 325°F, 170°C

As in Step 1, using a casserole about 3½ inches deep and perhaps 9 inches across. Cook 2–2½ hours, in bottom of oven. Liquid should be gently rippling, never boiling. This Carbonnade lends itself to advance preparation and very gentle reheating without boiling.

Green Peppercorn Steak

serves 6

2 lb	chuck steak, well trimmed	900 g
2 tbs	soya oil, or good beef dripping	2 tbs
2	large onions, thinly sliced	2
½ pt	white wine or dry cider	300 ml
	salt and pepper	
1	large garlic clove, crushed	1
2 tsp	brown flour	2 tsp
1 tbs	tomato purée	1 tbs
6 tsp	green peppercorns, drained	6 tsp
1 tbs	single or soured cream, or yoghurt (optional)	1 tbs

Electric slow cooker: preheat Pot on HIGH for 20 minutes

1. Cut the steak into slices about 5 inches (7·5 cm) long and 2 inches (5 cm) wide. Heat the oil or dripping until very hot, in a large frying-pan, quickly brown the meat all over. Remove and put into the Pot. Lightly brown the onion in the hot fat, drain well on kitchen paper and add to the meat.
2. Pour off almost all the remaining fat from the pan, add the wine, salt, pepper and garlic, and bring to the boil. Add to the meat and cook on LOW for 6 hours.
3. Remove the meat and onions and keep warm. In a blender or food mill, combine the sauce with the flour, tomato purée and four teaspoons of green peppercorns. Turn the Pot to HIGH, reheat the sauce until bubbling, then stir in the remaining green peppercorns and simmer for another 5 minutes. (For a rich, velvety sauce, stir in 1 tablespoon—no more—single cream, soured cream or yoghurt.) Pour over the steak and serve at once.

Casserole cooking: preheat oven to Gas 3, 325°F, 170°C

As in Steps 1 and 2, but put steak in a small, rather confining casserole, and cook about 2 hours. Have a look after an hour, and add a little more wine or cider if sauce is cooking down too much. Finish as in Step 3.

Glasgow Steak and Kidney Pie

serves 4

1 lb	good braising steak, well trimmed and cut into 2 inch (5 cm) cubes	450 g
8 oz	kidney, skinned, cored and cut up	225 g
2 tbs	lard, or beef dripping	2 tbs
1	large onion, thinly sliced	1
2	carrots, sliced	2
scant pt (1¼ pts)	stock or water	600 ml (750 ml)
	salt and pepper	
1	bay leaf	1
2 tbs	oatmeal	2 tbs
½ tsp	soy sauce	½ tsp
4 oz	mushrooms, sliced	100 g
	For the topping:	
8 oz	flour	225 g
2 oz	oatmeal	50 g
2 tbs	lard	2 tbs
2 tbs	butter	2 tbs
3 tbs	cold water	3 tbs
	pinch of salt	

Electric slow cooker: preheat Pot on HIGH for 20 minutes

1. Heat the lard until very hot in a frying-pan and brown the steak and kidney pieces. Add the onions and carrots, stir them around to colour them, add the water or stock, bay leaf, soy sauce, salt and pepper, and bring to the boil. Stir in the oatmeal and put into the Pot. Cook on LOW for 6 hours, until the meat is tender.

2. One hour before serving, add the mushrooms, remove the bay leaf and taste for seasoning. Turn the Pot to HIGH and cook for 20 minutes. Preheat oven to 400°F (200°C, Gas 6).

3. Make the pastry topping with the flour, oatmeal, salt, fat and enough water to make a firm dough. Knead lightly and pat out on floured board. If your Pot has a removable casserole, put a pastry lid on the steak and kidney, slash the top, and bake until crisp in oven. Or transfer the contents to a pie dish and proceed from there.

Casserole cooking: preheat oven to Gas 3, 325°F, 170°C

As in Steps 1 and 2, but omitting oatmeal in initial stage, and increasing stock to 1¼ pints (750 ml). Bring to boil, put in casserole with a tight lid, and cook in oven 1½ hours. Add mushrooms and put back in oven for half an hour. Then mix about 2 tbs oatmeal with 4 tbs cold water to a smooth paste, in a small saucepan. Stir in a little of the gravy from the casserole and cook a few minutes until thick. Stir all this back into casserole and mix well. Finish with pastry topping as in Step 3 above.

Sarah Morphew's Brown Stew with Ale

serves 6 to 8

This recipe came to me as a photocopy of a tattered newspaper cutting—I didn't know who Sarah Morphew was. I've just discovered that she is a bright spark who learned the brewing trade, went on to become a Master of Wine, and is now a wine buyer with a big trading group. And, I am sure, a very good cook. The stew must be made with **strong** *brown ale; beer will not do. Stout is just possible but gives an entirely different result. A half recipe can of course be made; but this stew freezes well, and makes a wonderful second-day dish topped with rounds of scone dough and baked for 40 minutes in a Gas 6 (400°F, 200°C) oven.*

3 lb	lean braising steak, well trimmed and cut into 1 inch (2·5 cm) cubes	1½ kg
½ pt	strong brown ale	300 ml
6	black peppercorns, crushed	6
2 tsp	mixed herbs	2 tsp
2 tbs	dark brown sugar	2 tbs
1½ tbs	brown flour, seasoned	1½ tbs
2 tbs	good beef dripping	2 tbs
6	medium onions, thinly sliced	6
	salt and pepper	
¼ pt (6 fl oz)	boiling water	150 ml (175 ml)
2 tbs	*beurre manié* (see p. 153) *or*	2 tbs
1 oz	instant potato (*optional*)	25 g

Electric slow cooker

1. Marinate the steak overnight in the ale with the peppercorns, herbs and sugar. Next day, drain very well, toss the meat in seasoned flour and brown in the hot dripping in a frying-pan. Blanch the onions for 1 minute in boiling water and drain.

2. Preheat Pot on HIGH for 20 minutes.

3. Pour the marinade into the frying-pan, scraping up the brown bits, and bring to the boil. Put everything into the Pot and add the boiling water. Cook on HIGH for 30 minutes, then on LOW for 6 hours.

   This makes a lot of bright, flavoursome brown gravy; if you like, you can thicken it with about 2 tablespoons of *beurre manié* or 1 oz (25 g) instant potato, stirred into a small saucepan of *boiling* sauce, then blended back into the Pot.

Casserole cooking: preheat oven to Gas 3, 325°F, 170°C

As in Steps 1 and 3 above, using a heavy casserole with good tight lid, and increasing the boiling water to about 6 fl oz (175 ml). Cook 2–3 hours, have a look at it at half time, give it all a good stir. The oven time depends on the tenderness of your braising steak.

Talismano Beef with Fennel

serves 6

2½ lb	lean braising steak, cut into 2 inch (5 cm) cubes	1 gen kg
1 tbs	olive or soya oil	1 tbs
1	onion, minced	1
1	celery stalk, diced	1
2	bacon rashers, minced	2
¼ pt	dry red wine	150 ml
5 fl oz	tin tomato purée	150 ml
1 tbs	brown flour	1 tbs
1 tsp	fennel seeds	1 tsp
1	garlic clove, crushed with 1 tsp salt	1

Electric slow cooker: preheat Pot on HIGH for 20 minutes

1. Heat the oil in a frying-pan, brown the meat cubes and remove and keep warm. Lightly brown the onion and celery in the same oil. (You may need to add a bit more oil.) Put the vegetables, bacon and meat into the Pot. Bring the wine to the boil in the frying-pan with the tomato purée and about 3 tablespoons boiling water. Put into the Pot. Cook on HIGH for 30 minutes, then on LOW for 6 hours.

2. Spoon about 3 or 4 tablespoons of the sauce out of the Pot into a small saucepan, stir in the flour and cook until it reaches the honeycomb stage. Stir into the Pot, add the fennel seeds and garlic (more if you like), taste for seasoning and cook on HIGH for another 30 minutes. You may of course reduce or increase the amount of fennel.

   This is very good with pasta shells.

Casserole cooking: preheat oven to Gas 3, 325°F, 170°C

As in Step 1, but cooking the meat and vegetables in oven in an uncovered casserole, about 1½ hours. Then as in Step 2, finish with flour, garlic and fennel seeds. If you have a flameproof casserole and boiling rings you can trust, this may be simmered slowly about 1 hour, then another half an hour after adding the fennel.

Veal Fricassee with Crisp Top★

serves 4

With an electric slow cooker this may sound a rather long process, but in fact the initial 6 hour cooking can be done the day before in the Pot, and the final stages done on the day of serving in the oven or on top of the cooker in a heatproof casserole.

1½ lb	pie veal, well trimmed and cut into 1½ inch (3·5 cm) cubes	700 g
½ pt (¾ pt)	boiling water	300 ml (450 ml)
1	chicken stock cube	1
1	bay leaf	1
1	medium onion, finely minced	1
1	celery stick, chopped	1
	small piece of lemon rind	
	salt and pepper	
	nutmeg, freshly grated	
4	small carrots, cut into matchsticks	4
4 oz	mushrooms, sliced	100 g
3 tbs	butter	3 tbs
3 tbs	flour	3 tbs
	For the topping:	
1	garlic clove, crushed	1
3 oz	breadcrumbs	75 g
3 oz	cooked ham, minced	75 g
1 tbs	parsley, chopped	1 tbs

Electric slow cooker: preheat Pot on HIGH for 20 minutes

1. Put the veal into a saucepan with the boiling water, stock cube, bay leaf, onion, celery, lemon rind and seasoning. Bring to the boil and put into the Pot. Cook on HIGH for 30 minutes, then on LOW for 6 hours. Remove the bay leaf and lemon rind. Blanch the carrots for 1 minute in boiling water and add, with the mushrooms, to the Pot. Turn the Pot to HIGH.
2. Melt half the butter in a saucepan, stir in the flour, and cook to the honeycomb stage, then dip out half the veal stock from the Pot into the butter/flour mixture. Stir well and cook until thickened and smooth. Put back into the Pot and cook until the carrots are tender. Taste for seasoning.
3. Just before serving, melt the remaining butter, simmer the garlic in it but do not brown, add the breadcrumbs and turn up the heat to brown them. Mix in the ham and parsley and thickly cover the veal at the last minute before serving.

Casserole cooking: preheat oven to Gas 4, 350°F, 180°C

As in Step 1, but increase liquid to ¾ pt (420 ml) boiling water. Put in a deep casserole, cover and simmer in oven 2 hours. Proceed with Step 2, making the thickened sauce and stirring it back into casserole. Cook, uncovered, another half an hour. Taste for seasoning. Finish with crumb topping, Step 3.

Vitello Tonnato

serves 6

The basic recipe, without sauce, makes an excellent braised veal dish.

3 lb	boned, rolled leg of veal	1½ kg
1	large onion, sliced	1
1	carrot, diced	1
2	garlic cloves, crushed	2
4	celery stalks, diced	4
¼ pt (8 fl oz)	dry white wine	150 ml (225 ml)
¼ pt	olive oil	150 ml
	pinch thyme	
1 tsp	parsley, minced	1 tsp
	salt and pepper	
	beurre manié (see p. 153) (*optional*)	
	For the sauce:	
1 tbs	onion, grated	1
3	anchovy fillets, finely minced	3
7 oz	tin good tuna in oil	175 g
4 oz	mayonnaise	120 g
2 tbs	capers	2 tbs

Electric slow cooker: preheat Pot on HIGH for 20 minutes

1. In a heavy saucepan, combine all (except sauce) ingredients and bring to the boil. Put into the Pot, and cook on LOW for 6 to 8 hours, or on HIGH for 3 to 4 hours. Let the meat cool in its juices (turn it out of the Pot into a basin, cover and cool in a sink of cold water).
2. Remove and cut into very thin slices. Mix the sauce ingredients together well with a wooden spoon.

If you prefer thicker juices, remove the meat, keep it hot, turn the Pot to HIGH and stir in 2 tablespoons of *beurre manié*, stirring and cooking until thickened to your taste.

Serve the veal with the sauce poured over.

Casserole cooking: preheat oven to Gas 2, 300°F, 150°C

As in Step 1, cooking in a casserole big enough to accommodate the veal rather snugly, and increasing wine to about 8 fl oz (225 ml). Cook 3½ hours, until meat is entirely tender. Glance at it from time to time, and add a little boiling water if it looks like drying. Finish with the sauce as in Step 2.

Fricandeau of Veal

serves 6

2 lb	shoulder of veal, boned, rolled and tied	900 g
½ lb	streaky bacon	225 g
2	medium carrots, thinly sliced	2
2	garlic cloves, cut in slivers	2
2	small onions, thinly sliced *or*	2
1	medium onion, thinly sliced	1
	salt and black pepper	
	a pinch of thyme	
¼ pt (½ pt)	chicken stock	150 ml (300 ml)
	butter or oil for browning	
1 tbs	potato flour	1 tbs
½ tsp	soy sauce	½ tsp
1 tsp	parsley, minced	1 tsp

Electric slow cooker: preheat Pot on HIGH for 15 minutes

1. Wipe the veal very dry and brown it quickly in the hot butter or oil in a frying-pan. Wrap it completely in the strips of bacon and skewer them firmly with cocktail picks or short metal skewers. Blanch the vegetables for 1 minute in boiling water (save the water for soup if you feel truly thrifty). Make a bed of vegetables in the bottom of the Pot and lay in the browned veal. Bring the stock to boil with the soy sauce and pour in. Add seasoning and thyme. Cook on HIGH for 30 minutes, then on LOW for 6 hours, or on HIGH for 3 to 4 hours until the veal is tender.
2. Blend the potato flour with an equal quantity of water to a thin paste. Remove the veal, slice and keep warm. Stir the potato flour mixture into the sauce, turn the Pot to HIGH and cook for 15 minutes.

Serve the veal on its bed of braised vegetables, with parsley and the sauce poured over.

Casserole cooking: preheat oven to Gas 1, 250°F, 130°C

As in Step 1 above, putting veal and vegetables in casserole and increasing chicken stock to half a pint (300 ml). Cook, uncovered, 2 hours, basting from time to time.

Fifteen minutes before serving, mix potato flour with ¼ pt (150 ml) boiling water, stir smooth, and brush or spread over meat. Increase oven temperature to Gas 6, 400°F, 200°C, and cook until lightly browned. Sprinkle with parsley and serve on bed of braised vegetables with sauce.

Giovanni's Osso Bucco

serves 4

This recipe came from the melancholy chef and owner of a wonderful New York restaurant, alas no longer there; the dish was never on the menu and had to be requested, as it was thought to be too bourgeois for the expense-account diners. Most recipes for Osso Bucco are unnecessarily tarted-up with southern Italian herbs and spices which merely mask the honest flavour of this Milanese dish.

2	veal shins, sawed into 2 inch (5 cm) lengths	2
2 tbs	butter	2 tbs
1 tbs	good oil	1 tbs
1	medium onion, very finely minced	1
2	garlic cloves, crushed	2
8 oz	(drained weight) tinned Italian peeled tomatoes	225 g
$\frac{1}{4}$ pt	dry white wine	150 ml
$\frac{1}{4}$ pt	chicken stock	150 ml
	salt and pepper	
1	small bay leaf	1
1 tbs	lemon rind, grated	1 tbs
2 tbs	parsley, minced	2 tbs

Electric slow cooker: preheat Pot on HIGH for 20 minutes

Heat the butter and oil until quite hot, and brown the veal shins all over. Put into the Pot and brown the onion and 1 garlic clove lightly in the same pan. Add the tomatoes, wine, stock and bay leaf and bring to the boil. Pour over the veal, season well, and cook on LOW for 8 hours.

Make Gremolata (a small handful of well-washed and dried parsley, grated peel of half a lemon, and a small clove of garlic crushed), and sprinkle over Osso Bucco as you serve it. An excellent accompaniment: a good risotto, and great quantities of grated Parmesan.

Casserole cooking: preheat oven to Gas 3, 325°F, 170°C

As above, putting pieces of browned veal shin in a casserole small enough to allow them to stand upright so the delicious marrow won't fall out. Cook, covered, in oven 2 hours, then uncover and cook another half an hour, to reduce sauce and glaze the meat. In the meantime, make the lemon and parsley Gremolata.

Spoon-Sliced Leg of Lamb

serves 6

This recipe is suitable only for a Pot wide and deep enough to contain the joint. Shop with your Pot dimensions and a tape measure! The meat of the shank should be folded back into a sort of pocket on the inside of the leg.

5 lb	leg of lamb, shank bone removed	2$\frac{1}{2}$ kg
1	large garlic clove, thinly slivered	1
	salt and pepper	
1 tbs	oil	1 tbs
1	medium onion, finely minced	1
2	medium carrots, diced	2
$\frac{1}{4}$ pt ($\frac{1}{2}$ pt)	dry white wine	150 ml (300 ml)
1$\frac{1}{2}$ tbs	tomato purée	1$\frac{1}{2}$ tbs
1 tbs	vegetable-yeast extract *or*	3 tbs
3 tsp	Chinese mushroom sauce	3 tsp

Electric slow cooker: Preheat Pot on HIGH for 15 minutes

1. Pierce the fat of the joint in many places with a thin-boned knife (a boning knife for preference). Insert the finely slivered garlic into the cuts and rub well with salt and pepper. Heat the oil in a large pan and brown the lamb all over. Put into the Pot. In the same fat gently brown the onions and carrots just to colour. Bring the wine, tomato purée and vegetable extract or mushroom sauce to the boil and add to the Pot.
2. Cook on LOW for 10 to 12 hours, until the meat is completely tender.
3. Remove and keep warm, skim or syphon off as much fat as possible. Strain and reheat the pan juices and taste for seasoning.

Serve if you can with a dish of well cooked haricot beans with some of the lamb juices mixed in, and a dish of coarse salt.

Casserole cooking: preheat oven to Gas 8, 450°F, 230°C

As in Step 1, putting the lamb and vegetables in a wide, fairly shallow casserole, in the hot oven for about 20 minutes. Then lower heat to Gas 2, 300°F, 150°C, cover casserole tightly and cook 5 hours more. Finish as in Step 3.

Marinated Lamb★   serves 4

1	small leg of lamb on the bone, cut into four slices by your butcher	1
4 oz	mushrooms	100 g
2	medium onions, cut into eighths	2
4	tomatoes, peeled and chopped	4
	For the marinade:	
¼ pt	good oil	150 ml
¼ pt	red wine	150 ml
1	garlic clove, crushed with 2 tsp salt	1
1 tsp	rosemary	1 tsp
1 tsp	basil	1 tsp
	black pepper	

Electric slow cooker

1. Marinate the lamb for 7 to 8 hours, turning occasionally.
2. Drain the marinade from the meat and reserve.
3. Preheat Pot on HIGH for 20 minutes.
4. Put the lamb into the Pot. Bring the marinade to the boil, add the mushrooms, onions and tomatoes and pour into the Pot. Stir well. Cook on HIGH for 4 hours, then on LOW for 2 hours.
5. Serve with some of the hot marinade poured over the lamb, and hand the rest in a heated sauceboat.

Casserole cooking: preheat oven to Gas 4, 350°F, 180°C

As in Steps 1, 2 and 4, putting all ingredients in casserole with well-fitting lid, and cooking in oven about 2 hours, or until lamb is tender. Glance at it after about an hour, and stir in a little boiling water if sauce is reducing too rapidly for your taste.

Golden Horn Lamb   serves 4

This recipe came many years ago from Clementine Paddleford's column in the late lamented New York Herald Tribune. *It possibly originated from an Armenian restaurant in New York called the Golden Horn. The addition of the curry powder is unusual in Armenian cookery.*

2 lb	lean loin lamb chops	900 g
1 tsp	groundnut or soya oil	1 tsp
1	medium onion, thinly sliced	1
8 oz	carrots, sliced	225 g
1 lev tbs	mild curry powder	1 lev tbs
1 lev tbs	flour	1 lev tbs
1	chicken stock cube	1
½ pt	boiling water	300 ml
3 lev tbs	pearl barley	3 lev tbs

Electric slow cooker: preheat Pot on HIGH for 20 minutes

1. Heat the oil until very hot in a large frying-pan, sauté the chops, remove and keep warm. Pour off all but 1 tablespoon of the fat in the pan and sauté the onions and carrots until they just begin to colour. Stir in the curry powder, flour and crumbled stock cube. Add the boiling water and barley. Mix very well and keep on the boil.
2. Arrange the chops in the bottom of the Pot and pour on the boiling vegetable and stock mixture. Cook on HIGH for 30 minutes, then on LOW for 4 hours, until the meat is fork-tender. Remove the meat and keep warm.
3. Pour the contents of the Pot into a heavy saucepan and cook down until it is thick and rich-looking, then pour over the chops.

Casserole cooking: preheat oven to Gas 3, 325°F, 170°C

As in Steps 1 and 2, cooking in a tightly lidded casserole about 1½ hours. After 45 minutes, have a look: add more hot stock if necessary. Pearl barley absorbs an amazing quantity of liquid, and you should have quite a nice lot of sauce at the end.

Kashmir Curry

serves 4 to 6

This mixture of dried fruit and lamb with curry is a characteristic Kashmiri dish. You can make it as mild or hot as you like, with whatever quantity of curry powder suits you.

1½ lb	lean lamb, cut into 2 inch (5 cm) cubes	700 g
½ pt	*natural plain yoghurt	300 ml
	curry powder as desired: 2 to 6 tablespoons	
2 tbs	oil	2 tbs
2	large onions, thinly sliced	2
2	garlic cloves, sliced	2
4 oz	dried apricots	100 g
2 oz	sultanas	50 g
	salt	
	juice of half a lemon	
1 oz	flaked almonds	50 g
(½ pt)	(boiling stock)	(300 ml)

Electric slow cooker

1. Marinate the lamb in half the yoghurt and all the curry powder for about 3 hours.
2. Preheat Pot on HIGH for 20 minutes.
3. Heat the oil in a frying-pan, and lightly brown the onion, remove and drain well on kitchen paper. Pour boiling water over the apricots, leave to stand until plump, then drain well. Pour off as much marinade as possible from the meat and set aside; fry the garlic and meat in the remaining hot oil for about 5 minutes. Put into the Pot with the onions, apricots, sultanas and the remaining marinade. Cook on HIGH for 30 minutes, then on LOW for 5 hours. The sauce will curdle, but this can't be helped and doesn't affect the taste *(but see 'To Stabilize Yoghurt', p. 155).
4. Taste for seasoning, add the salt and lemon juice. Stir in the remaining yoghurt with the flaked almonds just before serving.

Casserole cooking: preheat oven to Gas 3, 325°F, 170°C

As in Steps 1 and 3, using a casserole with well-fitting lid. Add ½ pt (300 ml) boiling stock to the meat. Cook about 1½ hours, until lamb is tender but not falling to shreds; look at it after about 45 minutes, add a very little boiling stock or water if sauce seems to be cooking down too much. This should be a richly sauced dish, into which you stir yoghurt, almonds and lemon juice at the finish.

Lamb with Tomato and Orange

serves 8

This must be made a day in advance if the Pot method is used, as it should cool and then be reheated. Choose a joint that, when boned, will fit into your Pot or casserole.

4 lb	boned rolled shoulder or leg of lamb	1·8 kg
2 tbs	oil	2 tbs
1	medium onion, finely minced	1
	juice and grated rind of 1 large orange	
	salt and pepper	
6	medium tomatoes, peeled, or their equivalent in Italian peeled tomatoes, well drained	6
	pinch of dried tarragon, or a sprig of fresh tarragon	
1 tbs	flour	1 tbs
½ pt	stock	300 ml

Electric slow cooker: preheat Pot on HIGH for 20 minutes

1. Trim the lamb of all excess fat, heat the oil in a large frying-pan and brown the meat all over. Put into the Pot. In the same frying-pan, gently sauté the onion until pale gold. Gradually stir in the flour, then add the orange juice, rind, tomatoes, herb and seasoning and put into Pot.
2. Bring the stock to the boil and pour in, mixing well. Cook on HIGH for 30 minutes then on LOW for 6 to 8 hours, until you can cut the meat very easily.
3. Remove from the Pot, put everything into a basin and cool as quickly as possible; skim off all the fat. Refrigerate. Reheat in an ovenproof casserole (not the Pot), in a moderate oven.

Slice the meat thinly and serve with some of the sauce poured over each slice.

Casserole cooking: preheat oven to Gas 2, 300°F, 150°C

Cook in oven, as in Steps 1, 2 and 3, using a casserole with well-fitting lid. It will take about 3½ to 4 hours, before cooling and reheating. An oval casserole that will hold the meat snugly is best.

Limerick Irish Stew★ serves 4

8	middle neck lamb chops	8
2 lb	potatoes, peeled and sliced	900 g
2	large onions, thinly sliced	2
1	celery stalk, sliced	1
	salt and pepper	
½ pt (¾ pt)	boiling water	300 ml (0·5 l)
2 tbs	cornflour	2 tbs
2 tbs	cold water	2 tbs
½	teacup parsley, minced	½

Electric slow cooker: preheat Pot on HIGH for 20 minutes

1. Trim as much fat as possible from the chops. Blanch the potatoes in boiling water. (Save the liquid for soup.) Put a layer of potatoes into Pot, then a layer of chops, a layer of onions, strew with celery, season lavishly with salt and black pepper; continue until everything is used up. Pour on just enough fiercely boiling water to come halfway up the layers. Cook on LOW for 8 to 10 hours.
2. Fifteen minutes before serving, blend the cornflour and cold water to a smooth paste and spoon out about ¼ pt (150 ml) of the cooking liquid. Slowly blend the hot broth into the cornflour, pour back into the Pot, turn to HIGH and cook until the sauce is slightly thickened. Add parsley.

Casserole cooking: preheat oven to Gas 1, 250°F, 130°C

As in Step 1, increasing boiling water to a generous ¾ pt (about half a litre), and cook about 2 hours.

Pour in a few more tablespoons of boiling water after about an hour, if it seems to be cooking dry. Finish as in Step 2, raising temperature of oven to Gas 5, 400°F, 200°C after pouring in cornflour mixture. This is neither Irish nor traditional, just a way of adding a pleasant creamy texture to the sauce.

Braised Lamb with Capers and Yoghurt serves 6

3 lb	shoulder or half leg of lamb	1½ kg
¼ pt	white wine or water	150 ml
3 tbs	capers	3 tbs
1	medium onion, sliced	1
½ tsp	dried tarragon	½ tsp
½ tsp	dried thyme	½ tsp
1 dsp	oil	1 dsp
5 oz	natural yoghurt	150 g

Electric slow cooker: preheat Pot on HIGH for 15 minutes

1. Trim the joint of as much fat as you can, removing the fell. Heat the oil in a pan and brown the meat very well. Blanch the onions for 2 minutes in boiling water and lay in the bottom of the Pot. Put in the lamb and add the herbs. Heat the wine or water almost to boiling point and pour in. Cook on HIGH for 30 minutes, then on LOW for 7 to 8 hours.
2. Fifteen minutes before serving, take out the lamb and keep it warm. Stir in the capers and yoghurt and heat on LOW until completely blended. You may want to remove the fat from the cooking juices before you stir in the yoghurt.

Casserole cooking: preheat oven to Gas 6, 400°F, 200°C

As in Steps 1 and 2 above, but put lamb in open casserole in hot oven for about 25 minutes, then reduce heat to Gas 3, 325°F, 170°C, and cover casserole. Cook another 3 hours, then finish with capers and yoghurt.

Navarin of Lamb

serves 4

2 lb	boned lean lamb, cut into 2 inch (5 cm) cubes	900 g
3	large onions, thinly sliced	3
	or	
10	small onions, thinly sliced	10
1 tbs	oil	1 tbs
¼ pt	white wine or dry cider	150 ml
1 tbs	flour	1 tbs
¼ pt	chicken stock	150 ml
1 lb	small carrots, cubed	450 g
	pinch of thyme	
	salt and black pepper	
8 oz	French beans	225 g
8 oz	peas, in pods	225 g
1 tbs	parsley, minced	1 tbs

Electric slow cooker: preheat Pot on HIGH for 20 minutes

1. Dry the lamb well. Heat the oil in a large, heavy frying-pan, brown the lamb lightly, remove and keep warm. In the same fat, brown the onions until just pale gold. Stir in the flour, then gradually add the wine, stock and thyme. Bring to the boil, stirring until smooth. Simmer on a low heat while you cut up the carrots and blanch them for 2 minutes in boiling water. Put the meat, carrots and sauce into the Pot and cook on LOW for 8 to 10 hours or on HIGH for 4 hours.
2. One hour before serving, top and tail the beans, shell the peas and blanch them in boiling water for 5 minutes. (If using frozen peas, thaw them completely.) Stir the vegetables into the Navarin, turn Pot to HIGH and cook for 1 hour until the vegetables are tender. Taste for seasoning and garnish with parsley.

If you prefer, you can turn the carrots—and later, the beans and peas—in hot butter for about 4 or 5 minutes before adding to the Pot. Personally, I think that this gives a better flavour.

Casserole cooking: preheat oven to Gas 7, 425°F, 220°C

As in Step 1, putting the ingredients in a casserole, uncovered, in the hot oven for 20 minutes. Then lower heat to Gas 4, 350°F, 180°C, cover, and cook 1 hour more before you add the French beans and peas. Stir well at this point, add a little more stock (or boiling water), and cook, covered, 30 minutes more or until vegetables are tender but not overcooked. Taste for seasoning, sprinkle on parsley.

Smothered Chump Chops★

serves 4

This recipe is most suitable for a wide, rather than deep, Pot or casserole, so that the chops may lie in a single layer.

4	thick chump lamb chops, well trimmed	4
	a little butter or oil	
4 tbs	horseradish sauce	4 tbs
4 tsp	single cream	4 tsp
8 tbs	soft brown breadcrumbs	8 tbs
	salt and pepper	

Electric slow cooker: grease and preheat Pot on HIGH for 20 minutes

1. Heat a very small quantity of oil or butter in a heavy frying-pan and quickly sear the chops on both sides. Mix the horseradish sauce and cream and thickly cover each chop. Lightly press on a layer of crumbs. (You will have some breadcrumbs left, save them for later.) Season quite lavishly.
2. Put the chops in a single layer in the Pot and cook on HIGH for 30 minutes, then on LOW for 4 hours; or on LOW for 5 to 6 hours. Brown the remaining breadcrumbs under the grill and half an hour before serving press them on to the chops (the original crumbs will have blended away into the sauce). That's all there is to it, and no one ever guesses the secret of the flavour.

Casserole cooking: preheat oven to Gas 4, 350°F, 180°C

Prepare as in Steps 1 and 2, cook about 1½ hours in a tightly-lidded casserole. Half an hour before serving, uncover casserole, cover chops with crumbs, and bake without lid until lightly browned.

Lamb with Rosemary and Mint★

serves 4

I owe this perfect recipe to Delia Smith's delightful cookery column in the Evening Standard. *In the slow electric cooker version the ingredients and, of course, the method, have been slightly modified to suit the ways of the Pot.*

3½ lb	shoulder or leg of lamb	1¾ kg
3 oz	softened (not melted) butter	75 g
1 tsp	fresh rosemary, crushed	1 tsp
1 tbs	fresh mint, chopped	1 tbs
1	garlic clove, crushed with 1 tsp salt	1
	black pepper	

Electric slow cooker: preheat Pot on HIGH for 15 minutes

1. Mix the butter, herbs, pepper and garlic/salt. With a narrow-bladed knife (a boning knife is perfect), cut slits all over the surface of the lamb and rub the herb butter well in. Wrap the entire joint in a large piece of aluminium foil, turning up and sealing the edges so that no juice drips out during cooking. Cook on HIGH for 30 minutes, then on LOW for 7 hours; or on HIGH for 4 hours.
2. You may serve the lamb as it is, slightly pinkish and fragrant with herbs, from its foil parcel. I myself think it is more attractive if you set it in a meat tin, turn back the foil, and brown it in a fairly hot oven (400°F, 200°C, Gas 6) for about half an hour.

Casserole cooking: preheat oven to Gas 5, 375°F, 190°C

As in Steps 1 and 2, putting the foil-wrapped parcel into a snug-fitting casserole. Cook, without lid, about 2½ hours, then lay it in a meat tin, turn back foil, raise heat to Gas 8, 450°F, 230°C, and brown for 15–20 minutes.

Baked Lamb Chops with Button Onions

serves 4

8	loin or best end of neck chops, well trimmed	8
24	pickling-size onions, peeled	24
	a little lard	
½ pt	hot stock	300 ml
	salt and pepper	
1 tsp	soy sauce	1 tsp
2 tsp	flour	2 tsp
	Worcestershire sauce	

Electric slow cooker: preheat Pot on HIGH for 20 minutes

1. Heat a heavy frying-pan until very hot, lightly grease with the lard and fry the chops on both sides. Simmer the onions in the boiling stock for about 5 minutes, drain and put into the Pot. Lay in the chops and add about 8 tablespoons of the hot stock, ½ teaspoon salt, pepper and the soy sauce. Cook on HIGH for 15 minutes, then on LOW for 5 to 6 hours until the chops are tender.
2. Remove the chops and onions with a slotted spoon and keep warm. Spoon or syphon off as much fat as possible. Put about 2 tablespoons of the sauce from the Pot into a saucepan and blend in the flour little by little until it is a smooth paste. Turn the Pot to HIGH and blend the mixture back into the sauce. Let it cook on until it is a thin cream consistency. Add as much or as little Worcestershire sauce as you like, taste for seasoning and pour over the chops and onions.

Casserole cooking: preheat oven to Gas 3, 325°F, 170°C

As in Step 1, putting all ingredients except flour and Worcestershire sauce in casserole (a fairly shallow, wide one suits best). Instead of the 8 tablespoons of hot stock specified in Step 1, use ¼ pt (150 ml). Finish as in Step 2.

Armenian Lamb with Apricots

serves 6

2 lb	lean, boneless lamb, cut into 2 inch (5 cm) cubes	900 g
2 tbs	oil or butter	2 tbs
1	medium onion, minced	1
1 tsp	salt	1 tsp
1	saltspoon black pepper, coarsely ground	1
8 oz	dried apricots, soaked for 10 minutes in boiling water	225 g
1 tsp	brown sugar	1 tsp
3 tbs	pine-nuts	3 tbs
¼ pt (½ pt)	boiling water	150 ml (300 ml)

Electric slow cooker: preheat Pot on HIGH for 15 minutes

1. In a heavy frying-pan heat the butter or oil until very hot but not brown. Brown the meat on all sides and put into the Pot. Sauté the onion until limp but not brown. Add to the Pot with the boiling water, salt and pepper. Cook on HIGH for 30 minutes, add drained apricots and cook on LOW for 6 to 8 hours.
2. Half an hour before serving, stir in the sugar and pine-nuts.

   Brown rice is an excellent accompaniment.

Casserole cooking: preheat oven to Gas 4, 350°F, 180°C

As in method above, but put lamb, onion, seasonings and ½ pt (300 ml) boiling water in casserole, cover and cook in oven 45 minutes. Add soaked, drained apricots and cook another 40–45 minutes. Five minutes before serving, stir in sugar and pine nuts. When you put in the apricots, you may want to add a few more tbs boiling water.

Tajin ★

serves 4

This Moroccan lamb dish has a flavour that takes a bit of getting used to: don't experiment on your more conservative friends. It can be made overnight, cooled quickly and refrigerated, then reheated in a saucepan.

2 lb	lean lamb cut into 2 inch (5 cm) cubes	900 g
8 oz	onions, finely minced	225 g
1 tsp	cumin	1 tsp
½ tsp	coriander	½ tsp
1 tsp	paprika	1 tsp
½ tsp each	ginger, curry powder	½ tsp each
	juice of a large lemon	
	salt and pepper	
(¼ pt)	(boiling water or stock)	(150 ml)

Electric slow cooker: preheat Pot on HIGH for 20 minutes

Mix together all the ingredients and bring to the boil in a heavy saucepan or frying-pan. Put into the Pot. Cover with aluminium foil and cook on HIGH for 30 minutes, then on LOW for 8 hours. Towards the end of the cooking time, taste for seasoning, and add more lemon juice or salt.

Serve with chutney, rice, yoghurt and sliced tomatoes.

Casserole cooking: preheat oven to Gas 3, 325°F, 170°C

As above, but add about ¼ pt (150 ml) boiling water or stock, and use a well-lidded casserole in oven for 2½ hours or until lamb is tender. Glance at it once in a while, add a few spoonfuls of water if it looks too dry. What you are aiming at is a thick, dense, flavourous sauce.

San Miguel Pork Chops

serves 4

This is a good dish to do in two stages. Brown the pork chops, sauté the onion and blanch the pepper, then refrigerate (not in the Pot or casserole). In the morning, bring back to room temperature while you preheat the Pot or casserole and boil up the tomatoes. A good cook-all-day recipe.

4	large loin chops, trimmed of fat	4
1 dsp	oil	1 dsp
1	medium onion, thinly sliced	1
1	medium green pepper, de-seeded and thinly sliced	1
12 oz	uncooked rice	350 g
28 oz	tin Italian peeled tomatoes, well drained	800 g
	salt and pepper	
5	drops hot pepper sauce	5
1 tbs	parsley, minced	1 tbs

Electric slow cooker: preheat Pot on HIGH for 20 minutes

1. Heat the oil in a frying-pan and brown the chops very well. Remove and keep warm. Sauté the onion in the same fat until pale gold. Put the onion into the Pot. Blanch the green pepper in boiling water for 1 minute and put it in with the onion. Lay the chops on top, season well and cover with the uncooked rice.
2. Heat the tomatoes to boiling-point, season, add the hot pepper sauce and parsley and pour into the Pot. Cover with aluminium foil and cook on LOW for 8 to 9 hours. Just before serving, gently prod the rice all over with a fork so that the grains separate.

Casserole cooking: preheat oven to Gas 2, 300°F, 150°C

As in Steps 1 and 2 using, if you have one, a fairly wide shallow casserole. Put a sheet of foil under lid and bake 3½ hours. Test rice with a fork, not a spoon. If it seems dry add about ¼ pt (150 ml) boiling water, cover again and cook another 20 minutes.

Rolled Pork with Beef Stuffing

serves 6

3 lb	pork loin, boned	1½ kg
2 tsp	soy sauce	2 tsp
8 oz	lean beef, finely minced	225 g
1	small garlic clove, crushed	1
2 oz	onion, minced	50 g
	salt and pepper	
2 tbs	barbecue sauce (see p. 150)	2 tbs
8 oz	mushrooms, sliced	225 g
3 tbs	fine dry breadcrumbs	3 tbs
2 oz	Parmesan, grated	50 g
2 tbs	oil	2 tbs

Electric slow cooker: preheat Pot on HIGH for 20 minutes

1. Cut the meat almost all the way through, lengthwise. Trim off most of the fat. Pound out to about ¾ inch (2 cm) thick with a meat hammer or rolling pin. Brush lightly with soy sauce on both sides. Mix together the minced beef, garlic, onion, salt, pepper and barbecue sauce, and spread evenly across the pork. Slice the mushrooms and press them lightly into this mixture. Cover with breadcrumbs and sprinkle on the cheese. Roll firmly, pressing the stuffing back in if—as it probably will—it oozes out around the sides. Tie with clean white butcher's string, or secure with cocktail sticks.
2. Heat the oil in a frying-pan, brown the pork all over and put into the Pot. Cook on HIGH for 4 hours, or on HIGH for 1 hour then on LOW for 5 to 7 hours.

For a darker finish, take the meat out of the Pot half an hour before serving and brown in a hot oven.

Casserole cooking: preheat oven to Gas 2, 300°F, 150°C

As in Steps 1 and 2. Put pork rolls in casserole, cover tightly, cook 3½ hours until tender. Brown under grill if you like, or raise heat to Gas 7, 450°F, 230°C, and bake uncovered for about 20 minutes.

Bigos

serves 4 to 6

This Polish 'Hunter's Stew' was traditionally based on whatever ingredients were at hand in the field; I have seen more than a dozen recipes, some with hare, some with lamb, but always with sauerkraut and mushrooms. The wonderful Polish (or Italian or French) dried mushrooms—those dilapidated little brown crumbles—soaked for a few minutes in warm water, are about ten times as flavourful as even the freshest field mushrooms.

8 oz	pork shoulder or leg, trimmed and cut into 2 inch (5 cm) cubes	225 g
4 oz	streaky bacon, diced	100 g
1	large onion, minced	1
2 tbs	flour	2 tbs
1 lb	sauerkraut	450 g
1	bay leaf	1
1 lb	firm white cabbage, shredded	450 g
2 oz	field (or dried) mushrooms	50 g
4 oz	cooked ham, cut into strips	100 g
2 tbs	tomato purée	2 tbs
¼ pt	red wine or cider	150 ml
1	garlic clove, crushed with 1 tsp salt	1
6 oz	Polish Kielbasa sausage, or a smoked boiling ring	175 g

Electric slow cooker: preheat Pot on HIGH for 20 minutes

1. Fry the bacon in a heavy frying-pan until the fat runs, and put into the Pot. Fry the onion in the bacon fat until limp and golden and add to the Pot. Blanch the cabbage in boiling water for 3 minutes, put into the Pot with ½ pt cabbage water and add the sliced mushrooms and ham. Put in the pork and add the tomato purée, red wine and garlic. Cook on HIGH for 30 minutes, then on LOW for 6 to 8 hours or overnight.
2. Two hours before serving, cut the sausage into 2 inch (5 cm) lengths, add to the Pot with flour and sauerkraut and cook on LOW. If you have cooked this dish overnight and refrigerated it, reheat it with the sausage in a saucepan on top of the cooker (not in the Pot) for 1 hour only.

3. Check for seasoning and add more salt if necessary.

Bigos should be just liquid, neither dry nor swamped. You can stir in some soured cream but it isn't necessary. This will need only good dark rye bread and some floury potatoes as an accompaniment.

Casserole cooking: preheat oven to Gas 3, 325°F, 170°C

As in Step 1, using a large casserole with well-fitting lid. Increase water from ½ pt to about ¾ pt (450 ml). Cook 3 hours in oven. About half an hour before end of cooking, cut up sausage and stir in. Heat through, taste for seasoning and serve very hot. (Halfway through cooking time, have a look at the amount of sauce: it should always just cover the meat and vegetables.)

Carbonnade of Pork

serves 4

I must warn you that this is a rather untidy, scrappy-looking dish, but the flavour is delightful. You can use any kind of mustard you like, except the strong ones containing things like horseradish; I like Moutarde de Meaux best.

2 lb	lean pork, trimmed and cut into 1 in (2·5 cm) cubes	900 g
3	large onions, diced	3
1	large cooking apple, peeled and diced	1
2	thick slices wholemeal bread	2
1 oz	lard	25 g
7 fl oz	beer or ale	175 ml
12 oz	carrots, sliced	350 g
½ tsp	coriander seeds	½ tsp
2 tsp	made mustard	2 tsp
	pinch of ground cloves	
	salt and black pepper	
2 tsp	made mustard	2 tsp

Electric slow cooker: preheat Pot on HIGH for 15 minutes

1. Melt the lard in a heavy frying-pan and brown the pork cubes. Drain well on kitchen paper. Season with salt and pepper. Gently soften the

diced apple and onion in hot fat and drain well. Pour surplus fat away and keep frying-pan hot.

2. Spread the bread with the mustard and cut into 8 squares. Put a layer of the onion and apple mixture in the bottom of the Pot, sprinkle with sage, cloves and coriander, add a layer of bread, a layer of pork cubes and continue until everything is used up. Pour the beer into the hot frying-pan, bring quickly to the boil and pour into the Pot, scraping up the brown bits from the pan.

3. Cook on HIGH for 30 minutes, then on LOW for 6 hours.

If you have a round, handleless colander that will fit into the top of your Pot, you may steam the sliced carrots for about 2 hours. Otherwise, steam them separately.

Casserole cooking: preheat oven to Gas 3, 325°F, 170°C

As in Steps 1 and 2, putting everything in a medium-size casserole, and simmering in the oven for about 2 hours and 45 minutes to 3½ hours. Halfway through, look to see if there is enough liquid, and top up with a little boiling water if necessary. 45 minutes before end of cooking time, set a steamer, or heatproof colander, over the carbonnade, and cook the sliced carrots in the fragrant steam.

Avignon Pork

serves 4

1¼ lb	pork loin (boned weight), trimmed	500 g
4 tbs	butter	4 tbs
½ lb	mushrooms, sliced	225 g
1	celery stalk, with leaves, diced	1
1	garlic clove, sliced	1
14 oz	tin Italian peeled tomatoes, with their juice	397 g
1 tsp	*each* thyme and basil	1 tsp
1	saltspoon fennel seeds	1
2 tbs	sherry	2 tbs
	salt and pepper	
1	saltspoon summer savory (*optional*)	1

Electric slow cooker: preheat Pot on HIGH for 20 minutes

1. Heat 3 tablespoons of butter to foaming in a frying-pan and sauté the mushrooms for about 2 minutes. Add the celery and leaves with the garlic and sauté gently until the garlic softens. Strain off about 6 fl oz (170 ml) of the juice from the tomatoes and add to the pan with half a teaspoon of mixed basil and thyme, salt and black pepper. Simmer, covered, for about 5 minutes, and pour into the Pot.

2. Dry the pork loin and, with a very sharp knife, slit it down the middle almost, but not quite, through. Rub the remaining herbs (basil, thyme, fennel seeds and summer savory if used) into the meat. In the same pan as previously used, heat the remaining butter until very hot. Brown the pork well and put into the Pot. Swill out the pan with the sherry, scraping out the brown bits. Add to the Pot with about 6 or 8 of the tinned tomatoes. Cook on HIGH for 30 minutes, then on LOW for 8 hours.

3. Remove the meat, keep warm, and arrange the vegetables around it. In a saucepan, reduce the pan juices to about one-third over high heat, taste for seasoning and add to the meat.

Casserole cooking: preheat oven to Gas 3, 325°F, 170°C

As in Steps 1 and 2, adding ¼ pt (150 ml) boiling water to frying pan with the sherry, and putting all ingredients in a deep casserole—the prettiest are those glazed brown earthenware round-bellied ones from Pearson's of Chesterfield, in my view. Cover, cook in oven about 3¼ hours until meat is tender to a kitchen fork. Turn off oven, put meat on heatproof dish and arrange vegetables around it to keep warm. Strain juices into saucepan and reduce briskly, stirring. Taste for seasoning and pour over meat.

Délices de Porc★

serves 6

1½ lb	pork fillet	700 g
1	garlic clove, crushed with ½ tsp salt	1
6 oz	lean ham, diced	175 g
4 tbs	butter	4 tbs
1 tbs	olive oil	1 tbs
1	medium onion, finely minced	1
2	small carrots, finely diced	2
2 lev tbs	flour	2 lev tbs
¼ pt (8 fl oz)	chicken stock	150 ml (250 ml)
¼ pt (8 fl oz)	white wine or dry cider	150 ml (250 ml)
	pepper	
2 tbs	parsley, finely minced (optional)	2 tbs

Electric slow cooker: preheat Pot on HIGH for 20 minutes

1. Beat out the pork fillet(s) very thin and cut into 6 even-sized squares, trimming neatly. Mince the trimmings with a sharp knife and mix with the crushed garlic/salt and diced ham. Spread this on the pork squares, roll up and secure with cocktail sticks. Melt the butter with the olive oil in a heavy frying-pan, sauté the onions and carrots for a few minutes, lower the heat and stir in the flour. Heat the stock to boiling-point and blend in; add the white wine and bring to the boil again.

2. Put the pork rolls into the Pot, sprinkle with the pepper and pour in the bubbling vegetable/wine mixture. Cook on HIGH for 30 minutes, then on LOW for 2 to 3 hours.

3. With a slotted spoon, carefully remove the pork packets and keep warm. Press the sauce through a food mill or whirl for a minute in a blender. Simmer for a few minutes in a saucepan, then stir in a very little butter to give a pretty glossy finish. Pour over the pork and sprinkle with parsley, if you like.

Casserole cooking: preheat oven to Gas 3, 325°F, 170°C

As in Steps 1 and 2, putting pork into a fairly deep, heavy casserole and increasing liquid to about ¾ pt (a scant half litre). Simmer in oven about 1½ hours, remove casserole lid and cook another 15 minutes. Finish as in Step 3, boiling down sauce on a high flame until you have about ½ pt (300 ml).

Navarin of Pork

serves 4

Don't be tempted to make this dish without the parsnip and turnip, eccentric as they may sound, as otherwise it is just a dull little pork stew. The Worcester sauce is needed for colour and the nutmeg is truly essential.

1½ lb	boneless lean pork, cut into 2 inch (5 cm) cubes	700 g
2 tbs	oil	2 tbs
2 tsp	flour	2 tsp
2	parsnips, peeled and cubed	2
½	white turnip, peeled and cubed	½
2	medium carrots, diced	2
1	medium onion, minced	1
½ pt (¾ pt)	chicken stock	300 ml (450 ml)
1 tsp	Worcester sauce	1 tsp
1	bay leaf	1
	salt and pepper	
	a little nutmeg, freshly ground	

Electric slow cooker: preheat Pot on HIGH for 20 minutes

Heat the oil in a heavy frying-pan. Dry the meat cubes well, toss in the flour mixed with the salt, pepper and nutmeg and brown in the hot oil. Blanch the vegetables in boiling water for 1 minute, drain and put into the Pot. Add the meat. Bring the stock and Worcester sauce to the boil in the frying-pan, scraping out the clinging bits, and add to the Pot with bay leaf. Cook on HIGH for 15 minutes, then on LOW for 6 hours.

Casserole cooking: preheat oven to Gas 3, 325°F, 170°C

As in recipe above, putting meat and vegetables in a fairly deep casserole, not a shallow wide one. Cover and cook in oven 45 minutes; add about ¼ pt (150 ml) of boiling stock and cook another 30 minutes. Taste for seasoning. If you prefer a thicker sauce, blend some of the hot sauce from casserole into a tablespoonful of flour, stir smooth, then return to casserole and cook another 15 minutes with casserole uncovered.

Bacon and Potato Casserole★

serves 4

4 tbs	flour	4 tbs
2 tbs	butter	2 tbs
1 pt	milk	600 ml
6	medium potatoes, peeled and thinly sliced	6
3	very large onions, thinly sliced	3
12 oz	*cooked gammon cut into pieces	350 g
	salt and pepper	
	about 1 saltspoon nutmeg, ground	

Electric slow cooker: butter and preheat Pot on HIGH for 20 minutes

1. Combine the flour, butter and milk in a saucepan and bring to the boil, stirring all the time. Lower heat and cook 1 minute longer, still stirring. Season well. Blanch the potatoes for 1 minute in boiling water, remove with a slotted spoon. Blanch the onions in the same water, remove and drain. Make alternate layers of potato, onion and gammon in the Pot. Pour in the sauce and separate the vegetables a little with a spoon so that the sauce goes all the way down. Cover with aluminium foil, cook on HIGH for 30 minutes, then on LOW for 6 hours.
2. If you have a removable casserole, you may like to take off the foil and finish off in a hot oven for 15 minutes, to brown the top.

You may stir in some grated cheese, or 2 tablespoons of bran for a nutty texture. Or add a diced, de-seeded green pepper. Or press on a layer of toasted brown breadcrumbs just before serving.

*Bacon rashers or the leftovers of a cooked ham—anywhere from 6 oz (170 g) to 1 lb (450 g)—can be substituted for the gammon.

Casserole cooking: preheat oven to Gas 5, 375°F, 190°C

As in Step 1, baking in heavy covered casserole for an hour, then lower heat to Gas 3, 325°F, 170°C, remove cover and bake another 1¼ hours. This wonderful family casserole can then sit, in a turned-off oven, for another half hour or so without coming to harm. Add grated cheese, diced green pepper or breadcrumbs if you want to, but the basic casserole is perfect as it stands.

Pork Chop and Apple Casserole

serves 4

4	thick pork chops	4
2 tbs	butter	2 tbs
1	small onion, minced	1
2	medium cooking apples, unpeeled, cored and cut up	2
2 tbs	brown sugar	2 tbs
1 tbs	crystallized ginger, or ginger in syrup finely minced	1 tbs
8 oz	soft brown breadcrumbs	225 g

Electric slow cooker: preheat Pot on HIGH for 20 minutes

1. Trim a little fat from the chops, heat it in a heavy frying-pan and brown the chops on both sides. Remove and keep warm. Add the butter to the fat, heat well and cook the onion until translucent and limp.
2. Pour away the fat, stir in the apples, sugar and ginger, then spread this mixture on the bottom of the Pot. Arrange the pork chops on top and cover with breadcrumbs. Lay a sheet of aluminium foil over the chops. Cook on HIGH for 30 minutes, then on LOW for 6 to 8 hours.

If your Pot has a removable casserole, you may like to put it, uncovered, in a hot oven for 15 minutes to brown the crumbs.

Casserole cooking: preheat oven to Gas 2, 300°F, 150°C

As in recipe above. Bake in heavy, fairly wide casserole, tightly covered, about 2½ hours. Uncover, raise heat to Gas 6, 400°F, 200°C, and cook another 20 minutes until lightly browned.

Spanish Pork

serves 4

The amount of salt given in this recipe is vital, as the dish otherwise tends to be slightly bland.

2 lb	boned leg or shoulder of pork, trimmed and cut into 1 inch (2·5 cm) cubes	900 g
2 tbs	butter	2 tbs
1 tsp	oil	1 tsp
8 oz	onions, coarsely chopped	225 g
2 lev tbs	flour	2 lev tbs
1 lev tsp	salt	1 lev tsp
½ tsp	thyme	½ tsp
12	juniper berries, crushed	12
2	garlic cloves, crushed	2
6 fl oz (¾ pt)	light red wine	175 ml (450 ml)

Electric slow cooker: preheat Pot on HIGH for 20 minutes

1. Toss the meat in the flour seasoned with salt and thyme. In a frying-pan, heat the butter with a little oil to keep it from burning, until it foams, and sauté the onions until limp and pale gold. Put the onions into the Pot and brown the meat in the remaining fat in small batches. Keep the meat cubes moving with a wooden spoon, as the flour coating tends to make them catch. You may need to add a little more butter or oil, but do this with caution, as the last thing you want is a film of oil in the finished dish.
2. Add the pork, juniper berries and garlic to the Pot. Pour the wine into the frying-pan, bring quickly to the boil and pour over the meat, scraping out the pan drippings. Cook on LOW for 6 hours. Taste for seasoning.
3. If you like a slightly thicker sauce, spoon out 4 tablespoons of the juices, blend with 1 tablespoon flour in a small saucepan and cook over low heat until it honeycombs. Stir back into the Pot and cook on HIGH for about 10 minutes.

Casserole cooking: preheat oven to Gas 3, 325°F, 160°C

As above, but increase wine to about ¾ pt (450 ml),

put everything in casserole with snug lid, and cook 2¼ hours in oven. Add a little more wine about halfway through cooking time, if sauce has reduced appreciably. Taste for seasoning, thicken if you like.

Somerset Pork with Honey

serves 4

1¼ lb	lean pork, cut into 2 inch (5 cm) cubes	500 g
1 tbs	groundnut or soya oil	1 tbs
1 tbs	butter	1 tbs
8 oz	cooking apples, peeled and sliced	225 g
½ pt (¾ pt)	dry cider	300 ml (450 ml)
	rind and juice of half a lemon	
1 tbs	clear honey	1 tbs
1 tsp	thyme	1 tsp
	salt and black pepper	

Electric slow cooker: preheat Pot on HIGH for 15 minutes

1. Dry pork well, sear in very hot oil and butter in a frying-pan. Remove to the Pot. Gently brown the apple in the pork fat, stirring with a wooden spoon. Drain off most of the fat, add the cider and bring to the boil, scraping up the clinging bits. Pour everything into the Pot and add the thinly cut lemon rind, thyme, salt and pepper. Cover and simmer gently on LOW for 6 hours. Add the lemon juice and about half a tablespoon of honey.
2. Turn the Pot to HIGH and cook for 30 minutes more, to reduce the sauce. Add more honey, to your own taste.
3. If you like a thicker sauce, strain off the juices into a saucepan and blend in a teaspoon of corn-flour.

Casserole cooking: preheat oven to Gas 2, 300°F, 150°C

As in Step 1 above, cooking in a heavy, fairly deep casserole with well-fitting lid in centre of oven for about 3 hours. Halfway through cooking time, add about ¼ pt (150 ml) more cider, cover again tightly. About 30 minutes before you want to serve it, turn heat to Gas 7, 425°F, 220°C, uncover casserole and cook until sauce is reduced a little. Finish as in Step 3 if desired.

Mustard Pork

serves 4

2 lb	pork loin	900 g
3 tbs	soft fresh brown breadcrumbs	3 tbs
½ tsp	sage	½ tsp
1 tsp	black peppercorns, crushed	1 tsp
1 tsp	salt	1 tsp
2 tbs	made mustard (Dijon, Moutarde de Meaux)	2 tbs
1 tsp	flour	1 tsp
¼ pt	dry cider	150 ml

Electric slow cooker: preheat Pot on HIGH for 20 minutes

1. Score the skin of the pork. (I keep a Stanley knife in the kitchen for just this purpose, as even the sharpest knife blade doesn't cut as cleanly as the razor-blade.) Then with a thin sharp knife carefully remove the skin and some of the layer of fat. Mix together the crumbs, sage, peppercorns and half the teaspoon of salt. Cover the pork evenly with mustard and press on the crumb mixture. Cook on HIGH for 6 to 8 hours. Do not skimp on time; it is essential that pork be completely cooked through.
2. Half an hour before serving, roast the pork skin and fat in a very hot oven, Gas 7–8 (450°F, 230°C). Pour off the melted fat and save it for another purpose. Keep the crackling hot. Pour out of the Pot all but about a tablespoon of the drippings and blend the flour gradually into the Pot. Heat the cider to boiling and when the flour mixture is bubbling slightly, gradually blend in the cider and stir until thick. Taste for seasoning.
3. Cut the meat into thick slices, serve the crackling with it and pass the hot gravy separately.

I think that cranberry sauce or redcurrant jelly is far nicer with this rather highly-flavoured dish than the traditional apple sauce.

Casserole cooking: preheat oven to Gas 3, 325°F, 170°C

As in Step 1, putting meat into a shallow, well-fitting casserole, with good tight cover. Cook on centre shelf of oven 3 hours, or until a meat thermometer pushed into centre of pork reads 180°F, 85°C. Pork must be well done. Finish as in Steps 2 and 3.

Szekely Goulash★

serves 8

This dish reheats beautifully—in fact, I think it is better cooked the day before you want to serve it. It doesn't freeze very well, however; the flavours seem to disappear.

3 lb	lean pork, cut into 2 inch (5 cm) cubes	1½ kg
3 lb	potatoes, peeled and grated	1½ kg
3	very large onions, minced	3
4 tbs	Hungarian paprika	4 tbs
4	peppercorns	4
1 lb	sauerkraut, drained	450 g
2 tbs	caraway seeds	2 tbs
8 fl oz	soured cream	225 ml
3 tbs	salt	3 tbs

Electric slow cooker: preheat Pot on HIGH for 20 minutes

1. Put the meat, potatoes, onions, paprika, peppercorns and salt into the Pot and just cover with boiling water. Cook on LOW for 10 hours until the meat is tender.
2. Halfway through the cooking time, add the drained sauerkraut and mix well.
3. During the last half hour of cooking, stir in the caraway seeds and taste for seasoning. At the last minute, stir in the soured cream.

Serve with thin black pumpernickel bread.

Casserole cooking: preheat oven to Gas 3, 300°F, 160°C

As in Step 1, but adding about ½ pt (300 ml) more water in the first place. Put in big casserole, with aluminium foil under the lid for a tight seal, and simmer in oven 3 hours. After two hours, add sauerkraut. Half an hour before serving, stir in 2 tbs caraway seeds, and at the last minute, away from heat, stir in the soured cream.

Juniper Gammon★   serves 4

2½ lb	joint of gammon or collar of bacon	1 gen kg
1 pt	dry cider	600 ml
1	small onion, stuck with 4 cloves	1
1	bay leaf	1
8	black peppercorns	8
	a small bunch parsley	
	For the sauce:	
1	small onion, finely minced	1
1	garlic clove, crushed	1
1	heaped teaspoon juniper berries, crushed	1
1 tbs	butter	1 tbs
1 tsp	flour	1 tsp
3 tbs	double cream	3 tbs
	salt and pepper	

Electric slow cooker: preheat Pot on HIGH for 20 minutes

1. If you think the gammon or bacon may be very salty, soak it overnight in cold water. Otherwise, cover with cold water, bring to the boil in a large saucepan, then pour off the water. Put the onion, bay leaf, peppercorns and parsley into the saucepan, add the cider, bring to the boil and put into the Pot. Cook on HIGH for 30 minutes, then on LOW for 8 hours, until the meat is tender. Remove from heat, skim liquor and keep gammon warm.
2. Melt the butter in a small saucepan and gently soften the onion, garlic and crushed juniper berries for about 10 minutes. Do not brown. Stir in the flour very slowly until smooth, then add ½ pt (300 ml) strained cooking liquor, stirring it in gradually to make a smooth sauce. Taste for seasoning. Cook gently for about 5 minutes, then stir in the cream and reheat gently, taking care not to let it boil.
3. Slice the gammon and pass the sauce in a warmed jug.

Casserole cooking: preheat oven to Gas 5, 375°F, 190°C

As in Step 1, using a heavy casserole and increasing liquid with about ¼ pt (150 ml) boiling water

added to cider. Cover, cook in oven for 45 minutes, then lower temperature to Gas 3, 325°F, 170°C, and simmer for another 2½ hours until gammon is tender. If you have a meat thermometer, push it into the thickest part of the gammon, and cook until it registers 160°F. Finish as in Steps 2 and 3.

Cabbage Stuffed with Sausages★   serves 4

1	large firm white cabbage	1
1 lb	very good pork sausages	450 g
4 oz	dry, spicy sausage (chorizos, Kabanos)	100 g
3 oz	butter	75 g
	salt and quite a lot of black pepper	

Electric slow cooker: preheat Pot on HIGH for 20 minutes

1. Slice and blanch the cabbage in boiling salted water for about 3 minutes and drain very well. Skin the pork sausages and break up the meat in a basin (ordinary sausage meat won't do, it is too well mixed with some sort of bulky filler).
2. Put half the butter in the heated Pot and swirl it around. Lay in some cabbage leaves, then a layer of sausage meat and some cut-up dry, spicy sausages, another layer of cabbage and another layer of sausage, ending with cabbage leaves. Salt and pepper between each layer and cut the rest of the butter over the top. Cook on HIGH for 30 minutes, then on LOW for about 4 hours, until the cabbage is completely soft.

Casserole cooking: preheat oven to Gas 4, 350°F, 180°C

As in Steps 1 and 2, putting cabbage and sausage meat, and cut-up dry sausages, in layers in buttered casserole, which should be deep rather than wide and shallow. End with cabbage leaves, dotted with butter. Cover and bake about 2–2½ hours, until cabbage is soft.

5. **Limerick Irish Stew** (p. 85): slow simmering makes the most of inexpensive cuts of lamb and seasonal vegetables
(*New Zealand Lamb Information Bureau*)

6. **Baked Apples with Mincemeat** (p. 138) and **Carbonade of Pork** (p. 90): two well-flavoured dishes for autumn, slowly cooked apples and a mustardy casserole of pork

(Fred Mancini; courtesy James Robertson & Sons Ltd and Colman's Mustard)

Choucroute Garni

serves 6

2 lb	sauerkraut	900 g
8 oz	garlic sausage (smoked Hungarian paprika sausage, or any well-smoked hard sausage)	225 g
4 oz	fat bacon	100 g
1	bouquet garni	1
1	medium onion, peeled and stuck with 2 cloves	1
2	garlic cloves, crushed	2
10	juniper berries, crushed	10
¾ pt	dry white wine or cider	400 ml
	Garnishes: very good frankfurters smoked loin of pork good flavoursome gammon roast pork loin cut into chops (any 1 or 2 of these)	

Electric slow cooker: preheat Pot on HIGH for 20 minutes

1. Put the sauerkraut into a colander and wash well under running cold water. Drain. Cut the fat bacon into slices and put half into the Pot. Add the sauerkraut and bury the bouquet garni, garlic and juniper berries in it, along with the onion and the garlic sausage. Pour on wine and, if necessary, a little boiling water, to bring the liquid just to the top of the ingredients. Cover with aluminium foil and cook on HIGH for 1 hour, then on LOW for 8 hours.

2. Put the meats for garnish on a heated platter in a warm oven, just to heat through. Almost all the liquid should have cooked into the sauerkraut, but if it looks watery, drain off the liquid into a saucepan and cook it down rapidly over high heat, then pour back into the Pot. Put the sauerkraut and its sausage in the centre of the platter with the other meats, and serve very hot with floury potatoes. If you have any sauerkraut left from this dish, make Sauerkraut Soup (p. 35).

Casserole cooking: preheat oven to Gas 2, 300°F, 150°C

As in Step 1, using a shallow, wide, heavy casserole of about 6 pts capacity (3 l, approx.). Add ½ pt boiling water. Cover tightly, cook in centre of oven for a total of 4 hours. After 2¼ hours, add some smoked loin of pork, cut in ½ inch slices, or some pieces of gammon. After 3 hours, put in some good frankfurters or pieces of roast pork, tucking them well under the sauerkraut. The liquid should have been almost completely absorbed into the sauerkraut at the end of 4 hours.

Kidneys in Red Wine★

serves 4

1½ lb	ox, veal or lambs' kidneys, skinned, cleaned and cored	700 g
1	large onion, sliced	1
½ pt (¾ pt)	red wine and water, half and half	300 ml (450 ml)
1 tbs	mixed dried parsley and marjoram	1 tbs
	salt and pepper	
	beurre manié (see p. 153)	

Electric slow cooker: preheat Pot on HIGH for 20 minutes

1. Soak ox kidneys for 2 hours in salted water or milk, drain and dry. The milder veal or lambs' kidneys should not need soaking. Cut the kidneys into small pieces. Blanch the onion slices for 1 minute in the boiling water and drain. Bring the wine/water mixture to the boil and add the herbs, salt and pepper. Put everything into the Pot and cook on LOW for 6 to 8 hours.

2. Thicken the sauce near the end of the cooking time with 2 tablespoons of *beurre manié*—use less for a thinner sauce. Taste for seasoning at the last minute.

Casserole cooking: preheat oven to Gas 3, 325°F, 170°C

As in Step 1, but increase water and wine to about ¾ pt (450 ml). Putting kidneys, onions and liquid in smallish casserole with seasoning. Cover tightly, cook about 45 minutes, adding a little more red wine and water mixed, if sauce seems to be cooking down too much for your liking. Then thicken with *beurre manié* about 10 minutes before end of cooking time.

Sicilian Lasagne

serves 4 to 6

The original of this recipe came to me from Josephine La Rosa, of the (originally Sicilian) pasta-manufacturing family of New York. It is totally unlike what most people know as lasagne, which is made with a creamy béchamel sauce. You may use oven-ready lasagne noodles, in which case omit Step 1.

8 oz	lasagne noodles	225 g
3 tbs	olive or sunflower oil	3 tbs
2	large garlic cloves, crushed	2
8 oz	*lean beef, minced	225 g
28 oz	tin Italian peeled tomatoes, well drained	800 g
	dash of hot pepper sauce	
1 tsp	*each* basil and oregano	1 tsp
1	bay leaf	1
12 oz	ricotta or cottage cheese	350 g
3 tbs	plain yoghurt	3 tbs
1	egg (size 3)	1
8 oz	Italian mozzarella or Gouda cheese, sliced thin	225 g
4 oz	Parmesan, grated	100 g

Electric slow cooker: grease and preheat Pot on HIGH for 20 minutes

1. In a really big saucepan, bring water to the boil and slide in the lasagne noodles, one at a time, stirring hard to keep them from sticking together. (A tablespoon of oil in the water will help.) Cook for 5 minutes, tip into a colander and run cold water over them. Put back into the saucepan and add hot water until the noodles float.
2. Heat the oil and sauté the garlic till golden, push aside and quickly sauté the meat just until it loses its red colour. Add the tomatoes, hot pepper sauce, basil, oregano and bay leaf and quickly bring to the boil. Beat the egg and mix with the ricotta (if you use cottage cheese press it through a sieve) and beat in the yoghurt.
3. Put 2 tablespoons of the sauce into the Pot and spread it around. Drain the noodles and put them in the Pot in a layer side by side, overlapping as little as possible. Spoon in some ricotta, then a few thin slices of cheese. Cover with sauce and some Parmesan. Continue to make layers, ending with sauce and Parmesan (save a tablespoon of grated cheese for use at serving time). Cover tightly with aluminium foil and cook on HIGH for 4 hours.
4. If you happen to be near the Pot, from time to time take off the lid, carefully lift off the foil and tip the accumulated water into the sink, then replace the foil, cover and go on cooking. You'll be surprised how much liquid has condensed on to the foil.

At serving time sprinkle with the remaining grated Parmesan.

*There are many possible variations:
Instead of the meat cooked in sauce, tuck in tiny meatballs flavoured with grated lemon rind.

Make the sauce without meat, and lay thin slices of Kassler Rippchen (German smoked pork loin) among the layers.

Or simply make a vegetarian version, with some thin-sliced carrots cooked in the sauce.

Casserole cooking: preheat oven to Gas 5, 375°F, 190°C

As in Steps 1, 2 and 3 above, arranging lasagne noodles, sauce, ricotta, cheese and Parmesan in layers in a rather shallow oiled casserole. Bake 45–60 minutes until cheese has melted and top is brown and bubbling. (Or: set oven at Gas 3, 325°F, 170°C, and cook it as long as 2 hours; then raise heat to Gas 7, 425°F, 220°C, to brown the top.)

Liver Pamplona

serves 4

1½ lb	lambs' liver, sliced	675 g
6	rashers streaky bacon	6
2 tbs	butter	2 tbs
6 oz	mushrooms	175 g
1	large onion, thinly sliced	1
1 tbs	flour	1 tbs
½ pt (¾ pt)	stock	300 ml (450 ml)
	salt, black pepper, pinch of thyme	
12–18	black olives, stoned	12–18
	juice of half a small lemon	

Electric slow cooker: preheat Pot on HIGH for 20 minutes

1. Roughly chop bacon, heat butter until hot but not brown, and quickly fry bacon. Remove, keeping pan hot, toss the sliced liver in hot fat until just sealed on all sides. Put in Pot, with bacon. Sauté mushrooms in pan and add to Pot. Blanch sliced onions in boiling water for 2 minutes and add to Pot.
2. Stir flour into remaining fat, cook for a minute, then gradually stir in stock and blend smooth. Add to Pot, with seasonings, cover and cook 30 minutes on HIGH, then 4 hours on LOW. Add olives just before serving, taste for seasoning, squeeze in lemon juice.

Casserole cooking: preheat oven to Gas 4, 350°F, 180°C

As in Steps 1 and 2, adding ¼ pt (150 ml) stock, and using a medium-sized casserole. Cover and cook 50 minutes to an hour. Add olives just before serving, taste for seasoning, finish with lemon juice.

Braised Tongue in Madeira★

serves 6 to 8

4 lb	ox tongue	1·8 kg
8	crushed peppercorns	8
2	bay leaves	2
1 tbs	wine or cider (*not malt*) vinegar	1 tbs
2 tbs	butter	2 tbs
2	large onions, thinly sliced	2
4	carrots, sliced	4
4	celery stalks, diced	4
5 tbs	madeira	5 tbs
	salt and pepper	
	bouquet garni	
1 oz	*beurre manié* (see p. 153)	25 g
1 tsp	tomato purée	1 tsp
2 tbs	parsley, chopped	2 tbs
(½ pt)	(beef stock)	(300 ml)

Electric slow cooker: preheat Pot on HIGH for 10 minutes

1. Soak the tongue in cold water, and drain. Place in a large saucepan, cover with fresh cold water, bring to the boil and simmer for 5 minutes. Drain and discard the water. Put into the Pot, cover with *boiling* water and add the bouquet garni, peppercorns, bay leaves and vinegar. Cook on LOW for 8 hours.
2. Heat the butter in a saucepan, gently sauté the prepared vegetables until golden, but take care not to let them brown. Remove the tongue from the Pot, pour off the liquid and reserve. Lay the vegetables on the bottom of the Pot and put the tongue on top. Bring 2 pts (1 generous litre) of the reserved liquid to the boil and pour over the tongue. Add madeira, season well and cook on LOW for another 2 to 4 hours, until tongue is tender when pierced at its thickest part with a thin skewer.
3. Remove the tongue, skin it carefully and pull away the small bones. Slice half of it, diagonally, in thinnish slices. Remove the vegetables, put on a serving dish, lay the sliced tongue over and keep warm in a low oven. Strain ½ pt (300 ml) of the liquid into a saucepan and heat, then flavour with tomato purée and parsley. Thicken the sauce with *beurre manié*, taste again for seasoning (add a little more madeira if you like) and pour some sauce over tongue; pass rest in a sauceboat.
4. Fit the remaining half of the tongue into a soufflé dish, or loose-based round cake tin, curling it back on to itself. Reduce the remaining stock over a hot flame, and pour on to the tongue. Cover with a snugly fitting saucer and weigh down with a heavy tin of food or a brick. Cool until firm, when it will have a nicely jellied surround.

Casserole cooking: First, soak and scrub the tongue and simmer it a good two hours, then peel it carefully as soon as it is cool enough to handle. Next preheat oven to Gas 3, 350°F, 170°C

Sauté vegetables as in Step 2, salt and pepper the tongue and put it in casserole just large enough to hold it comfortably. Put madeira, vinegar, seasonings and about ½ pt (300 ml) good beef stock in the sauté pan, bring to boil, pour over tongue and vegetables. Cook half an hour at above temperature, then lower heat to Gas 3, 325°F, 170°C, and braise for 2 hours. Turn it once or twice, test with a slender knife-blade, and cook another 30 minutes if needed. Finish as in Step 3.

Dolmathes★   serves 4

This is the easiest way to make dolmathes that I know. Cooking them the conventional way, one must test quite often to see that the water has not boiled away. 'Pot' Vine Leaves come out moist, tender and perfectly cooked. They are delicious warm or cold.

½ lb	beef, finely minced	225 g
1 lb	vine leaves	450 g
4 oz	butter, melted	100 g
½ lb	tinned Italian peeled tomatoes, well drained	225 g
2 tbs	mint leaves, chopped	2 tbs
3 oz	long-grain rice, parboiled for 5 minutes	75 g
2	medium onions, minced	2
	salt and pepper	
	juice of a lemon	
(¼ pt)	boiling water	(150 ml)
4	*For the sauce:* eggs juice of 2 lemons	4
3 tbs	boiling water	3 tbs

Electric slow cooker: preheat Pot on HIGH for 15 minutes

1. Pour boiling water over the vine leaves in a bowl. Leave to stand for 15 minutes, drain and rinse with cold water. Mix together all the other ingredients except lemon juice. Leave the leaves shiny side down, reserving any damaged ones for lining the Pot. Put a heaped teaspoon of the mixture in the centre of each leaf, laid on a plate. Fold the stem end over, then fold the sides in, then roll it up from the remaining end. The first two or three will seem impossible to do, then quite suddenly the knack develops.
2. Grease the Pot and line the bottom with the unused vine leaves. Lay in the little bundles. Place the second layer crosswise on top of the first. Squeeze the juice of 1 lemon over all and pour in boiling water about an inch deep. Lay a plate that will fit snugly into the Pot on top—this keeps the vine leaves from falling apart. Cover and cook on LOW for 5 to 6 hours.

To make the sauce: Remove the vine leaves with a slotted spoon and keep warm. Tip the liquid out into a saucepan, whisk in the eggs, lemon juice and boiling water, and stir over a low heat until thickened.

Casserole cooking: preheat oven to Gas 1½, 275°F, 140°C

As in Steps 1 and 2 above, putting rolled vine leaves in a fairly wide, rather than deep, casserole. Squeeze on lemon juice, and pour in about ¼ pt (150 ml) boiling water. Proceed as in Step 2, baking for about 2 hours. Add more water from time to time. Make sauce as above.

Sausages in White Wine   serves 4

1 lb	sausages with herbs	450 g
1 tsp	oil	1 tsp
1	shallot or very small onion, minced	1
¼ pt	white wine or dry cider	150 ml
	strip of lemon peel	
	juice of 1 lemon	
½ tsp	Dijon mustard	½ tsp
1 tbs	butter	1 tbs
1 tbs	flour	1 tbs
	salt and pepper	

Electric slow cooker: preheat Pot on HIGH for 20 minutes

1. Prick the sausages and brown them lightly in the hot oil, in a heavy frying-pan, for about 10 minutes. Pour off all but a tablespoon of the fat. Put the sausages into the Pot. In the frying-pan, gently sauté the shallot or minced onion for about 2 minutes, and add the wine, lemon peel and juice and seasonings. Bring to the boil and add to the sausages. Lay a sheet of aluminium foil over the sausages and cook on LOW for 4 hours.
2. In a small frying-pan, melt the butter, slowly stir in the flour and when it reaches the honeycomb stage stir in 2 tablespoons of juice from the Pot. Let it thicken, stirring, then stir back into the Pot.

Serve with lots of parsley or watercress, and plain steamed potatoes.

Casserole cooking: preheat oven to Gas 3, 325°F, 170°C

As in Step 1, putting sausages, shallot, wine, lemon and seasonings in small, deep casserole. Seal well with aluminium foil under lid, cook 1 hour in oven. Proceed with Step 2, stir sauce into casserole, and cook another 10 minutes.

Sausages Boulangère   serves 4

This dish isn't worth making unless you can lay your hands on some really good sausages— the ones called '90 per cent pork' are best. The kind made apparently from pork trimmings and rusk simply will not do. These quantities seem to come out better in a rather deep Pot or casserole—the wider, shallower ones are more suitable for a double quantity, for 6 to 8 people.

1 lb	very good sausages	450 g
1½ lb	potatoes, peeled and thinly sliced	700 g
2 tbs	butter	2 tbs
2 tbs	flour	2 tbs
¼ pt	milk	150 ml
1	medium onion, finely minced	1
1 tsp	salt	1 tsp
1 tsp	basil	1 tsp

Electric slow cooker: butter and preheat Pot on HIGH for 20 minutes

1. Brown the sausages in a little oil or butter. Blanch the potato slices for 1 minute in boiling water and drain well. Make a thinnish béchamel sauce with the butter, flour and milk. Put a layer of potatoes into the Pot, sprinkle with minced onion, salt and basil, and repeat this until the potatoes are used up. Lay the sausages on top and pour on the sauce. Cover with aluminium foil and cook on LOW for 4 to 6 hours.
2. If your Pot has a removable casserole, take off the foil and put it—uncovered—in a hot oven to brown for about 20 minutes.

Casserole cooking: preheat oven to Gas 2, 300°F, 150°C

As in Step 1 above, using a fairly deep, straight-sided casserole. Put a sheet of foil under the lid, and cook in centre of oven about 2½ hours. After about 1½ hours, look into the casserole and add a little more milk if sauce seems to be cooking down more than you like. At end of baking time, take off lid and foil, raise heat to Gas 6, 400°F, 200°C.

A Simple Cassoulet★   serves 4

This cassoulet—a very basic one—does not freeze, as the pork goes grainy.

8 oz	dried haricot beans	225 g
1 lb	salted belly of pork	450 g
2 oz	butter	50 g
2	garlic cloves, crushed with ½ tsp salt	2
4 oz	French garlic sausage	100 g
	To garnish: parsley	

Electric slow cooker: preheat Pot on HIGH for 20 minutes

1. Cover the beans with cold water in a saucepan, bring to the boil, boil for 2 minutes and leave to stand, covered, for 2 hours, off the heat. Drain well. Cut the rind off the pork and use it to line the bottom of the Pot. Cut the pork into thick rashers and then into 1 inch (2·5 cm) chunks, discarding bones. Mix the pork with the beans in the Pot. Cook on HIGH for 3 to 4 hours, with no liquid.
2. Melt the butter in a frying-pan and sauté the garlic for 2 minutes without browning. Pour over the pork and beans. Cut the sausage into pieces and add. Cook on LOW for 1 hour more. With scissors, cut the parsley very finely over the dish.

Casserole cooking: preheat oven to Gas 3, 325°F, 170°C

As in Steps 1 and 2, putting the basic ingredients in a deepish casserole, with a piece of foil under a well-fitting lid. Add about ¼ pt (150 ml) boiling water and cook 1½ hours, then finish as in Step 2, cooking another 30 minutes after sausage is added.

Cassoulet★

serves 8

This dish can, of course, be made the day before, refrigerated and reheated in the oven while you bake some floury jacket potatoes to go with it. In Pot cooking don't use more than the specified amount of liquid, since there is no evaporation from the Pot.

1 lb	dried haricot beans	450 g
4–8	good pork sausages	4–8
	salt and pepper	
2 lb	meat, made up of 2 or 3 from the following: bacon chops, cooked gammon, cooked chicken legs, small garlic sausages	900 g
4	garlic cloves, crushed	4
2 tsp	paprika	2 tsp
2 tbs	brown sugar *or*	2 tbs
1 tbs	black treacle	1 tbs
2	large onions, thinly sliced	2
4 oz	dried brown breadcrumbs	100 g
1 pt (1½ pt)	boiling water or stock	600 ml (750 ml)
¼ pt (½ pt)	red wine vinegar and water, half and half	150 ml (300 ml)

Electric slow cooker

1. Wash the beans, put into a saucepan with cold water to cover, bring to the boil, boil for 2 minutes, remove from heat and leave to stand for 2 hours.
2. Preheat Pot on HIGH for 20 minutes and put all the ingredients except the sausages and breadcrumbs into a large saucepan, bring to the boil and put into the Pot. Cover with aluminium foil and cook on LOW for 8 hours or overnight. An hour before serving, lightly grill or fry the sausages and add. Turn the Pot to HIGH.
3. If your Pot has a removable casserole, take it out, cover the cassoulet with breadcrumbs, press them down into the liquid and brown in a hot oven. Otherwise add the breadcrumbs when you put in the sausages and cook on HIGH until ready to serve.

Casserole cooking: preheat oven to Gas 1, 200°F, 130°C

As above, putting all ingredients except sausages and breadcrumbs in a very big casserole, laying a sheet of foil under lid, and increasing liquid to about 2 pts (a generous litre). Liquid should come about three-quarters of the way up the solid ingredients. Cook about 5–6 hours, glancing at it occasionally and adding more boiling water (or some red wine) if it looks dry. An hour before serving time, grill the sausages and add, and press a good layer of breadcrumbs over top. Shortly before serving, push the breadcrumbs down into the casserole, then raise heat to Gas 6, 400°F, 200°C, and cook without lid.

Bobotie★

serves 3

12 oz	very lean beef, minced	350 g
1	large onion, thinly sliced	1
½ pt	hot milk	300 ml
2	thick slices of brown bread, crusts cut off	2
3	eggs (size 3)	3
1 tbs	butter	1 tbs
1 tbs	cider vinegar	1 tbs
1 tbs	mild curry powder	1 tbs
½ tsp	salt	½ tsp
½ tsp	Chinese mushroom sauce (*optional*)	½ tsp

Electric slow cooker: grease the Pot well, and preheat on HIGH for 20 minutes

1. Blanch the onion slices for 1 minute in boiling water and drain well. Pour the hot milk over the bread in a basin and set aside until soaked. Beat 2 eggs with the minced beef and the vinegar, curry powder, salt and mushroom sauce if used. Strain off and reserve the milk from the soaked bread and beat the bread into the mixture. Shave in butter and add onion.
2. Put into the Pot, pressing well down. Whisk the milk and remaining egg until light and foamy and pour in. Cover with aluminium foil. Cook on LOW for 6 hours.

If you like, just before serving sprinkle finely chopped peanuts or crumbled potato crisps over the top.

Casserole cooking: preheat oven to Gas 4, 350°F, 180°C

As in Steps 1 and 2, but put all ingredients in a well-buttered casserole, allowing room for the Bobotie to rise and puff a little. Bake 1½ hours until golden brown.

Spiced Tripe

serves 4

This is one recipe I have not tried myself. It was given to me by a friend in whose cooking I have perfect confidence, but not even for her can I eat tripe.

2 lb	honeycomb tripe	900 g
½ lb	onions, thinly sliced	225 g
3 tbs	flour	3 tbs
	juice of half a lemon	
	salt and pepper	
1 tsp	capers, chopped	1 tsp
1 tbs	Worcestershire sauce	1 tbs
1 tbs	cider vinegar	1 tbs

Electric slow cooker: preheat Pot on HIGH for 15 minutes

1. Cut the tripe into narrow strips, blanch in boiling water. Put into the Pot with onions, lemon juice, salt and pepper and just enough boiling water to cover, and cook on LOW for 8 hours.
2. Half an hour before serving, brown the flour carefully in a small, heavy frying-pan, stirring often so that it does not burn. Blend some of the hot liquid from the Pot into the flour and stir to a thick smooth roux. Stir all this back into the Pot and add the Worcestershire sauce, capers, and vinegar (or an equal quantity of chopped gherkins if you like them better).

Serve with great quantities of toasted brown bread, to mop up the sauce.

Casserole cooking: preheat oven to Gas 2, 300°F, 150°C

If you are using parboiled tripe, skip Step 1. Otherwise, clean tripe, simmer in water to cover 2 hours. Then prepare sauce as in Step 2, using 8 fl oz (225 ml) boiling water. Put tripe and sauce in casserole, cover tightly, cook in oven 2 hours. Taste for seasoning, and add a little lemon juice mixed with boiling water if sauce seems too thick at end of cooking time.

Lentils and Sausages★

serves 4

This is rather a cheating dish, because it uses tins of Italian brown lentils. But it is quick to make in the Pot or casserole and almost equally delicious hot or cold, and nothing needs browning.

28 oz	(2 tins) Italian lentils	796 g
1 lb	boiling ring or other smoked sausage	450 g
4 oz	dry, spiced sausage (chorizos, Kabanos)	100 g
3 tbs	onion, very finely minced	3 tbs
1 tbs	yoghurt (*optional*)	1 tbs
(¼ pt)	(dry cider)	(150 ml)

Electric slow cooker: preheat Pot on HIGH for 15 minutes

1. Cut the boiling ring into 2 inch (5 cm) lengths, and the dry spicy sausages into ½ inch (1 cm) bits. Put everything into the Pot, cook on HIGH for 15 minutes, then on LOW for anywhere from 3 to 5 hours.
2. If you like a drier dish with less sauce, finish by putting into a hot oven, uncovered, for about 15 minutes.

You can if you like stir a tablespoon of natural unsweetened yoghurt into each serving; yoghurt and lentils have a natural affinity. Any leftovers make a rather strange looking but very good-tasting salad the next day, with some sliced tomatoes, olive oil (or olive and soya oil mixed half and half) and minced chives.

Casserole cooking: preheat oven to Gas 3, 325°F, 170°C

As in Step 1, putting ingredients in a heavy casserole with ¼ pt (150 ml) dry cider, covering and cooking about 1½–2 hours. Finish as above.

Oxtail

serves 4

Start this dish a good 24 hours before serving, if cooking in the Pot.

4 lb	*oxtail, cut up	1·8 kg
3 tbs	good dripping	3 tbs
2	onions, thinly sliced	2
1	bay leaf	1
3	carrots, thinly sliced	3
6	juniper berries, crushed	6
	pinch of powdered ginger	
2 tsp	salt	2 tsp
	or	
1 tsp	*each* salt and Chinese mushroom sauce	1 tsp
2	strips lemon peel	2
1	garlic clove, crushed	1
½ pt	red wine	300 ml
	beurre manié (see p. 153)	

Electric slow cooker: preheat Pot on HIGH for 20 minutes

1. Heat the dripping until very hot in a large, heavy frying-pan and brown the well washed and dried oxtail pieces. Put into the Pot with the onions, bay leaf, carrots, ginger, juniper berries, garlic, salt and lemon peel. Pour the wine into the frying-pan, bring to the boil, scraping up the clinging brown bits, and pour into the Pot. Cook on HIGH for 30 minutes, then on LOW for 8 to 10 hours or overnight.
2. Turn the contents into a basin, cool quickly, then chill until the fat solidifies and can be scraped off with a sharp knife.
3. Reheat over a medium flame and taste for seasoning. Thicken with 2 tablespoons of *beurre manié*.

   *James Beard, the famous American cookery writer, suggests adding a couple of pig's trotters, which would probably increase the rich and hearty character of this most substantial casserole; in this case, fish out the bones before chilling the dish.

Casserole cooking: preheat oven to Gas 1, 275°F, 140°C

As in Step 1, adding ¼ pt (150 ml) boiling water to red wine, and putting all ingredients except *beurre manié* in a big, heavy casserole. Cover and cook 4–5 hours; at halftime, look in and add a little more liquid if necessary. Finish as above.

Kidneys in Sherry

serves 2 to 3

To serve four, I would double the quantities. This dish should have a delicate flavour, so veal or lambs' kidneys are much preferable to ox kidneys.

8	veal or lambs' kidneys, skinned, cleaned and cored	8
1 tbs	vegetable oil	1 tbs
1	medium onion, finely minced	1
2	small garlic cloves, crushed	2
2 dsp	brown flour	2 dsp
¼ pt	hot stock	150 ml
1	sherry glass of dry sherry	1
1 tsp	soy sauce	1 tsp
	salt and pepper	
2 tbs	oil (olive or soya, preferably)	2 tbs
1	bay leaf	1

Electric slow cooker: preheat Pot on HIGH for 20 minutes

1. Heat the 1 tbs oil in a frying-pan, sauté onion until just translucent but not brown. Stir in the garlic and flour, lower the heat and stir with a wooden spoon until it reaches the honeycomb stage. Slowly blend in the hot stock, stirring well. Add the sherry, soy sauce, salt and pepper, and put into the Pot.
2. Wash out the frying-pan, heat the 2 tablespoons of oil and lightly brown the kidneys, turning often. Add to the Pot with the bay leaf, cook on HIGH for 15 minutes, then on LOW for 4 hours.

3. Taste for seasoning: you can if you like add a little more sherry about 10 minutes before serving. Remove the bay leaf.

Serve with very good white long-grain rice.

Casserole cooking: preheat oven to Gas 2, 300°F, 150°C

As in Steps 1 and 2 above, but putting the ingredients into a casserole with well-fitting lid, and cooking about 1¾ hours. Finish as in Step 3. This recipe has gone through many permutations: the original (from Jerez where the best sherries come from) actually simmered for only 5 minutes on low direct heat. I found by fiddling about with it that long, delicately-slow cooking makes it into a kidney casserole that converts even kidney-haters.

Hungarian Stuffed Cabbage

serves 4

The beauty of cooking stuffed cabbage in the Pot is that even an extra hour or two will not disintegrate the rolled leaves, nor leach out their flavour. This is a dish which can easily be converted to a vegetarian entrée by substituting cooked soy beans or soya mince for the beef.

12	large leaves from a Savoy cabbage	12
1 lb	lean beef, minced	450 g
3 oz	onion, minced	75 g
2 oz	butter	50 g
1	egg (size 3 or 4)	1
4 oz	rice	100 g
4 oz	streaky bacon	100 g
¼ pt (½ pt)	concentrated tinned consommé	150 ml) (300 ml)
4 oz	tinned Italian peeled tomatoes (drained weight)	100 g
	salt and pepper	
	pinch thyme or marjoram	
¼ pt	soured cream (*optional*)	150 ml

Electric slow cooker: preheat Pot on HIGH for 20 minutes

1. Cook the rice for about 5 minutes in boiling water in a saucepan and drain well. Blanch the cabbage leaves in slightly salted boiling water for about 5 minutes until just pliable, drain well and set aside. Heat the butter in a frying-pan and sauté 2 oz (50 g) of the onion until pale gold. Push to one side and lightly brown the minced beef. Mix the onion and beef with the beaten egg, drained rice, salt, pepper and herbs. Lay a cabbage leaf on a plate and put about 1 heaped tablespoon of the filling on it, roll up tightly, turning in the bottom and top first, then the sides, to make a neat sausage shape. Secure with cocktail picks or small thin skewers.

2. Lay the bacon rashers on the bottom of the Pot and put the cabbage rolls in. Sprinkle with the remaining minced onion. Bring the consommé and tomatoes to the boil in a saucepan, pour over and cover with aluminium foil. Cook on HIGH for 30 minutes, then on LOW for 5 to 7 hours.

3. Remove the rolls carefully with a slotted spoon, turn the Pot to HIGH, and stir in the soured cream if liked, let it just heat through and pour over the cabbage.

Casserole cooking: preheat oven to Gas 5, 375°F, 190°C

As in Steps 1 and 2, putting cabbage rolls in casserole (a wide one is best), and increasing consommé to about a scant ½ pt (300 ml). Cover tightly, cook about 2 to 2½ hours, until cabbage is tender. Strain off the sauce into a saucepan, boil down briskly to about half, stir in soured cream if you like it, and pour over cabbage rolls. Serve from casserole.

Meat Loaf   serves 2 to 3

If you find it more convenient, you can bake this inside your Pot in a small round casserole or small bread tin, with about ¼pt (150 ml) boiling water poured in around the sides. (See page 126 for aluminium foil 'lifter straps' to protect your hands.) The loaf is very good eaten cold, like a coarse country pâté. A double quantity serves 4 to 6. For another Meat Loaf, see Miriam's Terrine, p. 42.

12 oz	very good lean beef, minced	350 g
1	egg (size 3)	1
2 oz	oatmeal	50 g
1	medium onion, finely minced	1
1 dsp	piquant sauce	1 dsp
1 tsp	salt	1 tsp
	To decorate top: slices of tinned pimento	

Electric slow cooker: butter and preheat Pot on HIGH for 20 minutes

1. Lightly beat the egg and add to all the other ingredients. Mix well with your hands and form into a neat loaf shape that will fit into your Pot. Cook on HIGH for 3 hours. You can make a lattice pattern on the top with the tinned pimento before you put it in the Pot if you like, but I think this garnish gets a bit tasteless with long cooking; you might try decorating the loaf about halfway through the cooking time, but be careful not to burn your fingers.
2. Slip a big fish slice or a wide palette knife under the loaf to remove.

Casserole cooking: preheat oven to Gas 4, 350°F, 180°C

As in Step 1 above, lightly greasing a round or oblong casserole and pressing meat mixture firmly into it. Make lattice design with tinned pimento, cover top lightly with a sheet of foil, and bake 1 hour, then remove foil and bake uncovered another 40 minutes at Gas 2, 300°F, 150°C.

Vegetables and Pulses

The most important ingredient in the casserole cooking of vegetables must be good sense. After all, if tender young fresh peas (or good frozen ones, for that matter) cook to perfection in 10 minutes, why simmer the life out of them? And to me, a recipe for cooking courgettes in tomato sauce for 5 hours seems a great nonsense. But slow-cooking, in a good oven casserole or in the electric Pot can do rather miraculous things to all manner of vegetables. You can let them cook to melting deliciousness while you go about the more important things in life. The best stuffed cabbage rolls in the world; ratatouille that truly does equal in flavour any ever made in that mythical South of France kitchen; red cabbage with apples; braised leeks in a subtle soy-flavoured sauce. The key, it seems, is to choose vegetables that contain a good deal of natural moisture (tomatoes, courgettes, marrow, aubergines, okra, cabbage) and cook them in their own fragrant steam with very little added liquid. The harder root vegetables (carrots, swedes, turnips, big firm onions) remain maddeningly resistant unless cut into very thin slices or diced.

In the Pot, I have had better luck with a brief browning, or parboiling, of root vegetables. When they are put to cook with meat, always layer them under the meat so that they cook in extra heat and steam.

Frozen vegetables, for casserole or electric Pot cooking, should be completely thawed and put in at a late stage in the cooking. I tell you this for what it's worth, but as most frozen vegetables are really meant to be cooked swiftly in a minimum of water, it seems rather pointless to subject them to simmer-cooking.

The wonderfully useful pulses—lentils, haricot beans, black beans, Egyptian foul, speckled pinto beans, and rich mealy butter beans—need a bit of thought and preparation for casserole cooking whether it's in the oven or the Pot, but the results are extraordinary. I have found that the trick of bringing them to the boil in cold water to cover, boiling vigorously for 2 minutes, then setting to cool, off the heat, for 2 hours, is the best preliminary to Pot success.

Try to find a shop that does a brisk trade in dried vegetables (it's apt to be Syrian, Greek or Pakistani). Elderly pulses that have spent their best years on the shelf will take forever to cook. I have had variable luck with dried chick peas (cecci, garbanzos, kabli chana, whatever you want to call them), even with the pre-cooking method; you might try soaking them for 24 hours in cold water, draining, pre-boiling as above and then cooking on in a casserole. I must confess to some cheating here, buying good-quality Italian or Spanish tinned ones and then cooking them for 3 or 4 hours with other ingredients to bring out their rich, earthy flavour. The pulses are immensely nutritious, an astonishingly good source of protein, satisfying and filling, so it's worth spending a bit of time to find out what cooks best in an oven casserole, or in your own Pot.

Some recipes using a good proportion of vegetables or pulses (for example Choucroute Garni and Cassoulet) appear in the Meat section.

Boston Baked Beans★

serves 4 to 6

This is the real New England recipe, adapted for the Pot as well as for the casserole, without any of the additions of celery, diced green pepper, parsley or ginger which are sometimes suggested. It is traditionally served with Boston Brown Bread, which is not a true bread but a moist, steamed raisin loaf.

1 lb	dried haricot beans	450 g
12 oz	streaky pork (salt pork if you can get it)	350 g
1	large onion, minced	1
1 tsp	dry mustard	1 tsp
2 tbs	black treacle	2 tbs
3 tbs	brown sugar	3 tbs
2 tbs	tomato purée	2 tbs
2	bay leaves	2
1	large garlic clove, crushed	1
	salt and pepper	

Electric slow cooker

1. If you have a good, fresh source of dried pulses, pre-cook your haricots by boiling in a saucepan for 2 minutes, then removing from heat and leaving to stand, covered, for 2 hours. Or cheat a bit by pressure-cooking them, after soaking, until the skins burst. If you follow the 2-minute, 2-hour cooking method, finish them by returning to heat, bringing to the boil, then simmering, uncovered, for about 45 minutes to 1 hour. Salt pork should be soaked well.
2. Preheat Pot on HIGH for 20 minutes.
3. Drain the bean liquid into a basin and measure—you will need a scant pint (600 ml). Mix together the beans, onion, black treacle, brown sugar and flavourings and put into the Pot. Cut the streaky pork, or salt pork, into 2 inch (5 cm) cubes and push it down into the beans, leaving just a bit showing on the surface. Cook on HIGH for 30 minutes, then on LOW for 10 to 12 hours.
4. If you have a Pot with a removable casserole, you may finish it all off in a medium oven for half an hour, to reduce the liquid and brown the visible bits of pork a little. Or tip the contents of the Pot into a separate casserole and put into the oven. Stir in salt just before serving.

Casserole cooking: preheat oven to Gas 1½, 290°F, 140°C

1. As in Steps 1 and 3 above, putting all ingredients into a heavy (traditionally brown, glazed, round, deep) casserole. Pour in about ¾ pt (450 ml) of the bean liquid, saving the rest. Liquid should almost but not quite reach to the top of the beans.
2. Bake about 8–9 hours, adding a little boiling liquid every hour or so. When beans are tender, raise oven heat to Gas 4, 350°F, 180°C, and brown the top bits of pork a little. Salt and pepper at the last minute.

Chinese Braised Leeks

serves 4

This is delicious cold the next day, although there are seldom any leftovers.

*about 12	leeks	*about 12
2 tbs	butter	2 tbs
4 tbs	Chinese mushroom sauce	4 tbs

Electric slow cooker: preheat Pot on HIGH for 15 minutes

1. Wash the leeks thoroughly, split lengthwise and wash again. Cut into 4 inch (10 cm) pieces, approximately. Let the butter melt in the heated Pot, lay in the leeks, add the mushroom sauce, cover and cook on LOW for 6 to 7 hours. Do not salt or pepper, as the sauce is salty and strong.

* It is hard to be definite about the number of leeks you will need for four servings, because they vary so much in size and in the amount of white to green. I should think 2 lb (slightly less than 1 kg) of leeks, with a good proportion of white and pale green to the coarse green inedible bits, would do.

Casserole cooking: preheat oven to Gas 2, 300°F, 150°C

As in recipe above, putting leeks in a shallow, wide casserole if possible, and adding ¼ pt (150 ml) of boiling water. Cover tightly and simmer in oven about 2½–3 hours.

Pease Pudding

serves 4

8 oz	dried split peas	225 g
1	ham bone, or about 8 oz (225 g) bacon ends	1
1	medium onion, stuck with 3 cloves	1
1	large carrot, sliced	1
	good pinch cayenne pepper	
	salt and pepper	
1 tbs	butter	1 tbs
1	yolk of one large (size 2) *or*	1
2	of medium (size 3–4) eggs	2

Electric slow cooker

1. Wash the peas, put into a saucepan with water to cover, bring to the boil and boil for 2 minutes. Remove from heat, cover and leave to stand for 2 hours.
2. Preheat Pot on HIGH for 20 minutes.
3. Drain the peas, cover with fresh cold water in a saucepan and bring to the boil. Put into the Pot with the ham bone, onion, carrot, cayenne, salt and pepper. Cook on HIGH for 30 minutes, then on LOW for 8 hours.
4. Remove the cloves and ham bone, press the peas through a food mill or purée in a blender. Beat in the egg yolk and butter. Turn the Pot to HIGH. Put the peas in a greased pudding basin that will fit your Pot, cover securely and either make a handle with string, or use the aluminium foil 'lifter straps' as suggested on p. 126, for easy removal. Put into the Pot, pour in boiling water halfway up the bowl and steam for about 1 hour. Remove carefully, protecting your hands with oven gloves.

Turn out and serve with gammon steaks or sausages.

Casserole cooking: preheat oven to Gas 2, 300°F, 150°C

1. As in Steps 1 and 3 above, putting beans, ham bone, onion, carrot, and seasonings in ovenproof casserole with 1 pt (600 ml) extra boiling water. Cover tightly, and cook in oven 2½–3 hours until beans are tender.
2. Remove cloves and ham bone, purée peas, beat in egg and butter and pack into greased pudding

basin that will fit a deep ovenproof casserole. Cover basin tightly and pour boiling water half-way up sides. Cook 45 minutes in oven. (This last step can, if you prefer, be done in a steamer on top of your cooker.)

Haricots à la Gasconne

serves 4

This is very good with a plainly roasted joint of lamb or mutton. It makes rather a large quantity and can be reheated or even eaten cold the next day. It doesn't freeze well.

1 lb	dried butter beans	450 g
4 oz	fresh pork rind	125 g
	salt	
3	garlic cloves, crushed	3
2 tbs	pork dripping	2 tbs
1 tbs	parsley, minced, or chives, finely chopped	1 tbs

Electric slow cooker

1. Wash the beans, put into a saucepan with cold water to cover, bring to the boil, boil for 2 minutes, remove from heat and leave to stand for 2 hours.
2. Preheat Pot on HIGH for 15 minutes.
3. Drain the beans and put into the Pot with the pork rind and some salt and boiling water to cover. Cook on LOW for 8 hours or overnight.
4. Drain and mix with the crushed garlic which has been sautéed in the melted pork dripping. Scatter with the parsley or chives.

Casserole cooking: preheat oven to Gas 3, 325°F, 170°C

As above, putting beans, pork rind and boiling water to cover in ovenproof casserole. Bake about 2 hours, checking from time to time to see what's happened to the liquid. Finish as in Step 4. This can be made, successfully, in a flameproof casserole on low heat on top of your cooker, if necessary using an asbestos mat or metal 'gauze' flame-tamer.

Ratatouille

serves 4

1 lb	aubergines	450 g
1	green pepper (about 6 oz (175 g)), de-seeded and diced	1
1	large sweet onion, sliced or chopped	1
2 tbs	good oil	2 tbs
1	large garlic clove, crushed with 1 tsp salt	1
1 lb	tinned Italian peeled tomatoes, well drained (keep liquid from tin) *or*	450 g
12 ($\frac{1}{4}$ pt)	really ripe tomatoes, skinned (tomato juice)	12 (150 ml)
1 tsp	coriander seeds, crushed	1 tsp

Electric slow cooker: preheat Pot on HIGH for 20 minutes

1. Cut the unpeeled aubergines into slices about $\frac{3}{4}$ inch (2 cm) thick, salt well, put into a colander and cover with a plate, weigh down with something heavy and leave to stand for about half an hour. Drain off the liquid, rinse and dry well. Cut into rough cubes and sauté in hot oil in a frying-pan. Add all the other ingredients and put into the Pot. If the mixture looks dry, cautiously add some tomato juice, but very little.
2. Cover with aluminium foil and cook on HIGH for 30 minutes, then on LOW for 6 to 7 hours. The vegetables should still be bright in colour, with a soft but not mushy texture. Cool and then chill for 3 to 4 hours.

Casserole cooking: preheat oven to Gas 4, 350°F, 180°C

As in Step 1, putting all ingredients in a roomy casserole and adding liquid from tin of Italian tomatoes (or about $\frac{1}{4}$ pt (150 ml) tomato juice if using fresh ones). Cover tightly and cook in centre of oven about 2 hours, adding some tomato juice halfway through cooking time if mixture begins to look dry. Gently prod the aubergine cubes with a kitchen fork, and if they still seem firm after 2 hours cover and cook another half an hour. Finish by chilling.

Vegetables Varoise

serves 3 to 6

This makes 3 to 6 servings, depending on whether it is a main course, served with a big salad, or itself an accompanying vegetable.

4 oz	lean bacon rashers	100 g
1 oz	butter	25 g
1 lb	courgettes	450 g
1	medium onion, thinly sliced	1
4 oz	tinned red pimentos	100 g
8 oz	tomatoes, fresh or tinned	225 g
1 lev tsp	mixed herbs	1 lev tsp
1	garlic clove, crushed	1
	dash of hot pepper sauce	
4 oz	cheese, cut into $\frac{1}{2}$ inch (1 cm) cubes	100 g
	salt and pepper	

Electric slow cooker: preheat Pot on HIGH for 15 minutes

1. Trim the rind from the bacon and cut into squares. Heat the butter in a heavy frying-pan until hot, but do not let it brown. Gently sauté the onion until soft but not brown. Top and tail the courgettes, cut into $\frac{1}{4}$ inch ($\frac{1}{2}$ cm) slices. Thinly slice the pimentos. Peel and roughly slice the tomatoes. Add all the vegetables and the bacon to the pan with the onions, stir in the herbs and garlic. Add salt and pepper and a good dash of hot pepper sauce.
2. Put into the Pot and cook on LOW for 4 hours, until the vegetables are soft but not disintegrated. Stir the cheese into the hot vegetables.

Serve at once, with hot French garlic bread.

Casserole cooking: preheat oven to Gas 3, 325°F, 170°C

As in Step 1 above, putting the vegetables and herbs in a deepish casserole and covering tightly. Cook in oven 2 hours; lift lid after an hour and add a little tomato juice or about 4 tablespoons of boiling water if vegetables look dry. Stir in cheese at end of cooking time.

Aubergine Casserole   serves 4

This is rather like the Greek Pastitsio, adapted for the Pot as well as for the oven. It's a lovely hearty peasant casserole with an enigmatic flavour.

1	medium aubergine, unpeeled, sliced about ¾ inch (2 cm) thick	1
	salt	
4 tbs	oil	4 tbs
4 oz	short-cut macaroni	100 g
1 tbs	butter	1 tbs
1	medium onion, minced	1
1	garlic clove, crushed	1
4 oz	mushrooms, sliced	100 g
½ tsp	soy sauce	½ tsp
½ tsp	dry mustard	½ tsp
6 oz	cheese, grated	175 g
	few drops Worcestershire sauce	
1 tbs	sesame seeds	1 tbs
	For the béchamel sauce:	
1 pt	milk	600 ml
1 tbs	butter	1 tbs
1 tbs	flour	1 tbs

Electric slow cooker: grease and preheat Pot on HIGH for 20 minutes

1. Salt the aubergine slices well, put into a colander with a snugly fitting plate on top and weigh down. Leave to stand for half an hour, drain well, rinse and dry. In the meantime cook the macaroni in boiling water until almost tender, drain and put into the Pot. Heat the butter in a frying-pan and sauté the onion, garlic and mushrooms until the onion is translucent.
2. Make the béchamel sauce, stir in the soy sauce, mustard and Worcestershire sauce, then add the grated cheese. Mix well with the macaroni and the onion, garlic and mushroom mixture.
3. Heat the oil in the pan and sauté the aubergine slices until medium brown, then cut them into rough cubes and mix with the macaroni. Put into the Pot and cook on LOW for 4 hours. If your Pot has a removable liner, sprinkle the top with sesame seeds and brown in a hot oven for about 15

minutes; otherwise, merely scatter on the sesame seeds and serve.

Casserole cooking: preheat oven to Gas 5, 375°F, 190°C

As in Steps 1, 2 and 3, but put macaroni, aubergine and béchamel sauce in heavy casserole, press a layer of sesame seeds on top, and cook about 2 hours. Then raise heat to Gas 8, 450°F, 230°C, and brown the top, for about 15 minutes.

Sauerkraut with Gin   serves 4 to 6

I have made this dish without gin, thinking it a waste of a small but good martini in cooking, but I have to say that the gin does add an indefinable flavour to the sauerkraut.

3	streaky bacon rashers, roughly chopped	3
2 lb	sauerkraut	900 g
1	garlic clove, crushed	1
1	medium onion, minced	1
1 lb	potatoes, peeled and cut into eighths	450 g
6	small or 2 large carrots, diced	6
½ tsp	salt; black pepper	½ tsp
2 tbs	gin	2 tbs
¼ pt	white wine or cider	150 ml
1	bay leaf	1
1 lb	Polish Kielbasa sausage, or pork boiling ring	450 g

Electric slow cooker: preheat Pot on HIGH for 15 minutes

1. Fry the bacon rashers with the onion and garlic in a frying-pan until the onion is limp and translucent but not brown. Drain the sauerkraut well, put into a saucepan with the bacon, carrots, bay leaf, wine or cider and gin. Bring to the boil and keep hot. Blanch potatoes in boiling water, drain. Put everything into the Pot except the Kielbasa sausage, and cook on LOW for 8 to 10 hours.

7. **West Country Chicken** (p. 59): country cider and mushrooms give character to economical chicken joints

(Fred Mancini)

8a. **Brownie Pudding** (p. 133): a 'casseroled' pudding crammed with the dark richness of chocolate and nuts

(*Cadbury-Typhoo Ltd*)

8b. **Guinness Cake** (p. 132): a classic recipe, thick with fruit and enriched with stout, made the slow-cooking way

(*Fred Mancini*)

2. Half an hour before serving, cut the sausage into 1 inch (2·5 cm) slices, add to the Pot, turn to HIGH and cook just until thoroughly heated through.

Casserole cooking: preheat oven to Gas 4, 350°F, 180°C

As in method above, putting boiling sauerkraut, carrots, wine and gin in heavy casserole, covering, and cooking in oven 2½ hours. Then blanch potato pieces in boiling water 3 minutes, drain and add to casserole. Cook 30 minutes more, and stir in cut-up sausage. Cook just until sausage is heated through and potatoes are tender. The first step—cooking the sauerkraut, etc. in oven—can all be done a day in advance, if you like, and finished off with potatoes and sausage half an hour or so before serving time.

Vegetable Stew

serves 4

1	head of celery, cleaned and chopped	1
4	large carrots, sliced	4
4	large onions, sliced	4
1	leek, cleaned and cut into thin slices	1
1 pt	beef stock	600 ml
1 tbs	tomato purée	1 tbs
1 tsp	celery salt	1 tsp
	salt and pepper	

Electric slow cooker: preheat Pot on HIGH for 20 minutes

Bring everything to a rolling boil in a saucepan, and pour into the Pot. Cook on HIGH for 2 hours, then on LOW for 4 to 6 hours. The carrots and celery will retain an agreeable crispness.

Casserole cooking: preheat oven to Gas 3, 325°F, 170°C

As in recipe above, using a casserole that is deep rather than wide, covering closely, and simmering in oven about 2 hours.

Dhal★

serves 4

1 lb	red lentils	450 g
½ tsp	black peppercorns	½ tsp
3 tsp	salt	3 tsp
1 tbs	turmeric	1 tbs
1	large onion, finely minced	1
1	hot red chili, washed and de-seeded, finely minced	1
1 dsp	vegetable oil	1 dsp
3 inch	piece of whole cinnamon, broken into bits	7·5 cm
2	bay leaves	2
1 dsp	garam masala powder	1 dsp

Electric slow cooker: preheat Pot on HIGH for 15 minutes

1. Thoroughly wash and pick over the lentils. Put into a large saucepan, cover with cold water and bring to the boil. Put into the Pot, adding the flavourings. Wash the chili pieces in a small sieve and check them rigorously for seeds—which can inflict a very nasty burn. Mix into the hot lentils. Cook on LOW for 6 to 8 hours or overnight until the lentils are tender.

2. Half an hour before you are ready to serve, heat the oil in a frying-pan until very hot, fry half the onion dark brown and crisp. Stir into the lentils and top with the remaining raw minced onion.

This makes a delicious meal with, perhaps, good sausages. If there is any left, make it into soup: add enough water for a gruel-like consistency, a tablespoon of curry paste, and—probably—another teaspoon of salt.

Casserole cooking: preheat oven to Gas 2, 300°F, 150°C

As in Steps 1 and 2 above, but add 3 pts (1·5 l) of cold water to lentils, bring to boil, put with flavourings and chili in a large casserole. Cover and simmer in oven 3 hours until lentils are soft and most of the liquid has been absorbed. Finish with onion and oil, taste for seasoning, add salt if necessary.

La Potée

serves 8 to 12

This is a large semi-stew, semi-soup which makes a Sunday supper for 8 to 12 people with a lot of good bread and—apologies for the cliché—salad and fruit and cheese; or a wonderful hot first course on a cold night, with something like a quiche or a cheese soufflé to follow.

8 oz	dried haricot beans	225 g
3 lb	piece boiling bacon	1½ kg
6	Italian or English herb-flavoured sausages	6
3	leeks, cleaned and sliced	3
3	carrots, thinly sliced	3
½	small white cabbage, thinly sliced	½
	parsley and thyme	
	salt and pepper	
2	turnips, diced	2
2	celery stalks, diced	2
2	medium potatoes, peeled and diced	2
2	onions, finely minced	2
1	garlic clove, crushed	1

Electric slow cooker

1. Wash the beans, put them into a saucepan, with cold water to cover, bring to the boil and boil for 2 minutes, then leave to stand, covered, off heat, for 2 hours. Drain and reserve the liquid. Make it up to 4 pts (2·25 litres) with boiling water.
2. Preheat Pot on HIGH for 20 minutes.
3. Add the beans, herbs, bacon and seasoning to liquid and bring back to the boil. Add all the vegetables except the cabbage and boil for 5 minutes, then put into the Pot. Cook on HIGH for 30 minutes, then on LOW for 8 hours.
4. One hour before serving, gently brown the sausages in a frying-pan and cut each into three pieces. Drain the liquid from the Pot, cut the bacon into smallish pieces and return to the Pot, adding the sausages. Pour back enough liquid to give a soupy but not too liquid mixture, add the cabbage and cook on HIGH until the cabbage is soft. Taste for seasoning—it may need more salt at the end.

Casserole cooking: preheat oven to Gas 3, 325°F, 170°C

As above, putting beans, herbs and bacon in a huge casserole, and cooking 2½ hours in oven. Then add all the other vegetables except the cabbage, and cook another half an hour. Brown sausages and cut up. Strain contents of casserole in a big colander placed over a basin, saving the liquid. Put vegetables and sausage in casserole again, cut bacon into small pieces and stir in. Pour back enough hot liquid to make it soupy (you may need a little more boiling water here). Add cabbage and cook another 30 minutes, taste for seasoning and serve hot in large bowls.

Green Tomatoes Provençal

serves 4

A recipe which works best in a wide, shallow Pot or casserole.

1 lb	green tomatoes	450 g
3 oz	soft brown breadcrumbs	75 g
2	back bacon rashers, de-rinded and cut into strips	2
	black pepper	
1	garlic clove, crushed	1
2 tsp	(heaped) parsley, chopped	2 tsp
12	black olives, pitted and minced	12
2 tbs	oil	2 tbs
1 tsp	basil	1 tsp

Electric slow cooker: preheat Pot on HIGH for 20 minutes

1. Slice tomatoes in half, arrange in Pot, cut side up, in a single layer. Mix the breadcrumbs with the rest of the ingredients, taste for seasoning—it may need a pinch of salt. Press down on tomatoes, cover with foil, and cook on HIGH for 4 hours.
2. Remove foil and, if possible, brown quickly in a hot oven.

Casserole cooking: preheat oven to Gas 3, 325°F, 170°C

As in Step 1, putting tomatoes in a single layer in shallow casserole. Cover with lid or foil, and bake about 1½ hours. Turn up heat, to Gas 6, 400°F, 200°C, uncover and cook another 15 minutes until top is golden brown.

Tomato Casserole with Herbs

serves 4 to 6

2 lb	ripe tomatoes, or their equivalent in tinned Italian peeled tomatoes, well drained	900 g
1	large onion, very finely minced	1
4	large potatoes, peeled and sliced	4
8 oz	Cheddar cheese, grated	225 g
4 tbs	mixed herbs (basil, rosemary, marjoram)	4 tbs
2 tbs	paprika	2 tbs
¼ pt (7 fl oz)	single cream, or top of milk	150 ml (200 ml)
	salt and pepper	

Electric slow cooker: lightly oil and preheat Pot on HIGH for 20 minutes

1. Parboil the potatoes in boiling water for 1 minute. Drain well. Make layers in the Pot as follows: tomatoes, cheese, minced onion, herbs, paprika, salt and pepper, potatoes. Repeat, ending with potatoes topped with cheese. Pour in the cream, cover with aluminium foil. Cook on HIGH for 4 hours.
2. If your Pot has a removable casserole, put it in a hot oven for about 15 minutes, to brown the top.

Casserole cooking: preheat oven to Gas 4, 350°F, 180°C

As in Step 1, making layers of tomatoes, cheese, etc. potatoes and repeating, ending with potatoes and cheese. Increase cream or top of milk to about 7 fl oz (200 ml), put a sheet of aluminium foil under casserole lid, cover and bake about 2 hours. Remove foil and lid, raise heat to Gas 6, 400°F, 200°C, for another 20 minutes, to brown lightly.

Another Tomato Casserole

serves 4

This is very pleasant served with cold lamb or thinly sliced rare roast beef.

1 lb	fresh, ripe tomatoes, peeled and de-seeded, or their equivalent in tinned Italian peeled tomatoes, drained	450 g
3 tbs	butter with a little oil	3 tbs
4 oz	fresh brown breadcrumbs	100 g
1 tbs	onion, very finely minced	1 tbs
1 tsp	basil (or more)	1 tsp
	salt and pepper	
1	good dash of hot pepper sauce *or* saltspoon crushed red pepper flakes	1

Electric slow cooker: preheat Pot on HIGH for 20 minutes

1. Melt about 2 tablespoons of the butter in a small saucepan, stir in the breadcrumbs, onion, herb and seasoning, and mix well. Butter a 1½ pt (750 ml) soufflé dish and press a layer of the crumb mixture into the base. Roughly chop the tomatoes and put a layer on the top of the crumbs. Continue, alternating layers, until the dish is full. Cut the remaining butter in flakes over the top.
2. Cover tightly with aluminium foil, using aluminium foil 'lifter straps' as suggested on p. 126. Put on a trivet in Pot, add about ½ pt (300 ml) boiling water and cook on HIGH for 2 hours, or on HIGH for 1 hour, then on LOW for 4 hours.

Casserole cooking: preheat oven to Gas 3, 325°F, 170°C

As in Step 1, putting everything in a buttered fairly deep casserole, with a sheet of foil under its lid, and cook in oven about 1½ hours. Look at it then, and add a little tomato juice if it seems dry, and cook another 30 minutes.

Haricot Beans with Bacon

serves 4

Not for slimmers or for anyone on a low-cholesterol regime, but a joy for anyone else—especially on a cold, rainy night. It can all be done in advance, up to the point of frying the bacon, and reheated in a saucepan when wanted.

8 oz	dried haricot beans	225 g
2	medium onions, thinly sliced	2
1	bay leaf	1
½ tsp	thyme	½ tsp
1	celery stalk, diced	1
8	small streaky bacon rashers	8
1 tbs	butter	1 tbs
1	small garlic clove, crushed with 1 tsp salt	1
2 tbs	single cream	2 tbs
	black pepper	

Electric slow cooker

1. Wash the beans, put into a saucepan with cold water to cover, bring to the boil, boil for 2 minutes, remove from the heat, cover and leave to stand for 2 hours. Drain, put into the washed-out saucepan with fresh cold water and bring to the boil. Add the onion, bay leaf, pepper, thyme and celery.
2. Preheat Pot on HIGH for 20 minutes.
3. Put the contents of the saucepan into the Pot and cook on LOW for 10 to 12 hours or on HIGH for 4 to 5 hours, in which case you must stir the beans occasionally and if necessary add a bit more water.
4. Fry the bacon rashers crisp in a pan, remove and keep warm. Melt the butter in the same frying-pan, stir in the crushed garlic and salt and sauté until very pale gold. Drain the beans (keep the liquid, it makes wonderful soup) and mix in the garlicky butter. Tip in the bacon and stir in the cream.

Casserole cooking: preheat oven to Gas 2, 300°F, 150°C

As above, but adding about 1 pt (600 ml) extra cold water to the boiling process. Put vegetables and liquid in deep casserole with well-fitting lid, cover and cook in centre of oven about 4 hours, until beans are tender. Add more liquid halfway through cooking time if necessary. Finish as in Step 4.

Celery Madame Blanchard

serves 4

2	heads very good celery	2
1	medium onion, sliced	1
2	small carrots, diced	2
2	back bacon rashers	2
¼ pt (½ pt)	chicken stock	150 ml (300 ml)

Electric slow cooker: preheat Pot on HIGH for 20 minutes

1. Wash and trim the celery (save the trimmings for soup and dry the leaves for seasoning another dish). Cut the stalks into even lengths. Blanch in boiling water for 10 minutes, drain and put into the Pot. Keep the water boiling and blanch the onions and carrots for 1 minute. Drain and set aside. Trim the bacon of its fat, cut the fat into strips and blanch for 2 minutes, then drain and refresh in cold water.
2. Put the bacon fat in the bottom of the Pot, pushing it under the celery. Cover the celery with the onion and carrots and lay the rashers of bacon over all. Bring the stock to the boil and add to the Pot. Cook on HIGH for 3 hours.
3. Remove the vegetables and keep warm. Tip the juices into a small saucepan and boil rapidly over high heat to reduce.

This is a pale dish; for a little more colour dust with finely minced parsley or minced chives.

Casserole cooking: preheat oven to Gas 4, 350°F, 180°C

As above, putting celery in casserole, laying in onion and carrots and covering with bacon strips. Increase stock to a scant ½ pt (300 ml), bring to boil, pour over vegetables. Cover tightly, and bake 1½ hours. Increase heat to Gas 6, 400°F, 200°C, take off lid and cook another 20–30 minutes to crisp the top a little. Remove bacon and dice. Make sauce as above. Stir bacon bits into vegetables, and cover with sauce.

Greek Casserole

serves 4

2	small aubergines (about 1½ lb)	700 g
1 lb	courgettes, sliced	450 g
1	small onion, peeled and thinly sliced	1
4 tbs	oil	4 tbs
2	garlic cloves, crushed	2
1½ lb	ripe tomatoes, or their equivalent in tinned Italian peeled tomatoes, sliced	700 g
	salt and pepper	
1 tsp	mixed herbs	1 tsp
3 tbs	fresh brown crumbs	3 tbs
1	small tin anchovy fillets	1

Electric slow cooker: preheat Pot on HIGH for 20 minutes

1. Cut the aubergines into ½ inch (2·5 cm) slices, salt well, put into a colander or on plates, weigh down heavily and leave to drain for 30 minutes. Drain, rinse and dry well with kitchen towels. Separate the onion slices into rings. Heat the oil in a frying-pan and gently sauté the onion and garlic until just translucent. Put into the Pot. Sauté the courgettes in the same pan and remove. Fry the aubergine slices in the same oil—you may have to add more—for about 3 minutes on each side.
2. Mix the aubergines and courgettes and put half this mixture into the Pot, cover with half the tomatoes. Repeat and season layers well with salt, pepper and herbs. Cover with the breadcrumbs. Cut the anchovy fillets into very narrow strips and make a lattice on top of the crumbs. Cook on LOW for 8 hours.

Casserole cooking: preheat oven to Gas 2, 300°F, 150°C

As in Steps 1 and 2, using a casserole well-brushed with oil, covering tightly and cooking in centre of oven about 3 hours. Uncover for the last half hour and raise heat to Gas 6, 400°F, 200°C, for a brown crusty top.

Loubia

serves 4 to 8

This does very well as a hot first course for 8 people, or serves 4 as an accompanying vegetable. The initial cooking can be done beforehand (overnight in the Pot) and the mixture refrigerated, to be reheated in a saucepan with tomato and garlic—how much of the latter I leave to your taste.

8 oz	dried haricot beans	225 g
4	garlic cloves	4
2 tsp	salt	2 tsp
	several sprigs of parsley	
2 tsp	cumin	2 tsp
3 tsp	paprika	3 tsp
2 tbs	olive oil	2 tbs
1	large ripe tomato, or its equivalent in tinned Italian tomatoes	1
1½ tbs	flour	1½ tbs

Electric slow cooker

1. Wash the beans, bring to the boil in a saucepan with cold water to cover, boil for 2 minutes, remove from heat and leave to stand, covered, for 2 hours. Drain, cover with cold water and bring to the boil.
2. Preheat Pot on HIGH for 20 minutes.
3. Crush 2 of the garlic cloves with salt and parsley. Put into the Pot with the beans. Cook on LOW for 8 to 10 hours.
4. Heat the oil in a saucepan, cook chopped tomatoes, 2 more garlic cloves (sliced) and spices until the mixture thickens. Remove the garlic, stir in the flour and about a teacupful of the cooking sauce from the Pot. Cook 1 minute more, then stir all this back into the Pot. Taste for seasoning.

Casserole cooking: preheat oven to Gas 3, 325°F, 170°C

As in Steps 1 and 3, putting beans, garlic salt and parsley in a large casserole, and adding enough boiling water to rise an inch above the beans. Cover and cook in oven about 3 hours, until beans are tender. Finish as in Step 4, cooking another 10 minutes in oven after adding tomato mixture.

October Casserole

serves 4

8 oz	carrots, thinly sliced	225 g
8 oz	potatoes, peeled and diced	225 g
1	leek, washed and sliced	1
1	onion, finely minced	1
2	tomatoes, coarsely chopped	2
1	medium cauliflower, broken into florets	1
3 tbs	butter	3 tbs
2 tbs	flour	2 tbs
2 tsp	Worcestershire sauce	2 tsp
	salt and pepper	
½ pt	stock	300 ml
	For the topping:	
8 oz	self-raising flour	225 g
½ tsp	dry mustard	½ tsp
2 tbs	butter	2 tbs
2 oz	grated cheese	50 g
	milk to make a soft dough	

Electric slow cooker: preheat Pot on HIGH for 20 minutes

1. Heat the butter in a saucepan and gently sauté the vegetables for about 5 minutes. Add the flour, Worcestershire sauce, salt and pepper and stir in the stock. Bring to the boil, stirring, and put into the Pot. Cook on LOW for 5 hours.
2. Half an hour before serving, preheat oven to Gas 6, 400°F, 200°C.
3. Sieve the flour with the mustard, rub in the butter and stir in the grated cheese and enough milk to make a scone dough. Mix well, pat out and cut into 12 rounds. If your Pot has a removable casserole, put the scone rounds on top and bake in oven for about 20 minutes until well risen and brown. With a fixed-casserole Pot, tip the contents into baking dish and proceed as above.

Casserole cooking: preheat oven to Gas 3, 325°F, 170°C

As in Steps 1 and 3, simmering vegetable mixture in a casserole in centre of oven for 2 hours, then raising heat to Gas 6, 400°F, 200°C, to bake the scone topping.

Carrot Ragoût

serves 4

Make this only when you can get large 'old' carrots; the tender little spring ones cook to pieces.

2 lb	carrots	900 g
8 oz	small, even-sized onions	225 g
3 tbs	butter	3 tbs
8 oz	small mushrooms	225 g
2 oz	raisins or sultanas	50 g
½ tsp	fennel seeds	½ tsp
¼ pt (½ pt)	white wine or dry cider	150 ml (300 ml)
1 lev tsp	salt	1 lev tsp
½ tsp	cider vinegar (*optional*)	½ tsp

Electric slow cooker: preheat Pot on HIGH for 20 minutes

1. Scrape the carrots and cut them into neat shapes about 2 inches (5 cm) long. Peel the onions (drop them into boiling water for 2 minutes, which will blanch them and allow their skins to slip off). Melt the butter in a heavy frying-pan and turn the vegetables over just to colour them. Add the wine or cider, raisins, salt and fennel seeds, bring to the boil and put into the Pot. Cook on LOW for 6 hours until the vegetables are tender but still slightly crisp.
2. Take out the vegetables with a slotted spoon and keep warm. Pour the sauce into a small, heavy saucepan, taste for seasoning, add vinegar if you like and boil rapidly to reduce to a thick syrupy glaze. Pour over the vegetables.

Casserole cooking: preheat oven to Gas 2, 300°F, 150°C

As in Steps 1 and 2 above, putting everything in a fairly deep casserole. Increase wine or cider to ½ pt (300 ml). Cook for 3 hours until carrots are tender but not mushy. Finish as in Step 2.

Vegetable Curry

serves 4

3	carrots, diced	3
8 oz	new potatoes, with skins rubbed off	225 g
1 tbs	oil	1 tbs
1	onion, minced	1
1	cooking apple, diced	1
1 tbs	mild curry paste*	1 tbs
8 oz	tin baked beans in tomato sauce	225 g
1 tbs	flour	1 tbs
1 tsp	tomato purée	1 tsp
¼ pt	plain yoghurt	150 ml
2	eggs, hardboiled	2

Electric slow cooker: preheat Pot on HIGH for 20 minutes

1. Blanch carrots for 1 minute in boiling water to cover, remove with a slotted spoon and keep the water boiling. Add more water to make up to ½ pt (300 ml) and blanch the potatoes for 2 minutes. Heat the oil in a pan, gently sauté the onion and apple and add the curry paste and the still-boiling vegetable stock. Stir well and add the baked beans. Mix the flour with the tomato purée and stir slowly into the simmering mixture. Put into the Pot and cook on LOW for 4 hours or on HIGH for 2 hours.
2. Stir in the yoghurt and garnish with hardboiled eggs cut into eighths.

  * If you have no curry paste, mix 1 teaspoon or more mild curry powder into the oil before sautéing the onion and apple.

Casserole cooking: preheat oven to Gas 2, 300°F, 150°C

As in Step 1, put everything except yoghurt and eggs in a large casserole, and cook in centre of oven for about 1½–2 hours. This is a most amenable curry, and can stand for another hour in an oven turned down to Gas ½, 250°F, 130°C, if you like. Finish as in Step 2.

Lentil Pot

serves 6 to 8

You may halve the quantities of this recipe, or put the remainder aside for another lunch or dinner.

1 lb	bacon joint	450 g
½ lb	brown lentils	225 g
2	medium onions, roughly chopped	2
2	carrots, diced	2
2	bay leaves	2
3 tbs	bacon dripping	3 tbs
1	garlic clove, crushed	1
	pinch of thyme	
	pinch of sage	
	salt and pepper	
1¼ pt (1¾ pt)	boiling water	750 ml (1 gen l)
1	extra garlic clove	1
	parsley, chopped	

Electric slow cooker: preheat Pot on HIGH for 15 minutes

1. Cut off bacon rind and cut bacon into 1 inch (2·5 cm) cubes. Wash and carefully pick over lentils. Cover bacon with cold water in a saucepan, bring to boil and drain well. If it seems very salty, do this twice. (Or soak overnight.)
2. Heat the dripping, sauté onions until transparent. Add all the other ingredients, except extra garlic and parsley, and bring to the boil. Put everything into the Pot, cook on HIGH for 30 minutes, then on LOW for 6 hours, until the lentils are tender and the liquid is absorbed.
3. Mix the parsley with the extra clove of garlic, crushed, and some bacon dripping and stir into the Pot. Check for seasoning. If you like, you can cover this Lentil Pot at the last minute with a thickish layer of toasted brown breadcrumbs—in which case it becomes a sort of bastard Cassoulet.

Casserole cooking: preheat oven to Gas 3, 325°F, 170°C

As in Steps 1 and 2, increasing water to about 1¾ pts (1 l), bring it all to the boil, put in casserole, cover and simmer in oven about 1½ hours. Remove lid, cook another half an hour until liquid is absorbed. Finish as in Step 3.

Turnips à la Barrière

serves 4

The turnip slices darken in colour and look most unusual, but they are utterly delicious. Even people who usually hate turnips like this dish.

1 lb	firm white turnips	450 g
2	fat bacon rashers	2
1 tbs	butter	1 tbs
	salt and pepper	
	nutmeg, grated	
2 tbs	parsley, chopped	2 tbs

Electric slow cooker: preheat Pot on HIGH for 20 minutes

Peel and slice the turnips thinly. Cut the bacon into really fine dice and fry in a frying-pan until the fat begins to run. Add the butter and let it melt, put in the turnip slices, stir around until completely coated, season, then put into the Pot. Cook on LOW for 6 hours.

Serve hot, sprinkled with parsley.

Casserole cooking: preheat oven to Gas 3, 325°F, 170°C

As in recipe above, using a rather small casserole with close-fitting lid, and cooking in oven about 2½ hours. About halfway through cooking time, look in and add a few tablespoons of boiling water if turnips look dry.

Lentils with Bacon

serves 4

8 oz	red lentils	225 g
4	back bacon rashers	4
3 tbs	oil or dripping	3 tbs
2	medium onions, minced	2
2	large garlic cloves, crushed with ½ tsp salt	2
1 tbs	flour	1 tbs
	black pepper	

Electric slow cooker

1. Wash and carefully pick over the lentils. Bring to the boil in a saucepan with water to cover, remove from heat and leave to stand, covered, for 2 hours. Cut the rind and bones from the bacon and cut into small squares. Preheat Pot on HIGH for 20 minutes while you are preparing the next step.
2. Sauté the onions in hot oil in a frying-pan until limp and golden, then stir in the garlic/salt and bacon and cook for about 5 minutes but do not brown. Drain the lentils but reserve the liquid; put the vegetables, bacon and flour into the Pot, then add ¼ pt (150 ml) hot lentil liquid. Cook on LOW for 5 hours. Taste for seasoning and add quite a lot of freshly ground pepper.

If any lentils are left after serving this dish, purée half of them, keep the rest whole for a nice texture, add some well-seasoned stock and make a pleasant little soup.

Casserole cooking

As in Step 1 above. After pre-cooking lentils, drain well, reserving liquid, and make it up to 4 pints (2·25 l) with boiling water. Preheat oven to Gas 3, 325°F, 170°C.

Proceed as in Step 2, using a casserole with well-fitting lid, and simmering in oven 2½ hours until lentils are tender. Taste, and add salt if necessary, and plenty of black pepper.

Sweet and Sour Onions

serves 4

1 lb	*small, even-sized onions	450 g
2 tbs	juice of 1 large lemon *or* cider or tarragon vinegar	2 tbs
¼ pt (½ pt)	water	150 ml (300 ml)
1 dsp	tomato purée	1 dsp
1 tbs	oil	1 tbs
1	garlic clove, crushed	1
1 tsp	salt	1 tsp
2 oz	raisins or sultanas	50 g
	pinch of thyme	

Electric slow cooker: preheat Pot on HIGH for 20 minutes

Mix together the water, lemon juice, oil, tomato purée and thyme in a saucepan, bring slowly to the boil and stir well. Crush the garlic with the salt and add to the pan, then put in the peeled onions and raisins. Put everything into the Pot and cook on LOW for 6 hours. Then cool in the liquid.

Serve as part of mixed hors d'oeuvres, or as a cold vegetable with something like braised veal.

* If you cannot get small, pickling-size onions, choose small to medium, even-sized onions and cut them in halves or quarters.

Casserole cooking: preheat oven to Gas 3, 325°F, 170°C

As in recipe above, putting everything in a rather deep casserole, and increasing liquid to about ½ pt (300 ml) water. Simmer in oven 2½ hours and cool.

Potato Soufflé   serves 4

This dish can be made with instant mashed potato. The chives (or very finely minced spring onion tops) give it a pretty green-flecked look as well as a certain flavour. Filling enough for a luncheon dish, with salad.

1 lb	cooked mashed potatoes	450 g
3 oz	grated cheddar	75 g
2 tbs	chives, finely minced	2 tbs
	salt and pepper	
	grated nutmeg	
3	eggs (size 3) separated	3
	butter	

Electric slow cooker: preheat Pot on HIGH for 20 minutes

Butter well the inside of a soufflé dish or casserole that will fit into your Pot. Mix the potatoes, cheese, chives, salt, pepper and nutmeg with the beaten egg yolks. Whisk the whites until stiff but not dry. Blend a tablespoon of the potato mixture into the beaten whites to slacken them, then lightly cut the whites into the potatoes with a metal spoon. Pile into the soufflé dish, smooth the

top and cover loosely with aluminium foil, using aluminium foil 'lifter straps' as suggested on p. 126. Pour in boiling water halfway up the sides of the soufflé dish. Cook on HIGH for 2½ hours until well risen.

Casserole cooking: preheat oven to Gas 4, 350°F, 180°C

As above, putting mixture into well-buttered ovenproof casserole. Bake, uncovered, 45 minutes until well risen and golden.

Marrow with Rosemary   serves 4

If you can lay hands on fresh rosemary you might want to make up a bottle of rosemary oil: ½ pt (300 ml) olive oil and about 5 sprigs of rosemary, allowed to mellow together for a few weeks. This makes a deliciously flavoured oil to sauté onions in for a dish like this, but of course you will then reduce the amount of dried rosemary.

1½ lb	marrow, peeled and diced	700 g
1	onion, coarsely chopped	1
1	garlic clove, crushed	1
2 tbs	oil	2 tbs
1	tinned red pimento, cut into strips	1
½ tsp	rosemary	½ tsp
	salt and pepper	

Electric slow cooker: preheat Pot on HIGH for 20 minutes

Heat the oil in a frying-pan and sauté the onions and garlic until just limp but not brown. Put into the Pot, add the pimento, marrow and seasonings. Cook on LOW for 6 hours, until the marrow is tender but not mushy.

Casserole cooking: preheat oven to Gas 2, 300°F, 150°C

As in recipe above, putting all ingredients in a deepish casserole with a tight lid, and simmer in oven about 2½ hours. Taste for seasoning when marrow is soft as butter.

Grimaud Onions

serves 6

This is a distant cousin of the Provençal dish called Tian of Onions, named in fact for the actual shallow baking dish in which it is customarily baked. Don't make it with corn oil or the ordinary mixed vegetable oil used for frying.

3 lb	large onions, thinly sliced	1½ kg
5 tbs	good oil (olive or sunflower and olive, half and half)	5 tbs
4 tbs	flour	4 tbs
¼ pt	milk	150 ml
	salt and pepper	
	nutmeg, grated	
5 tbs	*To garnish:* breadcrumbs	5 tbs

Electric slow cooker: preheat Pot on HIGH for 20 minutes

1. Blanch the sliced onions in boiling water to cover for 3 minutes. Remove with a slotted spoon and put into the Pot. Keep the onion liquid hot. In a small heavy saucepan, heat the oil, stir in the flour and cook, stirring, until it honeycombs. Take off heat and gradually stir in ¼ pt (150 ml) of the onion liquid, and then the milk. Cook and stir until slightly thickened, then mix with the onions in the Pot. Season well. Cover tightly with aluminium foil and cook on LOW for 4 hours.
2. While the onions are cooking, toast the bread-crumbs or dry them in a medium oven, until they are nicely brown. Strew them on top of the onions just before serving. If you have a Pot with a removable casserole, you may like to pop it into a hot oven for a few minutes, to brown the top, but this doesn't affect the flavour.

Casserole cooking: preheat oven to Gas 4, 350°F, 180°C

As in Step 1, putting a layer of sauce in a heavy casserole, then the blanched onions, and finishing with remaining sauce. Sprinkle with bread-crumbs, and trail a little more oil over the surface. Bake in oven about 2 hours. For a crisp brown finish, put casserole under grill for 5 minutes, or turn up oven to heat to Gas 8, 450°F, 230°C.

Potato and Anchovy Casserole

serves 4

2	large onions, thinly sliced	2
2 lb	potatoes, thinly sliced	900 g
1	can anchovy fillets in oil	1
4 oz	mushrooms, sliced	100 g
2 tbs	butter	2 tbs
¼ pt	single cream	150 ml
	black pepper	

Electric slow cooker: grease and preheat Pot on HIGH for 15 minutes

1. Blanch the onion and potato slices in boiling water for 1 minute. Heat the butter and sauté the mushrooms for 3 minutes only. Line the bottom of the Pot with a layer of potatoes, then a layer of onions, mushrooms and anchovies. Repeat, ending with a layer of potatoes. Season lightly with pepper but no salt. Pour on half the oil from the anchovy tin and half the cream. Cook on HIGH for 20 minutes, then on LOW for 4 hours. Pour on the remaining anchovy oil and the rest of the cream.
2. If you have a Pot with a removable casserole, put it in the top of a hot oven, to brown the top. A shallow, wide casserole can go under a hot grill for a few minutes.

Casserole cooking: preheat oven to Gas 2, 300°F, 150°C

As in Step 1 above, using a casserole that is deep rather than wide, and slipping a sheet of foil under the lid. Bake in centre of oven 2½ hours, then raise heat to Gas 7, 425°F, 230°C, remove lid and foil, and move casserole to top shelf of oven to brown.

Red Cabbage with Apples

serves 6

1	large firm red cabbage, finely shredded	1
2	onions, thinly sliced	2
2 oz	butter	50 g
2	cooking apples, peeled and sliced	2
2	dessert apples, peeled and sliced	2
1 tbs	brown sugar	1 tbs
1 tbs	vinegar	1 tbs
	pinch of ground cloves	
	salt and pepper	

Electric slow cooker

Soak the cabbage in warm water for 1 hour. Pre-heat the Pot on HIGH for 20 minutes. Fry the onions in hot butter in a frying-pan until limp and golden. Add the drained cabbage, apples, sugar, vinegar, cloves and salt and pepper and bring to the boil. Put into the Pot and cook on HIGH for 4 hours. Taste for seasoning.

You can cook this on HIGH for 30 minutes, then on LOW overnight, but it loses a good deal of its colour this way.

Casserole cooking: preheat oven to Gas 3, 325°F, 170°C

As above, but put all the ingredients in an earthenware, glass or enamelled steel casserole with a good tight lid, and add about 4 fl oz (100 ml) boiling water. Cover tightly, bake 2 hours, adding a little more boiling water if necessary from time to time.

Leek and Vegetable Ragoût with Dumplings★

serves 4

1 lb	leeks, well washed and quartered	450 g
12 oz	potatoes, peeled and diced	350 g
12 oz	lean bacon, diced	350 g
	salt and pepper	
1 tsp	soy sauce or Chinese mushroom sauce	1 tsp
$\frac{1}{2}$ pt ($\frac{3}{4}$ pt)	chicken stock	300 ml (450 ml)
	For the dumplings:	
8 oz	self-raising flour	225 g
$\frac{1}{2}$ tsp	salt	$\frac{1}{2}$ tsp
4 oz	shredded suet	100 g
	just enough water to make soft dough	

Electric slow cooker: preheat Pot on HIGH for 20 minutes

1. Wash leeks again and cut into 3 inch (7·5 cm) lengths. Bring the stock to the boil, put everything into the Pot (except dumplings) and cook on LOW for 6 hours. Turn the Pot to HIGH while you prepare the dumplings.
2. Mix dumpling ingredients well and pat into rounds about 1 inch thick on a floured surface. Cook in a saucepan of boiling water with a very tight lid, until well risen and light. Put into the Pot on top of the stew and cook for another 10 minutes.

Casserole cooking: preheat oven to Gas 3, 325°F, 170°C

As in Step 1, putting all ingredients in a fairly shallow, wide casserole, tightly covering and simmering in oven about 2 hours. Add another $\frac{1}{4}$ pt (150 ml) hot chicken stock after an hour. Prepare dumplings as in Step 2, raise oven heat to Gas 6, 400°F, 200°C, and add cooked dumplings to ragoût, covering tightly and simmering on 10 minutes.

Bread, Cakes and Puddings

Baking in a casserole? At such low temperatures? I didn't believe it until I tried it. Cakes bake to an excellent moist texture, with a fine even surface, in an earthenware casserole or a heavy Le Creuset enamel pot. Peasant Bread comes out of a casserole crusty and sturdy, a firm-textured unpretentious loaf. (It can even be made in the Pot, on High, without rising or proving, cooking for 3 hours or more.) I find casserole cooking of breads and cakes a useful stratagem on days when I can't nip into the kitchen every 45 minutes; and it's not hard to find a space in the oven to slot in a smallish (half recipe perhaps) fruit cake when you're cooking two or three other casseroles at a time.

You can even bake cakes beautifully in the Pot, using a casserole that will fit into the width and depth of its internal container. Innsbruck Honey Bread and Guinness Cake are worth trying, both for taste and for the ease and freedom slow cooking can give you. Best of all, perhaps, are the steamed cakes and puddings: Date Cake, Light Christmas Pudding and, beyond anything, American Spice Cake. The Pot is, after all, merely the twentieth-century edition of the heavy black iron 'kettle' of American colonial days.

For baking and steaming, experiment with a variety of containers to set within the ceramic or glass liner of your Pot. I have used, with success, 2 lb marmalade tins, soufflé dishes, oven-glass casseroles, a 1-pint (500 ml) glazed French mixing bowl, and even a cluster of three soup tins, well scrubbed and freshened with bicarbonate of soda (used to steam small loaves of tea bread). Always, for baking, use a trivet to raise your chosen container off the base: old saucers, biscuit cutters, small wire cake-racks, jam jar lids, or an oven-glass custard cup inverted in the base of the Pot, will do. If you use a loose-bottomed tin, make sure that the trivet(s) will support the rim and not merely the centre of the tin. For complete protection against burning out the heating element, it is wisest to pour about $\frac{1}{2}$ pt (300 ml) hot water around the dish after it is in the Pot.

But do remember that the water and the inside container are going to be *hot* at the end of the cooking time. An easy way to remove the dish or tin is to make two 'lifter straps' of aluminium foil folded four times for strength, crossed under the dish and brought up over the top to give a good hand-hold. Keep a pair of these 'lifters' near your Pot—they last nearly for ever. And protect your hands from steam with a pair of strong but flexible oven gloves, or those well-padded pockets connected by a strap.

Peasant Bread (makes 1 large loaf)

This is very much like the deep-crusted Central European breads and is light-years away from shop-bought bread.

1 tbs	dried yeast	1 tbs
12–18 fl oz	warm water	350–475 ml
2 tsp	brown sugar	2 tsp
	softened margarine for greasing the Pot	
1 lb	flour: half wholemeal and half strong white *or* three-quarters white and one-quarter brown	450 g
1 tbs	salt	1 tbs

Electric slow cooker: grease and preheat Pot on HIGH for 20 minutes

1. Dissolve the yeast in ¼ pt (150 ml) warm water (100°–115°F (40°–45°C)), add the sugar, stir well, cover and keep in a warm place for about 10 minutes until it froths up. Measure all but about half a teacup of flour into a large basin, and save the rest for kneading. Mix in the salt. Tip in the yeast mixture and add about three-quarters of the warm water. Mix vigorously with your hands, adding a little more water if the dough is very stiff. When it is thoroughly mixed and leaves the sides of the bowl clean, transfer to a lightly floured board.

2. Sprinkle the dough sparingly with flour, and flour your hands. Press down on the ball of dough, push it away from you, turn it, pull it towards you and fold it over on itself. Continue kneading until the dough feels springy and 'live'. To test the dough, make a hole with your fingers; it should spring back quickly. Shape the dough into a ball that will fit your Pot, rub it with softened margarine, and press well down into the Pot.

3. Cover the opening of the Pot with 4 or 5 layers of kitchen paper towel, put the lid on and cook on HIGH for 3 hours without raising the lid. At the end of this time, remove the lid, take off the towels and test the top of the bread. If it feels really soft, put on another layer of 3 or 4 towels, replace the lid and cook on HIGH for another half hour or so. Remove and allow to cool on a wire rack.

Because of the steam which is inseparable from Pot cooking, the loaf will feel rather damp when you remove it. I think it is better when it is a day old. You will have a compact, chewy, deliciously flavoured loaf which has not risen very high, and has a dense, crusty exterior. You will need a very sharp knife, and it isn't for anyone with insecure teeth!

Casserole cooking

As above, but mix the dough vigorously in the bowl, tip it out on a floured board, roll it into a ball and grease it well. Put it in a 3 pt (1·75 l) round earthenware, glass or enamelled-metal casserole, cover lightly with oiled plastic film, and let rise until double in bulk. Remove the plastic film and bake in oven that has been preheated to Gas 4, 350°F, 180°C, for approximately 1¼ hours. Tip it out and turn upside down on a sheet of foil on oven shelf, and bake it another 15–20 minutes, until it is crusty all over and sounds hollow when firmly tapped with your knuckles. This one-rise method, as all true bread people will instantly recognize, is a sort of homage to Doris Grant, *Your Daily Food* (Faber & Faber).

Innsbruck Honey Bread

8 oz	white or finely sifted brown flour	225 g
1½ tsp	baking powder	1½ tsp
1 tsp	(or less) cinnamon	1 tsp
½ tsp	salt	½ tsp
¼ tsp	nutmeg	¼ tsp
½ tsp	grated lemon rind	½ tsp
5–6 oz	caster or light soft brown sugar	150–175 g
7–8 fl oz*	milk	200–250 ml*
3 tbs	honey	3 tbs
1 tbs	butter	1 tbs

Electric slow cooker: preheat Pot on HIGH for 20 minutes

1. Well grease and flour a bread or cake tin that will fit into your Pot.
2. Sift together the flour, baking powder, spices and salt, then add the sugar and lemon rind. Heat the milk, honey and butter in a saucepan until the butter melts, then stir in the flour/sugar mixture. (*Use the lesser amount of milk, you can add more later if necessary. The mixture should be of a rather heavy dropping consistency, not slack; as flour varies immensely in its capacity to absorb liquid, be cautious with the milk.) Pour the mixture into the tin, cover tightly with aluminium foil and use the aluminium foil 'lifter straps' as suggested on p. 126. Put the tin on a trivet in the Pot (see p. 126) and pour around it ½ pt (300 ml) hot water. Cook on HIGH for 3 to 3½ hours, until a thin skewer pushed into the centre comes out clean.
3. Remove from the Pot and leave to stand on a wire rack for 15 minutes until it shrinks from the sides of the tin, then slide out.

   This is very good sliced thin and lightly toasted under a grill for tea or breakfast.

Casserole cooking: preheat oven to Gas 4, 350°F, 180°C

As in Step 2, putting the batter into a buttered and floured round casserole, and baking about 1¼ hours, until a skewer in the centre comes out dry. Finish as in Step 3.

Colorado Cake

This is an eggless, milkless cake, with very little fat—rich and satisfying nonetheless—which will keep for a fortnight in an airtight tin. This quantity makes about 8 to 10 slices. A half recipe can be made in a small-sized Pot.

6 oz	brown sugar, light or dark	175 g
2 oz	margarine	50 g
½ pt	boiling water	300 ml
10 oz	sultanas or raisins	300 g
9 oz	fine brown flour	250 g
1 tsp	cinnamon	1 tsp
½ tsp	ground cloves	½ tsp
	or	
1½ tsp	mixed spice	1½ tsp
1 tsp	bicarbonate of soda	1 tsp

Electric slow cooker: preheat Pot on HIGH for 20 minutes

1. Well grease a cake tin that will fit into your Pot.
2. Mix together the sugar, margarine, boiling water and raisins in a saucepan and boil for 5 minutes, then cool quickly in a sinkful of cold water. Sift the dry ingredients together and mix with the fairly cool batter. Stir very well.
3. Pour the mixture into the tin. Cover with aluminium foil and use the aluminium foil 'lifter straps' as suggested on p. 126. Put the tin on a trivet in the Pot (see p. 126) and pour around it ½ pt (300 ml) hot water. Cook on HIGH for 4 hours or until a skewer pushed into the centre comes out clean.

Casserole cooking: preheat oven to Gas 1, 250°F, 130°C

As above, pouring the well-mixed batter into a buttered casserole and bake 2 hours, until a skewer pushed into the centre comes out clean. I have baked this in a greased and lined cake tin, but a heavy casserole, perhaps because it transmits heat in a different way, seems to make a moister, better-keeping cake.

Date Cake

The bottom and sides of this cake will look very crumbly and strange. It isn't a pretty cake, but an exceedingly good, moist and luscious family sweet. It keeps well and freezes beautifully.

4 oz	dates, chopped	100 g
3 oz	light soft brown sugar	75 g
8 oz	self-raising brown flour	225 g
	or	
8 oz	plain flour and 2 level tsp baking powder	225 g
$\frac{1}{2}$ tsp	cinnamon	$\frac{1}{2}$ tsp
$\frac{1}{2}$ tsp	nutmeg, freshly grated	$\frac{1}{2}$ tsp
5 tbs	milk (sour if possible)	5 tbs
1	egg (size 3) beaten	1
4 oz	butter	100 g

Electric slow cooker: preheat Pot on HIGH for 20 minutes

1. Well grease a cake tin that will fit into your Pot.
2. Cut the butter into the sifted flour, spices and sugar. Mix in the dates and toss until they are completely coated. Whisk the egg and milk and stir into the date mixture. It will be quite soft. Pour the mixture into the tin and cover with aluminium foil. Use the aluminium foil 'lifter straps' as suggested on p. 126. Set on a trivet in Pot (see p. 126). Pour in $\frac{1}{2}$ pt (300 ml) boiling water and cook on HIGH for 3 to $3\frac{1}{2}$ hours.
3. Take the tin out carefully, allow to cool slightly, run a palette knife around edge to loosen. Turn out on to a wire tray, then invert so that the top is uppermost.

Casserole cooking: preheat oven to Gas 4, 350°F, 180°C

Grease a round, fairly deep casserole, and follow Step 2, levelling top of cake batter after you have poured it in. Bake, uncovered, in centre of oven about $1\frac{1}{4}$–$1\frac{1}{2}$ hours. Finish as in Step 3.

American Spice Cake

4 oz	butter	100 g
8 oz	light soft brown sugar	225 g
1	egg (size 3)	1
1 tsp	vanilla essence	1 tsp
8 fl oz	plain yoghurt	225 ml
10 oz	white or fine brown flour	300 g
8 oz	sultanas	225 g
1 tsp	ground nutmeg	1 tsp
1 tsp	cinnamon	1 tsp
1 tsp	bicarbonate of soda	1 tsp
$\frac{1}{2}$ tsp	ground cloves	$\frac{1}{2}$ tsp
$\frac{1}{2}$ tsp	salt	$\frac{1}{2}$ tsp

Electric slow cooker: preheat Pot on HIGH for 20 minutes

1. Grease a cake or loaf tin that will fit into your Pot.
2. Cream the butter and sugar together until light and fluffy. Beat the egg with the vanilla essence, mix well with the yoghurt and blend into the butter/sugar mixture. Sift the dry ingredients and toss the sultanas well until completely coated. Add slowly to the first mixture and mix, but do not overbeat. Spoon the mixture into the baking tin and set it on a trivet (see p. 126). Use the aluminium foil 'lifter straps' as suggested on p. 126.
3. Cover the tin with a loosely fitting plate, pour in $\frac{1}{2}$ pt (300 ml) hot water. Bake on HIGH for 4 hours. Remove the plate cautiously, using oven gloves, and lift out the cake tin. Let it cool for a few minutes, then turn out on to a rack.

This may be iced with any plain white icing when cool; or serve it with cream cheese.

Casserole cooking: preheat oven to Gas 2, 300°F, 150°C

As in Step 2, spooning the mixture into a well-greased round (or oblong) oven-glass casserole. Bake in centre of oven for 2 hours, cool in casserole and turn out on a rack. Let it cool very well before icing.

Whisky Cake

¼ pt	whisky	150 ml
1	large lemon	1
6 oz	sultanas or raisins	175 g
8 oz	butter	225 g
8 oz	light soft brown sugar	225 g
3	eggs (size 3), separated	3
8 oz	fine brown flour	225 g
1 tsp	baking powder	1 tsp
	pinch of salt	

Electric slow cooker

1. Well grease a cake tin that will fit into your Pot.
2. Grate the lemon (wrap the denuded lemon in plastic cling-film and refrigerate for future use). Mix the whisky and sultanas and leave to stand for 3 or 4 hours.
3. Preheat Pot on HIGH for 20 minutes.
4. Cream the butter and sugar, lightly beat the egg yolks and add the yolks to the butter/sugar mixture alternately with tablespoons of flour, beating after each addition so that it will not curdle. (I have done this whole operation—creaming and mixing—in a blender when pushed for time.) You will have quite a lot of flour left. Mix the whisky and sultanas with half the remaining flour, then mix it carefully into the egg/sugar/flour mixture. Sift the baking powder with the rest of the flour and fold in. Whisk the egg whites and salt until they will stay in the bowl when you carefully turn it upside down (not over your head as I once did). Cut them into the cake mixture with a metal spoon, blend well but don't beat all the air out.
5. Pour into the cake tin. Cover with foil and use the aluminium foil 'lifter straps' as suggested on p. 126. Set the tin on a trivet in the Pot (see p. 126) and pour around it ½ pt (300 ml) hot water. Bake on HIGH for 3½ hours. Don't lift the lid even once. The cake is done when a thin skewer pushed into the centre comes out clean.

Casserole cooking: As in Steps 2 and 4 above, greasing a round, fairly deep casserole and lining base with greased greaseproof paper. Steep sultanas in whisky 3–4 hours. Then preheat oven to Gas 4, 350°F, 180°C. Cover batter with greased foil, and bake half an hour at the above temperature, then lower heat to Gas 2, 300°F, 150°C, and bake another 1 hour and 45 minutes. Remove foil halfway through the cooking time, to let top of cake 'set'.

Mrs O'Leary's Chocolate Cake

1 oz	instant potato	25 g
	or	
3 oz	freshly cooked potato, sieved	75 g
¼ pt	boiling water	150 ml
3 oz	plain dark chocolate	75 g
4 oz	butter	100 g
5 oz	caster or light soft brown sugar	150 g
2	large eggs (size 2)	2
6 oz	plain flour, sifted with 1½ tsp baking powder	175 g
	pinch of salt	
2 tbs	milk	2 tbs

Electric slow cooker: preheat Pot on HIGH for 20 minutes

1. Grease a cake tin that will fit into your Pot.
2. Whisk together the instant potato and boiling water to a light, creamy consistency. (Or use 3 oz (75 g) freshly cooked, sieved potato.) Cream the butter and sugar and beat in the potato. Melt chocolate in a basin over hot water and add to the potato mixture. Whisk the eggs. Sift together the flour, baking powder and salt. Add the egg and flour alternately to the first mixture, then blend in the milk.
3. Pour the mixture into the tin and smooth the top with a palette knife. Cover tightly with aluminium foil and use the aluminium foil 'lifter straps' as suggested on p. 126. Put the tin or dish on a trivet in the Pot (see p. 126) and pour around it ½ pt (300 ml) hot water. Cook on HIGH for 3½ hours until well risen and lightly firm to the touch.
4. Remove from the Pot and allow to cool for a few minutes. Turn out of the tin and invert on a wire rack to dry out for an hour or two, before splitting into two layers and icing; or spread each layer with stiffly whipped cream.

Casserole cooking: preheat oven to Gas 3, 325°F, 170°C

As above, putting cake mixture into a very well-greased, heavy, fairly deep casserole (a round enamelled cast-iron one is ideal), and baking in centre of oven for about 1½ hours. Let cool in casserole until it shrinks slightly from sides, before removing to a cake rack. Finish as above.

Almond Fruit Cake

8 oz	butter	225 g
8 oz	light brown sugar	225 g
4	eggs (size 2)	4
4 tbs	milk	4 tbs
8 oz	self-raising flour	225 g
4 oz	plain flour	100 g
2 oz	ground almonds	50 g
12 oz	mixed fruit	350 g
4 oz	cut mixed peel	100 g
2 oz	split almonds	50 g

Electric slow cooker: preheat Pot on HIGH for 20 minutes

1. Grease a cake tin that will fit into your Pot.
2. Cream the butter and sugar until light. Beat in the eggs one at a time. Add the milk and mix well. Mix together the flour and ground almonds, toss fruit and peel in this mixture, then add to the butter/sugar/eggs and blend well.
3. Pour the mixture into the tin and decorate the top with concentric circles of halved almonds. Cover tightly with aluminium foil and use the aluminium foil 'lifter straps' as suggested on p. 126. Put the tin on a trivet in the Pot (see p. 126), and pour around it ½ pt (300 ml) hot water. Cook on HIGH for 3½ hours or until a skewer inserted in the centre comes out clean. Remove carefully and allow to cool slightly before turning out of the tin.

Casserole cooking: preheat oven to Gas 3, 325°F, 170°C

Grease a fairly deep casserole, about 7–8 inches (200 mm) diameter, and line base with greased greaseproof paper. Proceed as above, and bake (uncovered) about 1¾ hours. Let cool about half an hour before running a sharp knife around edge and turning out; or just cut in wedges from the casserole.

The Healthy Fruit Cake

This cake benefits from standing at least 24 hours before being sliced; wrapped in a cling-film it will keep in a cool place for about a week.

3 oz	soft brown sugar, light or dark	75 g
½ pt	milk	300 ml
4 oz	coarse bran	100 g
4 oz	fine brown flour	100 g
2 tsp	baking powder	2 tsp
4 oz	mixed peel	100 g
4 oz	mixed dried fruit	100 g
	juice and rind of half a lemon	

Electric slow cooker: preheat Pot on HIGH for 20 minutes

1. Heavily grease an oblong or round cake tin that will fit into your Pot.
2. Whisk together the milk and sugar, stir in the bran and leave the mixture to stand for about half an hour. Sift the flour and baking powder and toss the cut peel and dried fruit in it. Add to the mixture, then stir in the lemon juice and rind. Fill the tin with the mixture. Cover the tin with aluminium foil and use the aluminium foil 'lifter straps' as suggested on p. 126. Put the tin on a trivet in the Pot (see p. 126) and pour around it ½ pt (300 ml) hot water. Cook on HIGH for 3½ to 4 hours.
3. Remove from the Pot and leave to cool in the tin before turning out. The cake will be moist, succulent and rather heavy.

Casserole cooking: preheat oven to Gas 3, 325°F, 170°C

As in Step 2, putting mixture in a round, straight-sided, fairly deep casserole, stand it in a baking tin with about an inch of hot water, and cook in centre of oven about 2½ hours, until a skewer in the centre comes out clean. Finish as in Step 3.

Guinness Cake

This cake should be kept for at least a week before cutting.

6 oz	butter, softened	175 g
6 oz	dark brown sugar	175 g
3	eggs (size 3)	3
8 oz	flour	225 g
½ tsp	salt	½ tsp
1½ lev tsp	mixed spice	1½ lev tsp
6 oz	raisins	175 g
6 oz	sultanas	175 g
3 oz	mixed cut peel	75 g
3 oz	walnuts, chopped	75 g
¼ pt	Guinness	150 ml

Electric slow cooker: preheat Pot on HIGH for 20 minutes

1. Brush a cake tin that will fit into your Pot with fat, and line the base with a piece of greased greaseproof paper cut to fit.
2. Cream the butter and sugar until as light and fluffy as possible. Break the eggs into a small bowl, whisk lightly, then gradually blend into the butter/sugar mixture. Sift the flour with the spices and salt, mix in the dried fruit, peel and nuts and toss until completely coated. Add to the creamed mixture with four tablespoons of Guinness and fold together but do not overbeat.
3. Pour the mixture into the tin, cover with aluminium foil and use the aluminium foil 'lifter straps' as suggested on p. 126. Put the tin on a trivet in the Pot (see p. 126) and pour around it ½ pt (300 ml) hot water. Cook on HIGH for 4 to 5 hours, until a thin skewer pressed into the centre comes out clean.
4. Remove the tin from the Pot and let the cake cool in the tin. Then turn out on to a cake rack, and stand this on a large plate. Stab the bottom of the cake with a skewer, spoon the remaining Guinness over it and let it soak in. Wrap in foil and keep for at least a week.

Casserole cooking: preheat oven to Gas 3, 325°F, 170°C

As in Step 2, greasing a round deep casserole and lining bottom with a piece of greased, greaseproof paper. Use only half the Guinness in the cake mixture. Turn batter into casserole, bake 1 hour at the above temperature, then lower heat to Gas 2 300°F, 150°C, and bake another 1 hour and 45 minutes. Let cake cool, then turn out on rack set in a large plate. Prick base of cake (which is now uppermost) with a thin skewer, and pour on remaining Guinness. When it is all absorbed, wrap in foil and don't cut it for a week.

Creamy Rice Pudding serves 4

This is a recipe for the smallest Pot or casserole; if you have a large Pot, use a well-buttered soufflé dish or basin that will fit easily inside, set it on a trivet, use aluminium foil 'lifter straps' as suggested on p. 126, and pour about ½ pt (300 ml) boiling water around it.

3 oz	pudding rice	75 g
1 pt	milk	600 ml
2 tbs	sugar	2 tbs
1 tsp	butter	1 tsp
½ tsp	vanilla essence	½ tsp
	or	
½ tsp	grated lemon or orange rind	½ tsp
	nutmeg, freshly grated	

Electric slow cooker: butter and preheat Pot on HIGH for 20 minutes

Before heating the Pot, make sure that the sides and bottom are well buttered, otherwise you'll burn your fingers. Mix the well washed rice with the milk, sugar and vanilla essence and put into the Pot. Cut bits of butter over the surface. Cover with aluminium foil and cook on LOW for 8 hours or overnight.

Sprinkle with freshly grated nutmeg before serving.

Casserole cooking: preheat oven to Gas 2, 300°F, 150°C

As in recipe above, buttering casserole well. Set casserole into a deep oven tin and pour in hot water halfway up the sides. Cook for 2 hours or more, until creamy and thick.

Brownie Pudding

serves 4

This recipe is most suitable for baking in a rather deep Pot or casserole. If you have a wide, shallow one, I suggest you use a well buttered cake tin or pudding basin which will sit on a trivet, or a large jam-jar lid, in your Pot or casserole.

2 oz	sifted flour	50 g
1 tsp	baking powder	1 tsp
½ tsp	salt	½ tsp
3 oz	light soft brown sugar	75 g
1 tbs	cocoa powder	1 tbs
4 tbs	milk	4 tbs
½ tsp	vanilla essence	½ tsp
1 tbs	melted butter	1 tbs
2 oz	walnuts, chopped	50 g
	For the sauce:	
4 oz	light brown sugar	100 g
2 tbs	cocoa powder	2 tbs
¼ pt	boiling water	150 ml

Electric slow cooker: butter and preheat Pot on HIGH for 20 minutes

1. Mix the flour, baking powder, salt, sugar and 1 tablespoon of cocoa, and sift all together. Add the milk, butter and vanilla. Mix until just barely smooth and add the nuts. Put into the Pot.
2. Mix together the 4 oz (100 g) brown sugar and the 2 tablespoons cocoa powder, and sprinkle evenly over the batter. Pour on the boiling water quickly—this makes the chocolate sauce sink to the bottom. Cover with aluminium foil, and cook on HIGH for 3 hours or until set.

Serve warm or cold, but not hot.

Casserole cooking: preheat oven to Gas 4, 350°F, 180°C

As in Steps 1 and 2, using a deep, rather small, round or oval casserole. Bake in centre of oven 45 minutes. A slightly different result is obtained by baking it for 2 hours at Gas 2, 300°F, 150°C—no matter how you make it, it is richly fragrant of chocolate and nuts, and designed to be eaten inelegantly with a spoon.

Mocha Pudding Tart

serves 4 to 6

1	*large tin condensed, sweetened milk	1
¼ pt	hot strong coffee	150 ml
	or	
4 dsp	coffee essence	4 dsp
2 tbs	chopped walnuts	2 tbs
	For the tart crust:	
20	digestive biscuits, finely crushed	20
3 tbs	melted butter	3 tbs

Electric slow cooker: preheat Pot on HIGH for 20 minutes

1. Put the *unopened* tin of milk into boiling water in the Pot and cook on HIGH for 3 hours. Remove the tin, very carefully, with two big spoons, protecting your hands with oven gloves. Cool quickly in a saucepan of cold water (or leave to stand overnight). In the meantime, make a tart crust with the digestive biscuits stirred into butter, pressed into a buttered 8 inch (200 mm) dish and chilled.
2. When the milk is cold, open the tin and spoon it into a large basin. Add the hot coffee or coffee essence and whisk until thick and smooth. Pile into the tart shell and sprinkle with chopped walnuts. Chill until ready to serve.

If you have a big Pot, use the boiling water to caramelize two or three small-sized tins of condensed milk when you're steaming another pudding, and store them, unopened, in the fridge for a week or ten days until you feel like making a quick, rich and sumptuous-looking Mocha Tart.

* Do *not* attempt this recipe with evaporated milk; according to the manufacturers the tins are made differently and will not withstand boiling.

Casserole cooking: this is something to put in a corner of a well-filled oven set at about Gas 5, 375°F, 190°C—not much point in heating up an oven merely to steam a tin of milk!

However, it's a very easy way to make a most rich and luscious-tasting coffee pudding. Put your unopened tin of milk in boiling water in a deep casserole, cover it, and let it cook away for 3 or 4 hours while you're making a beef stew or an oxtail casserole. Then finish as above.

Indian Pudding

serves 6 to 8

8 oz	yellow maize meal (American cornmeal), or polenta	225 g
1½ pt	milk	750 ml
2	eggs (size 3)	2
3 oz	suet, shredded	75 g
4 oz	light soft brown sugar	100 g
6 oz	black treacle	175 g
	nutmeg, freshly grated	
¼ tsp	ground cloves	¼ tsp
¼ tsp	cinnamon	¼ tsp
¼ tsp	ginger	¼ tsp
¼ tsp	allspice	¼ tsp
1 tsp	salt	1 tsp

Electric slow cooker: grease and preheat Pot on HIGH for 20 minutes

1. Heat the milk in a saucepan to just below boiling-point. Gradually sift in the maize meal and stir constantly on a medium flame until it thickens. Cool slightly. Whisk the eggs and add to the maize meal mixture. Add all the other ingredients and mix very well.
2. Pour into the well greased Pot, cover with 5 or 6 layers of paper towels, put on the lid and cook on HIGH for 4 hours. This pudding may, alternatively, be steamed: pour into a well greased container that will fit your Pot and cover tightly with aluminium foil. Use the aluminium foil 'lifter straps' as suggested on p. 126. Put the dish on a trivet in the Pot and pour around it 1 pt (600 ml) hot water. Cook on HIGH for 5 hours. If you have a small-sized Pot, you can make a half quantity of this recipe, and steam it in a 1 lb (450 g) coffee tin, well greased.

Serve fairly hot and, traditionally, with vanilla ice cream to melt over it. Rum butter makes a good accompaniment too.

Casserole cooking: preheat oven to Gas 3, 325°F, 170°C

As in Step 1. Pour mixture into buttered 8 inch (200 mm) round casserole, cover tightly with foil under lid, and bake 2 hours. Serve as above.

Cuban Pudding

serves 4 to 6

Start this pudding the day before you want to serve it.

6 oz	sultanas or raisins	175 g
¼ pt	red wine	150 ml
6 oz	dry, fine breadcrumbs	175 g
8 oz	caster sugar	225 g
½ tsp	salt	½ tsp
3	eggs (size 1 or 2), well beaten	3
2 oz	butter, melted	50 g
8 fl oz	milk	225 ml
4 oz	slivered almonds	100 g
1 tsp	cinnamon	1 tsp
½ tsp	ground cloves	½ tsp

Electric slow cooker

1. Soak the dried fruit in wine overnight or longer.
2. Preheat Pot on HIGH for 20 minutes.
3. Mix together the breadcrumbs, sugar, salt and spices. Whisk together the eggs, butter and milk, and mix in nuts and dried fruit in its liquid. Combine both mixtures and turn into a buttered 2 pint (1 litre) mould, basin or soufflé dish. Put into the Pot and cover with several thicknesses of kitchen paper towels. Use the aluminium foil 'lifter straps' as suggested on p. 126. Put the dish on a trivet in the Pot and pour around it ½ pt (300 ml) hot water. Cook on HIGH for 3 to 4 hours.
4. If you can turn the pudding out of the mould, do so—I have found it difficult for some reason.

Good with lightly sweetened whipped cream, but exceedingly rich.

Casserole cooking: preheat oven to Gas 4, 350°F, 180°C

As in Steps 1 and 3 (soaking fruit overnight first). Bake in buttered, fairly deep, round or oval casserole, uncovered, and set in baking tin with hot water halfway up sides of casserole. It will take about 1½–2 hours, and in fact if you want to lower the heat to Gas 2, 300°F, 150°C, you can leave it in the oven another hour without harm. Finish as in Step 4.

Baked Chocolate Custard

serves 4

¼ pt	rich milk	150 ml
¼ pt	single cream	150 ml
3 oz	dark plain chocolate	75 g
3 oz	sugar: half caster and half light soft brown	75 g
2	eggs (size 2) *or*	2
3	eggs (size 3–4)	3
	pinch of salt	
1 tsp	vanilla essence	1 tsp
1 tsp	almond essence (*optional*)	1 tsp

Electric slow cooker: preheat Pot on HIGH for 20 minutes

1. Heat the milk and cream in a small saucepan, to just below boiling-point, remove from the heat and stir in the broken-up chocolate and half the sugar. Stir until the chocolate melts. Whisk the eggs with the salt and the remaining sugar, vanilla and almond essence if used. Allow the hot milk mixture to cool slightly and gradually whisk in the egg/sugar mixture.
2. Butter a 1 pint (600 ml) mould (or 4 small ramekins if your Pot will accommodate them), and pour in the mixture. Cover with aluminium foil in a loose tent, as the pudding will rise slightly as it bakes. Use the aluminium foil 'lifter straps' as suggested on p. 126. Put the pudding(s) on a trivet in the Pot and pour around about ½ pt (300 ml) hot water. Cook on HIGH for 2½ to 3 hours, until a thin skewer pushed into the centre comes out clean.
3. Remove from Pot and cool for half an hour.

Serve warm or cold, but not hot. With a dish of lightly sweetened, whipped cream, this is an intensely luxurious pudding.

Casserole cooking: preheat oven to Gas 3, 325°F, 170°C

As in Steps 1 and 2; you may use 4 ramekins, or a casserole if that suits you better. Either way, set it or them in a deeper casserole of hot water, and bake about 1 hour, until a thin-bladed knife pushed into the centre comes out clean. Cool before turning out, then chill or gently reheat in oven at Gas 1, 250°F, 130°C.

Euphrates Pudding

serves 6 to 8

If your Pot or casserole is small, you may, of course, make a half-size pudding.

12 oz	sifted wholewheat flour	350 g
1 lev tsp	bicarbonate of soda	1 lev tsp
1 lev tsp	baking powder	1 lev tsp
6 oz	butter	175 g
4 oz	chopped dates	100 g
2 lev tsp	black treacle	2 lev tsp
¼ pt	and 2 additional tbs milk	150 ml

Electric slow cooker: preheat Pot on HIGH for 20 minutes

1. Grease a 3½ pint (2 litre) pudding basin and a piece of greaseproof paper to cover it. Sift the dry ingredients, pressing out any lumps in the bicarbonate of soda and making sure it is well mixed throughout. Rub in the butter, and toss the dates well to coat them. Add the treacle and enough milk to make a good dropping consistency. Put into the basin, cover with greaseproof paper, wind string around the basin to secure it, and make a loop over the top for a handle. Put on a trivet in the Pot, pour in boiling water halfway up, and cook on HIGH for 3 hours. Check occasionally that the water level is not dropping too much.
2. Remove carefully, protecting hands with oven gloves. Allow to cool slightly, then turn out.

Serve with a custard sauce, pouring cream or yoghurt. This is a very black, sweet pudding, and portions should be small. Any leftovers are very good cold, even 3 or 4 days later.

Casserole cooking: preheat oven to Gas 5, 375°F, 190°C

As in Steps 1 and 2, putting the pudding mixture into a casserole, covering it loosely with buttered foil, and setting it on a trivet in a deep baking dish with hot water three-quarters of the way up the casserole sides. Oven-steam about 2½ hours, adding more boiling water halfway through cooking time if necessary. This is the easiest way to steam a pudding that I know, and keeps the kitchen free of all that floating vapour.

Chocolate Piece Pudding

serves 4 to 6

4 oz	plain chocolate, cut into small pieces	100 g
6 oz	self-raising flour	175 g
1 lev tsp	baking powder	1 lev tsp
3 oz	fresh white or brown breadcrumbs	75 g
4 oz	suet, shredded	100 g
1	egg (size 3)	1
4 oz	light soft brown sugar	100 g
¼ pt	and 4 additional tbs milk	150 ml
	For the chocolate sauce:	
4 tbs	drinking chocolate	4 tbs
2 lev tbs	cornflour	2 lev tbs
½ pt	cold water	300 ml

Electric slow cooker: preheat Pot on HIGH for 20 minutes

1. Choose a pudding basin that will fit your Pot, grease it, and grease a piece of greaseproof paper to cover. Break the chocolate into small neat pieces. Sift together the flour and baking powder, cut in the suet and mix to the fine breadcrumb stage. Beat in the egg, sugar and milk and stir well. Add the chocolate pieces and breadcrumbs.
2. Put the mixture into the pudding basin and smooth the top. Make a pleat in the greaseproof paper, as this pudding will rise, and cover the basin. Tie securely with string, and make a string loop for a handle, or use the aluminium foil 'lifter straps' as suggested on p. 126. Put the basin on a trivet in the Pot and pour around it ½ pt (300 ml) hot water. Cook on HIGH for 3 hours.
3. Make chocolate sauce by blending drinking chocolate with cornflour, then gradually stirring in the cold water. Bring to boil in a saucepan, stirring, and cook until lightly thickened.
4. Remove the pudding carefully from the Pot and turn out on to a rather deep plate. Spoon over some of the chocolate sauce and pass the rest separately.

Casserole cooking: preheat oven to Gas 3, 325°F, 170°C

As in Steps 1 through 4, putting mixture into buttered casserole, with a piece of buttered greaseproof paper or foil cut to fit loosely over the top. Set casserole in a baking tin with 2 inches of hot, not boiling, water and bake 2 hours until centre of pudding is firm but not dry. Finish as in Steps 3 and 4 with chocolate sauce.

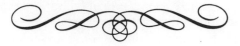

Oxford Pudding

serves 4

3 oz	white or fine brown flour	75 g
1 lev tsp	baking powder	1 lev tsp
1½ tbs	caster sugar	1½ tbs
2 oz	currants	50 g
3 oz	soft brown breadcrumbs	75 g
½ tsp	salt	½ tsp
3 oz	shredded suet	75 g
	rind of 2 oranges, grated	
2 tbs	orange juice	2 tbs
2	eggs (size 2)	2
6 tbs	orange marmalade	6 tbs

Electric slow cooker: preheat Pot on HIGH for 20 minutes

1. Sift the flour and baking powder together and toss currants in it. Mix together crumbs, sugar, salt, suet and orange rind, then stir into the flour mixture. Beat the eggs with orange juice and add to dry mixture. Stir well. The mixture should be of a good dropping consistency; if not, add a little more orange juice. Blend in 2 tablespoons of the marmalade.
2. Grease a 1½ pt (1 litre) pudding basin very well and spread the remaining marmalade in the bottom. Spoon in the mixture, smooth the top, cover with a pleated piece of greaseproof paper. Tie down well, wind string around and make a string loop across the top for a handle, for easier removing from the hot Pot. Or use the aluminium foil 'lifter straps' as suggested on p. 126.
3. Put on a trivet in the Pot, pour in boiling water halfway up the basin and steam for 3 to 4 hours on HIGH. Turn out, and serve with custard sauce.

Casserole cooking: preheat oven to Gas 5, 375°F, 190°C

As in Steps 1 and 2, using a deep straight-sided round casserole well-greased. Cover with a piece of greased foil, pleated to allow pudding to rise. Set in a deep baking tin and pour in boiling water nearly to the rim of the casserole. Oven-steam about 3 hours, adding more boiling water halfway through or whenever necessary.

This isn't the traditional pudding-shaped pudding with rounded top when it's turned out, but it tastes exactly the same and cuts into neat pieces. My first casserole-steamed pud was made the day I dropped my only deep pudding basin on a stone floor, and since then I have made endless ones in casseroles ranging from a 1 pt flowered French porcelain oven dish, to a huge brown glazed earthenware affair—Oxford pudding for 16, that was.

Orange Custard serves 4

A very rich custard.

	rind of half a Seville orange *or* of 1 small sweet orange and 1 small lemon	
	juice of 1 orange	
1 tbs	brandy	1 tbs
2 oz	caster sugar	50 g
2	egg yolks (size 1 or 2)	2
½ pt	double cream	300 ml

Electric slow cooker: preheat Pot on HIGH for 15 minutes

1. Thinly peel the orange rind, cut into slivers, boil in water to cover until tender. Drain well, mince very fine and mix with the brandy, orange juice, sugar and egg yolks. Heat the cream gently to just below boiling-point. Slowly stir in the orange mixture.
2. Pour into 4 small buttered ramekins, if your Pot is wide enough to hold them, or a buttered soufflé dish, cover with a layer of aluminium foil, and use the aluminium foil 'lifter straps' as suggested on p. 126 and put on a trivet or wire rack in the Pot. Pour

about ½ pt (300 ml) hot water around it. Cook on HIGH for 3 hours.

Serve warm or chilled, with perhaps a few slivers of preserved ginger.

Casserole cooking: preheat oven to Gas 4, 350°F, 180°C

As in Steps 1 and 2, using buttered individual ramekins, or an attractive glass, earthenware or glazed porcelain casserole. Set in a baking tin with hot, not boiling water, halfway up sides of casserole, and cook in centre of oven about 45 minutes until centre of pudding is just set. Remove from the hot water bath at once, and serve either warm (not hot) or chilled.

Bag Pudding serves 4

This is a pudding best served piping hot. It will be a rather odd shape, but a lovely soggy, fruity pud.

12 oz	fresh brown or white breadcrumbs	350 g
4 oz	dried mixed fruit and nuts	100 g
4 oz	butter, cut into pieces	100 g
¼ pt	milk	150 ml
6 oz	dark or light brown sugar	175 g
	an oven roasting bag	

Electric slow cooker: preheat Pot on HIGH for 20 minutes

Mix together all the ingredients, pour into the oven roasting bag, fasten the neck loosely and put on a trivet in the Pot. Pour around it about ½ pt (300 ml) boiling water. Cook on HIGH for 4 to 5 hours.

Turn the pudding out and serve with a sprinkling of brown sugar and double cream.

Casserole cooking: preheat oven to Gas 4, 350°F, 180°C

As in recipe above, putting all ingredients in an oven-roasting bag, fastening the neck not too tight and putting on a trivet in a casserole. Do not cover. Bake 1 hour, turn out and serve as above.

Light Christmas Pudding

(2×2 lb (900 g) puddings)

To be made well in advance of Christmas.

1 lb	fresh white breadcrumbs	450 g
1 tsp	powdered ginger	1 tsp
1 tsp	mixed spice	1 tsp
1 tsp	salt	1 tsp
8 oz	suet, shredded	225 g
8 oz	soft brown sugar	225 g
4 oz	mixed cut peel	100 g
4 oz	currants	100 g
4 oz	sultanas	100 g
1 lb	carrots, grated	450 g
5 tbs	milk	5 tbs
2 tbs	golden syrup	2 tbs

Electric slow cooker

1. Select from your collection 2 straight-sided tins which will fit together in your Pot. (In a wide Pot, perhaps 2 of those useful 2 lb marmalade tins.) Grease well. Mix together the dry ingredients, then blend the milk and syrup and stir into the first mixture. Stir well and leave to stand for an hour or so.
2. Preheat Pot on HIGH for 20 minutes. Divide the mixture between your two containers. Cover well with aluminium foil and use the aluminium foil 'lifter straps' as suggested on p. 126. Put the tins on a trivet in the Pot and pour around it 1 pt (600 ml) hot water. Cook on HIGH for 7 hours. Halfway through cooking time top up boiling water if necessary.
3. Remove and cool, then store in a cool dry place until you are ready to use.
4. To re-heat, preheat Pot on HIGH for 20 minutes, put the tins on a trivet; pour around it ½ pt (300 ml) boiling water and cook on HIGH for 2 to 3 hours.

Casserole cooking: preheat oven to Gas 5, 375°F, 190°C

You can make this in two 2 pt (1·2 l each) straight-sided casseroles which will fit, side by side, in a deep oven tin half-filled with boiling water. Pro-ceed as in Steps 1 and 2 above, covering each casserole with greased aluminium foil and a well-fitting lid. Cook in centre of oven 8 hours, topping up oven tin with boiling water from time to time. Obviously, this is a Christmas pudding to make when you are filling your oven with other dishes to bake at the same temperature. Wonderfully trouble-free, and the kitchen isn't steamy all day long. Admittedly, the shape is far from traditional. To reheat, steam another 2 hours, covered with a fresh piece of buttered foil or greaseproof paper.

Baked Apples with Mincemeat

serves 4

4	medium Bramley apples	4
8 tbs	mincemeat	8 tbs
1	large juicy orange	1
2 lev tbs	soft brown sugar, light or dark	2 lev tbs

Electric slow cooker: butter and preheat Pot on HIGH for 15 minutes

1. Wash and dry the apples. Take out the cores, cutting a hole straight through to the bottom. Make a shallow cut right round the circumference of each apple, to keep the skins from splitting. Mould a piece of aluminium foil under each. Fill the holes with mincemeat, pressing well down. Put into Pot.
2. Squeeze the orange and if necessary make up the juice to 4 fl oz (100 ml) with cold water. Stir in the sugar, bring to the boil and pour over the apples. Bake on LOW for 3 hours. Let the apples cool slightly and lift out carefully with a slotted spoon. Remove the foil.

There will be a lot of juice: spoon some over each apple. Serve lukewarm or cold, with pouring cream. They are wrinkled as an old woman's cheek, but the slow-cooked flavour is incomparable.

Casserole cooking: preheat oven to Gas 6, 400°F, 200°C

As in Steps 1 and 2, putting filled apples in a buttered shallow casserole. Cover, bake about 1 hour, basting once during cooking time.

Apricot Nut Pudding serves 6

1 lb	dried apricots	450 g
3 tbs	soft brown sugar	3 tbs
3 oz	melted butter	75 g
6 oz	dry brown breadcrumbs	175 g
4 oz	walnuts, chopped	100 g
	pinch of salt	

Electric slow cooker: preheat Pot on HIGH for 20 minutes

1. Wash apricots well, cover with boiling water and simmer with 1 tbs brown sugar about 10 minutes. Drain, reserving juice.
2. Mix remaining butter, sugar, dry breadcrumbs and walnuts, with salt. Arrange a layer of apricots in bottom of Pot, cover with crumb mixture, and repeat until all ingredients are used up. Pour on the apricot juice. Cook on HIGH 30 minutes, then on LOW for 4 hours. Serve warm or cold, with lightly whipped cream.

Casserole cooking: preheat oven to Gas 3, 325°F, 170°C

As in Steps 1 and 2 using a well-buttered casserole. Cook, covered, in oven about 1 hour, then uncover and cook 1 hour more. Serve as above.

Apples and Sultanas serves 4

This is probably the world's simplest pudding, which takes less than 3 minutes to prepare for the Pot.

3	large Bramley apples	3
	or	
4	smaller ones	4
4 oz	sultanas	100 g
1 tsp	butter	1 tsp

Electric slow cooker: preheat Pot on HIGH for 20 minutes

1. Peel and core the apples and cut them into uniform slices. As you cut them, drop them into a basin of cold water with a pinch of salt added. Then drain and put into a tightly lidded saucepan with no extra liquid. Cook on a high flame for

about 2 minutes until the apple slices begin to soften slightly.
2. Put into the Pot with the sultanas and butter, no liquid. Cover with aluminium foil. Cook on LOW for 2 to 3 hours.
3. Remove from the Pot, allow to cool, and dust with nutmeg if you like.
   Serve with single or double cream.

Casserole cooking: preheat oven to Gas 2, 300°F, 150°C

As in Steps 1 and 2, using a casserole with a tight-fitting lid. Cook in oven about 1½ hours, let cool, serve with cream (and freshly grated nutmeg if you like it).

Baked Bananas with Orange serves 4

4	firm ripe bananas	4
1½ tsp	cornflour	1½ tsp
3 fl oz	orange juice	75 ml
	or	
3 tbs	orange marmalade, slightly thinned with water	3 tbs
2 tbs	brown sugar	2 tbs
1 tbs	butter	1 tbs
3 oz	desiccated coconut	75 g

Electric slow cooker: butter Pot with half the butter and preheat on HIGH for 20 minutes

1. Cut the bananas crosswise, then lengthwise, so that you have 16 pieces. Combine the cornflour, orange juice or marmalade and half the sugar and bring to the boil in a saucepan. Put bananas into the Pot and pour on the mixture. Dot with the remaining butter and sprinkle on the rest of the brown sugar and the coconut.
2. Cook on LOW for 4 hours, until the sauce is thickened and glossy and the bananas are tender.

Casserole cooking: preheat oven to Gas 2, 300°F, 150°C

As in Step 1, buttering a shallow casserole, and cooking the bananas for about 2 hours until they are soft and the sauce is fairly thick.

Baked Custard

serves 4

For the electric slow cooker recipe I have tried baking this on LOW for 6 to 7 hours, starting with cold water in the Pot—not pre-heated. The result is softer and less firmly set, but quite delicious with poached plums or fruit compote.

4	eggs (size 1 or 2)	4
1 oz	caster or light brown sugar	25 g
1 pt	milk, heated to just below boiling-point	600 ml
½ tsp	vanilla essence or rum	½ tsp
	pinch of salt	

Electric slow cooker: preheat Pot on HIGH for 20 minutes

1. Whisk the eggs lightly, beat in sugar, salt and vanilla essence, then gradually whisk in the milk. Use only a scant pint, not more.
2. Strain into a buttered 1 pint soufflé dish or 4 buttered ramekins if your Pot is wide enough to hold them. Cover tightly with aluminium foil and use the aluminium foil 'lifter straps' as suggested on p. 126. Put the pudding(s) on a trivet in the Pot and pour around about ½ pt (300 ml) hot water. Bake on HIGH for 3 hours, until set.
   Serve with a dusting of nutmeg.

Casserole cooking: preheat oven to Gas 3, 325°F, 170°C

Proceed as for Baked Chocolate Custard (p. 135), baking in a water-bath for about 45 minutes at the above temperature, or at Gas 2, 300°F, 150°C, for 1 hour 45 minutes to 2 hours.

Danish Apricot Cream

serves 4

4 oz	very good apricot jam	100 g
3	eggs (size 3)	3
¾ pt	milk	400 ml
1½ oz	and 1 extra tsp caster sugar	40 g
½ tsp	vanilla essence	½ tsp
4 fl oz	double cream	100 ml

Electric slow cooker: preheat Pot on HIGH for 20 minutes

1. Butter a soufflé dish and spread the jam evenly over its base. Break two of the eggs into a basin. Separate the third egg and beat its yolk with the other two. Reserve the white. Heat the milk in a saucepan until the surface just shivers; it must not boil. Cool slightly and add the 1½ oz (40 g) caster sugar and the vanilla essence. Stir gradually into the eggs. Strain into the soufflé dish.
2. Cover with aluminium foil and use the aluminium foil 'lifter straps' as suggested on p. 126. Put the dish on a trivet in the Pot and pour around it ½ pt (300 ml) hot water. Cook on HIGH for 2½ to 3 hours. Remove carefully and allow to cool completely.
3. Whisk cream and 1 teaspoon caster sugar with the reserved egg white, and pile in on top of the pudding.

Casserole cooking: preheat oven to Gas 5, 375°F, 190°C

As in Steps 1 and 2, but set soufflé dish into baking tin. Pour in hot water halfway up dish, cover securely with foil, and cook about 1 hour. Finish as in Step 3 after it has cooled.

Rum Raisin Rice

serves 4

1½ pt	milk	750 ml
4 oz	long-grain rice, parboiled	100 g
3	eggs (size 3)	3
2 tsp	vanilla essence	2 tsp
4 oz	sultanas or raisins	100 g
2 oz	caster sugar	50 g
1½ tsp	lemon rind, grated	1½ tsp
	nutmeg, freshly grated	
2 tbs	butter	2 tbs
3 tbs	dark rum	3 tbs

Electric slow cooker: butter Pot and preheat on HIGH for 20 minutes

1. Heat milk to just below boiling-point, pour over rice. Blend together the eggs, vanilla, sultanas, sugar and lemon rind, and mix into the rice.
2. Put into the Pot and sprinkle with nutmeg, as

much or as little as you like. Shave the cold butter in flakes over the surface. Cook on LOW for 4 to 6 hours; it can if necessary stand for another hour in the turned-off Pot.

3. Turn out in a serving-dish, and stir the rum through it with a fork.

Serve moderately warm, not hot. It can be accompanied by lightly sweetened, stiffly whipped cream, but this makes a very rich pudding indeed.

Casserole cooking: preheat oven to Gas 2, 300°F, 150°C

As in Steps 1 and 2, using a largish casserole attractive enough to put on the table: put everything in, cover, cook 2½ hours. Finish as in Step 3.

Brazilian Pudding serves 4 to 6

¾ pt	milk	450 ml
4 oz	fine dry breadcrumbs	100 g
2 tbs	butter	2 tbs
4 oz	Brazil nuts, coarsely chopped	100 g
2	eggs (size 3)	2
4 oz	light soft brown sugar	100 g

Electric slow cooker: preheat Pot on HIGH for 20 minutes

1. Bring the milk to the boil, stir in the breadcrumbs and butter and allow to cool. Lightly toast the nuts under grill (watch them, they burn easily). Whisk together the eggs and sugar, add the nuts and mix into the milk/breadcrumbs.
2. Heavily butter a pudding mould or soufflé dish—if you have a wide, shallow Pot, you might use 6 ramekins. Put the mixture into the mould or cups. Cover with aluminium foil and use the aluminium foil 'lifter straps' as suggested on p. 126. Put the mould or cups on a trivet in the Pot and pour around it ½ pt (300 ml) hot water. Cook on HIGH for 3 hours.
3. Carefully remove the mould or cups and allow to cool for about 10 minutes, then unmould.

This can be served warm or cold, as you like, with thin pouring cream; or with a sauce made of liquidized, cooked dried apricots, which have a miraculous affinity with the Brazil-nut flavour.

Casserole cooking: preheat oven to Gas 3, 325°F, 170°C

As in Steps 1 and 2, cooking in casserole covered with aluminium foil for about 1¾ hours, until a skewer thrust into the centre comes out almost dry.

Soft Apple Crumble serves 4

This will not be a crunchy apple crumble, as the topping is soft, but the apples cook to a wine colour and flavour. In a Pot with a non-removable casserole, you can make this in a buttered soufflé dish set on a trivet, with about ½ pt (300 ml) boiling water around the dish.

5	large Bramley apples, peeled and thinly sliced	5
4 oz	soft brown sugar	100 g
2 oz	white or fine brown flour	50 g
2 oz	porridge oats	50 g
1 tsp	mixed spice	1 tsp
3 oz	butter, softened	75 g
	pinch of salt	

Electric slow cooker: butter and preheat Pot on HIGH for 20 minutes

1. As you peel and slice the apples, drop them into a basin of lightly salted cold water. Then drain, put into a saucepan, cover and cook on a medium heat for about 2 minutes, until the apple slices are just beginning to soften.
2. Mix the flour, oats, salt, brown sugar, mixed spice and butter, to a crumbly stage. Put the apple slices into the Pot, cover with the crumble mixture, lay a sheet of aluminium foil on top and cook on LOW for 5 hours.

Casserole cooking: preheat oven to Gas 2, 300°F, 150°C

As in Steps 1 and 2, using a heavy and fairly shallow casserole, and covering it loosely with aluminium foil. Bake 2 hours, then uncover, turn up oven heat to Gas 4, 350°F, 180°C, until top is golden but not crunchy.

Ritz Compote

serves 8

1 lb	dried figs	450 g
1 lb	dried apricots	450 g
8 fl oz	dry red wine	225 ml
8 oz	caster sugar	225 g
1 tbs	lemon rind, grated	1 tbs
	For the sauce:	
4 tbs	milk	4 tbs
¼ pt	double cream	150 ml
1	egg yolk	1
2 tbs	caster sugar	2 tbs
¼ tsp	vanilla essence	¼ tsp

Electric slow cooker: preheat Pot on HIGH for 20 minutes

1. Pour boiling water on to the well washed figs and apricots and let them soak until they begin to look plump. Drain well. Put into a saucepan with the wine, sugar, lemon rind and about half a teacup of boiling water, bring to the boil and put into the Pot. Cook on HIGH for 30 minutes, then on LOW for 3 hours, until the fruit is tender. Cool.
2. To make the sauce: bring the milk and half the cream slowly to the boil. Whisk the egg yolk with the sugar, stir in a tablespoon of the cream mixture, then gradually add the rest, stirring. Cook on top of a double boiler until the mixture coats the back of a spoon. Cool, then chill.
3. When ready to serve, whisk the remaining cream and vanilla essence and fold into the chilled sauce. Let each person take as much sauce as wished—it's rich and rather filling.

Casserole cooking: preheat oven to Gas 2, 300°F, 150°C

As in Step 1, putting ingredients in a fairly large, deep casserole with well-fitting lid. Cook in oven about 1½ hours until fruit is soft but not mushy. Finish as in Steps 2 and 3 above.

Coconut Custard

serves 4

¾ pt	milk	400 ml
3	eggs, lightly beaten (size 3)	3
3 oz	caster sugar	75 g
1 tsp	vanilla essence	1 tsp
	good pinch of salt	
4 oz	desiccated coconut	100 g
	nutmeg, freshly grated	

Electric slow cooker: preheat Pot on HIGH for 20 minutes

1. Heat the milk in a saucepan to just below boiling-point and cool slightly. Whisk together eggs, sugar, vanilla and salt. Whisk a little of the milk into this mixture, then beat it all back into the milk. Lightly toast 1 oz (25 g) of the coconut under the grill, and set aside. Mix the remaining coconut into the milk mixture.
2. Pour into a buttered soufflé dish or 4 smaller ramekins if your Pot is wide enough to hold them. Cover with aluminium foil and use the aluminium foil 'lifter straps' as suggested on p. 126. Put the pudding(s) on a trivet in the Pot and pour around it ½ pt (300 ml) hot water. Cook on HIGH for 3 hours.
3. Remove from the Pot and sprinkle the top of the pudding with toasted coconut and grated nutmeg.

Serve warm or chilled, but not hot.

Casserole cooking: preheat oven to Gas 3, 325°F, 170°C

As in Steps 1, 2 and 3 above, pouring the custard mixture into 4 buttered ramekins or a soufflé dish. In either case, stand it or them in a baking tin with about 2 inches of hot, not boiling water, and bake for about 45 minutes for ramekins, 1 hour for larger casserole or soufflé dish. The custard should be set and firm to a light touch of the finger. Finish as in Step 3.

Blackberry and Apple Pudding

serves 4

1 lb	blackberries	450 g
4 oz	caster sugar	100 g
1 lb	apples, peeled, cored and sliced	450 g
	For the topping:	
4 oz	porridge oats	100 g
4 oz	light soft brown sugar	100 g
3 oz	butter, softened	75 g

Electric slow cooker: butter and preheat Pot on HIGH for 20 minutes

1. Wash the blackberries well, put into a saucepan with caster sugar (do not add any water) and cook on a high heat for about 5 minutes until just soft. Press through a Mouli-légumes or a sieve, to remove the pips. Peel and slice the apples and drop them into a basin of salted water; then drain and cook on high flame without any added water until they just begin to soften.
2. Put a layer of blackberry purée in the Pot, then a layer of apples and add the rest of the purée.
3. Make a crumble topping of softened butter, brown sugar and oats, and press it thickly on to the fruit. Cover tightly with aluminium foil, and cook on LOW for 4 to 5 hours.

Casserole cooking: preheat oven to Gas 4, 350°F, 180°C

As in Steps 1, 2 and 3, making layers of blackberry purée and apples, ending with crumble mixture, in a rather deep casserole. Bake, uncovered, in centre of oven about 1 hour, for a crunchy top: or for 2 hours at Gas 2, 300°F, 150°C, with aluminium foil over top of casserole—a soft, mellow autumn pud.

This and That

Much best to make the various hot punches that follow, either in the electric Pot or simmering on the top of your cooker! But do consider casserole cooking for all the tomato sauces (Bolognese, Stracotto, and so on), and the chutneys and marmalades and butters. Long, slow oven simmering develops flavours wonderfully, and cooking without watching and stirring does make life so much simpler. The heavier the casserole the less worry. Use every corner of your oven when you can: the slow-cooking apple butter could usefully cook alongside a three-hour casserole meant for a main dish. The electric Pot, of course, is completely 'cooking without looking': infinitely useful if you are doing sauces, preserves and so on for bottling or freezing.

Cider Punch

2 pts	dry cider	1 gen 1
4 oz	caster sugar	100 g
12	whole cloves	12
1	stick cinnamon	1
8	allspice berries	8

Electric slow cooker: preheat Pot on HIGH for 20 minutes

Combine everything in a saucepan, bring to the boil and pour into the Pot, stirring until the sugar dissolves. Simmer on LOW for 2 hours and strain into warmed glasses. Keep the punch warm in the Pot, on LOW.

Glögg

This is a powerful drink, served at Scandinavian Christmas parties: be not deceived by its sweetness.

1	bottle gin or vodka	1
2	bottles heavy red wine	2
4 oz	caster sugar	100 g
3 oz	raisins or sultanas	75 g
1	stick cinnamon	1
6	cloves	6
	peel of 1 lemon, thinly shredded	

Electric slow cooker: preheat Pot on HIGH for 20 minutes

1. Pour half the gin and all the wine into a big saucepan, with the dried fruit and sugar. Tie the cinnamon stick, lemon peel and cloves up in a bit of gauze (a strip of wide surgical gauze bandage does the trick), and add. Bring slowly to the boil and put into the Pot. Allow to cook on LOW for 2 to 3 hours.
2. Remove the spices, add the remaining half-bottle of spirits and instantly set it alight.

Serve in *heated* punch cups with handles. The Pot serves wonderfully—still on its LOW setting—to keep the Glögg warm as long as the party lasts.

Apple Warmer

This recipe is non-alcoholic—for a party, you can add 8 fl oz (225 ml) Calvados, or inexpensive brandy, 15 minutes before serving.

4 pts	apple juice	2·2 l
6 oz	light brown sugar	175 g
1 tsp	allspice berries	1 tsp
3	sticks cinnamon	3
	nutmeg, grated	

Electric slow cooker: preheat Pot on HIGH for 20 minutes

Heat 1 pt (600 ml) apple juice with the sugar, stirring, until the sugar dissolves. Put into the Pot with the remaining apple juice. Tie the spices up in a muslin bag, and add. Heat on LOW for 2 to 3 hours. Remove the spice bag, grate on nutmeg and serve in hot mugs.

Portobello

2	lemons	2
2	cloves	2
2 pts	port	1 gen l
1 pt	boiling water	600 ml
1 tsp	mixed spice	1 tsp
2 oz	lump sugar	50 g

Electric slow cooker: preheat Pot on HIGH for 20 minutes

1. Stud one of the lemons with the cloves, and cook it for about 10 minutes with the boiling water and the spice.
2. Then add the port to the lemon-and-spiced boiling water and heat to simmering-point. Rub the lump sugar over the skin of the second lemon, squeeze the juice and mix with the sugar. Pour the port mixture into the Pot and add the sugar and lemon. Turn the Pot to LOW and keep it warm until you are ready to serve, in warmed, footed glasses, or in punch cups with handles.

Kate Crosby's Tomato Juice

This is an excellent way to use up a glut of tomatoes.

12	large ripe tomatoes	12
2	celery stalks	2
1	diced carrot	1
1	large green pepper, de-seeded and sliced	1
	salt and pepper	
1 tbs	sugar	1 tbs
	dash of Worcestershire sauce	

Electric slow cooker: preheat Pot on HIGH for 20 minutes

Wash but do not dry the tomatoes. Take out the hard central core. Put the tomatoes into the Pot with the vegetables and seasoning. Cook on LOW for 6 hours, then sieve, whizz in a blender or press through a Mouli-Légumes and then sieve. Cool, and bottle.

Increase the other vegetables but not the tomatoes, and you will have a very good spicy mixed vegetable juice.

Casserole cooking: I have to say that I have never made this in a casserole in the oven. My friend Mrs Crosby (who grows and cooks her own) did this superb tomato juice in her electric Pot, and neither of us has ever done it any other way. I should think, though, that it could be done in a casserole in an oven about Gas 3, 325°F, 170°C, for about 3 hours, or at even lower heat and a longer time. This is only a guess.

Stracotto

serves 6 with spaghetti

In Italian, this means something like 'very well cooked' or 'extra cooked'. A good change from Bolognese or Marinara sauce for spaghetti. It can be made well in advance, cooled quickly and refrigerated, then reheated while spaghetti is cooking. It freezes well.

1 lb	lean beef	450 g
4 oz	butter	100 g
2	medium onions, finely minced	2
1	large celery stalk, finely chopped	1
1	large carrot, finely chopped	1
	big handful parsley, minced	
2 oz	mushrooms, chopped	50 g
4 fl oz (8 fl oz)	concentrated tinned consommé	100 ml (225 ml)
$\frac{1}{4}$ pt	Marsala or sweet sherry	150 ml
2 tsp	grated lemon rind	2 tsp
1 tsp	salt	1 tsp
	good pinch of cayenne	
$\frac{1}{2}$ tsp	black pepper	$\frac{1}{2}$ tsp

Electric slow cooker: preheat Pot on HIGH for 20 minutes

1. Chop the meat very finely with a sharp knife, or put through the coarse blade of a mincer. Heat the butter in a large heavy frying-pan, add the meat, cook gently but do not brown. Stir in the onions, celery, carrot and parsley. Stir over high heat for 5 minutes. Add the mushrooms, consommé, Marsala and lemon rind. Season and bring to the boil.
2. Put into the Pot and cook on LOW for 7 hours, or on HIGH for 4 hours, in which case check it occasionally and add a little more consommé or Marsala if it looks dry.

Casserole cooking: preheat oven to Gas 2, 300°F, 150°C

As in Step 1, increasing concentrated consommé to 8 fl oz (225 ml) and putting all ingredients into large casserole with tight-fitting lid. Simmer $3\frac{1}{2}$ hours; after 2 hours glance in, and top up with a very little more liquid if it's too dry.

Bolognese Sauce

This quantity is sufficient for 4 average servings of pasta.

8 oz	lean beef, minced	225 g
1 tsp	oil	1 tsp
4	medium onions, finely minced	4
7 fl oz	beef stock	200 ml
2 tbs	tomato purée	2 tbs
1 tsp	basil	1 tsp
	salt and pepper	
1 tbs	cornflour	1 tbs
2 tbs	*Chinese oyster sauce *(optional)*	2 tbs

Electric slow cooker: preheat Pot on HIGH for 20 minutes

1. Fry the minced beef in the hot oil in a frying-pan until it just loses its red colour. Stir in the onions and cook gently for about 5 minutes. Add the stock and bring to the boil. Add the tomato purée, oyster sauce, if used, and seasonings, and put into the Pot. Cook on HIGH for 2 hours, then on LOW for 3 hours.
2. Half an hour before serving, slake the cornflour with a little cold water and stir in well. Let the sauce cook on until thickened.

   * This recipe is much 'beefier'-tasting with the Chinese oyster sauce; if you have none to hand, you may want to add more salt.

Casserole cooking: preheat oven to Gas 4, 350°F, 180°C

As in Steps 1 and 2, putting all ingredients except cornflour in a heavy casserole with well-fitting lid. Cook in oven 2½ hours; it may be quite thick at the end of this time but if not, add cornflour as in Step 2, and cook another 10 minutes in oven.

Super Tomato Sauce

This is delicious with fish and can be served hot or cold. Try a teaspoon in any simple fish dish; or stir 2 tablespoons into a big pot of mussels. Very good with fishcakes, or even with toasted cheese sandwiches.

2 lb	ripe tomatoes, or their equivalent in tinned Italian peeled tomatoes	900 g
¼ pt (½ pt)	white wine or cider	150 ml (300 ml)
	juice of 1 lemon	
1 tbs	oil (soya or groundnut)	1 tbs
2	garlic cloves, crushed	2
2 tbs	butter	2 tbs
2 tbs	anchovy essence *or*	2 tbs
2	pounded anchovy fillets	2
1 tsp	basil	1 tsp
2 tbs	parsley, chopped	2 tbs
	horseradish sauce	

Electric slow cooker: preheat Pot on HIGH for 20 minutes

1. In an *enamel* saucepan, bring the tomatoes, lemon juice, wine and oil to the boil. In a heavy frying-pan, heat the butter and sweat the garlic with the anchovy essence until well blended. Stir into the tomato mixture and put into the Pot. Cook on LOW for 8 to 10 hours or overnight. (The sauce can be prepared up to this point, then quickly cooled and frozen, to be reheated over a medium heat before the herbs and horseradish are added.)
2. Stir in the basil and parsley and cook on HIGH for another 30 minutes. Taste for seasoning, and stir in as much or as little horseradish sauce as you like. Pour into a basin, and leave to stand for an hour so that the flavours blend.

Casserole cooking: preheat oven to Gas 2, 300°F, 150°C

As in Step 1, using a large heavy casserole, and increasing wine or cider to about a scant ½ pint (300 ml). Simmer in oven 4 hours, stirring once in a while, and continue to cook until it is rich and thick—perhaps another hour, depending on your oven. Finish as in Step 2.

Concentrated Tomato Purée
makes about 1 pint (600 ml)

This is highly concentrated. Use it to enrich a not very interesting spaghetti sauce, stir a tablespoon into mayonnaise for cold fish salad, or use it to season a dish of cooked white beans for a good Mediterranean flavour.

28 oz	tin Italian peeled tomatoes, or their equivalent in very ripe fresh tomatoes	800 g
1½–2 tbs	olive oil	1½–2 tbs
1	large onion, finely minced	1
2	large garlic cloves crushed with 1 tsp salt	2
1 tsp	grated orange rind	1 tsp
	pepper	
1 tsp	mixed herbs: oregano, basil, thyme	1 tsp
1	bay leaf	1
2 tsp	light brown sugar	2 tsp
	dash of hot pepper sauce	

Electric slow cooker: preheat Pot on HIGH for 20 minutes

1. Heat the oil in an enamel saucepan and simmer the onion and garlic/salt until soft and translucent. Add the tomatoes, orange peel, herbs, sugar and some freshly ground black pepper. Bring to the boil and put into the Pot. Cook on LOW for 10 hours or overnight. It should reduce to a thickish paste; if too liquid, turn the Pot to HIGH and continue to cook. Add a little hot pepper sauce, to your taste, and check for seasoning.
2. Put into hot sterilized jars with a tight screw top, or freeze in ice cube trays, then turn out the cubes of purée into a plastic bag and return to freezer.

Casserole cooking: preheat oven to Gas 1, 250°F, 130°C

As in Step 1, putting all ingredients in a medium-size casserole with a sheet of foil under the lid to make an airtight seal. Simmer at least 5 hours, or longer if you can, until it is thick and dark. Stir a few times during the cooking process, and seal again. Finish as in Step 2.

Barbecue Sauce
makes about 1 pint (600 ml)

This will keep well in the fridge for a month or 6 weeks.

14 oz	bottle tomato ketchup	400 g
4 oz	ripe tomatoes, coarsely chopped	100 g
4 dsp	wine vinegar	4 dsp
2 oz	dark brown sugar	50 g
2 tbs	lemon juice	2 tbs
2 tbs	Worcestershire sauce	2 tbs
2 tbs	made mustard	2 tbs
1 tsp	dry mustard	1 tsp
2 tbs	oil	2 tbs
1	garlic clove, minced	1
	good pinch of salt, and pepper	

Electric slow cooker: preheat Pot on HIGH for 15 minutes

Combine all the ingredients in a large *enamel* saucepan, bring quickly to the boil, tip into the Pot and cook on LOW for 5 hours. Bottle in clean, sterilized jars.

Casserole cooking: preheat oven to Gas 3, 325°F, 170°C

As above, putting all ingredients in a large casserole and adding about ¼ pt (150 ml) boiling water. Cover, simmer in oven 3 hours, stirring from time to time. Or: cook at Gas 1, 250°F, 103°C, for about 5–6 hours, if you prefer; stirring two or three times if you are near the cooker.

Tomato Chutney

makes about 6 lb (about 3 kg)

This is a recipe to cook overnight or all day if you are following the Pot recipe. It is rather like the American 'chili sauce', a misnomer for a mild, spicy, thick sauce which is not at all hot. Very good with cold beef, cold lamb, cheese, or hamburgers.

3 lb	ripe tomatoes, peeled and chopped	1½ kg
4	large firm cooking apples, peeled and chopped	4
3	large onions, finely minced	3
6 oz	sultanas or raisins	175 g
1 lb	light brown sugar	450 g
1 pt	cider vinegar	600 ml
2	cloves	2
	pinch of cayenne	
2 tsp	salt	2 tsp
1 tsp	dry mustard	1 tsp
1 tsp	ginger	1 tsp
½ tsp	coriander seeds	½ tsp

Electric slow cooker: preheat Pot on HIGH for 20 minutes

Put everything into a big *enamel* saucepan, bring to the boil, pour into the Pot and cook on LOW for 10 to 12 hours, or overnight, until thick. Bottle and seal as for any chutney.

Casserole cooking: preheat oven to Gas 1, 250°F, 130°C

As in recipe above, simmering in a large casserole with a piece of foil under lid, for a perfect seal, about 6 hours. Stir a few times while it cooks, and bottle as you would any chutney. You may want to add about ¼ pt (150 ml) boiling water halfway through cooking time, if it seems to be cooking down too much.

Apple Butter

makes about 3 lb (1½ kg)

This is a recipe to make when someone gives you a lot of windfalls, or when there is a glut of apples in the market. It takes a lot of fruit to make a fairly small amount of apple butter—just as well, perhaps, as fruit butters don't keep as well as marmalades and jams. Very good on scones and toast and especially good on pancakes.

4 lb	apples, washed and cut up	1·8 kg
3 pts (4 pts)	half water and half cider	1·5 l (2·4 l)
12 oz	brown sugar for each pound of apple pulp	350 g
½ tsp *	powdered cloves	½ tsp
3 inch *	piece whole cinnamon	3 inch
1 tsp	salt	1 tsp

Electric slow cooker: preheat Pot on HIGH for 20 minutes

1. Cut away any brown spots on the apples, do not peel or core. Bring the water and cider to the boil and pour over the apples in Pot. Cook on LOW for 10 to 12 hours or overnight. Sieve, weigh the pulp and add the recommended amount of sugar. Stir in the spices and salt and return to the washed-out Pot. Cook on HIGH for 3 hours.
2. Ladle out (it will be very hot, so be extremely careful), into sterilized jars and pot as for marmalade.

   * The amount of spices you use is to your own taste: you may like to add allspice, mace or nutmeg in addition to the essential clove and cinnamon.

Casserole cooking: preheat oven to Gas 2, 300°F, 150°C

As in Steps 1 and 2, increasing water/cider mixture to about 4 pts (2·4 l). Cook in oven, stirring occasionally, about 5 hours. Then sieve, weigh pulp, add recommended amount of sugar, spices and salt, and cook in oven another hour. With a flameproof casserole, and boiling rings that will stay on a steady simmer, you can do this on your cooker top in half the time; but keep an eye on it, apple pulp catches and burns easily.

Tomato Cumin Chutney

makes about 1½ lb (about 675 g)

This is sweet, hot and spicy. You can make it hotter, with more crushed red pepper flakes, but don't use more than the given quantity of mustard seeds.

28 oz	tin Italian peeled tomatoes	800 g
1 tsp	oil	1 tsp
½ tsp	whole cumin seeds	½ tsp
¼ tsp	whole mustard seed	¼ tsp
½ tsp	whole allspice	½ tsp
¼ tsp	ground nutmeg	¼ tsp
	good pinch of Italian red pepper flakes	
½	lemon cut into pieces	½
3 oz	sultanas	75 g
3 oz	caster or granulated sugar	75 g

Electric slow cooker: preheat Pot on HIGH for 20 minutes

1. Heat the oil in an enamel saucepan and sauté the seeds until they begin to pop, stirring so that they don't burn. Crush the allspice and add, then pour in all the other ingredients except the sugar. Bring to the boil, simmer for 15 minutes, stirring frequently. Add the sugar and put into the Pot. Cook on HIGH for 2 hours, then on LOW for 4 hours, until thick.
2. Remove from the Pot, allow to cool, bottle and seal as for any chutney.

Casserole cooking: preheat oven to Gas 3, 325°F, 170°C

As in steps 1 and 2. Cook in a well-lidded casserole for about 3–4 hours, until thick, stirring two or three times so that it doesn't catch. Add about ¼ pt (150 ml) boiling water after first hour of cooking. Taste for seasoning after 3 hours, and add some salt if you like. Finish as in Step 2.

Davenport Chutney

makes about 4 lb (about 2 kg)

I am indebted for the original of this recipe to Philippa Davenport's cookery column.

8 oz	dates, stoned and chopped	225 g
8 oz	dried figs, chopped	225 g
2 lb	cooking apples, peeled and chopped	900 g
1 lb	onions, minced	450 g
2 tbs	mustard seed	2 tbs
1 lb	brown sugar	450 g
2 tbs	coriander seed	2 tbs
1 tbs	salt	1 tbs
1	saltspoon black pepper	1
½ tsp	ground cinnamon	½ tsp
1 pt	tarragon vinegar	150 ml

Electric slow cooker: preheat Pot on HIGH for 20 minutes

1. Put everything together in an *enamel* saucepan, bring to the boil and put into the Pot, giving it a good stir. Cook on HIGH for 1 hour, then on LOW for 4 hours; or on LOW for 10 hours or overnight.
2. Stir well. Pot in hot, sterilized jars, cover with greaseproof paper lids and seal. This will keep in a cool larder for at least 3 months.

Casserole cooking: preheat oven to Gas 3, 325°F, 170°C

As in Step 1, after bringing it all to the boil, tip into a heavy casserole and simmer, uncovered, for about 1½ hours. Stir once in a while, make sure it isn't catching, and add a little bit of boiling water if it seems to be thickening too much. Finish as in Step 2.

Tomato-Lemon Marmalade

makes about 2½ lb (1 gen kg)

An American recipe with a strange, sweet, piquant taste, a pleasant change from orange marmalade for breakfast, and interesting served with cold ham or tongue.

2½ lb	ripe tomatoes, or their equivalent in Italian tinned peeled tomatoes, well drained	1 gen kg
1	large juicy lemon, thinly sliced	1
1 tsp	ground ginger	1 tsp
2 lb	light soft brown or granulated sugar	900 g

Electric slow cooker: preheat Pot on HIGH for 15 minutes

1. Skin and roughly chop the tomatoes. Put into a large *enamel* saucepan with the lemon and ginger. Bring to the boil, put into the Pot, cook on LOW for 8 hours or overnight.
2. Stir in the sugar, and in an enamel saucepan, bring to the boil and boil rapidly to setting point (just like marmalade, put a blob of the mixture on to a cold plate, put in the fridge for 5 minutes, if it wrinkles when you touch it with a finger it's ready to set). Pot in hot sterilized jars.

Casserole cooking: preheat oven to Gas 3, 325°F, 170°C

As in Step 1, putting boiling tomatoes, lemon and ginger in a preheated heavy casserole. Cover and simmer in oven for 3½ hours. Stir in sugar, pour into enamel saucepan and finish as in Step 2.

Beurre Manié

Equal quantities of softened butter and flour, worked together on a saucer into a smooth paste. To thicken a mixture in the Pot, stir in lumps about the size of an olive, with control set on HIGH. This isn't the easiest thing in the world to do, but it does give a perfect texture. An alternative method: tip all the sauce, or as much as you can manage, from the Pot into a saucepan, set it over a medium heat and stir the bits of *beurre manié* in, little by little, until it's all smoothly thickened, then stir back into the Pot.

Homemade Browning

4 oz	caster sugar	100 g
¼ pt	boiling water	150 ml

In a small, heavy saucepan, on a low heat, let the sugar dissolve until it is dark brown but not burnt. Stir once in a while. Take off the heat, cool completely, and very, very slowly add the boiling water, stirring with a long-handled wooden spoon. It is splashy and hot and a drop of it burns your hand badly. Stir until completely dissolved, and cool and store in a plastic 'squeezy' bottle, to add drop by drop to give colour to a pale dish. It is not sweet.

Porridge

serves 4

4 oz	oatmeal, the coarser the better	100 g
1½ pts	boiling water	750 ml
	*salt to taste	

Electric slow cooker: preheat Pot on HIGH for 20 minutes

Put the oatmeal into the Pot with the salt and pour on the boiling water (make sure your Pot is really hot). Stir well and cook on LOW overnight.

* The amount of salt to use is such a touchy subject that I hesitate to specify; if you like your porridge as in Scotland where it is customarily eaten sprinkled with salt, not sugar and cream, you may want to under-salt it in the basic cooking.

Casserole cooking: preheat oven to Gas 1, 200°F, 130°C

Rinse out casserole with boiling water, put in oatmeal, salt and boiling water as above, and cook 2 hours or as much longer as suits you. Obviously, there's no point in doing this with quick-cooking oatmeal, and the length of time you slow-cook it will depend largely on your own convenience, when your family breakfasts, and indeed what kind of oats you are using. If your oven can be set, steadily, as low as Gas ¼–½, about 225°F, 110°C, you can cook your porridge all night long, in which case increase boiling water to about 2 pts (1·2 l).

Cheese Monkey
serves 3 to 4

Why 'Monkey'—who knows? This will rise beautifully, but will fall when you take it out—which doesn't affect the flavour at all. It is more filling than a soufflé, not so airy.

8 fl oz	milk	225 ml
6 oz	cheddar cheese, grated	175 g
1 tbs	flour	1 tbs
2	eggs (size 3) separated	2
½ tsp	salt	½ tsp
½ tsp	dry mustard	½ tsp
	good pinch of cayenne	

Electric slow cooker: preheat Pot on HIGH for 20 minutes

1. Heat the milk in a saucepan but do not boil; melt the cheese in it over a low heat. Mix about 3 tablespoons of this mixture with the flour until smooth, then blend this well into the remaining milk/cheese. Allow to cool slightly, add the well beaten egg yolks and seasoning. Whisk the egg whites stiffly and lightly cut them into the mixture.
2. Put into a well buttered soufflé dish or casserole that will fit into your Pot, cover with a loose tent of aluminium foil to allow room for the mixture to rise, and use the aluminium foil 'lifter straps' as suggested on p. 126. Set on a trivet. Pour boiling water around the dish to a depth of about 2 inches. Cook on HIGH for 2½ to 3 hours.

Casserole cooking: preheat oven to Gas 4, 350°F, 180°C

As in Steps 1 and 2, using a well-buttered casserole with straight sides, about 7–8 inches (200 mm) in diameter. Bake about 45 minutes at the above heat. A somewhat different, but very pleasant dish results if you cook it 1½ hours at Gas 2, 300°F, 150°C. Increase heat to about Gas 6, 400°F, 200°C, to brown the top.

Roux

8 oz	butter	225 g
8 oz	flour, sifted with 1 tsp salt and ½ tsp pepper	225 g

In a small saucepan melt the butter but do not let it 'oil'. Very gradually, stirring all the time, mix in the seasoned flour. Stir on low heat until completely blended and smooth, then put into the top half of a double boiler over simmering water, stir again, cover and allow to cook for half an hour, stirring once in a while. (If it lumps despite all this titivating, push it through a sieve or liquidize it.) Cool and store in a tin with an airtight cover; refrigerate—it will keep for at least a fortnight—or freeze. Add to the hot liquid in the Pot as needed to thicken, stirring in a tablespoon at a time, with control set on HIGH.

Scone Mix

It is endlessly useful to have this on hand to make a quick topping for steak and kidney stew, or vegetable ragoût, or chicken fricassee. I make up rather a large batch of dry scone mixture, and store it in an airtight tin (the kind powdered milk comes in, or a well-scrubbed coffee tin).

1 lb	plain flour (white or finely sifted wholewheat)	450 g
2 tsp	bicarbonate of soda	2 tsp
4 tsp	cream of tartar (or, if you prefer, 6 rounded tsp baking powder)	4 tsp
½ tsp	salt	½ tsp
4 oz	of whatever cooking fat you like best	100 g

Rub the fat into the sifted dry ingredients until it feels like coarse breadcrumbs. Store in the fridge or deep freeze. It's easy to measure out exactly what you need, and stir in milk to the right consistency.

Seasoned Salt

This is a more highly flavoured version of the commercial seasoned salt available in little jars. Because of its accentuated flavour it is particularly suitable for Pot cooking.

8 oz	fine sea salt	225 g
1	dried bay leaf	1
½ tsp	freshly ground black pepper	½ tsp
¼ tsp	turmeric	¼ tsp

Crush the bay leaf finely and mix all the ingredients together. To this basic mixture you can add special seasonings for whatever dish you cook most: for lamb, *oregano*; for beef, *ground cloves*; for tomatoes, *crushed basil*; for fish, *dillweed*. Keep each mixture in its own small jar, of course.

Yoghurt

I have made yoghurt according to several methods and with varying degrees of success in the Pot. It never comes out as thick and creamy as when made in more traditional ways; but as in our house any yoghurt is better than none, I give you the recipe for what it is worth. Home-made yoghurt in the Pot works out at about 15p a pint, infinitely cheaper than the shop variety.

1 pt	Long Life milk	600 ml
2 tbs	natural, unsweetened yoghurt	2 tbs
3 tbs	dried non-fat milk	3 tbs
	(or, for a low-fat yoghurt, use *all* dried non-fat milk powder: 5 heaped tablespoons whisked into 1 pint (600 ml) water)	

Electric slow cooker: preheat Pot on HIGH for 20 minutes

1. Warm the milk until a drop on the inside of your wrist feels neither cold nor hot—this is about 110°F (42°C). Add dried milk. Mix a tablespoon of milk into the natural yoghurt 'starter', then whisk this into the remaining milk. While you are doing this, heat about 1 pt (600 ml) water to simmering point and pour into *pre-heated* Pot. Turn the milk mixture into a heatproof plastic container which has been swilled out with hot water and dried, cover it tightly, and put into the Pot. Turn to LOW and leave it for 1 hour, then turn the Pot off completely and allow the yoghurt to stay in it until the water cools—about 2 hours or so.
2. Remove and cool. Chill. You may then flavour with sweet or savoury things.

To Stabilize Yoghurt

Yoghurt will always curdle in long slow cooking—unless it is the true Middle Eastern kind made with goats' milk only. You can, however, do something to alleviate this: if you are going to be doing several dishes within a week's time, say, it pays to make up 2 pints (1 generous litre) and store it in a tightly-lidded container in the fridge.

2 pts	natural unflavoured yoghurt	1 gen l
1	egg white, lightly beaten *or*	1
1 tbs	cornflour slaked with a little water	1 tbs
½	rounded teaspoon of salt	½

Beat the yoghurt until it is liquid and add the egg white or the cornflour paste. Put into a heavy-based saucepan, bring very slowly to the boil, stirring constantly with a wooden spoon in one direction only. When it is just on the boil, reduce the heat to the lowest possible, and let it barely simmer—the surface should just shiver, not bubble—for about 10 minutes. Do not on any account cover it, as a drop of steam falling into it will ruin it. At the end, it should look thick and rich. You can now use this stabilized yoghurt in the Pot.

Appendix

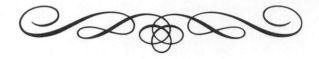

Be not dismayed at the apparent discrepancies between the wattages of the various slow cookers. Each has its own way of controlling heat—by thermostat or variable switching on and off—and they all give very much the same results. Timing, when all is said and done, is not all that critical when you're dealing with 6, 7, 8 hours and not with minutes.

DESCRIPTION OF THE POTS

Kenwood Cookpot: 5 pints (2·8 litres)

Bright plastic exterior, removable interior casserole of brown glazed earthenware, clear plastic lid with knob. Casserole is 11 in (230 mm) wide at top, tapering slightly to base and $5\frac{1}{2}$ in (140 mm) deep. It will take a cake tin or soufflé dish up to $8\frac{1}{2}$ in (215 mm) wide and $3\frac{3}{4}$ in (95 mm) deep. Rocker switch. Fixed flex. Wattage: 70 on Heat I (LOW), 170 on Heat II (HIGH), thermostatically controlled.

Kenwood Automatic Slow Cooker: 5 pints (2·8 litres)

Buff plastic exterior shell, glazed dark brown earthenware casserole, plastic lid. Casserole is 8 in (200 mm) wide, $5\frac{1}{4}$ in (135 mm) deep. Wattage: 85 on Low, 170 on HIGH.

Pifco Slow Cooker: 5 pints (2·8 litres)

Orange aluminium exterior shell, removable deep brown glazed earthenware casserole, glass lid. Casserole is $7\frac{3}{4}$ in (197 mm) at top, tapering to 7 in (178 mm) at base, and 4 in (114 mm) deep. It will take a cake tin or soufflé dish up to 7 in (178 mm) wide and 5 in (125 mm) deep. Lighted dial switch, with OFF, LOW and HIGH. Removable flex. Wattage: 260, thermostatically controlled.
Note: The Pifco heats more quickly and cooks at

higher temperatures than the other Pots; approximately 80°C, 175°F on LOW and 100°C, 210°F on HIGH. Cooking times can be up to 25 per cent faster than other makes. Consult Pifco for details. Light in dial switches off when cooking temperature is reached.

Pifco Corning Ware Casserole Slow Cooker: 4·4 pints (2·5 litres)

Squarish painted aluminium exterior, removable white casserole of Corning Ware, which goes from freezer to flame to slow cooker, guaranteed for life against breakage from heat or cold. Clear glass lid, 8 in (205 mm) by $3\frac{3}{4}$ in (95 mm). Lighted dial switch: OFF, LOW, HIGH. Removable flex. Wattage: 80 on LOW, 130 on HIGH.

Prestige Crock Pot: $3\frac{1}{4}$ pints (1·8 litres)

Coloured plastic exterior shell, removable caramel-coloured glazed earthenware casserole, earthenware lid. Casserole is $9\frac{1}{4}$ in (235 mm) wide, $3\frac{1}{2}$ in (90 mm) deep. It will take a cake tin or soufflé dish up to $8\frac{1}{2}$ in (215 mm) wide and $2\frac{3}{4}$ in (70 mm) deep. Ceramic lid has steam hole. Fixed flex. Wattage: 115 on LOW, 160 on HIGH. Lighted rocker switch: LOW and HIGH.

Prestige Crockette: 2 pints (1·5 litres)

Orange lacquered-finish painted steel exterior, fixed interior casserole of caramel-coloured earthenware with a smoke-coloured translucent plastic lid. Casserole is $5\frac{1}{2}$ in (130 mm) wide and $3\frac{1}{2}$ in (90 mm) deep. It will take a 1-pint (0.5 litre) pudding basin or a soufflé dish $5\frac{1}{4}$ in (135 mm) wide and $2\frac{3}{4}$ in (70 mm) deep. Operates on LOW setting only. Fixed flex. Wattage: 55.

Prestige '3100' Crock Pot: $5\frac{1}{4}$ pints (3 litres)

Bright lacquered-finish painted steel exterior, fixed interior casserole of caramel-coloured earthenware with matching lid. Casserole is 7 in (178 mm) wide and 5¾ in (145 mm) deep. It will take a 1½-pint (800 ml) pudding basin, or a soufflé or baking dish 6¾ in (170 mm) wide and 5 in (125 mm) deep. Lighted rocker switch. LOW and HIGH settings. Removable flex. Wattage 80 on LOW, 140 on HIGH.

Tower Slo-cooker: 3½ pints (2·1 litres)

Tan plastic exterior, fixed interior casserole of brown glazed earthenware; earthenware lid. Interior of casserole 7¼ in (185 mm) wide by 3½ in (90 mm) deep. It will take a soufflé dish or pudding basin up to 6½ in (165 mm) wide and 3 in (78 mm) deep. Rocker switch. Removable flex. Wattage: 75 on LOW, 120 on HIGH.

Tower Slo-cooker: 6 pints (3·5 litres)

Tan plastic exterior, fixed interior casserole of brown glazed earthenware; earthenware lid. Interior of casserole 7¼ in (185 mm) wide, tapering slightly to base, and 5¾ in (145 mm) deep. It will take a cake tin or soufflé dish up to 7 in (178 mm) wide and 5½ in (140 mm) deep. Rocker switch. Removable flex. Wattage: 75 on LOW, 130 on HIGH.

Tower Automatic Slo-cooker: 6 pints (3·5 litres)

Tan plastic exterior, removable brown glazed earthenware casserole; earthenware lid. Interior of casserole 9¼ in (235 mm) wide, tapering slightly to base, and 4½ in (110 mm) deep. It will take a cake tin or soufflé dish up to 8½ in (215 mm) wide and 3¾ in (95 mm) deep. Rocker switch: LOW, HIGH and AUTOMATIC. Removable flex. Needs no pre-heating: Automatic setting preheats, cooks on HIGH for suitable time according to contents of casserole, then switches to LOW for balance of cooking time. Wattage: 120 on LOW, 180 on HIGH.

These particulars were correct when my manuscript went to press; it should, however, be remembered that manufacturers sometimes modify their products and that new models come on to the market.

Index